THE WORLD AT HER FEET

"Dan!" Mary cried. She ran to him, breathless. "I was afraid you weren't coming."

"Did you think anything could keep me away?" He gazed into her eyes, lost in their dark blue depths. He wanted to hold her, to press his lips to hers, but he knew he could not, not yet. "You take a feller's breath away, Mary Kilburne," he said.

Mary smiled, charmed by his playful manner. "Would that be a compliment?"

"You do me proud, Mary Kilburne."

"I want to."

Mary's simple statement touched Dan's heart. He was warmed by her innocence, moved as he had never been before. "Mary," he said so softly it was a caress. "Mary, I love you, my darling girl."

"Oh, Dan, I love you." Tears stood in her eyes. She blinked them away, smiling. "Isn't it amazing what's happened to us?"

"You're amazing."

"The whole world's different now. I'm so happy. You make me so happy . . . It's like a dream."

"Ah, it's better than a dream. Dreams end. What we have will never end. I promise you." Dan kissed Mary's lips. "Come," he said hoarsely. "I've a whole world to show you."

EXCITING BESTSELLERS FROM ZEBRA

STORM TIDE   (1230, $3.75)
by Patricia Rae
In a time when it was unladylike to desire one man, defiant,
flamehaired Elizabeth desired two! And while she longed to be
held in the strong arms of a handsome sea captain, she yearned
for the status and wealth that only the genteel doctor could provide—leaving her hopelessly torn amidst passion's raging
STORM TIDE . . . .

PASSION'S REIGN   (1177, $3.95)
by Karen Harper
Golden-haired Mary Bullen was wealthy, lovely and refined—and
lusty King Henry VIII's prize gem! But her passion for the handsome Lord William Stafford put her at odds with the Royal
Court. Mary and Stafford lived by a lovers' vow: one day they
would be ruled by only the crown of PASSION'S REIGN.

HEIRLOOM   (1200, $3.95)
by Eleanora Brownleigh
The surge of desire Thea felt for Charles was powerful enough to
convince her that, even though they were strangers and their marriage was a fake, fate was playing a most subtle trick on them
both: Were they on a mission for President Teddy Roosevelt—or
on a crusade to realize their own passionate desire?

LOVESTONE   (1202, $3.50)
by Deanna James
After just one night of torrid passion and tender need, the dark-
haired, rugged lord could not deny that Moira, with her precious
beaty, was born to be a princess. But how could he grant her
freedom when he himself was a prisoner of her love?

*Available wherever paperbacks are sold, or order direct from the
Publisher. Send cover price plus 50¢ per copy for mailing and
handling to Zebra Books, 475 Park Avenue South, New York,
N.Y. 10016. DO NOT SEND CASH.*

THIS CHERISHED DREAM

BARBARA HARRISON

ZEBRA BOOKS
KENSINGTON PUBLISHING CORP.

ZEBRA BOOKS

are published by

KENSINGTON PUBLISHING CORP.
475 Park Avenue South
New York, N.Y. 10016

First Printing: June, 1984

Printed in the United States of America

This Cherished Dream

*For Bentley Kolodny
With love*

Prologue

Hexter, England—1905

A bitter wind blew across the moors. It whistled eerily through bare, skeletal trees, through copses of blackened thorn, through the crags and hollows that composed the grim landscape. When finally the wind stopped, silence settled on the dark land. Now the air was utterly still and it seemed as if time itself had stopped.

In the middle of this desolate place suddenly appeared the tall, slender figure of a young girl. She wore a shabby coat, outgrown years before, and beneath it, the plain gray servant's uniform of Abbeywood Manor. Her hair, released from tight braids coiled at the back of her neck, tumbled freely in chestnut waves, now and again brushing her pale ivory cheeks. Her step was quick but cautious, for she knew these moors, with their sharp rises and drops, their jagged rocks, their tangled bramble, and she feared them as she feared nothing else.

Mary Kilburne was fourteen years old, her childhood already lost to memory in some far corner of her mind. And indeed it had been a brief childhood, ending, as it ended for most of the children of Hexter, at the age of nine. In her ninth summer she had entered service at Abbeywood Manor, becoming a scullery maid, and three years later, Cook's helper. The work was hard and often without respite, for Cook was a stern woman with a hearty dislike of her young charge. Many times over the years she had tried to break the girl's spirit, to humble her; when she realized she could not, she buried her in chores morning to night.

Mary never complained. She did her work, she endured the petty tyrannies of upper servants, and she minded her manners. Such behavior was, in part, instinctive, for she had been taught from the cradle to know her place and obey her betters. But it was also a matter of pride; Mary Kilburne would not give in to despair, nor would she concede defeat.

And so, on this bleak March day, Mary strode resolutely along the path through the moors, evading the rocky debris in her way, deftly snatching her skirts from the grasp of outstretched thorns. She smiled, contemplating the package clutched in her arms. It held the leftover food that Cook gave her every Saturday—some ham, a ham bone juicy with bits of meat and fat, three sausages, half a cabbage, pickles, a wedge of cheese. It was enough for their supper, thought Mary, and, if she was careful, for Sunday tea as well.

Mary's smile vanished when she looked at the darkening sky. Frowning, she picked up her skirts and began to run, for soon it would be night and thick black mists would descend on the moors. The air was already damp. Mary could feel the dampness on her skin, on her hair, in each breath she took. She ran faster, her slim frame tilted forward into the wind.

In 1905 the village of Hexter looked much as it had fifty, even a hundred years before. The little main street was narrow and unpaved, deeply scarred by the rumblings of carriage wheels. It had a pub, the Crow and Oyster, a small grocery and dry goods, a butcher shop, an apothecary, and a tobacco shop that also served as the local post office. Some distance away was the old church, its stones smooth and gray with age. Just behind the church was the cemetery where generations of villagers lay beneath simple white grave markers.

To the east was Shepherd Lane. There, fewer than half-a-dozen large houses were set on broad lawns behind high, black, iron fences. They were the houses of the mill owners and, although they were expensive by the standards of Hexter, they were unremarkable, without the slightest grace or charm. There were no flowers to brighten the paths, no fountains to offer water to thirsty birds; the very idea of such frivolity would have shocked the rich and powerful men of Shepherd Lane.

Almost at the foot of the moors, in the path of storms, swirling winds, and perpetual black mists, was Hexter Oval, home to the workingmen and their families. All the cottages were uniformly dark and ugly, crouching like cats upon an oval of land that was little more than mud. Children played in the mud, bent spoons and discarded pots their only toys, and parents watched, resigned, for they had been born to poverty and in poverty they would live out their lives. Their

11

battles were the ordinary, urgent battles of the poor: to put food on the table every day, to put shoes on a child's feet, to keep sickness and death at bay.

Eighteen shillings a week, the highest wage for mill hands, did not go far, and those who dwelled on Hexter Oval made their meals of cabbage and mash, home-baked bread, and weak tea. Bacon was a Sunday treat, the drippings carefully saved to use in cooking throughout the week. Chicken was served only after weddings and funerals. Beef was served, sparingly, at Christmas. This strict frugality went beyond meals. Men who allowed themselves an extra pint of ale on a Saturday night felt guilt for days afterward, and men who did this too often were scorned by their neighbors as weaklings who took food from their children's mouths.

The people of Hexter Oval had every reason to curse their fate. Strangely, they did not. They went about their lives, men, some of the women, most of the children leaving for work before dawn, returning home after sundown. Inside their miserable cottages they froze in winter and sweltered in summer. Rain poured through cracks in roofs, snow blew against loose windows, mists rotted beams and floorboards. The cottages were old, and over all of them hung the smell of ashes and decay and cabbage boiling on the stove.

It was to one of these cottages that Mary so eagerly hurried now. Her skirts flew up about her ankles as she ran, drawn by the warm familiar call of home. Golden lamplight shone at the undraped windows and she pictured her family sitting at the round oak table, cozy and snug by the hearth. At the door of the cottage she paused, bending to the lilacs she had planted. They were stunted and very pale, but their scent was true and she inhaled their sweetness over and over again. Gently, she plucked several blossoms from the small bush and placed them atop her package. "We'll have a centerpiece tonight," she whispered, smiling. "Just like gentry."

But Mary's good humor was interrupted by angry shouts coming from within the cottage. Worry came into her dark blue eyes, for her father and her brother George were arguing again. In the four years since her mother's death, they seemed to be arguing all the time. Often it was in fun, but more often it was not, and on those occasions their strong, determined voices became weapons fighting each other for the last, furious word. George usually won the final say, though it was his father who always won the argument. He won it with a slap to his son's face, a slap so hard the impression of his hand remained for long moments after. A hush would fall upon the cottage then as John sat by the fire, smoking his pipe, and George sulked. They managed to make up their arguments, but Mary wondered if such anger, once spoken, could ever really be resolved. "What's this?" Mary asked now, opening the door to the kitchen. "At it again? What's to become of the two of you, screaming like the zanies in Bedlam?" She closed the door and put her package on the table. The lilacs, forgotten, slipped to the floor. "Mark me," she said, her glance moving from her father to her brother, "they'll be carting you off."

"Eh, he's the zany in this house," George replied angrily, throwing a black look at his father. "He's plain daft."

John spun around. His eyes flashed dangerously. "I won't have talk like that!" he shouted, shaking his fist. "I'll have respect! Do you hear me, lad?"

"Aye, I hear you."

Mary watched father and son glare at each other. Two peas in a pod, she thought, for they were so much alike. Brown-haired, brown-eyed, they were both tall and broad through the chest, with thick forearms and hands as big as hams. Both were moody and quick to anger, though George, at fifteen, was the more reckless of the two. He goaded his father, almost daring him to respond with violence.

Mary had inherited the role of peacemaker after her mother's death. Now, she draped her coat over a hook on the door and stepped swiftly between John and George. She put her hands on George's chest, pushing him back. "Fill the soup pot with water, Georgy. I've a nice bone in my package this week. We'll have broth." George stayed where he was and Mary pushed him again. "Go on with you," she said. "Do you want your supper, or do you want to argue all the night?"

Muttering, George stomped away to the cupboards. He grabbed the iron pot from its shelf, slammed it down, and began pumping water into it. Mary waited a moment, then turned to her father. "Pa?" she asked quietly. "What started it this time?"

John shook his head, waving his big hands in the air. He took a few steps to the hearth and stared tiredly into the fire. "The lad has no respect. He needs a proper thrashing, that's what. Nothing like a strap across the back to get the sass out of a lad."

Mary went to her father's side. She linked her arm in his. "You don't mean that, Pa. Georgy's not so bad. It's just high spirits."

"High spirits, eh?" John turned his head and stared at Mary. In the glow of the fire her chestnut hair sparkled with golden lights and her dark blue eyes, so large and trusting, shone. "Well," he said slowly, "you have a kind way of putting it. Your Ma would have put it the same way. Aye, I can hear her now." John smiled faintly. There was a long pause before he continued. "You remind me of her, lass. I could always count on your Ma and I can always count on you. A man needs that. He needs to know his loved ones will . . . understand."

Mary was pleased by her father's words, but his manner troubled her. He was subdued and too thoughtful, as if he were struggling with a problem to which there was no answer. "Pa, what did you and Georgy argue about?"

"We'll talk about it later," John sighed, returning his glance to the fire. "You'd best see to supper."

"Pa—"

"Do as I say, lass."

It was an order and Mary instantly obeyed. She went to the table and unwrapped her package, putting ham and cheese in the cold-box, arranging pickles and sausages on a plate. She quartered the cabbage and added it to the potatoes cooking on the stove. Every few minutes she peered over her shoulder at her father; a frown deepened on her brow, for she knew something was wrong.

George, muttering loudly now, finished filling the soup pot and slammed it on the stove. "Go easy, George," Mary scolded. "You'll spill our supper on the floor."

"Supper! Is that all you can think about?"

"What else would I be thinking about at seven o'clock on Saturday night?"

George took Mary by the shoulders and shook her. "Didn't Pa tell you yet?" he demanded, his face scarlet.

"Don't you know?" He shook her harder, oblivious to everything but his own rage. "Answer me!"

John was across the room in a flash. He wrested George away from Mary and struck him full in the face. He pinned his arms behind his back, pushing him roughly toward the door. "Bloody fool! Bloody, bloody fool! Touch your sister again and I'll have your hide on a stick. By God I will." John's voice was low, ominously low. He had only one thought—to get George out of the cottage before he killed him.

Color began to drain from George's face, for even he realized he had gone too far. "I'm sorry, Pa," he said, writhing in his father's viselike grip. "I didn't mean it. I wouldn't hurt Mary. You know that, Pa."

"I know a bloody fool when I see one." John opened the door and pitched George outside. "A walk will do you good. Go fetch Rose from Mrs. Warren."

"Aye, Pa." George nodded earnestly, rubbing his aching wrists. "I will. I'm sorry, Pa."

John did not know if his son's contrition sprang from fear or from genuine regret, nor did he care. He closed the door and leaned against it, breathing heavily. Perspiration beaded his upper lip, and his hands were clenched in tight fists.

"Pa, are you all right?"

John looked around to see Mary, very still and pale, once again standing at his side. "Eh, lass, you're a comfort to me." He patted her head, touched her cheek. "There now, you look like you need comforting yourself. Did Georgy hurt you?"

"No, but I don't understand. What was he talking about?" Mary anxiously searched her father's eyes. "What did he mean?"

Slowly, as if every step were a great effort, John

walked back to the hearth. He lowered himself into a narrow, straight-backed chair and lit his pipe. Plumes of lazy gray smoke swirled around him; he was silent.

"Pa, what did Georgy mean? What am I supposed to know?"

"Well, lass, I've some news. A surprise, you could call it. And there's no cause to fret. You're the sensible one. You'll see it's all for the best."

Mary was not reassured. She shifted nervously from foot to foot, waiting for her father to continue. When he did not, her pale face grew paler. It must be bad news, she thought, and that's why Georgy's so upset. "Will you tell me, Pa? Please?"

"Aye, but later. After supper. After Rose is in bed." John looked up. He smiled wanly. "See to the meal, lass, or we'll be eating at midnight."

Mary, her dark blue eyes downcast and cloudy with tears, returned to the stove. Absently, she dropped the soup bone into the pot, adding pepper, cloves, and a few sprigs of parsley and thyme she had taken from the herb garden at Abbeywood Manor. Carrot tops went in next, and then tiny wild onions, fragrant and pink.

Mary enjoyed cooking and she was good at it. For the past year she had done some of the cooking and all of the baking at Abbeywood, making the rich, elaborate confections she could not afford to make for her own family. Her family got by on scraps, though they were tasty scraps indeed, for everyone knew that Mary could do more with odds and ends than Cook could do with a full larder. Now she moved away from the broth and began to heat bacon drippings in a small pan. She crumbled sausages into the pan, leaving them to cook while she set the table.

John watched his daughter bustle about the table,

her movements as sure as those of someone twice her age. He was not an especially reflective man, but it occurred to him that he often forgot how young she really was. She was hardly more than a child, a child whose youth was being destroyed by the work and worry that marked every day of her life. A poor, bare life, he thought to himself, that would soon take its toll on Mary; soon her eyes would not shine so brightly; her hair would not sparkle with golden lights; her smile would not come so quickly. Years and years before her time, she would be old.

John had wanted better for Mary. He knew she was the smartest of his three children. He knew, too, that she had courage and strength and kindness. His late wife Elizabeth had had the same qualities, though in the end, in the final, desperate poverty of Hexter Oval, they had not saved her. Her death had been blamed on the influenza epidemic that swept the village in 1901. John blamed it on other things, on a damp, drafty cottage, on poor skimpy meals, on years of hard work and hard times.

John sighed again. He drew deeply on his pipe and gazed around the kitchen. The cottage consisted of three tiny bedrooms and this kitchen, which was also the parlor. It was sparsely furnished with table and chairs, stove, cold-box, cupboards, and an old cedar chest. A large tub, used for bathing and for laundry, sat in one corner of the room. A single shelf held a Bible and a book of sonnets that had belonged to Elizabeth. Not much to show for my thirty-five years on earth, thought John, more in sorrow than pity.

"Eh, look who's here!" George's voice boomed in the stillness of the cottage. He carried his sister Rose in his arms and both John and Mary rushed to greet her.

Rose was five years old, the pride and joy of the Kilburne family and of all Hexter Oval, for she was a truly beautiful child. She was small boned and delicate, with huge, pale blue eyes and hair the color of spun gold. Her skin was so fair it was almost translucent; her lips were a sweet and tender pink. "There now, Rose," George said, kissing her silky cheek, "go on to Mary."

Mary took the child and held her close, nuzzling her golden curls. Rose was her darling, more daughter than sister, and she loved her with all her heart. "How are you, lass?" she asked softly. "It's been so terrible damp. Are you all right?"

Rose nodded. She tilted her head, looking at Mary through long, golden lashes. "Did you bring my candy?" she asked.

"Aye, I did. I've two peppermints for you, but only if you've been a good lass. Have you?"

"Mrs. Warren says I'm the best lass in all the world. Look"—Rose beamed proudly, holding out her hand—"she gave me an egg."

"An egg! Well, you can have it with your bacon tomorrow. Won't that be nice?"

Rose shook her head from side to side. The corners of her pretty little mouth drew into a pout and her pale eyes were suddenly cold. It was a harsh look, startling in one so young. "Tonight," she said sharply, clearly. "I want the egg tonight. It's *my* egg, Mary."

Mary hesitated. She found it painful to deny Rose anything, though in matters of food, she knew she had to be firm. "No, Rose. I've some sweet pickles for you tonight. They're just the way you like them. And they're just for you."

Rose clapped her hands together, smiling again. "Just for me," she chirped happily, delighted to have something that did not have to be shared. "Just for me," she repeated, looking pointedly at George.

George threw his head back and laughed. "You little imp, I'm no thief." He winked, tweaking one of Rose's curls. "What's yours is yours. That's fair. Eh, Mary?"

Mary was not at all certain it was fair. Was it fair, she wondered, to give extra food to Rose when the men barely had enough to eat? Rose was growing and needed her nourishment, but the men worked hard and they needed their nourishment too. Mary shook her head, unable as always to resolve her dilemma. With a shrug, she put Rose down. "Go along to Pa now," she said quietly. "I'll fetch our supper."

Rose wrapped her fingers around John's hand and walked with him to the hearth, sitting in the small, high-backed chair he had carved for her fifth birthday. Mary had made the tufted chair cushion and Rose liked to bounce on it, swinging her short legs back and forth. She was content, for, atop her cushion, she would pretend she was a royal princess. It was an old game, begun by Mrs. Warren, the woman who cared for her during the week. Rose never tired of it.

John watched as Rose smoothed her skirts and held an imaginary scepter aloft. His eyes became soft, immensely gentle. He loved all of his children, but he loved his youngest child most of all, and this was so even though he knew her faults. He knew she had a selfish streak, knew she was growing vain of her looks. He suspected she would turn her nose up at work, when the time for work came. In truth, John dreaded the coming of that time. He pictured Rose trudging across the blackened moors to Abbeywood Manor, there to slave in a steaming kitchen or laundry room, there to waste her life. *No,* thought John fiercely, banging his fist against his knee; I won't let that happen. By God I won't!

"Pa," Mary called. "Supper."

The Kilburnes took their places around the table, bowing their heads while John said grace. It was a brief blessing, followed immediately by the clattering of spoons and bowls as everyone began to eat. There were no polite pauses for conversation, no neat dabbings of napkins on mouths. The Kilburnes were hungry. They devoured their meal, every crumb, and when the dishes had been cleared and they sat with their tea, they pretended they were full.

It was past nine when Mary set her mending basket in her lap and threaded a needle. Rose had been bathed and put to bed. George paced the room in silence, glancing expectantly at John. John felt his son's eyes on him. He cleared his throat once or twice. He lit his pipe. He crossed and uncrossed his legs. Finally, having delayed as long as he could, he looked up. "All right now," he said with an assurance he did not feel, "I've something to tell you."

Mary jumped at the sound of her father's voice. A tightness came into her chest and her pulse throbbed. In her nervousness she stuck her thumb with the needle. It stung, but she was so tense she hardly felt it. "We're listening, Pa, Georgy and me."

"I'll have no tantrums." John looked sharply at his son, holding his gaze. "I've made my decision, so there's no use to zany carrying on."

"Aye." George nodded, though his eyes blazed and his jaw was as unyielding as granite. "Aye."

"All right then. Lass, we'll be leaving Hexter Oval

21

soon. We're leaving England, going far away." The words exhausted John. He drew weakly on his pipe, looking down at the splintered floor boards. He could endure George's scorn, but not Mary's, and he prayed that she would understand. "Lass, we're going to America."

Mary stared at John for a long time. The air in the cottage seemed to crackle around her; the fire rose and roared up the chimney in a rush of blinding yellows and reds. She did not speak. She continued to stare at John, her eyes wide, filled with an odd intense light.

"Did you hear me, lass?"

"America," Mary whispered. An expression of astonishment, and then sudden elation and joy passed across her face. "America!" she cried, jumping to her feet. She stumbled over her fallen mending basket, staggered around the table. When she reached her father she bent and flung her arms about his neck. "It's true, Pa? America?"

"Aye, lass. You . . . fancy the idea?"

"America's all I've dreamed about. It's not dead, like here. There's *life* in America." Mary was crying now, great, happy tears splashing down her cheeks. "Thank you, Pa," she said, hugging him. "You won't be sorry. I'll work hard. Aye, I will. What a grand life we'll have, Pa. It's a miracle. A miracle!"

John had not been prepared for such a reaction. He sat openmouthed as Mary danced around the room, and for the first time that night he breathed easily.

George had not been prepared for her reaction either. He had expected Mary to join him in battle against their father. Now he realized the battle was lost and, viciously, he kicked the wall. I'll never forgive them, he thought, bitter tears standing in his eyes;

never, as long as I live.

"Georgy," Mary said, "try to think of the good in this. There's no life for us here in Hexter. But in America we'll have our chance. It's a new start. Don't you see?" George did not reply. Mary went to him and laid her hand lightly on his arm. "Georgy, do you want to live and die in Hexter?"

"What if I do? What's wrong with that?" He shook off Mary's hand, glaring at her. "I suppose you're too good for Hexter, Miss High-And-Mighty. Nobody else complains. Two hundred families living in Hexter and nobody complains but you. Well, it's good enough for them and it's good enough for me." George took a step toward Mary, his mouth twisting in contempt. "I don't have your grand notions. My nose isn't stuck in the air."

"Nor is mine."

"Aye, it is." George walked away. He paced in a small circle and then turned, pointing at Mary. "Airs and graces from a scullery maid! I never saw the like. Have you forgotten who you are, Mary Kilburne? You're a mill hand's daughter, no more than that."

"And not ashamed of it."

"Eh, you've been at Abbeywood Manor too long. It's changed you."

Mary had remained calm under her brother's assault, but now she colored and a fiery light burned in her dark blue eyes. "Aye, it's changed me," she said, her voice trembling. "I've seen things. I've seen how there's people born to everything and people born to nothing. How you're born is all that matters in Hexter. In America it's different."

"America! I've heard about America. It's a mean place, full of foreigners and blackamoors and Indians.

And papists! Do you want to live with papists?"

"It's none of my account how people worship God. Even papists."

"Do you want to live with them? Is that what you want?" George was very close to Mary, his dark and furious face only inches away from hers. "Do you want to *live* with papists?"

"I want to live anywhere there's no black mists choking us," she said vehemently. "Anywhere there's enough food, and a dry roof over our heads."

"The lass is right." John had been listening closely to his children and he decided it was time to intervene. He stood up, folding his arms across his chest. "We've nothing in Hexter, Georgy. We're poor as church mice. And church mice we'll be 'til the day we die. That's the truth of it."

"Aye, but . . ." George stopped. He stared curiously at his father. "How can church mice afford to go to America? The trip costs dear. We've no money."

Mary's hand flew to her throat. "Pa, the money!" she cried in alarm. "Where will we get the money?"

"Don't fret, lass. I've enough for our trip."

"How?" George asked. There was accusation in his voice and satisfaction, for he was sure he had found the flaw in his father's plan. "It's all talk, isn't it? There's no money."

John regarded his son in silence. His eyes were without expression; though, finally, a small smile lifted the corners of his mouth. "There's money."

"How?" George shouted.

"Four years ago . . . when your ma died . . . Cousin Bob sent money for us to go to America. There was the funeral, all the expenses. Doctor's bills. I had to use some of Bob's money to pay all that. But every month since I've put a little back. A few shillings here and there." John walked to the other end of the hearth. He was thinking about Elizabeth, remembering their years together. She had made life in Hexter bearable, but she was gone and life was not bearable anymore. "Well," he said quietly, "there's enough now. It's not much, but it'll get us to America."

"You're sure, Pa?" Mary asked.

"Aye. I went to Wayfarers Inn and telephoned to the ship company. There's a way to travel called steerage. We've enough for that."

"It's settled then?"

"Aye, lass."

The tension in Mary's face disappeared. She smiled so radiantly that light actually seemed to fall from her. "America," she sighed.

George turned away in disgust. He opened his mouth to speak, changed his mind, then changed his mind once more. "If you've all this money, Pa, why don't you use it here? You could fix our cottage good as new."

"Are you daft? I'd sooner throw the money down the well. Listen here, lad, even if the cottage *was* new, what would we have? Nothing, that's what. I'm offering you a new life in America. Work hard and you can be whatever you want to be."

"I want to be *here*," George snapped. "I want to have a farm *here* someday."

John slowly shook his head. "There's no getting through to you. Georgy, stop any ten fellers in the road and nine will say they want to have a farm someday. I ask you, when does this someday come? Never. It's only a dream. A dream you'll carry to your grave."

"I'm strong. I'll work and I'll save."

"Eh, you could work two lifetimes and be no closer

to your farm than you are today. It's slave wages we get, lad. You, in the mill five years and earning only eight shillings the week. Can you buy land on eight shillings the week?"

George hurled himself into a chair. His eyes were twin pools of misery, still and dark and blank.

"Lad," John said kindly, "we're going to live with Cousin Bob in a place called New York City. It's a grand place. Why, they say the streets are paved with gold!" John sat down next to George. He reached over and patted his hand. "Cousin Bob wasn't much older than you when he went to America. He went with empty pockets and big dreams. People all over Hexter called him a zany. I remember how they laughed. But it's Bob who's laughing now, 'cause his dreams came true. He has a big tavern in New York City, five men working for him. And he lives in a big flat, with fancy carpets and furniture and all. Lives like a bloody lord!"

George looked sideways at his father. "How do you know so much about it?" he asked. "Eh, you're telling a fairy story."

"No, it's true. Cousin Bob wrote a long letter after your ma died. He told me how it was in America."

"That was four years past."

"Aye, but we've kept in touch. And in September I wrote to say I had enough money put by." John reached into his pocket, withdrawing a white envelope. "Here's Bob's letter." It was a short letter, covering less than a page, and John had read it so often he knew it by heart. "He says he'll meet us at a place called Ellis Island and take us to his flat. The flat's in a place called Yorkville. Yorkville." John smiled, as excited as a child. "I'll wager that's the fancy part of the town."

George showed no interest in Bob's letter; he pushed

26

his chair back and looked away. But Mary came forward, peeking over her father's shoulder at the words that called them to a magical new land. Soon she would meet the writer of those words, she thought in wonder, amazed at the idea of having a rich relative. John had mentioned his Cousin Bob before, usually in stories about their youth. In those stories Bob was a hero of sorts, spirited and strong, good at games, at sport, at making people laugh.

"See, lass," John said, taking Mary's hand, "Bob says there's plenty of room for us."

"Aye, Pa. It's grand."

"Eh." George glared again at Mary. "You're daft, plain daft, the both of you. Going to a strange country to live with strangers. It's nothing to me if he's rich. My home's in Hexter."

John had had enough of his son's stubbornness. Angrily, he crashed his fist on the table. He crashed it again and then grabbed George by the collar of his shirt. "Bloody fool!" he roared, all patience gone. "I've tried my best to make you understand, but now I'm through trying. Do you hear me, lad? We're going to America in the steerage and that's that." John stood suddenly. He strode the length of the cottage, his hands chopping at the air. "We're going! By God we're going! I'll not have my children bowing and scraping to gentry all their lives. 'Aye sir, no sir, kick-me-in-the-backside-sir.' Maybe that's all right for you and Mary . . . but is it all right for our Rose?"

George flinched, as if from a blow. He had given no thought to Rose or her future, but now he imagined her in the years ahead—working, like Mary, from dawn to dark, working for four shillings a week and table scraps. "No, Pa," he said, slumping in his chair. "It's not all right for Rose."

Mary ran to George and embraced him. "That's a good lad, Georgy," she smiled, radiant once again. "You see it, don't you? In America Rose can be a lady!"

"Aye." George rested his head wearily on Mary's shoulder. His eyes were vacant, his jaw slack. "Aye, in America."

The argument was over at last and John went to his son, clapping him vigorously on the back. "You'll like it once we're there. The place is full of money! And Cousin Bob is a fine feller, always ready with a smile and a joke."

George passed his hand across his face. He got up slowly, glancing at John. "It's late. I'll be off to bed. Good night."

"Good night, lad."

"Good night, Georgy," Mary called. She watched her brother walk away, his head down, his shoulders hunched. It was the walk of an old man, an old man trapped and, ultimately, defeated. She saw him pause briefly outside his bedroom and then go inside, closing the door behind him. "Poor Georgy. He's terrible sad."

"Well, lass, home is home. Even a black place like Hexter. It's not easy to leave." John emptied his pipe in the hearth. If he was worried about his son he gave no sign; he seemed relaxed, more relaxed than he had been in years. "Eh, the lad will soon change his mind. When the shillings gather in his pockets, he'll change his mind."

"I hope so. When do we leave, Pa?"

"I've booked our passage for July. Georgy'll be used to the idea by then, if that's what's worrying you." John smiled at Mary, tilting her young face to him. "Don't fret. It's a new life we're beginning. Be glad."

"I am. Oh, I am . . . but Georgy—"

"Eh, have a thought for yourself once in a while. No harm in that." John turned. He lowered the lamps, cloaking the kitchen in a shadowy half-light. "You're tired. Take yourself off to bed."

"I've chores."

"Chores," John said softly, slowly. "Always chores. I'll be glad to see the last of this bloody country and that's a fact." He bent, kissing the top of Mary's head. "Don't be too long. Morning comes early."

"I won't, Pa."

John walked toward his bedroom and Mary noticed the sudden lightness of his step. "Good night, Pa."

"Good night. Eh, Mary, there's something else. Don't tell of our trip to anyone at Abbeywood Manor yet. They'll get two weeks' notice and no more. What a row there'll be when they hear you're leaving!"

Mary shrugged her slim shoulders. "They won't miss me, Pa," she said, her eyes twinkling, "only my cakes and puddings."

"Aye, and that's reason enough to start a row. It's a terrible thing when gentry has to do without. A terrible thing!" John repeated, laughing wickedly.

The mending had been done. The floor had been scrubbed, and the hearth, and the stove. Six loaves of dough, enough for the week, had been kneaded and turned into bread pans, ready for baking after church in the morning. Now Mary sat at the round oak table, staring dreamily into space. Feeling giddy, a little dazed, she recalled her father's extraordinary announcement: *We're going to America.* The words echoed sweetly in her mind and she smiled. "America," she murmured.

The night grew later. Drifting winds brushed against the windows, and from the moors came the lonely cry of an owl. The moon disappeared, swallowed whole by the vast black sky. It was after midnight, but still Mary made no move to go to bed. She sat in the dim and shadowy lamplight and dreamed her dreams, hardly able to believe the good fortune that had touched their lives.

Book One

One

The dark and stormy waters of the Atlantic churned restlessly. Small ripples became great waves, driven and tossed by rampaging winds. Above, lightning turned the sky to silver while thunder exploded in rapid volleys as loud as cannon.

The British steamship *Royal Star* had been at sea for three days and three nights. The days had been balmy, full of sun; the nights had been like this one, buffeted by nature's vast sound and fury. Many of the passengers suffered seasickness, but nowhere was the suffering worse than in steerage. There, in the very bowels of the ship, well away from the more stable center, the passengers felt every pitch and roll of the hull. They were unable to sleep, unable to keep food down, unable to do anything but lie in their narrow bunks and suffer. Some bore their pain in silence, others with moans or whispered prayers. Only three days out of port, the stench of unwashed bodies, of sickness, overwhelmed the airless compartments.

The Kilburnes had not known what to expect when they boarded the ship in Liverpool. There had been crowds and noise and chaos, a happy kind of chaos that brought a smile even to George's sullen face. None of the Kilburnes had ever seen so many people before and they gaped unashamedly at the throngs. The ship, itself, had been a wonder to them, large beyond imagination, sitting proudly atop the water like some omnipotent sea creature. Eyes wide, they had taken in every line of the *Royal Star,* from its tall gray smokestacks to its railed decks covered with scurrying crewmembers. There had been brightly colored flags, and a band, and much laughter. In this spirit of high excitement, the Kilburnes had boarded the *Royal Star.*

In 1905 the officers and crew of the *Royal Star* were no different, no better or worse, than the officers and crews of other ships. They all had in common a deep and abiding contempt for steerage passengers. They had as little to do with them as possible, and when contact was necessary they were rude, sometimes cruel. It was said, not in jest, that the ships had four classes: first, second, livestock and steerage. Travelers were treated accordingly.

The steerage deck to which the Kilburnes had been sent was dirty and oppressive. It was divided into two large compartments, one for men, one for women, each packed top to bottom with two hundred single bunks. In these compartments there were no amenities of any sort; indeed there was barely room to stand. To the left of the compartments, at the end of an unlit passageway, was the dining hall. Stuffy, redolent of cabbage and dried grease, the room held two long refectory tables bordered by hard wooden benches. Roaches searching for crumbs skittered over the benches, over the grimy floor. At the far end of the passageway were the lavatories, so foul they made Mary gasp.

Prohibitions abounded in steerage. Printed signs

warned that passengers were to use the outside deck only at specified times of day, and never when the heavy metal chains were up. They were to speak to crew members only when spoken to, or in case of emergency. They were not to leave their compartments at night. They were not to sit on the stairs. They were not to go to the upper decks for any reason. Thus chastised, steerage passengers settled in for their journey.

Mary had been appalled by their new circumstances, but stubbornly, she refused to lament. "It's not forever," she said briskly. And whenever George cursed or Rose cried, she repeated those words. She meant them. It was, after all, *not* forever; discomfort, no matter how severe, was a small price to pay if it led them to America. That was how she saw it.

John admired her stubbornness. He was grateful, too, for he could not have faced George and Rose alone. The hurt look in Rose's beautiful eyes was almost more than he could endure. He ached for her all the time and only Mary offered solace. The anger in George's eyes bothered him less, but it did bother him. Again, Mary was there with solace. He had begun to rely on her. She is Elizabeth all over again, he said to himself, taking refuge in the thought.

Mary was unaware of her father's thoughts. As fierce waves pounded at the *Royal Star,* tossing it from side to side, she was crowded into Rose's bunk, her long legs drawn up practically to her chest. She was there because Rose would not sleep alone, but since two of them were packed into a space scarcely big enough for one, neither of them slept. Mary swept the damp curls from Rose's brow. She held her little hand and murmured the words of an old lullaby. The child was not mollified. She tried to turn, to kick her legs free. There was a mighty struggle that nearly knocked Mary to the floor. "Rose," Mary pleaded, pulling herself back into the bunk, "please try to lie quiet. Close your eyes and you'll sleep."

"My stomach hurts. I want to go home."

"We're going to our new home. It won't be long. I promise."

"I want to go *home.*"

"Soon."

"Now," Rose shrieked. Tears coursed down her flushed cheeks. She beat her fists on Mary's knee. "Take me home *now."*

"Hush, lass," Mary said soothingly. With a sigh, she untangled her arm and used the sleeve of her dress to wipe the perspiration from Rose's face. "Try to sleep."

"Won't you take me home?"

"Rose, we're way out in the ocean. Soon . . ."

The rest of Mary's sentence was lost, for Rose had begun to cry in earnest. Great piercing screams shook her small body. Her hands flailed the air. Her legs, wedged into a corner of the bunk, trembled.

Mary realized there was no way to calm her sister. She lay as still as she could and let Rose cry it out. Her cries joined those of the other children in the compartment, for they too suffered from the heat and the stench and the constant rolling of the ship. The noise was deafening. Exhausted mothers closed their eyes and tried not to hear.

Mary turned slightly, gazing at the occupants of the bunks around her. They were children, some only babies; young women, middle-aged women, and old women, white-haired, wrinkled, dressed all in black.

36

Her glance lingered longest on the old women. She knew how hard it must have been for them to leave their homes, to leave whole lifetimes behind them; she knew how hard it must be for them now, at their ages, to stand the hardship of this ocean crossing. She thought: But they're doing it 'cause they want a better life. They want a bit of hope before they die. They want it to be better for the little ones. They're no different from me, even if they're old. And Irish.

There were 374 steerage passengers. Of these there were the British Kilburnes, a pair of Russian Jews, father and son, who neither spoke nor understood English, and 368 Irish who had boarded at Queenstown. The Jews were ignored. It was as if they were not there at all, and that attitude seemed to please them. The attitude of the Kilburnes toward the Irish, and the Irish toward the Kilburnes, was far less pleasing. It was, in fact, hostile. Animosity and mistrust ran deep, for both had been learned, ingrained over many years. The small quarters in which they lived did not help. They were forced to eat together, to sleep together, to walk the meager deck together; there was no escape.

John tried as best he could to stay out of the way. He tried to keep George out of the way as well, but this was proving more and more difficult each day. It had become clear that George yearned for an argument, perhaps even a fight. It had become equally clear that several strapping young Irishmen would be happy to oblige him.

If this worried John, it scared Mary. She knew her brother. She knew there was no real harm in him, no evil, but there was recklessness. She considered his quick temper, his unpredictable moods, and fear clutched her heart. John had called him a born brawler, but Mary knew that if a brawl started on this ship it would not end until someone dropped. Men have no sense, she thought, not for the first time.

Mary took a breath, trying to slow her racing mind. She looked at Rose, who slept peacefully now, lost in childish dreams. Carefully, making no sound, she climbed down from Rose's bunk and went to her own. She lay there, dozing but not sleeping. There was quiet in the compartment. The storm had veered away and soon it would be morning. The *Royal Star* sailed on.

"Here, Rose," Mary said. "I saved my bread for you. And Pa saved his tea."

"I don't want it. It tastes terrible bad."

"Lass"—John stroked his daughter's golden curls—"you'd best eat. You'll be hungry later. It's a long time off 'til lunch."

"It tastes *bad.*"

"Eh, that's just the sea air you're tasting. Go on with you now. Eat your food and be glad of it."

Rose took a tiny bite of bread. She chewed it very slowly, scowling all the while. John and Mary waited patiently for her to finish. They were the last people in the dining hall because Rose had first refused to eat and then had dawdled over her food. No one really blamed her. Breakfast, like all other meals in steerage, always arrived late and cold. The oatmeal was a thin, watery paste, the bread stale, the tea bitter. It was portioned out by surly cabin boys who felt they had better things to do than attend a roomful of ragged immigrants. These cabin boys never smiled, never spoke; they divided the stingy rations and quickly left, not to return again until lunch. Lunch was broth, bread, and tea. Supper, when finally it came, was cold meat, a potato, cabbage, bread, and tea. Grace was said before each meal, led by Father Malone, a wiry young priest on his way to a parish in New York.

"That's a good lass." Mary smiled. "You're halfway through. A few more bites and we'll have a nice walk on the deck. Won't it be nice to feel the sun on your face?"

"Aye." Rose nodded, eager for sun after the long dark night. She lifted her huge eyes to Mary and a smile spread across her face. It was a beautiful smile, full of the innocence and mystery of childhood. "You're a good lass too, Mary," she said. "You take good care of me."

Mary gathered Rose into her arms and hugged her. "Aye, I always will."

"Forever?"

"Aye."

Rose thought about this. "But someday," she said after a while, "I'll have a husband. I'll marry a prince, Mrs. Warren says. Then *he'll* take care of me."

"A prince!" John laughed fondly, winking at Mary. "The lass has her sights high set. I hope there are princes in Yorkville."

"Are there, Mary?" Rose asked.

"And why not? But you must eat. A prince doesn't want a starveling on his doorstep."

Rose giggled. She stuffed a chunk of bread into her mouth and washed it down with a gulp of tea. Mary watched in pleasure as the child ate. Always sensitive to Rose's moods, Mary was happiest when Rose was happy. She basked in the sweetness of her smile, in the

39

clear, pale light that danced in her eyes. She wanted so much to please her, to give her all the things she had not had. In America, she thought, Rose will have everything.

"Well, lass," John shook Mary's shoulder, "have you been to the moon again?" Mary laughed at her father's question, for it was an old joke between them, trotted out whenever she looked dreamy or far away. "Tell me then," John went on, "is the moon really made of green cheese?"

"Oh, Pa, I was only thinking about America. I know things will go our way there."

"Aye. It's hard, this trip, but we'll be glad in the end. I wish Georgy—"

"Where is Georgy?" Mary asked. Her dark blue gaze roamed the room and then settled on John. "He's not here, Pa. Where is he?"

"Likely he's out on deck." John's face became serious. He stared at Mary, a deep frown creasing his brow. "What's bothering you, lass? Are you fretting about Georgy again? He'll be fine once he gets to America."

"It's not that, Pa." Mary hesitated, trying to find the right words. "You've seen him these days past. You've seen how he is. He's looking for trouble."

"Eh, he's always looking for trouble."

"And finding it. The way he's been acting with the Irish lads. He's . . . daring them. It makes them terrible mad."

John nodded slowly, rubbing his eyes. He knew that Mary was right and he knew that he had to try, yet again, to reason with his unreasonable son. The prospect was wearying, for every confrontation with

George took its toll. Even now he could see the stony set of George's jaw, the black and glaring anger in his eyes. They would argue, he knew; they would argue until they were both exhausted and still nothing would be resolved. Abruptly, John stood up. "I'll have another talk with him," he said. He smiled slightly. "There has to be a way to get through his thick head. I'll find it."

"I can go with you, Pa."

"No. See to Rose. See she finishes her breakfast." John walked a few steps, then turned and looked at Mary. "You're a great comfort, lass. Like your ma." He walked swiftly to the door and stepped into the passageway. At the end of the passageway was a door and, to the left, another passageway leading to a set of stairs. John climbed the stairs quietly, composing his thoughts as he went.

The sunlight was bright out on deck and when it fell on John's face it only accentuated his pallor. He had aged during their trip. Seasickness had made him thinner by several pounds and there were sharp new lines around his mouth and eyes. There were dark hollows in his cheeks that had not been there before. His walk was different too, not slower exactly, but somehow unsure. He seemed diminished. Such changes had come upon many of the men traveling in steerage, for, no matter how brave their talk of a new land and a new life, they had known moments of doubt, of desperate fear. Had they been right to uproot their families and take them across an ocean to America? There were no ready answers. Better the devil you know, thought one disheartened Irishman, lying sleeplessly in his bunk.

Now, John edged his way around the crowded deck toward the rail. The waters of the Atlantic were tranquil, a shimmering, sun-dappled blue. The air, cleansed by last night's storm, was clear and warm, ruffled every few minutes by feathery breezes. John could only imagine the scenes on the upper decks—rich people strolling leisurely in fine clothes, clean and well fed and attended by fawning crew members. Here no one strolled. Passengers staked out places for themselves and then guarded those places. The women held children in their arms or in their laps and turned their faces to the sun. The men, at the other end of the deck, talked and joked, content to enjoy the sweet summer day.

John leaned against the rail, looking toward the men. There, near a group of six or seven young Irishmen, was George. He threaded in and out of their group, gesturing, his lips moving. John could not hear what George said, but he could guess his intentions. He thought: The lad's trying to get the Irishers riled. But they're smarter than he is. They're paying him no mind. That's good. Let Georgy learn the sun doesn't rise and set on him and his bloody big mouth.

Someone else was watching George, and with concern. Father Patrick Malone's keen blue eyes had been fixed on George all morning. They followed his every movement, measured his provocations, and knew that trouble was brewing. In truth, Father Malone had been concerned since the first day of the journey. He had known boys like young George Kilburne before, boys full of shapeless anger and black moods. There was trouble wherever they went, for trouble was what they wanted and, inevitably, what they got. His glance shifted across the deck to John. He wondered why the boy's father simply stood there and watched.

George, the center of this attention, was blithely unaware of both his father and Father Malone. He had been taunting the young Irishmen since breakfast, and now, seized by a dangerous excitement, his taunts became bolder. "Papists," he said quite clearly, cutting into the circle they had formed. "Dirty heathen papists!"

One of the young men, as tall as George and as broad, took a step forward. Quickly, he was pulled back by his friends. "He's not worth dirtying your hands, Sean," one of them said, also quite clearly. "The dirty Sassenach!"

There was raucous laughter and much slapping of backs. George, infuriated, turned and spat at the young man. "Tell me," he shouted, "why is it you papists kiss the Pope's ring? Is it because you can't reach his ass?"

A gasp rose from the group and now Sean leaped at George, fists flying. He landed the first punch, catching George squarely on the chin. Lusty cheers filled the air as George fell to the deck. He lay there a moment, but he came up swinging and the fight was on.

Sean Ryan had grown up with five older brothers and so was an expert fighter. He was quick and light on his feet; he bobbed and weaved like a seasoned professional, easily avoiding George's wild swings. His own swings were hard and on the mark. They were so fast George never saw them coming. Sean's left hand was deadly. With it he split George's lip and bloodied his nose, staggering him. "And have you had enough, Sassenach?" Sean called over the excited shouts of the crowd. "Or would you be wanting more?"

George bent over to catch his breath. He was drenched in sweat. Blood streamed from his nose, from his mouth, from his bruised and aching hands. He knew he had no chance to win this fight, but fury drove him on. "I'll have enough when you're lying on the bloody deck, bloody papist!"

"Sure and that'll be the day. Come on then; don't keep a proud Irishman waiting."

From opposite sides of the deck, John and Father Malone were struggling to push their way through the surging, cheering crowd. "Let me through!" John shouted, pounding on unresponsive backs. "Let me through! It's my son! Are you all daft? . . . That's my son there! Let me through!"

Two men moved, opening a small space, and John threw himself into it, elbowing his way to the front. He and Father Malone arrived at the same time and with the same idea. Father Malone went after Sean, wrestling him away; John went after George, grabbing his arms, locking them behind his back. George squirmed, but not for long. He was exhausted and he was in pain, bruised, bloody, soundly beaten by the hated papist. He could not bring himself to look at his father. It was just as well he did not, for John was as angry as he had ever been in his life.

Neither John nor George spoke for several minutes. When at last John was able to speak his voice was bitter. "Are you satisfied? Did you get what you wanted?"

"Pa, I can explain."

"Not to me." John released his son. He turned him around and stared into his puffy, reddened eyes. "I don't understand you, lad. I'll never understand you if I live to be a hundred. Look at you! Your face half torn off . . . your hands scraped down to bone. And why? Because you always have to go too bloody far, that's why. I saw you with the Irish lad. You kept at him . . . jeering him, daring him, until he finally had to bash you." George tried to speak but John silenced him. "Eh, there's nothing to say. You do the same thing to me all the time. Keep at me and keep at me until I finally have to bash you. I never understood why. I don't understand now." John turned away. He stared down at the blood-stained deck and shook his head angrily back and forth. His mouth was a thin and trembling line. "By God, it has to stop!"

"Pa," George said, wiping blood from his streaming nose, "if you'll listen to my side of it."

"*Your* side? Eh, there's nothing but trouble on your side. Trouble and heartache all around." John put his hands on George's shoulders. He shook him violently. "You have to stop this carrying on, lad. You *have* to. Do you hear me?"

"Aye, Pa. I'm sorry, Pa."

"You're always sorry. Always when it's too late. I'm at the end of my rope, lad, and that's the truth."

"Pa, I'll—"

"No!" John threw up his hands. "No more talk. I've had my fill of talk that takes us nowhere."

Without another word, John walked away. He was preoccupied, still angry; he did not see the small pool of blood in his path. He took a step and slipped, falling with a crash to the deck. Cursing, he got up, but his footing was unsure and he fell again. He was pitched forward, into the heavy metal chains coiled at deckside.

He rolled over once and then lay absolutely still.

"Pa," George screamed. He ran to John and bent over him. "Pa, are you all right?" John did not move, did not speak. Blood trickled from his temple. "Pa?"

Now a crowd gathered for the second time that morning. Father Malone broke through, followed closely by Mary and Rose.

"What happened?" Mary cried. She saw her father lying in a widening circle of blood and she dropped to his side. "Pa, it's Mary. Can you hear me, Pa?"

"Give the man air," Father Malone shouted, pushing the curious crowd back. "Sean, run and fetch the doctor. *Run,* boyo." The priest joined Mary at John's side. He took a handkerchief and pressed it to his wounds. Gently, he patted John's face. "Wake up now. Open your eyes and talk to us. . . . Wake up . . . wake up. . . . Ah, that's better."

John opened his eyes. He blinked and, slowly, Mary's face swam into focus. "Lass," he whispered.

"Pa, the doctor's coming," she said anxiously. "You'll be fine. He'll fix you good as new." She took her father's hand and held it tightly. "You'll be fine, Pa . . . Pa, can you hear me?"

John stared mutely at Mary. He felt strange, very sleepy and weak. Dimly, he remembered falling, remembered the metal chains smashing into his skull. There was an odd taste in his mouth and he realized it was the taste of blood. "Lass . . ."

"Aye, Pa, I'm here," Mary said, her voice breaking. "Just hold fast to my hand, Pa. The doctor's coming. You'll be fine."

"Lass . . ."

"Aye, Pa. I'm here."

John's lips moved but no words came. Mary leaned closer to him, her fingers gripping his hand like bands of iron. "Don't try to talk, Pa. You've been . . . hurt." She turned stricken eyes to Father Malone. "He'll be all right." She nodded urgently. "Aye, he'll be all right."

Father Malone put his strong arm around Mary's shoulder. He had no illusions. He had seen men die before and he knew John did not have long. Dear Lord, he prayed silently, give this poor child strength. She has no one but a useless brother and a wee sister. Dear Lord, help her.

"Lass," John whispered. Blood ran from the corner of his mouth. His face was as white and cold as marble. "Lass, promise me . . . you'll . . . always take care of . . . our Rose."

"Aye, Pa, but . . . Pa?" Mary gasped. *"Pa?"*

Father Malone reached out and closed John's eyes. "I'm sorry," he said quietly.

"What? Sorry? No!" Mary cried. "No, it can't be. It can't."

"It was God's will, child." Father Malone spoke automatically and without great conviction, for, secretly, he doubted that God involved Himself in every life, every death. God allows accidents, he thought; perhaps there's a reason, perhaps there isn't. He could never have spoken such a heresy to his fellow priests, but he thought it.

Mary had begun to sob. Father Malone took her head on his shoulder and rocked her gently. Out of the corner of his eye he saw George standing rigidly, his mouth agape, his eyes wide and staring. Rose was near the ship's stern, sitting in the motherly lap of an Irishwoman from Cork, Father Malone's own county.

A profound silence had fallen over the deck. Children had stopped playing, women had stopped talking, and men who earlier had been so boisterous in their cheers, now hung their heads, ashamed of themselves.

The silence was shattered by the sound of footsteps and raised voices. Sean Ryan appeared on the stairway, followed by the uniformed figure of the ship's doctor, the latter clearly annoyed. "I'm apologizing, Father," Sean said, "but I had the divil of a time getting the good doctor to . . ." Sean looked at all the somber faces. He looked at George's face, at his wildly staring eyes, and he knew that John was dead. Quickly, he made the sign of the cross.

"What's going on here?" the doctor demanded. "I intend to speak to the captain about you . . . you people. How dare you send that boy above deck? He is steerage. He is not allowed above deck. How dare you bother me with—"

"Doctor," Father Malone said firmly, keeping Mary close to him, "not to interrupt you, but there's been a terrible accident. A man is dead."

"Oh?" Dr. Edwin Carlyle took his eyeglasses from his pocket and put them on. "Who are you?"

"Patrick Malone. Father Patrick Malone."

"Catholic. I suppose you're all Catholic down here." He wrinkled his nose. "Irish Catholics. Well, it can't be helped."

"It's kind you are to see it that way," Father Malone said dryly. "But the man who died didn't happen to be Irish or Catholic. He was an Englishman."

"An Englishman?" Dr. Carlyle's icy glance went from one end of the deck to the other. He wondered how any decent Englishman could allow himself to travel with the filthy Irish. Another question occurred to him then and he stepped back, toward the stairs. "Was he set upon by your . . . your people?"

"He slipped on the deck," Father Malone replied, no longer amused. "His head hit the chains. If you don't mind my saying so, Doctor, the man's children are here and it's not good for them to be hearing talk like this."

"Very well. I certainly have no wish to prolong the conversation."

"And I'm thanking you for that."

Dr. Carlyle's eyes narrowed. He knew he had been insulted, but surrounded as he was by hulking Irishmen, he did not know what to do about it. He decided to do nothing. "Shall we get on with business?" he asked crisply. "Where is the body?"

"Here." Father Malone gestured and a path was cleared for the doctor. "The man is John Kilburne."

Mary heard her father's name and she began to sob again. Her cries seemed to fluster Dr. Carlyle. He looked at Mary, at the body of John Kilburne, at Father Malone. "Get her to her compartment. Get everybody to their compartments."

Father Malone nodded. At his signal, men and women and children filed quietly to the stairs. Rose was taken inside but George and Mary remained. "You too," Dr. Carlyle said. "Go along."

"Father," Mary pleaded, choking on her sobs, "I can't leave Pa here. All alone."

"It's best you go inside, child. You can be helping your brother. I'll stay with your Pa, and I'll be coming to get you as soon as the doctor's done."

Mary hesitated. She wiped her wet eyes and tugged at her long chestnut braid. She was dazed, unable to make a decision. Father Malone saw this. He took Mary on one side, George on the other, and led them to the stairs. "Listen to me, child," he said to her. "Your brother's needing help. But you're a brave girl. You can help him. You must, he trusts no one else."

Mary had given no thought to George. She looked at him now and was newly shocked, for his face was swollen and caked with blood and his eyes were the eyes of a madman. "Georgy," she said, swallowing hard, "come along with me. I'll get some water for your cuts. Come, Georgy." She took his arm, guiding him down the steps. "It's all right. Come, Georgy, that's a good lad."

Father Malone watched them go, two young people in pain, leaning on each other. When he could watch no more, he returned to Dr. Carlyle.

Dr. Carlyle had finished with John. He stood by the rail, writing in a black leather-bound book. "Oh, it's you," he said curtly as Father Malone joined him. "My report is almost completed. Concussion, I should think. Nasty business. Died within minutes." He continued writing, not bothering to look up. "I thought I heard you to say this fellow was not a Catholic."

"He wasn't."

"Why are you so involved with his children? Trying to convert them, are you?"

"Ah," Father Malone sighed. "I don't go about converting people. I've all I can handle with my own . . . I'm involved with the children for they've nobody else."

"No mother?"

"No."

"Orphans." Dr. Carlyle shook his head impatiently.

50

"They will be deported back to England, of course. Another expense for the ship company. These . . . people are nothing but trouble."

Father Malone's eyes darkened. He ran his hand through his unruly thatch of black hair. "The children might not be deported. They might be going to relatives in America."

"Relatives indeed! What could their relatives be but miserable creatures like themselves? Do you suppose their relatives will be anxious to have orphans on their hands? More mouths to feed. Less room in their grimy slums. No," Dr. Carlyle snorted, "they will surely be deported." He snapped his book shut and stared at Father Malone. "I shall notify the captain. Crewmen will come down shortly. An hour."

"An hour?"

"Yes." Dr. Carlyle looked at his watch. "Yes, I should say an hour. The Kilburne fellow will be slipped over the side then. Family will be allowed on deck. Clergy, of course. No others."

Father Malone winced at the doctor's coldness. He knew the nature of man, knew that cruelty lurked in many hearts, but still he was saddened. "It'll be hard," he said quietly, "on the children."

"That is not my problem."

"I'm wishing there was another way."

"Another way?" Dr. Carlyle laughed. It was a thin, dry laugh, as thin and dry as the man himself. "I have often wondered why America wants . . . steerage people in her country. As a source of cheap labor, no doubt. Well, whatever her reasons, America does not want steerage corpses. No, there's no other way. The Kilburne fellow goes over the side. You have an hour to

51

prepare the children, if preparation is necessary."

Dr. Carlyle turned on his heel and was gone. Father Malone stared up at the serene blue sky, imploring God to give him the right words to speak to the children. "Help me to ease their burden," he prayed fervently. "They're only children. Your children. Give them strength. Give me strength to see the way." He prayed for a long time, prayed to the God he loved, but did not always understand. When he had finished, he knelt over John. He drew the cloth from his face and gazed at him. "I'll do my best for the little ones," he said. "Godspeed, John Kilburne."

The steerage passengers had put aside their hostilities and rallied around the Kilburne children. Molly Brosnan kept Rose with her, brushing her beautiful golden curls, singing songs, telling stories. Peg Finnery saw to Mary. She found a fresh shirtwaist for her. She mended her torn skirt. She managed to produce a cup of tea, liberally spiked with the poteen she carried in her traveling bag.

The men did their part. They cleansed George's wounds with strong, homemade powders they had brought from Ireland. They combed his hair and bound his bloodied knuckles with clean rags. Sean Ryan contributed a white shirt, Tom Kennedy a tie. They fed him poteen spoon by spoon. George never noticed what was being done to him. Like a zombie, mute, unseeing, he stood their pushings and proddings, offering not even a murmur of protest.

Now, Father Malone sat with Mary and George in the empty dining hall. Rose was absent, for Mary had decided to spare her the ordeal of their father's funeral. "She wouldn't understand," Mary had said to Father Malone, and that settled the matter.

Mary was still dazed, but she had begun to collect her thoughts. She had responsibilities now; George was sick and would need her attentions; to Rose she would have to be both mother and father. She looked at George, sitting across from her on the bench, staring blankly into space. An hour had passed since John's death, yet he had not cried, had not said a single word.

Father Malone, as if reading Mary's mind, spoke softly. "It's the shock, child. I've seen it many a time before. He'll come round."

"Father, you know we're not Catholic. The . . . service . . ."

"Ah, don't worry about that. It's your Bible I have here. I'll be reading a few psalms from it, that's all."

"Thank you, Father."

"If you're ready, we should be going outside. I'll take the boyo."

The three proceeded in silence, through the passageways and up the stairs. Outside, the late morning sun was hot and bright, shining everywhere on the deck. Mary was blinded for a moment. She shielded her eyes against the fierce light. When her vision cleared she began to cry, for she saw her father's body, wrapped in a shroud of black cotton and strapped to a simple wooden frame.

"'Urry up then," one of the four crew members called. "We 'aven't got all the day."

"Have you no respect?" Father Malone said sharply, looking at each man in turn. "What if it was your pa there? Wouldn't you be wanting to say a proper goodbye?" He did not wait for their reply. He led Mary and George to their father and then opened the Bible.

Father Malone had a wonderful voice, deep and resonant and rich with the accents of County Cork. He loved the ancient words of the Bible and on his lips they found their true splendor. Mary listened, mesmerized. Her grief was eased, for in the soaring beauty of the psalms she felt God's grace. She felt strengthened, infinitely reassured. The crew members listened as if under a spell. They turned rapt faces to Father Malone, utterly lost in the moment.

He concluded with the Twenty-third Psalm, closing the Bible and giving it to Mary. "It's time, child." He nodded. "You must say goodbye now."

Mary hugged the Bible to her chest. She went to her father and knelt by him. Gently, she kissed the black cloth that covered his lips. "I love you, Pa," she whispered. "Godspeed."

Father Malone helped her up. He grasped George's arm and took him to his father. "Have you anything to say, boyo?" he asked. "Ah well, your pa knows you love him, and that's enough."

The crew members, all reverence now, looked down at the shrouded body of John Kilburne. "Father," one of them said, "the way I'm thinking, we 'ave our job to do, but the children don't 'ave to see it."

"Sure and they don't. Come along, Mary. We'll be going back inside."

Mary took the hand Father Malone offered. She paused, looking back once more at her father, and then started to walk to the door. They were almost inside when suddenly George stopped. "Pa!" he cried. He turned around just in time to see his father's body thrown into the ocean. *"Pa . . . Pa,"* he screamed.

George broke away from Father Malone. He ran screaming toward the rail. Mary and Father Malone ran after him. "Stop him!" Father Malone shouted, for he knew what the boy wanted to do. "Stop him!"

The four crewmen formed themselves into a semicircle. They caught George as he made a leap for the rail. They wrestled him to the deck, but in a burst of insane strength, he escaped their grasp. He leaped again at the rail. He had one leg over the side when Father Malone grabbed him about the waist and pulled him down. Father Malone handled George the way John had; he pinned his arms behind his back and held him there. Father Malone gave no ground. After what seemed like an eternity, George's shoulders sagged and he collapsed to the deck. He cried. He cried as if his heart were breaking.

Mary sat next to her brother. She stroked his head. "He'll be all right now," she said. "It's good for him to cry."

Father Malone smiled at Mary. The girl has sense, he thought. Sense and kindness too. She won't go far wrong.

The *Royal Star* was two days out of New York Harbor. No one was more aware of the schedule than Mary Kilburne, for she had heard talk, frightening talk that she and her brother and sister would be deported. *Deported.* The word struck fear in the hearts of steerage passengers. To Mary it was unthinkable. Her family had not come so far, had not suffered so much, only to be turned back. This was their chance and, if they lost it, they would not have another.

This morning, while Rose played with Molly Brosnan and George napped in his bunk, Mary decided to seek the advice of Father Malone. It was a hard decision to make, for she had been raised to distrust outsiders, but she liked the young priest; despite the teachings of her Hexter childhood, she trusted him. The question thus decided in her mind, she marched up the steps and out to the deck.

Father Malone stood by himself near the rail, reading his breviary. He smiled as Mary approached. "Ah, good morning to you, child. And isn't it the prettiest morning yet?"

"Aye, Father." Mary glanced away for a moment, trying to think how to begin. She was not used to initiating conversations and she was uneasy. Father Malone watched her. He had an idea of what was coming, but he said nothing, waiting instead for her to speak. "Father," she said hesitantly, blushing, "I wonder if I could . . . ask you something?"

"Certainly you can. Anything at all."

"Well . . . I've heard the women talking. I've heard that we'll be deported . . . Rose and Georgy and me. Is it . . . do you think it's true?"

"Tell me, have you any family at home in England?"

"Family? We've two aunts and a cousin. But they're old, all of them. They couldn't take us in. Father, we've given up our jobs and our cottage. We've no money. We can't go back. There's nothing for us back there."

"Have you family in America then?"

"Aye, our cousin Bob. He's a rich man, Pa said. It's settled we're to live with him and his family. Not on charity," Mary said quickly. "Bob's found jobs for

Georgy and me." She reached into the pocket of her skirt and withdrew Bob's last letter. "Look," she said, giving the letter to Father Malone.

He read the letter carefully. It did not, to his shrewd eyes, appear to be the letter of a rich man. It was full of veiled warnings, speaking too often of "expenses," of the jobs he had arranged for them. And such lowly jobs too, thought Father Malone. "So you're to be a scullery maid?"

"Aye. I was scullery maid to Lady Worsham four years over. I have references. Father," Mary said, her voice almost a plea, "I can do maid's work or cook's work. I can read and write and do sums. I'll work. I'll earn our keep."

"I've no doubt of that, child," Father Malone nodded. He thought: Your little Rose is already pettish and vain. She won't be one for work. And your Georgy, he's over his shock but he's turned inward, away from the world. He'll be no use at all. Sure and you'll be earning the keep for everybody. "Child," he said finally, "we've all heard how the streets are paved with gold in America. Be wary of that. There's poverty there and plenty of it. You'll be working your fingers to the bone, just as you did in England."

"Aye, Father. I'm happy to, because there's one thing different. In America our Rose can be a lady!"

"Ah, I see." Father Malone was not entirely surprised by Mary's answer. He knew the Kilburnes were besotted with Rose. Clearly, some of his own Irishwomen had become besotted with her. She had that effect on people. It's a pity, he thought. Surely it's a waste. Father Malone looked at Mary. He studied her face, her fine ivory skin, her eyes dark as the sky at .

57

midnight, her shining chestnut hair. She'll be a beautiful woman, he thought, but what good will it do her, locked away in a scullery somewhere? "America's what you want, child? What you really and truly want?"

"Aye, Father."

Father Malone, at twenty-seven, was a practical man. He believed problems had to be faced squarely, and if a few white lies were necessary to solve them, so be it. "I'm not promising," he said after a while, "but I'll do my best to get you what you want. You must listen carefully, child. Listen, then be telling me what you think."

"Aye."

Now Father Malone's eyes were intent on Mary. His voice was firm. "Be wary what you tell the immigration people. Don't tell them you have jobs waiting. It's against the law and they'll deport you for it. The law was made to protect immigrants from becoming slave laborers, and that's one way of looking at it. The other is that they don't want greenhorns taking good jobs from Americans. Do you understand, child?" Mary nodded and Father Malone continued. "You can tell them you're going to live with your cousin . . . but that may not be enough. There's many a man who takes his relatives in one week and throws them out the next. So, if you're willing, I'll vouch for you. I'll promise to be responsible for the Kilburnes if need be."

"Father," Mary said, astonished. "I couldn't ask it."

"I'm offering. It's the only way I know."

Mary's thoughts tumbled one on top of the other. She knew her father, were he alive, would be angered by such a suggestion, angered and ashamed. To accept help from a Catholic, from a Catholic *priest,* was humiliating. And yet . . . Well, thought Mary, Pa's gone and I'm responsible for us. I can't follow the old ways. I don't even want to. No one's ever been kinder to us than this man, this Father Malone.

"We have two days, child. You don't have to be deciding right off."

Mary raised her head. Her eyes met Father Malone's. "I've decided." She smiled. "I'll be glad of your help, Father. Aye, and proud too."

Two

It was morning, the last Friday in July, when the *Royal Star* slid into its berth at the edge of the Ellis Island pier. Three hundred seventy-three cheering steerage passengers, clutching bags, cloth sacks, and boxes tied with rope, disembarked. On American soil at last, their faces held the special wonder and joy known only to those who had sought, and then found, a promised land. Many wept. One woman fell to her knees and kissed the ground.

Immigration officials had, over the years, become inured to such sights. Impassively, they hurried the new arrivals along. "This way. Step lively . . . this way. Step lively," was their continuous, uninflected refrain.

The immigrants walked beneath a glass and steel canopy, past a grassy, sycamore-shaded yard, and through a two-story archway into the grand hall. There they climbed a stairway to a reception room of tiled, vaulted ceilings and curved windows reflecting the Manhattan skyline. Now the attitudes of the immigrants began to change. Joy was replaced by fear, for they realized they were under observation. Two old men, out of breath when they reached the top of the stairs, were stopped by officials. A large *H,* immigration code for a bad heart, was pinned to their shirts. The men, doomed to deportation, hung their heads. There were other dreaded letters: *L* for lameness; *C* for coughs; *E* for eyes that were running or inflamed.

Father Malone thought the system haphazard and unfair. It angered him, but because the power of immigration officials was absolute, and because he was a prudent man, he kept his temper. He busied himself amongst the immigrants. To some he offered words of encouragement, to others words of consolation. He smiled into tired, anxious faces and, at least for a while, eased their waiting.

The wait for inspection was long and it was uncomfortable. Immigrants sat shoulder to shoulder on parklike benches of hard wooden slats. The benches stretched out in row after endless row, reaching even into the corners of the cavernous room. Aisles formed by iron dividers were prowled by immigration officials watching for signs of illness or suspicious behavior.

Under the circumstances, Mary had concluded that it was wisest to blend unnoticed into the crowd. She admonished both Rose and George to keep silent, keep still. "We mustn't do anything to call attention," she said over and over again.

Rose hardly heard her sister's warnings. She was in a world all her own, fascinated by her new surroundings. In awe, she stared at the high ceilings of the room, at the many windows sparkling with sunlight. The room was larger than any she had seen before, larger than any she had imagined. It was, she thought, like a room in a great palace. She pretended it was her palace. Sitting in Mary's lap, she stared at the sea of black-clad immigrants and pretended they were her servants.

George, too, was in a world of his own. He was bewildered. So much had happened that he had trouble keeping his thoughts in order. He remembered leaving Hexter, remembered arriving in teeming Liverpool, remembered the *Royal Star*. His head began to throb as he remembered his fight with Sean Ryan and, then, his father's death. The two events were locked together in his mind; if he had not fought with Sean, his father would be alive now. He shut his eyes, trying to shut out the terrible pain.

It was past noon when the Kilburnes were summoned for inspection. The health inspection was thorough, with special attention given to skin and eyes and lungs. Immigrants with rashes, with infected eyes or congested lungs were sent to the contagious-disease wards on the grounds. Some of them—those with tuberculosis or small pox—would die there.

Mary had heard about the wards, about the crematorium. During the wait, she had seen men and women and children being led away in tears, admittance to America denied. She had seen their pain, and felt it as if it were her own. Now, guiding Rose and George to their inspections, she straightened her back and held her head high. Determination glittered in her dark blue eyes. "Mind your manners," she said firmly to George. "You too, lass. We're in America and in America we'll stay!"

It was a smiling and radiant Mary, health certificates in hand, who ran up to Father Malone. "We're passed," she cried. "All of us, we're passed!"

"I'm congratulating you, child. Sure and your smile

tells the whole story." Impulsively, Father Malone reached out and hugged Mary. "I'm thinking you're the happiest girl in the room today. Would I be right?"

"Aye, Father. I only wish . . ." Mary's face became quiet, thoughtful. "I only wish Pa was here with us. It was his dream that brought us here."

Father Malone saw an odd look come into George's eyes. "That it was," he said quickly. "So let's have the dream come true. Here, stand here with me. The inspectors have some questions to ask."

There were indeed questions, twenty-one standard questions asked of all immigrants. There were also forms to be completed and papers to be stamped. Long lines of immigrants waited; they might have waited forever but for the efficiency of inspectors who rushed most of them through in less than five minutes. Suspected criminals and prostitutes were immediately marked for deportation. The others proceeded smoothly, close now to the end of their journey.

Mary watched, heartened by what she saw. Only one woman in her line had been marked for deportation, a woman not from the *Royal Star,* but from a German ship that had docked at about the same time. She did not know why the woman had been rejected, for she was innocent in such matters, but Father Malone knew. He watched the woman's obscene gestures as she was taken away and he shook his head sadly. Father Malone, young as he was, had seen many things. He had seen families thrown off their land, left to starve by greedy landlords. He had seen men turn to drink. And he had seen women turn to the streets. It was a puzzle to him that life could be so cruel to some, so kind to others.

The woman's protests grew more violent and instinctively Father Malone moved to shield Mary and Rose from the sight. "Pay no mind," he said softly. "The poor woman's upset." But Rose was intrigued. She craned her neck for a better view. Father Malone grasped her tiny wrist and pulled her away. "Come, Miss Rose, that's nothing for you to be looking at."

The rest of their wait was uneventful. After forty minutes or so, they reached the head of the line. Their inspector, a balding bespectacled man in his fifties, did not glance up from his papers. He began the litany of questions, stopping only when he heard the ages of the immigrants at his desk. Now he looked up. He saw Mary, neatly dressed, her chestnut braids pinned at the nape of her neck. Old enough to support herself, he thought, his eyes moving to George. Old enough to support himself, he decided, looking then at Rose. "Well," he said, startled by the huge pale eyes looking back at him. "Well." The inspector cleared his throat. "Where're the child's parents?" he asked.

"They're dead," Father Malone answered quietly. "The mother four years ago. The father during the crossing of the *Royal Star.*"

"Orphan! Do you think America's here just to take in starving orphans? Think again!"

"Inspector," Father Malone's voice was calm, patient, "the Kilburnes, all of them, are to live with their cousin Bob Kilburne in Yorkville."

"Cousin! I know cousins, and aunts and uncles for that matter. You can't count on 'em." The inspector wagged a bony finger at Father Malone. "They'll let you down every time. Especially a cousin. A cousin ain't even a close relation. A cousin's got his own problems. This child'll end up a public charge."

"No, Inspector. Because I'll vouch for the Kilburnes, the three of them. If their cousin doesn't want them, I'll see to their care."

"Is that so?" The inspector removed his glasses. He wiped them with his sleeve and then replaced them on his nose. "Why would you do that? Are they Catholics?"

"No. But their father put them in my care before he died."

"Is that so?" The inspector was not persuaded. He stared at the Kilburnes, settling finally on Mary. "Is that so, young lady? Did your papa give you over to the priest here?"

"Aye." Mary nodded. "We heard him, my brother and me. Father Malone promised to see to us."

"Is that so, young man?"

George nodded.

"What's the matter with you? Cat got your tongue? Speak up, young man!"

Mary glanced anxiously at George. She kicked him and the sudden action seemed to clear his mind. He recalled Mary's detailed instructions; they had been more like orders than instructions, but he was too tired to offer any challenge. "Aye." He nodded again. "The Father's to see to us if Bob won't."

"You"—the inspector pointed at Father Malone—"you're taking a lot on your plate."

"I'm agreeing with you there. But the church has facilities for orphan children."

The inspector hesitated, his hand poised halfway between the tags for deportation and the tags for admittance. He was a conscientious man who hated to make mistakes and so he debated with himself. A full minute went by. "All right," he said finally. With a flourish, he completed the forms, stamped the papers, and issued the appropriate tags. "Welcome to America. Move along. . . . Next!"

Mary's face lit up. Her eyes glistened and her cheeks colored a deep pink. "It's true then?" she asked Father Malone. "We're passed?"

"It's true."

Mary clapped her hands together in an old gesture of childhood. She was beside herself, laughing and crying at the same time. Her exultation was so great, so pure, it caused everyone to smile. The other immigrants watched her and they remembered what it was to be young, to stand at the joyous beginning of life.

"It's a miracle you've done for us, Father," Mary said when she was able to speak. "A miracle! I thank you for it." She kissed the priest's cheek, then spun around and kissed George. In one graceful motion, she lifted Rose into her arms and hugged her. "Oh, lass"—she beamed—"what a grand life you'll have! Aren't you glad to be in America?"

"Aye." Rose shrugged, dropping her head to Mary's shoulder. "Can we go home now? I'm sleepy. I want to go home."

Downstairs, in a long and sunny hall near the door, fewer than fifteen people were gathered to greet the newly arrived immigrants. German, Irish, and Italian, they clustered in little groups, glancing often to the staircase. The appearance of a beloved relative brought elated shouts, then tears, as brothers embraced brothers and mothers embraced sons.

Off to the side of the hall, one man stood alone. He was tall, very thin. The planes of his face were sharp and angular; his cheeks were gaunt. Every few moments he raised sad, bloodshot eyes toward the stairs and as he did so his hands trembled. Nervously, he paced back and forth, a lonely figure oblivious to the happiness around him.

Bob Kilburne was forty years old. He looked sixty. His hair, once a dark, vibrant brown, was shot through with gray. His walk was slow and stiff. Deep lines were etched about his mouth and on his forehead. His clothes had lost whatever fit they may have had; they hung loosely on him, two sizes too big for his fleshless frame. Anyone who had known Bob Kilburne in the old days, in the days of laughter and money, would not have recognized him now.

He knew what he had become. His wife and children knew too, though they never reproached him, never said an unkind word. "Papa's not feeling well today," was all that was ever said. It was enough. Bob had learned to live with such gentle deceptions, but now, awaiting the arrival of family he had not seen in many years, he was ashamed. His shame touched other chords in him: anger, resentment, self-pity. He rued the day he had invited the Kilburnes to come to America.

Rueful was Bob's state of mind when his cousins appeared in the hall. They were strangers to him, yet he recognized George right away. He stared at the boy and in his face he saw the face of a young John Kilburne. The resemblance was extraordinary. For a moment he was transported back to Hexter, back to the raucous times of his youth.

Wearily, Bob rubbed his eyes. He took a few halting steps toward George. "You're John's son?" he asked. "John Kilburne's son?"

"Aye."

"Where is he? Where's John?"

George looked in confusion at the tall, thin man looming over him. He felt a sudden panic and turned to Mary for reassurance. But Mary, too, was confused. She knew the man had to be Bob Kilburne, yet she could not reconcile him with John's merry description. "A fine feller, always ready with a smile and a joke" . . . "his dreams came true" . . . "rich" . . . "he lives like a lord." Mary realized there was no truth in any of it. She looked at Bob's poor clothing, his frayed cuffs, his trousers shiny from too many pressings, his patched shoes, and she knew he was not rich; she looked into his sad eyes and she knew he had not smiled in a long, long time.

Mary took a deep breath. "Cousin Bob," she said, trying to sound cheerful, "I'm Mary. This is Rose, and that's our brother Georgy."

"Yes, but where's John? Where's your papa?"

Father Malone had been watching everyone very closely. With sinking heart, he had noted Bob's ravaged face and ashen complexion; sure signs, he thought, of a man destroyed by drink. What, he wondered, would happen to the children now? "Mr. Kilburne," he said, stepping forward, "if I could be having a word with you?"

"What?"

"A word with you, Mr. Kilburne. There're some things you should know."

Bob glared at Father Malone's clerical collar. He

shook his head. "I don't know what you want," he said, "but whatever it is, I'm not interested. I've no use for you and your kind."

"It's important. It's about John Kilburne."

"What have you to do with John?"

"That's what I want to talk to you about. Let's go where we can talk in quiet. I'm promising I won't take long."

Bob was annoyed by the priest's insistence, but he was also curious. "I'll hear you out," he snapped. "See you're quick about it."

"I'll do my best. Come along over here," Father Malone gestured, leading Bob a short distance away. "I'm afraid I'm bringing you bad news."

Mary stayed where she was. She shifted Rose's weight in her arms and then turned all her attention to the two men. Only Father Malone spoke. He spoke without pause for several minutes, his eyes never leaving Bob's face. At one point, when Bob seemed to falter, he offered his arm in support. Mary saw Bob glance swiftly in her direction. When he glanced back at Father Malone his eyes were wild with indignation. He began to yell, but his words tumbled so rapidly they made no sense.

"Mary," George said, "what is it? I don't understand. Who's that feller?"

"Why, that's cousin Bob."

"Him? Cousin Bob? No . . . Pa said . . ."

"Aye, Georgy. I remember." Mary gazed thoughtfully at her brother. She knew he was still not well. He had moments of clarity, and in those moments he was his old self. But those moments were rare; most of the time he was withdrawn, unable or unwilling to follow

70

the simplest conversation. All the details of their lives he left to Mary to decide. "Georgy, that's our cousin Bob. And we must be nice to him. He's . . . had hard times."

George studied the man arguing with Father Malone. He frowned. His head started to ache again. "Mary . . ."

"Aye, Georgy?"

"What will we do?"

"Don't fret, lad. We'll get by. We're in America now. One way or the other, we'll get by."

Mary's words had been intended to soothe George and they did. Some of the tension left his face. His hands, held so stiffly at his sides, relaxed. "Aye, if you say so, Mary."

George had the reassurance he sought. He drifted back into his thoughts, far away from the commotion of Ellis Island. His eyes became paler and softer, focused inwardly on a place only he saw. Mary was concerned about him, but in the aftermath of John's death, she had learned to order her concerns. Right now, safely in America, her concern was to make a place for her family.

Sighing, Mary lifted Rose in her arms once more. She patted the sleeping child, taking comfort in her sweet young scent. "There's a good lass," she murmured. Mary looked up to see Bob and Father Malone returning. Now her heart began to pound and her breath came quickly.

Neither man smiled. Father Malone started to speak but Bob turned on him in anger. "Stay out of our affairs! We don't need Papists and their meddling. You've caused enough trouble."

71

"Cousin Bob," Mary said anxiously, "Father Malone helped us. If it hadn't been for him—"

"And that's my point! You did a bad thing, Mary. You shouldn't be here, not with your papa . . . gone. You should be on your way back to England, where you belong. Where there's people to look after you." Bob's voice was loud, raspy. His hands shook, whether from rage or illness, Mary was not sure. "Did you expect to live off me? Did you expect I'd be the support of three orphans?"

Mary had not been prepared for such an assault. She was startled, and hurt. Tears stood in her dark blue eyes. Stubbornly, she refused to let them fall. "No, Cousin," she said. "I can work and so can Georgy."

"Oh, you'll work all right. There's no doubt of it. But without your papa's wages it's a bad bargain."

Mary said nothing, for there was nothing to say. She faced her cousin, looked into his eyes, and waited.

"Do you think money grows on trees? Four years ago I sent money for your passage. It's still owed me."

"We'll pay what we owe. We'll pay every shilling. I can work and so can Georgy."

There was an uncharacteristic look of defiance about Mary. Father Malone was glad to see it. She'll need a bit of iron in her spine, he thought, if she's to make a decent life here.

Bob, too, had noticed the abrupt change in Mary. In the determined thrust of her chin, the square set of her shoulders, she seemed more woman than young girl. He exhaled a great breath, running his hand impatiently through his graying hair. "Well, there's nothing to do about it now. I can't send you back. I can't be throwing good money after bad."

"Father Malone offered to see to us."

"Father Malone!" Bob roared furiously. "Are you out of your mind? Are you mad? Do you think I can have John Kilburne's children raised by *papists?* Do you think I can sink so low?"

"Father Malone's been kind to us. His religion's no account of mine."

"Kind? Is it kindness you're after? You're in the wrong country for that. You're in the wrong *world* for that."

Bob's angry voice awakened Rose. She stirred, yawning drowsily. "Georgy," Mary said, "hold our Rose for a while . . . Georgy?"

George took the child. He cradled her gently in his arms and she fell back asleep.

"Cousin Bob"—Mary looked at him—"we've all our papers . . . we're in America and glad of it. I'm not after kindness, only a chance to work and earn our way. It's not much to ask."

Bob recognized the challenge in Mary's voice. He was taken aback by it, for he was used to children like his own, children who would be bullied. "You have a sharp tongue on you," he said slowly. "I don't like it. I'm the head of your family now. You'd best remember that, and your place too."

"Aye." Mary flushed, surprised and embarrassed by her daring. "I'm sorry if I spoke wrong."

"That's better." Bob nodded in satisfaction. "That's respectful." He looked at the big round clock on the wall. "We have some traveling ahead of us and it's getting late. Follow me, children. . . . Don't dawdle."

Mary sent her brother and sister after Bob, then turned to Father Malone. "I'll never be able to thank you for all you've done," she said. "I'll . . . I'll miss you, Father."

"Ah, but we'll be living in the same city now. Sure and our paths are bound to cross one day."

"I hope so."

"And if you ever need anything, child, you can come to me. You have the address of the rectory."

"Aye, it's tucked safe away. . . . Hell's Kitchen sounds terrible bad."

Father Malone laughed. He took both of Mary's hands and held them in his own. "It's fitting. A priest's needed most in hell."

"Aye . . . Well . . ." Mary's eyes clouded, for it was time to leave and she was truly sorry to leave the man who had been such a kind friend. "Goodbye, Father."

"God keep you, Mary Kilburne."

After traveling by ferry, by streetcar, and on foot, the Kilburnes arrived in the section of Manhattan known as Yorkville. It was a sprawling neighborhood of tenement buildings, small shops, restaurants, and saloons. It was also a neighborhood of children. Boys and girls played on stoops, on sidewalks, even in the streets, nimbly dodging the horse-drawn carriages and wagons that came their way. There were peddlers selling vegetables and fruit from wooden carts, and roving street musicians who sang for pennies.

Mary, accustomed to the quiet lanes of Hexter, was dazzled by the noise and color of her new neighborhood. Everything seemed big and loud: people, voices, buildings; the sun itself seemed to shine with a special intensity. "It's a festival here, Cousin Bob," she said in amazement. At that, Bob stopped walking and glared at her. "It's no festival. It's a hard life. The sooner you learn that, the better. You're too old for girlish notions."

Mary said nothing more. Gazing around the bustling streets of Yorkville, she felt the energy and strength that, she was certain, lay at the heart of America. There was no gold in the streets, but there was life and it was everywhere. She thought about the choking black mists of Hexter. She laughed.

The building Bob took them to was a five-story tenement on Eighty-first Street near First Avenue. They passed through a small vestibule into a dim hall and Bob pointed to the stairs. "It's four flights up. Get moving."

Rose was bleary-eyed with fatigue. She managed two or three steps, then turned to George and held out her arms, waiting to be picked up. George was no less tired, but dutifully, he bent and swept the child from the stairs. Huffing and puffing, he carried her the rest of the way.

Mary carried their bags, though their weight did not slow her. She flew up the stairs, her face radiant, her eyes aglow, as if in pursuit of some great treasure. When the door was opened to the Kilburne flat, she alone was smiling.

"Welcome to our home," Anna Kilburne said, hastily wiping her hands on her aprons. "Come in, come in." She was a pretty, blond-haired woman in her late thirties. Like her husband, she was very thin; unlike him, she had a wholesome look and a sweet, calm manner that put everyone at ease. Mary looked at her and knew she had found a home. "Sit down," Anna said, settling the children around the kitchen table. "I have tea ready . . . oh"—she shook her head—"but the little one needs bed more than tea. I'll take her." Even before introductions had been made, Anna Kilburne scooped Rose into her capable arms and carried her into a back room.

"That's my wife," Bob mumbled. "Anna. Now drink your tea. Nothing goes to waste around here."

When Anna returned, Bob led her to a corner of the kitchen and spoke a few words. Her reply obviously angered him, for his face reddened and his mouth curled in derision. "Don't be a damn fool," he yelled, stomping off to the bedroom.

Anna did not appear flustered by her husband's temper. She joined Mary and George at the table, folding her hands on the clean white cloth. "I'm sorry about your papa," she said softly, "but I'm happy you're here with us. You'll meet my children later. Harley is about your age." She nodded at George. "And Jane is just Rose's age. The girls will go to school together, come September. Everything will turn out fine. Don't worry."

Tears of relief came into Mary's eyes. Anna was a good woman, she thought, and though Bob would be their enemy, Anna would be their friend. "Thank you, Cousin Anna. I know it's hard, having us here and all. But we'll be good. And we'll work. We'll earn our keep."

Anna was touched by Mary's earnestness. She was impressed by her strength, for she knew what Bob must have put the girl through. She wondered if, in the same circumstances, she would be as brave.

Anna rose. She refilled their cups and put a plate of

bread-and-butter sandwiches on the table. "I'll bet you haven't eaten all day," she said. "This will see you 'til supper."

George came to life at the sight of food. He gobbled one sandwich and was starting a second when Mary stopped him. "Mind your manners, Georgy. Say thank you to Cousin Anna."

"Aye, thank you. Can I take another?"

"Help yourself. I know what growing boys are like. And growing girls too. Mary, have some before they're gone."

Mary ate slowly, savoring the taste of sweet butter on her tongue. It was the best meal she had had in weeks and, because it was her first meal in America, she wanted to remember it. George finished three sandwiches in the time it took her to finish one.

"I can't offer you any more to eat." Anna shrugged. "But would you like to rest awhile? I made up the beds fresh this morning."

"Aye." George got to his feet. "I'm terrible tired."

"Mary?"

"I'm too excited to sleep."

"Come with me, George. You can sleep in Harley's bed. Well, it's your bed too, from now on. You'll be sharing." Anna led George from the kitchen into a small hall at the end of the flat. There were three bedrooms, each of them long and narrow, with only enough space for a bed and a chest of drawers. "Here we are. I hope . . ." Anna did not have a chance to finish her sentence, for George had fallen on the bed, asleep even before his head hit the pillow. Anna removed his boots and opened the top buttons of his shirt. "Sleep well," she whispered. "You'll need all your strength."

Mary stood up when Anna entered the kitchen. "I'll wash the dishes, if that's all right?"

"Leave them for now. Sit down, Mary. I'd like to talk to you."

"Aye."

"It's just that . . . well, I think you have an explanation coming. Bob's letters . . . He never wrote about what happened. You see, things changed for us. Four years ago we had everything. Now we have very little. We get by—don't think we don't—but it's day to day. Like most everybody."

"You don't have to explain, Cousin." Mary's eyes were wide with concern, for she sensed Anna's discomfort. "We had a poor life in Hexter. It was terrible bad there. We're glad to be gone. We're glad to be in America." Mary stopped speaking as Bob walked into the kitchen. She was quiet, watching him warily.

"The girl thinks it's a festival here," he said, annoyed. "She'll soon learn." Bob, despite his annoyance, was calmer than he had been earlier. He had accepted the situation and, though far from pleased, he was resigned. "I'll see she learns. Anna, I'm going to work now. Don't wait up for me. Get your rest."

Anna smiled slightly. "I like to wait up for you."

Bob touched his wife's shoulder lightly. He stared at her and a look passed between them. It was not a look of passion, but of tenderness, of years and memories shared. "I'll try to be early. Mary, I expect you to help Anna with supper . . . and with all the other work around here."

"Aye, Cousin Bob. I'm glad to do it."

Bob went to the door and let himself out. Anna waited until she heard his footsteps on the stair and then smiled at Mary. "I wish you'd known Bob before. He was the happiest man I'd ever seen. How he loved to tell jokes! How he loved to laugh!"

"Pa told us. He said Bob was a fine feller."

"He was. He still is. He's a good man, Mary. But he's had so many bad things happen." Anna sighed. She clasped her hands in her lap, gazing into space. "Bob had a big tavern downtown. It was busy day and night . . . he was so good with the customers, you see. We lived in a fine flat, with fine furniture and carpets thick as clouds. We had a carriage. The children had nice clothes. . . . Well, a year ago there was a fire in the tavern. It burned to the ground. Bob lost everything."

"Oh, I'm sorry," Mary said, genuinely dismayed. "Poor Bob."

"We'd had such a good life, too good it turned out, because we owed money. A lot of money. With the tavern gone, there was no way to pay. We sold everything we could. Furniture, carpets, the fancy dishes. Bob sold his watch. We sold most of our clothes. It took awhile, but we managed to pay our debts. Then Jane got sick. She was sick for weeks. It cost so much for doctors and medicines." Anna smoothed her skirts. She brushed the sleeve of her plain white shirtwaist and smiled grimly. "Bob tried to borrow money from his friends. It was *hard* for him to do that, Mary. He's a proud man."

"Did they help him? His friends?"

Anna hesitated. Her green eyes became dark and still. "A few did what they could. . . . Bob says you know who your friends really are when you need money. Maybe he's right, I don't know. Bob started working at two jobs. We were almost paid up when he fell and broke his ankle. The doctors, the bills started all over again. Bob started to . . . Mary, I don't want you to think I'm talking behind Bob's back. But you'll find out anyway, it's best you find out from me. That way you'll understand. Bob started to drink after his accident. He . . . he never stopped. Maybe he has cause. Everything was taken from him. His *pride* was taken from him. And when a man loses his pride . . ."

"Aye." Mary nodded gravely. "I saw it happen in Hexter. Things keep going wrong 'til a feller can't stand it anymore. Then he's in the pub all the night. It happened to our own neighbor. There was some who called him bad names. But he wasn't bad. Just a feller."

Anna smiled at Mary. "I'm grateful you understand," she said. "Not everybody does. People can be cruel sometimes. But I know better. I know Bob's a good man. I've always known."

Anna Wagner, the daughter of German immigrants, had met Bob Kilburne in the spring of 1886. She had loved him almost from the first moment of their meeting and, over the fierce objections of her family, had married him the following year. The marriage had caused estrangement from her parents, prosperous merchants who had chosen a young German lawyer to be her husband. The marriage had caused estrangement from her friends, who thought she was marrying beneath her. It had caused pain and tears and separation from everyone and everything she had known.

Anna had no regrets. She had loved Bob Kilburne in that spring of 1886 and she loved him still. She had borne six children, and in the two who survived she took constant and unabashed delight.

"With your troubles and all, we're a burden," Mary said quietly. "The money—"

"You're no burden. Don't think that. It's true we don't have much money, but there are people worse off than we are. Harley has a job on Wall Street. Bob works weekends at the Rathskeller. We manage."

Anna and her family managed on approximately six dollars a week. Harley worked as a runner on Wall Street and contributed two dollars of his meager wages to the family's finances. Bob was weekend bartender, sweeper, and handyman at the nearby Rathskeller. He kept his tips for himself, but his wages he always gave to Anna. Not a penny was wasted. She cooked simple meals, relying on soups, day-old bread, homemade noodles, and a few cents worth of this and that to see them through each week. They paid no rent, for she was janitress of the building. Most months she was able to earn extra money doing fancy sewing for Mrs. Preston Sinclair. It was not much, but money was money and never scoffed at.

"Georgy and me want to help," Mary said eagerly. "When can I begin at my job?"

"Soon. Mrs. Sinclair comes back to the city in September. If she agrees, you'll start then. It's as scullery maid. Mrs. Sinclair has a cook who doesn't want anyone interfering in her kitchen."

"Aye, I know how cooks are."

"Well," a young male voice came from the doorway, "how are they?" Harley Kilburne smiled. "Are they mean and ugly with warts on their noses?"

"Don't tease Mary." Anna laughed. "She'll get the

wrong idea of you."

"So this is Mary."

"Hello, Harley," Mary said. "I'm glad to meet you."

"My son's an awful tease. He likes his little jokes. . . . But he's a good boy."

"Aw, Ma."

"Never mind that. You're a good boy and I'm not ashamed to say so." Anna looked at the packages he was carrying. "Did you remember everything?"

"Twenty cents worth of ground round. Five cents worth of carrots. Two onions." Harley put his packages on the table and sat down. "I saw Jane outside. She's playing marbles with Frannie. She said she'll be up soon."

"Good. You talk to Mary while I get supper started."

"I'll help," Mary offered quickly.

"No, stay where you are and get to know Harley."

Mary looked at her cousin. He was almost seventeen, not handsome but pleasant looking, with Bob's dark eyes and Anna's easy smile. His hair, a sandy brown, fell carelessly over his forehead. He was a comfortable sort of person and Mary liked him right away.

Harley leaned back in his chair, lacing his fingers behind his head. He stared at Mary. "Tell me about England."

"Oh, it's a terrible place." Mary blushed, embarrassed by the bluntness of her reply. She lowered her eyes and started again. "I mean . . . our part of it, Hexter, is a terrible place. It's dead there."

Harley was silent. He continued to stare at Mary. She felt his gaze and was puzzled by it. "Hexter's not so bad for gentry," she went on. "Or for Lord and Lady

Worsham. But for the rest of us . . ."

"You're going to like it in America, Mary. Leave it to me."

An odd smile flickered about Harley's mouth. His eyes were very bright, for he thought Mary Kilburne was the prettiest girl he had ever seen.

Three

In August a heat wave gripped the city. The sun was relentless, yellow fire burning in a sky of unclouded blue. Temperatures reached into the nineties every day and, it was claimed, steam rose from the sidewalks of New York. People seeking a breath of air fled to fire escapes, to stoops, to rooftops, to any place offering relief from stifling flats. Mr. Caruso's ice wagon was the most popular sight in all of Yorkville.

Among the seven Kilburnes, only Mary seemed unaffected by the intense heat. She saw to it that George left for work with Harley each morning. She got Rose washed and dressed and fed and out to play with Jane. She did the breakfast dishes and made the beds. Then, at the sound of the mailman's eight o'clock whistle, her day began.

Mary had insisted on helping Anna with her chores. Anna, overwhelmed by Kilburne stubbornness, had agreed. Together they cleaned the flat. It did not take long, for though there were three bedrooms, a kitchen and parlor, the rooms were small and practically without furniture. When they finished with the flat, they gathered buckets, mops, and strong brown soap and cleaned the building.

Mary and Anna started in the cellar, emptying the dumbwaiter shelves of garbage, hauling the filled cans up to the street. On hands and knees, they scrubbed the hallways and the stairs. They cleaned the spokes of the banisters with oiled cloths. Last, they polished the bell plates in the vestibule, and the mailboxes. They finished in time to make lunch for Jane and Rose. Afterward, over a cup of tea, Anna told Mary all the things she needed to know about America.

Mary learned to think in dollars and cents instead of pounds and shillings. She learned the geography of the city and the routes of streetcars and the Third Avenue El. Walking around the neighborhood, she came to know Yorkville's many shops and many accents: German, Irish, Jewish, Austrian. She discovered the public library and got a library card; from books read late at night she learned the history of her new country.

September came and with it brisk, cleansing breezes. The air was suddenly cooler. The sky was a darker blue. To adults the change of season meant only a change of weather, but to children it meant school. Anna was worried about the start of the school term, for she knew both Jane and Rose needed clothes. "I have just over a dollar saved," she said to Mary one day. "That's enough to buy middies for the girls, and maybe stockings if the pushcart man comes by. What will we do about skirts?"

"There's my old skirt, Anna. We can cut it down."

"You need it for yourself. If your good skirt gives out you'll have only your petticoats."

"Aye. But there must be something. . . . Anna." Mary brightened. "There's something. There's my winter uniform from Abbeywood Manor. It's good sturdy wool, lots of wear left in it."

"Thank God."

Mary had brought few possessions to America. She had two skirts, three shirtwaists, a threadbare coat, boots, several pairs of patched black cotton stockings, several petticoats and shifts. Packed beneath her petticoats was her Abbeywood uniform. Smiling, she carried it into the kitchen and showed it to Anna. "There's more than two skirts here, if we cut careful."

"Oh, that's wonderful." Anna looked at the gray wool cloth; from the delighted expression on her face, she might have been looking at cloth of gold. "Sometimes I think God really *does* provide."

Mary measured and cut the cloth. Anna sewed it. By late afternoon they had four little skirts and, proudly, they inspected their handiwork. "It's a fine job, Mary, even if I do say so myself."

"Aye. Do you think Rose and Jane will like them?"

"They'd better. We can't afford to be choosy around here. We make do with what we have." Anna closed her sewing basket and smiled at Mary. "Don't worry. Most of their classmates will be wearing hand-me-downs."

"I know. It's just . . . I want Rose to get off to a good start in school. She doesn't fancy the idea."

"Of school? Children never do. But they get used to it." Anna laughed. "Some even get to like it."

"I hope so. Rose can make a terrible bad fuss, when she has a mind to."

"Don't worry about anything. I'll handle Rose."

But when the first day of school arrived it was Jane, not Rose, who burst into tears and refused to leave the kitchen. She sat at the table, shaking her head adamantly from side to side. "No, Mama. I don't want to go. I don't. I don't." She was a pretty child, a small copy of Anna, with green eyes and straight blond hair. Her hair was in long braids now and she pulled at them, twisting them in front of her face. "I don't like school, Mama," she said through her tears. "I don't want to go."

"But you have to. All the little girls and boys are going. All your friends . . . Frannie and Irene . . . and Rose. Look at Rose. She's not crying."

"I don't care."

"If Rose can—"

"Rose, Rose, Rose." Jane cried harder. "I don't care about her. She's silly."

"Jane!" Anna was startled by her daughter's outburst, for it was uncharacteristic. She had always been a happy child, a child who liked everyone she met. She had seemed to like Rose too, at least up until the past week; sometime during the past week her attitude had changed. "Jane, I want you to apologize. Right now."

"I'm sorry." Jane sniffled.

Rose smiled across the table at her cousin. It was a sweet smile but also a pleased smile, as if she were enjoying Jane's distress. Anna saw it and was bothered, though only briefly, for she told herself she was imagining things.

Anna brought a wet cloth and wiped Jane's face. "It's time to go, dear. No more foolishness. You can't be late your first day."

"Mama—"

"Right now, Jane."

Reluctantly, Jane slid off the chair. She turned her back on Rose and went to the door.

"You too, Rose," Anna said. "Come along."

Mary leaned over and kissed her sister. "Be a good

lass. Do as teacher says. . . . Anna, maybe I should go with you."

"No, I won't be long. And when I get back we're going to Mrs. Sinclair's, so you'd best get ready. . . . Children, out the door with you."

Mary watched them go, two little girls in middy blouses, gray skirts, black cotton stockings, and polished black shoes. She thought they looked adorable; especially Rose, whose smile was like the sun.

A makeshift bedroom had been set up for Mary in the parlor and she went there now. It was furnished with a stove, a daybed, and a wooden crate in which she kept her few clothes. Her best shirtwaist was neatly folded atop the pile. Mary put it on, carefully buttoning all the many buttons. She brushed her long hair, braided it, and wrapped the braids in a bun at the back of her neck. Returning to the kitchen, she scrubbed her face until it was sore.

The morning chores would not be done today, for the visit to Mrs. Sinclair was more urgent. Mary realized just how urgent it was; she had to have a job, and soon. Funds were perilously low in the Kilburne household. Anna had not complained, but there was a certain tension in her face when she prepared meals. With three extra mouths to feed, and no extra money save George's two dollars a week, she had been forced into new economies. Milk, butter, and sugar were rarely seen on the table anymore; meat was not seen at all. They had soup and day-old bread. On the most recent Friday before payday, they had only soup.

"Well," Anna said, coming into the flat, "that's done. They're schoolgirls now."

"Did Rose give you a fuss?"

"She was an angel. . . . But I don't know what got

into Jane." Anna went to the sink and splashed water on her face. She washed her hands, dried them, and then turned to Mary. "I think there's some trouble between the girls. I don't know what. I'll talk to Jane after supper."

"Aye, I'll have a word with Rose."

"Good. We'd best go now, Mary. We have more than twenty blocks to walk. Are you ready?"

"Aye." Mary's brows knitted in a frown. "But what do I call her? She wouldn't be Lady Sinclair, would she?"

"Call her Mrs. Sinclair or ma'am," Anna said, amused. "There are no titles in America, even if some people do live like royalty."

Mr. and Mrs. Preston Sinclair lived in a five-story townhouse on east Sixty-third Street off Fifth Avenue. It was a lovely house, twice the width of the others on the block, trim and graceful of line. Its long windows were draped in pale silk. Its four front steps were immaculate, swept and scrubbed and sparkling in the morning light.

Anna and Mary went to the side of the house, walking down a short flight of stairs to the service entrance. Anna rang the bell. "Don't be scared," she said, squeezing Mary's hand. "They won't bite."

The door was opened by the Sinclair cook, Elsie Jadnick, a small, round woman of fifty with close-set brown eyes and a perpetually quizzical expression. "Who is it?" she blinked. "Oh, it's you, Anna. Come in, come in. This must be Mary."

"Yes. Mary, this is Mrs. Jadnick."

"Hello, Mrs. Jadnick." Mary ducked her head, for

she was inches taller than the woman. "I'm glad to meet you."

"We'll see about that. Follow me, we can wait in the kitchen 'til Mrs. Sinclair's ready for you. Anna, did you have a good summer? You look thin to me. Well, I have biscuits fresh from the oven, and butter and jam. Come along, come along."

Anna smiled, accustomed to Elsie's constant chattering. She guided Mary through the hallway to the kitchen and, once inside, sat her at a long table of bleached oak. "Elsie, something smells delicious."

"That's my biscuits. And I made tea for you. We drink coffee most of the time, but I have tea for you. Mary, do you want tea with your biscuits or coffee? It makes no difference to me."

"Tea. Thank you."

"You're polite," Elsie nodded. "Some girls you get these days are fresh as paint. No manners at all. You wonder what kind of folks they came from. In my day, you learned your manners or you got the strap. But no more. Folks are too easy on their children nowadays." Elsie poured the tea. She put a tray of hot biscuits on the table, and then pots of cream and jam and sweet butter. "Go ahead and eat," she said. "Help yourselves. There's plenty. I'll be insulted if you don't finish every bit of it. What's the use of cooking if nobody eats?"

"Elsie, it's kind of you, but we can't eat all of this. We've had our breakfast."

"You can stand another meal. Look at you, the both of you . . . nothing but skin and bones. And don't tell me I'm wrong. I have eyes. I can see. Pride's all well and good, but it doesn't fill the belly. Besides, if you don't eat my food I'll be insulted." Elsie put her hands on her broad hips and stared at Anna. "Do you want to insult me?"

"No," Anna laughed. "I'd never do that."

"Then eat. What're you waiting for?"

Anna smiled fondly at Elsie, their little ritual concluded. She was a practical woman who never declined an offer of food, but she also knew the rules here; manners required her to demur, to be urged to eat by Elsie Jadnick. She took a biscuit, covered it with butter and jam, and bit into it. "Elsie, you still make the best biscuits in New York."

"Do you think so?" Elsie smiled, greatly pleased by the compliment, for, though she had no personal vanity at all, she was vain about her cooking. "What do you have to say, Mary? I hear tell you cooked for royalty back in the old country. Could you do any better than me?"

"Oh no," Mary answered quickly, munching on a biscuit. "These are the best I ever tasted. I'd be glad of the recipe."

Good girl, thought Anna; that was the right thing to say and the right way to say it.

Elsie, too, was gratified by Mary's reply. She had been expecting an uppity young girl with uppity ways. But the girl sitting in her kitchen now was polite, and knew how to give credit where credit was due. Elsie decided she liked Mary Kilburne. "Maybe I'll give you the recipe. Maybe I won't. We'll see about that later. First thing I have to do is fatten you up."

"Aye, ma'am."

"Don't call me ma'am. I'm Mrs. Jadnick. And the word's 'yes,' not 'aye.' You're in America, talk American."

"Yes, Mrs. Jadnick." Mary was not put off by the woman's rebuke, for she saw beyond the stern façade.

She saw warmth and not a little kindness. "I'll remember," she said.

Elsie poured a cup of coffee and sat down to talk to Anna. Mary continued to eat and while she did so, she looked around. It was a fine kitchen, newer and much brighter than the kitchen at Abbeywood Manor. It was painted a cheery light yellow and had starched white curtains at the windows. The stoves and ovens were wide, spotlessly clean. Two rocking chairs with cherry red seat cushions were placed near the stone hearth.

Mary ate four biscuits and drank three cups of tea— a whole day's ration at Abbeywood Manor, where all food and drink had been strictly apportioned. Abbeywood servants had not been allowed cream, or jam for their bread. They had been allowed but one teaspoonful of sugar a day. Mary was amazed at the generosity of Mrs. Sinclair's kitchen.

A bell sounded and they all looked at a panel on the wall. Elsie saw a light flash on. She stood. "That's Mrs. Sinclair. She's ready for you. The housekeeper's off doing errands, so I'll take you up. Do you have your letters? Your references?"

Mary reached into her pockets. "Aye . . . yes, Mrs. Jadnick."

"Then come with me. It won't do to keep Mrs. Sinclair waiting. She's a busy woman. She has responsibilities to her position. Come along, come along."

Elsie was small but she was quick and Mary had to hurry to keep up with her. Holding her skirts, she followed the woman up two flights of stairs to a long and carpeted hallway. They passed two closed doors and stopped at the third. "The morning room," Elsie said, knocking at the door.

"Come in."

Elsie opened the door. "Here's Mary Kilburne, from England. Anna's cousin."

"Thank you, Elsie. You may go."

"Yes, ma'am." Elsie stepped back and turned to Mary. "Remember your manners," she said. "Don't speak 'til you're spoken to."

"You may go, Elsie," Mrs. Sinclair called. "Mary, come in."

Mary smoothed her hair. She squared her shoulders and walked into the room, pausing just inside the door. In a glance, she saw pale silk walls, antique rugs, delicate rosewood furniture. She saw flowers, great masses of them in polished silver bowls.

"Come over here where I can get a look at you."

"Yes, ma'am." Mary crossed the room, taking care to walk lightly, the way she had been taught. She reached the small desk at which Mrs. Sinclair sat. She curtsied.

"My servants do not curtsy to me, Mary," Mrs. Sinclair said. "Nor do they go about with eyes downcast."

"Yes, ma'am."

Mary looked at Mrs. Sinclair. Her eyes widened, for the woman regarding her with such amusement was not the woman she had expected. She had expected someone on the order of Lady Worsham, drab and dour and graying. Mrs. Sinclair was none of those things. She was beautiful, barely thirty years old. Her hazel eyes twinkled vivaciously. Her hair was coppery and, contrary to the style of the times, swept atop her head in glossy ringlets that tumbled prettily about her brow when she moved. She had a voluptuous figure which even the discreet lines of her morning gown could not hide.

"Do I surprise you?"

"I'm sorry, ma'am. I . . ." Mary colored bright red. She hated herself for her awkwardness. "I thought . . . you'd be older."

"Don't be sorry. I'll take that as a compliment."

"Aye . . . yes, ma'am."

"May I see your references?"

Mary took the letters—one written by the Abbeywood housekeeper, the other written by Lady Worsham in a rare burst of good feeling—and gave them to Mrs. Sinclair.

"Thank you. Sit down while I read these."

Mary, feeling impossibly clumsy, was grateful for the security of a chair. She sat very straight and tried to be still. Every few moments she glanced at Mrs. Sinclair, awed by the extravagance of her beauty.

Cynthia Sinclair was used to such looks. Before her marriage to Preston Sinclair, a man almost twice her age, she had been on the stage. She had had many admirers. She had had many suitors too, though none so determined, so generous as Preston Sinclair. A widower of two years, he had wooed the beautiful Cynthia with jewels and furs and visions of a respectable life. The latter point had won her and, in 1896, they were married.

It was a satisfying marriage. As much as it was possible for Preston Sinclair to love anyone, he loved Cynthia. And Cynthia, in her way, loved her husband. She was a thoughtful wife who honored the bargain she had made.

"These are impressive references," Cynthia said now. She sat back in the ivory silk chair and smiled. "You must tell me about Lord and Lady Worsham."

"I only saw them when I served at table." Mary remembered those times. She remembered the enormous dining room, the enormous table laden with silver and crystal and elegant foods. Lord and Lady Worsham had presided, two cold, unsmiling people who looked at servants as if they were the lowest form of life. She had feared and disliked them. "That was only at big dinners. When people came from London."

"The servants were treated well?"

Mary cleared her throat, searching for a polite answer. "Lady Worsham left that to the housekeeper."

"You are a diplomat!"

"Ma'am?"

"I mean"—Cynthia Sinclair laughed—"that your answers were quite proper. I find gossip distasteful and so I give all prospective servants a little test. Most fail. They are . . . indiscreet. You didn't fail. You answered properly."

"Thank you."

"We have a housekeeper, of course. But I make it a point to see that my servants are treated well. They're paid well and they eat well. I try to be fair."

"Yes, ma'am."

"You may have the job, Mary. The salary is three dollars a week. You will eat what we eat, and you will have a room of your own. Every Thursday off, half a day Sunday."

Once again, Mary's eyes widened. "Three dollars! That's terrible kind of you."

"In return, I expect you to work hard. I also expect your loyalty."

"Oh yes, ma'am. I promise. You'll have no trouble with me."

Cynthia leaned forward. She propped her chin on

her hand and stared into Mary's eyes. "Now listen to me carefully. There are two things I will *not* tolerate. One is stealing. The other is . . . socializing with my stepsons. They're fourteen and sixteen, impressionable ages. Most of the time they're away at school. But there are holidays and vacations."

"I don't understand."

"It would be best, when my stepsons are home, if you stayed out of their way. Boys will be boys, after all. And you are so pretty."

Mary finally grasped Mrs. Sinclair's meaning. She was incredulous. "Pretty? Me?"

"Hasn't anyone ever told you you're pretty?"

"It's my sister Rose who has the looks in the family, ma'am. There's no worry about your boys. Boys take no account of me."

Cynthia's hazel eyes twinkled. She laughed. Her laugh was hearty, as hearty as it had been years ago in her native Brooklyn. A succession of voice teachers had been able to tame her diction, to train it, but they had given up on her laugh. "You're an amusing girl, Mary. And far too innocent, I fear. When you go home today, look in a mirror." She stood up, concluding the interview. "Do not forget what I told you about my stepsons."

Mary jumped to her feet. She nodded, unsure of what to say. She looked quickly and warily around the room, as if expecting obstacles to bar her path.

Cynthia came around the side of the desk. She had a smooth, measured walk, a stage walk, and it gave her the appearance of height. "Anna will sew your uniforms," she said. "You may begin work on Monday next. I hope you will be happy here, Mary."

"Yes, ma'am. I will. I know it."

"Elsie will explain your duties. In time, when you've gained her confidence, she will let you help her with cooking and baking. Apart from her famous biscuits, she really hates to bake. I gather you're good at it."

"Thank you, ma'am."

"Mr. Sinclair enjoys desserts. Particularly sweet and creamy desserts. Perhaps you will keep that in mind?"

"Oh yes, ma'am. It was the same at Abbeywood Manor."

They were almost at the door when Cynthia stopped and plucked a handful of red roses from a silver bowl. "Please give these to Anna with my regards. I admire her very much," Cynthia said slowly. "She has character. If you are half the worker she is, we will get along quite well."

"I'll try my best. . . . I want to thank you, Mrs. Sinclair, for giving me the chance."

"Can you find your way back to the kitchen?"

"The way I feel now, I could float all the way there."

It was a giddy walk home for Mary and Anna. They felt as if they had been rescued and, in relief and exultation, they giggled like schoolgirls. Anna was as radiant as a schoolgirl, for suddenly she had money in her purse. She had been given two lengths of black wool to make winter uniforms for Mary, and a basket of sewing for Mrs. Sinclair. For this work she had been given five dollars, an enormous sum. She knew it had to last, yet she was determined to do something special. "We have to celebrate," she said finally. "I've made up my mind. We're going to have a *real* supper tonight. I'll make stew. With meat and vegetables and everything."

"Can we afford it, Anna?"

"Everybody needs a treat once in a while. I've made up my mind. Tonight the Kilburnes celebrate!"

They stopped first at the butcher shop, where Anna astonished Mr. Schultz by ordering seventy-five cents worth of stewing meat. At the greengrocers she bought a whole bunch of carrots, a whole pound of potatoes, and a whole pound of small white onions. She bought two loaves of day-old bread, a half-pound of sweet butter, and a quart of milk. Lastly, feeling very wicked indeed, she bought five cents worth of hot red paprika from the Viennese spice store. "I'm not sorry," Anna said, as much to herself as to Mary. "Maybe it's wrong, but I'm not sorry."

They were walking home, their arms full of packages, when Mary tripped. She righted herself quickly, taking Anna's arm for support.

"Did you hurt yourself?" Anna asked.

"I'm fine," Mary said, though she did not move. She stood in the middle of the sidewalk, staring at the busy street corner.

"What is it, Mary? Is something wrong?"

"I was just . . . looking at that lad there."

"Where?" Anna followed Mary's gaze. "Oh, I see." She smiled. "He's quite a sight, isn't he? That's Dan McShane. One of the many McShanes. There are eight children in that family, all redheads, all beautiful. When they line up to go to Mass on Sunday . . ." Anna saw that Mary was not listening. She saw the pink color in her cheeks, the dark intensity in her blue eyes, and she sighed. "Mary, did you have a boyfriend at home in Hexter?"

"What? . . . A boyfriend?" The word jolted Mary. She looked at Anna, embarrassed. "Oh, boys don't fancy me."

"They will. And you'll fancy them. But one boy you *can't* fancy is Dan McShane." Anna's expression softened, for she knew how it was when a young girl felt the first stirrings toward the opposite sex. It was confusing, especially for a sheltered and innocent girl like Mary. "Come along," she said firmly, propelling Mary through the street. "We have things to do at home."

"Yes. I'm sorry, Anna. I don't know what's the matter with me."

A handsome young boy's the matter with you, thought Anna. She glanced at Dan McShane, so tall and square-jawed, so splendid in the sunlight. His hair was like flame. His eyes, even at a distance, were the most compelling blue she had ever seen. All the girls in the neighborhood were after him, and some of the women too. Anna understood why.

Once inside, Anna hurried Mary up the stairs and into the flat. She closed the door, leaning against it. Jane and Rose were at school, Harley and George were at work, and Bob was off drinking somewhere, as he always was during the day. Anna was glad they were alone; she wanted no mention of Dan McShane to reach Bob's ears. After a moment, she began to sort her packages. Some went into the icebox, others into the cupboard. The sewing she took into her bedroom.

When Anna returned to the kitchen, she found Mary standing over the sink, splashing cold water on her face. "Are you all right?" she asked.

Mary turned around. "I don't feel so well, Anna. I feel . . . queer."

Anna studied Mary's flushed face. She felt her forehead. "You don't have a fever, thank God. It's probably the excitement. Does your stomach hurt?"

"No. But my legs are shaky. And my heart's beating terrible fast. The worst is my head. It feels full of fog."

All the symptoms of a girl's first crush, thought Anna. Mary had looked at Dan and something had happened. It would pass; such things always did. "Mary, I want you to lie down for a while. You'll feel better after a nice rest."

"I hate to leave all the chores to you."

"Don't worry about that. Have your rest. You don't want to get sick, not now."

"No. Thank you, Anna."

Mary went off to her improvised bedroom. She sat at the edge of the bed and removed her good shirtwaist, folding it carefully away. She got out of her boots and then lay back against the pillow. She closed her eyes. She slept. In her dreams, she saw a tall young man with hair of flame.

Anna looked in on Mary from time to time, but she did not wake her. She scrubbed the kitchen floor, sorted the laundry, cleaned the stove. At noon, when Jane and Rose came home for lunch, she gave them bread-and-butter sandwiches and tea with milk. The girls ate in silence, not looking at one another, not speaking. Anna watched them, shaking her head. "I thought you two would be bursting with things to tell me," she said. "Don't you want to tell me about school? Jane? . . . Rose?"

"Teacher says I have pretty hair." Rose smiled proudly. "Teacher says—"

"Rose is teacher's pet," Jane interrupted. "She has her own desk in the front of the room. I sit in the back and I have to share my desk." There was no rancor in Jane's voice but there was resignation, as if she had concluded that Rose would always be at the front of

101

things, enjoying privileges denied to others. "It's not nice in the back. We bump our elbows."

"Well, your teacher probably puts the taller children in the back of the room. And you're taller than Rose."

"That's not why, Mama."

"It's because I'm pretty." Rose beamed.

"Rose"—Anna patted the child's small hand—"it's rude to brag. Little girls should be modest."

Rose gazed at Anna. Her expression was unchanged, though a cool light came into her eyes. "Teacher says I'm pretty."

"Have it your own way." Anna sighed impatiently. "But be quiet about it." She took plates and cups from the table and put them in the sink. "Time to go back to school now. Frannie's mother is doing me a big favor, seeing you two back and forth for lunch. Don't keep her waiting."

"Do I have to go, Mama?"

"You know the answer to that." Anna bent and hugged Jane. "I think *you're* pretty," she said quietly. "Inside and out."

After the children had gone, Anna sat at the table and thought about Rose. Her thoughts were not kind. She forced herself to remember that Rose was only six years old, surely unaware of her irritating ways. The child was spoiled, but that was not her fault. It was a phase, she insisted to herself, and children grew out of phases.

All the Kilburnes were at the table for Anna's celebration supper. The sight of so much food put everyone in a happy frame of mind. Even Bob, usually belligerent after a day's drinking, smiled. He joked with

Harley, who told a few jokes of his own. George told a riddle with a silly answer. The girls laughed loudly and clapped their hands. Mary, refreshed by sleep, laughed too. Often during the course of the meal, she felt Harley's eyes on her. She was still puzzled by his attentions, but in the levity of the moment, she gave them little thought.

After supper, Mary took Rose and George into her bedroom and closed the door. "Sit down," she said, gesturing to the bed. "We've things to talk about. With my job and all, I won't be home much anymore. I want to know the two of you will be all right."

"I'm all right." Rose nodded vigorously.

"Are you? Are you getting on with Jane? You must try, lass."

"I don't do anything. It's *her.*"

Mary sat next to Rose. She slipped her arm around the child's shoulder. "Have you done anything to upset Jane? Tell the truth. Have you been sharp with her? Have you been bad?"

"No," Rose said, all outraged innocence. "I'm a *good* lass."

Rose believed she was telling the truth. It did not seem bad to her to have demanded Jane's prettiest marbles, to have cried until she got them. It did not seem bad to have taken Jane's doll, to have refused to return it until she had finished playing. Little things, such as monopolizing the bed they shared, or the mirror, certainly did not seem bad. She believed herself to be good, above blame.

"Lass." Mary tried again. "There must be a reason why Jane's acting like she is. Something must have happened between you."

Rose shrugged. "Well . . . Mrs. Goodman from the

candy store gave me a licorice whip."

"Yes? And?"

"And I ate it."

"Didn't you share with Jane?"

"No."

"That wasn't very nice, was it, lass?"

"Mrs. Goodman gave *me* the licorice whip. She said—"

"Rose"—Mary shook her head—"from now on you're to share everything with Jane. No excuses. You must promise to be nice to Jane and to obey Anna. Do you understand?"

"Aye, Mary."

"Let me hear you promise."

"I promise."

Mary kissed Rose's silky curls. "That's my good lass. Run along now. Get ready for bed."

"Good night, Rose," George said as the child skipped out of the room. He waited until the door closed and then turned to Mary. "Why do you take Jane's side? What's a bit of candy anyway?"

"I wasn't taking Jane's side. I just want Rose to do right. Anna and her family took us in. It's little enough we can do to share what we have. Even a bit of candy."

"They take all my wages."

"Not all."

"All that's left after I pay carfares and lunch. I haven't a penny to myself."

"Anna feeds us with that money. . . . Georgy, I know it's hard, but things will get better."

"When?"

George lifted his big hands and then dropped them to his lap. He had grown taller in the last month, thinner; two weeks from his sixteenth birthday, he seemed all arms and legs and shoulders. He had recovered from his depression, though there were times when his eyes looked haunted. He showed very little of his old spirit, none of his fight, and Mary could not decide if that was good or bad.

"Georgy, when we've been here longer, when we've saved some money, things will be better."

"How can we save? We're next door to starving, just like in Hexter. Eh, we're no better off."

"That's wrong. It's different here. There're chances. We'll save our money, and when we see our chance we'll take it."

"How?"

"We have our jobs and that's—"

"I hate my job." George put his head in his hands, staring down at the floor. "I hate it, Mary. I run around like a zany all the day . . . from one place to another to another. I hate it all, even the going and coming. You haven't been on the El train. You don't know. It's up so high. It makes me dizzy. And when it goes fast on that skinny little track . . . I keep thinking it'll go off . . . just crashing down."

"Georgy, they wouldn't have it in the city if it wasn't safe."

"I hate it, Mary. The bloody El . . . the bloody job." George began to cry and Mary held him as she would a child. After some moments he sat up. He wiped his eyes with the back of his hand. "I knew it'd be like this. All for nothing . . . *nothing.*"

"For a better life. And we'll have it, Georgy. I promise you we will. It'll take time, but we'll get our chance."

George stared at Mary. His eyes were flat, empty. "Well, you have your way of looking at things and I have mine."

Mary was sitting on her bed, reading a book, when a knock came at the door. She jumped up, crossing the small room in five steps. "Harley," she said, surprised to see him standing there.

"Can I come in for a minute? It's still early, and I want to ask you something."

Mary stepped aside. "Come in then."

There was no place to sit but the bed and so they both stood. Harley smiled. "I was wondering, Mary . . . you haven't seen much of the city. Would you like to go to Central Park on Sunday? We could take sandwiches and have a picnic."

"You want to take me to the park?"

"Why not?"

"Oh, it's kind of you, Harley. Are you sure you haven't better things to do?"

"I'm sure. Would you like to go?"

"Yes, if it's all right with Anna. I'll ask her."

"I already did. She said to have a good time." Harley laughed. He brushed a strand of hair from Mary's brow. "We'll leave about noon."

"Thank you, Harley."

"Good night."

"Good night."

Mary went back to her bed and her book. She wondered about Harley's invitation, but briefly, for she decided he was merely being thoughtful; it was like him to be thoughtful. An hour passed and Mary closed her book. She undressed, stepped into one of Anna's old nightgowns, and got into bed. She was opening the window when she happened to look outside and saw, in the glow of the streetlight, Dan McShane. He was with a group of other young boys, all of them laughing at something he had said. She pressed her nose against the window. She smiled, only dimly aware of the fluttering of her heart.

Four

Eight servants were employed by the Sinclairs, though only five lived in. Their rooms, on the top floor of the house, were not overly large but they were comfortable, made so by Cynthia Sinclair. Mary's room had flower-sprigged wallpaper, curtains at the window, a dresser with mirror atop, and a rocking chair. Warm quilts were folded at the foot of the single bed. A circular blue rug lay on the wood floor. Mary had never had such a room before and she took meticulous care of it, dusting, sweeping, polishing until every surface shone. It was, Elsie often joked, the cleanest room in the house.

Mary's work day began at seven-thirty. Her chores were no different from those she had had at Abbeywood Manor, but the atmosphere was vastly different and she reveled in it. No matter how hard she worked, no matter how late, she was never tired. Sometimes she and Elsie sat up past midnight, rocking themselves by the kitchen hearth while they talked, or planned the week's menus.

Elsie and Mary had become friends. They trusted each other. They understood each other too, for both had come from poverty, both knew the meaning of work. Mary did most of the baking now and she was delighted to be doing what she did best. Thick sweet puddings, buttery tarts, and her special Tipsy Cake, luscious with rum and cream, appeared regularly on the Sinclair table. Preston Sinclair often sent his compliments; occasionally his compliments took the form of a bonus in her pay envelope.

Mary was happy. The happiest day of all was Sunday, for then she received her wages and a basket of food to take home. Cynthia Sinclair had directed that the baskets be generous and they were, usually containing a whole ham or chicken, sometimes a whole roast of beef. Her Thanksgiving basket had contained a twelve-pound turkey, as well as cranberries and sweet potatoes. Sunday dinner at the little flat in Yorkville became an event, eagerly anticipated all week.

Each Sunday, after the meal, Mary and Harley went for a walk. She liked him, liked his easy laugh, his casual good humor, and she confided in him. All her hopes, her plans for the future, she told to Harley. He gazed into her eyes and listened to every word. He thought she was beautiful and wonderful and smart, but far too serious. "You haven't left any time for fun," he would say. "What's life for, if not for fun?" It became an argument between them, though a very small one; it was impossible, Mary discovered, to have a real argument with Harley Kilburne. On her fifteenth birthday, he surprised her with an exquisite collar of fine Irish lace. "You probably wanted something practical, like flannel knickers," he joked. "But I wanted to splurge. What's life without a splurge now and then? Someday you'll have a dress to go with that collar. Leave it to me."

Christmas drew near. Mary was busier than she had ever been, for the Sinclairs planned endless holiday dinners and teas. She baked fruitcakes by the dozens, cookies by the hundreds. She baked pies and cakes and logs of chocolate filled with jam and iced with whipped cream. On her Thursday off, she walked about Yorkville, looking dreamily at all the Christmas gifts on display.

Anna had insisted that Mary keep fifty cents from each pay envelope. "Save it or spend it, but it's yours," she had said, firmly closing the discussion. And so, each week, Mary put fifty cents into an old evaporated milk can she kept on her window sill. She made a few modest purchases—satin hair ribbons for Rose and Jane, stockings for Anna, some penny postcards to send to Father Malone—but most of her savings were intact. She had almost six dollars. It was a fortune, and she decided to spend it on Christmas presents for all the Kilburnes. Three Thursdays in a row she browsed among the shops and pushcarts, trying to decide what to buy.

There was a great deal to choose from, for Christmas was a special time in Yorkville. Every store window was filled with treats, decorated with holly and pine and bright red bows. The neighborhood's one department store had a huge Santa Claus in the window, his sled spilling over with toys and dolls and games. Gaily trimmed pushcarts lined First Avenue for blocks. Some sold toys and trinkets, others candies and bags of nuts and dried fruits. The "women's carts" sold bottles of scent and hand lotion, stockings, gloves, dainty lace-edged handkerchiefs, and frilly petticoats. Men sold Christmas trees from stands on street corners. Other men sold hot roasted chestnuts, eight for a penny.

On this last Thursday before Christmas, Mary went directly home, anxious to collect her savings and begin her shopping. She bounded up the four flights of stairs, smiling as she entered the flat. "Good morning, Anna. Elsie sent biscuits and sweet butter."

"Elsie's a good woman." Anna left the sink, drying her hands on her apron. "My," she said, staring at Mary, "don't you look happy today!"

"This is the day I do my Christmas shopping. Will you come with me?"

"I'd love to. I have a little money put aside myself." Anna took the package from Mary and put it on the table. "Do we have time for a cup of tea, or do you want to go now?"

"Oh, we've time for tea. Elsie says to eat the biscuits while they're still warm." Mary removed her coat, hanging it on a hook behind the door. "But I'll just fetch my money so I don't forget."

"Not much chance of that." Anna laughed. "You've been looking forward to this day for a long time."

"That's the truth." Mary tossed her head and her long chestnut hair rippled over her shoulders. Her eyes glowed. Her face was pink with excitement, with youthful joy. "It's a grand day. And it'll be a grand Christmas, Anna. It's the first Christmas there'll be presents. . . . I already know what I'm going to buy for everyone. Wait 'til you see what I've picked out." She ran to Anna and hugged her. "Wait 'til you see!"

Mary turned and ran off to her bedroom. She ran to the window, plucking the evaporated milk can from the sill. She frowned, for the can felt very light. She looked inside and saw that it was empty. Desperately, she began to search. She searched behind the bed, under the bed, in the bed itself, tearing sheets and blanket away. "Anna!" she called. "Anna!"

"What is it, Mary?"

"My money. It's gone."

"Gone? It can't be gone."

Mary held out the empty can. "Look," she said.

"I don't understand." Anna began her own search. She, too, looked behind and under and in the bed. She looked into every corner of the room, and when she had finished, she looked in the stove. "I don't understand. No one's been in here but . . ." Anna put her hand to her head. She was pale, utterly still.

"Anna, are you sick? Here, let me help you." Mary took her to the bed and sat her down. "I'll fetch a cold cloth."

"No, wait. I . . . I have something to tell you." Anna looked away, twisting her thin gold wedding band around and around. "It's Bob. Bob was in here early this morning. I didn't pay any attention. I never thought about your money. He . . . he must have taken it."

"Bob?"

"He's the only one who's been in here. He knew about the money. I was so proud of you, Mary. I told him about your savings." Anna covered her face with her hands. "I'm sorry. My God, I'm sorry."

"It's all right. Don't cry, Anna. It's all right."

"It's *not* all right. You worked so hard, denied yourself things, and now . . ." Anna could not go on. She was overwhelmed by sadness, by shame. Always in the past she had been able to find excuses for Bob's actions, but not now. She felt as if her whole world had been turned upside down. "I'm sorry. I don't know what else to say."

"If Bob needed—"

"Needed? What does that mean? We've had our hard times. Times when there was no money to pay the doctor, or to buy a ten-cent bag of coal, or to buy *food*. But we managed somehow. Without stealing."

"Anna—"

"Stealing is stealing. It's a terrible thing. It's terrible how life can change a man. If only you'd known Bob before . . ." Anna sighed. She dried her eyes and looked at Mary. "Well, I have two dollars saved. I'll get it for you."

"No, Anna. I couldn't take your money."

"You have to. I want to put things right. Two dollars isn't much, not compared to what you had, but it's a start. I want you to have it."

Mary shook her head. She set her chin stubbornly and stared back at Anna. "We owe you everything. You took us in and made us welcome. You got us our jobs. You helped us. . . . The last thing I'll do is take your money."

"But what about *your* money?"

Mary glanced at the empty can she held in her hand. She smiled slightly. "It's not the first time I've been without. I'll start saving again."

"What about Christmas? You had such plans."

"There'll be other Christmases. Maybe it's best this way. Maybe I learned a lesson."

Anna did not dare ask what lesson she had learned, for there had been too many lessons in too short a time. Mary was old beyond her years. It was unfair, thought Anna, but then life was unfair. "I can't let you do this,"

114

she said.

"There's only one thing. Would you get Rose a little Christmas present? So long as Rose has something, I'll be happy." Mary turned, walking quickly out of the room. "I'll put water on for tea."

"Mary, please—"

"It's all settled."

Anna cried for a while. When she had no more tears left, she went into the kitchen and had tea with Mary. There was no further mention of Christmas. They did their chores. They greeted Jane and Rose when the girls came home for lunch. They got through the day. Mary returned to the Sinclair house early, leaving Anna to ponder what she would say to Bob.

It was after one in the morning when Bob Kilburne let himself into the flat. He had been drinking heavily and it showed in his red-rimmed eyes, in his lurching walk. Anna let him sleep it off, but at six o'clock the argument began. Bob was sitting on the edge of the bed, holding his aching head. Anna, already dressed, walked into the bedroom and closed the door. "Where's Mary's money?" she asked.

"What?"

"Mary's money. Where is it?"

"Not now. Don't talk to me now. I have a headache."

"I wish I could say I was sorry."

Bob, muddled as he was, heard the cold anger in Anna's voice. He looked up. "And what's that supposed to mean?"

"Bob, I want you to return Mary's money. Give it to me. I'll take it to Mrs. Sinclair's myself."

"I don't have it." Bob rubbed his throbbing temples. He coughed and each cough brought a wince of pain.

"Don't bother me now, Anna. Can't you see how I feel?"

"How you feel? It's always how *you* feel. Are you the only person in the world? Is that what you think?" Anna's face was pale, rigid with anger. She had had many hours to think about what Bob had done, and in those hours her anger had become a stone in her heart. "Other people have feelings. *I* have feelings. *Mary* has feelings. How do you think she felt when she found her savings gone?"

"Goddamn it all, that money was coming to me. It was owed me. Four years ago I sent their passage money. It's time I was paid back."

"Mary gives you all her bonus money toward that debt. What more do you want?"

"I want what's coming to me." Bob stood up. He steadied himself, then took a few halting steps toward the door. Anna blocked his way. "I'm in no mood for this today," he said.

"I don't care. Where is the money? Gone? Which bar did you spend it in this time?"

Bob blinked. His lips parted. He was stunned by the coldness in Anna's voice. "I don't believe what I'm hearing. How can you say such a thing to me?"

"It's true, isn't it?"

"No. I took the money. It was coming to me. But I didn't take it for drink. I took it so my children could have a decent Christmas. They'll have presents this year. A roomful of presents bought and paid for."

"My God, Bob! Bought and paid for with stolen money!"

Bob colored a dark and ugly red. His mouth shook. "Are you calling me a thief?" he roared. "Your own husband? Are you?"

"You sneaked into Mary's room and took her money. That makes you a thief. Can't you see the truth? Can't you see what you've become?"

Fury swept over Bob. Before he could stop himself, he slapped Anna's face. "Damn you! Damn you for making me do that!"

Anna sank down on the bed. She saw Bob rush from the room, heard the door slam. She turned her head and stared unseeing into space, all too aware of what had happened. Anna and Bob had had arguments before, but they had not been serious. No damage had been done. Now, in only a few moments, their marriage had been changed forever. Bob would not forget that his wife had called him a thief; Anna would not forget that her husband had hit her.

"Ma, are you okay?"

"Yes, Harley. I'm sorry you heard us."

"We all heard. Can I do anything?"

"No one can do anything. Not now."

A light snow began falling early on Christmas Day. Lacy little flakes danced in the wind before settling on roofs and sidewalks and carriages. Within hours, the city lay under a cover of pure and perfect white. "Isn't it beautiful, Elsie?" Mary asked, gazing out of the window. "I love to watch it."

"Everybody loves to watch it. Walking in it, that's another story. You'd better be on your way. There's no telling if we're in for a blizzard."

"It's funny not to be working Christmas Day. In Hexter I always worked Christmas Day."

"Not here. Mrs. Sinclair says Christmas is for families. So all the servants have the day off. Not many mistresses are as kind as her. Be grateful."

"Oh, I am, Elsie."

"You don't look it. I thought you'd be in a big hurry to get home, but here you are moping around. What's bothering you?" Elsie left the table and walked over to Mary. She turned her around, staring up into her eyes. "You can tell me. What's bothering you?"

"Nothing. I was just watching the snow."

"Well, I'm not one to stick my nose in. But if you ask me, something's wrong. A week ago you were going on and on about Christmas. Now it's like all the excitement's gone out of you. It's Christmas, Mary. Let me see a Christmas smile."

Mary smiled. "Don't worry about me," she said. "I'm fine. And I'm on my way home this minute." She went into the hall, opening the closet door. "Elsie? I don't see my coat."

"That's right. It's in here."

Frowning, Mary returned to the kitchen. "What's it doing in . . . That's not my coat, Elsie."

"Yes it is." Elsie was holding up a coat of rich brown wool lined with silk. It had a velvet-trimmed hood and tiny velvet buttons. "It's your coat now. It used to belong to Mrs. Sinclair, but she had Anna make it over for you. No arguments. Mrs. Sinclair has a dozen coats. She wanted you to have this one."

"But . . . why?"

"Well, for a Christmas present."

"She already gave me a present. She gave me two dollars."

"I know. This is something extra. I happened to

mention how your coat was old and worn out. Mrs. Sinclair can't have her servants going around like ragamuffins, can she? What would people think?"

"Elsie, that's a coat for a lady. I can't take it."

"Don't talk foolish. I have no use for a smart girl who talks foolish. Why should this coat wind up in the clothes box at the church? You need it and it's been made over to fit you. So hold out your arms. Let me see how it looks. . . . That's it. How does it feel?"

"Oh, it's so nice and warm."

"Of course it's warm. Do you think Mrs. Sinclair would go around in a coat that wasn't warm?" Elsie stepped back and looked at Mary. "It's a little short, 'cause you're taller than Mrs. Sinclair, otherwise it fits perfect."

Mary stroked the soft wool. She spun around, watching the folds of the coat billow about her ankles. "It's too good to wear, Elsie."

"Maybe we should put it in a museum." Elsie shook her head impatiently. "You have some strange ideas about things," she said. "Is that what they taught you in England? I'm glad we're no part of it, if that's what they taught you. How can a coat be too good to wear? A coat's meant to be worn, isn't it? Come over here. Let me see the hood." She drew the hood up until it framed Mary's face. "There." She smiled. "Mrs. Sinclair said the brown would show off your skin. She was right, like always. No *lady* every looked better."

Mary spun around again. "I can't believe it's mine."

"It's yours. And if you reach in the pockets you'll find something else that's yours."

"Oh," Mary said, removing a pair of kidskin gloves the same dark brown as the coat. "They're beautiful.

I can't—"

"No more talk. That's my Christmas present to you and that's that."

Mary looked at the gloves. She looked at Elsie and burst into tears.

"My goodness, Mary, presents are supposed to make you happy. What in the world are you crying about?"

"It's just . . . just . . ."

"Just what?"

Mary wiped her eyes and blew her nose. When she could speak, she explained about her savings, about Bob Kilburne and the empty milk can. "So that's why I have nothing to give you," she finished, sniffling. "I'm sorry, Elsie."

"Well, you poor girl. I know the kind of man who does things like that. There's more of them around than you think." A scowl darkened Elsie's small round face. She felt sorry for Mary but she felt sorrier for Anna, who had wasted her life on such a man. "I suppose he had an excuse." She sniffed. "They always have excuses. Never mind. You'll keep your savings here from now on. There's no stealing in this house."

"Yes, Elsie. I will."

Elsie glanced at the watch clasped to her shirtwaist. "There's still time for you to buy some things for your sister and the others. You have your two dollars. Make the best of it."

"It's Christmas. The shops are closed."

"Not the pushcarts. I know Yorkville. I had a nephew lived there. Those pushcarts stay all Christmas Day, hoping for stragglers."

"Really?"

"Sure."

A vast smile spread across Mary's face. Christmas would not be ruined after all, she thought; she could still buy a present for Rose. "I'll hurry then."

"That's the girl. Here, before I forget . . ." Elsie took a red-wrapped package from a drawer and gave it to Mary. "This is for Anna, from Mrs. Sinclair."

"Thank you. I'll give it to her first thing." Mary bent and put her arms around Elsie. "Thank you for everything. Merry Christmas."

"Merry Christmas. And don't forget tomorrow's a work day."

"I won't. I'll be here in the morning, sharp at seven. Merry Christmas, Elsie."

Mary, bundled up in her new coat and gloves, did not feel the cold as she rushed through the snowy streets. Twice she almost stepped into the path of oncoming carriages. Their drivers' loud and obscene curses rang in her ears, but she was not dismayed. Her spirits were high, for the day would be happy after all. That, too, was a lesson to her; in Hexter the days ended as they had begun, but in America anything could happen.

Pushcarts were out in force on First Avenue. Mary went from one to another, examining both merchandise and price tags with great care. She bought two small, pretty porcelain dolls, one blond, one brunette, for Rose and Jane. She bought scented hand lotion for Anna, and wool mufflers for George and Harley. She had no desire to buy anything for Bob but, after debating with herself, she bought him a tie.

Balancing her packages in her arms, Mary started for home. She was two blocks from the flat when she saw Dan McShane walking toward her. A thrill of excitement ran along her spine. Her heart began to pound and her breath caught in her chest. She felt warm, light-headed; for a moment she thought she was going to faint.

Dan McShane was dressed in his good Sunday suit, a coat thrown jauntily over his shoulders. Snowflakes glittered in his mane of bright red hair. His eyes were an intense blue, focused directly and deliberately on the young girl coming his way. "Hello, Mary Kilburne," he said, stopping in front of her. "Merry Christmas to you."

Mary looked into Dan McShane's handsome face. She looked into his blue eyes. She tried to speak, but found she had no voice.

Dan laughed. His laugh, like his voice, was deep. It was at once playful and insinuating. "Aren't you going to wish me a Merry Christmas?"

"How . . . how did you know my name?"

"I saw you and I asked about you."

"Saw me?"

"You were walking with your cousin, Mrs. Kilburne. I asked around the neighborhood and found out who you were and where you lived."

"You did all that?"

"For you, Mary Kilburne, I would have done much more."

Mary's heart skipped a beat. Her face shone with rosy light. She gazed at Dan and suddenly she wondered if she had misunderstood. "Would you be teasing me?"

"No. I'm serious." And so he was. Dan McShane had always known his own mind. In matters large and small he had always known exactly what he wanted.

What he wanted, he went after. "I've planted myself on the street outside your window many a Thursday and Sunday night. You've seen me there. I know you have."

Mary blushed. She lowered her eyes. "Yes, I have. But not for two weeks now."

"Ah, I was hoping you'd noticed. Well, Mary Kilburne, let me take your packages. I'll walk you home."

They walked slowly, looking often at each other. When they reached the corner, Dan took Mary's arm and helped her across the street. His touch, light though it was, nearly took her breath away. She gasped.

"I didn't mean to startle you."

"No, it's not that," Mary said, trying to hide the awkwardness she felt. "It's just . . . you have such nice manners."

"Beat into me by my old Irish granda." Dan smiled. "There are eight children in my family, and Da, and Granda. Granda sets the rules. It's school, work, church, and mind your manners. Or it's Granda's strap. Bless him, but he has the devil's own temper."

Mary was too distracted to follow what Dan was saying. She was distracted by very blue eyes and very red hair, by a square jaw and clefted chin, by broad shoulders and powerful arms. She felt Dan's closeness and was intoxicated.

Dan was not yet seventeen, but he knew the effect he had on women. Sometimes he found it useful; most of the time he found it amusing. A stern upbringing kept him from vanity. He was charming, but naturally so, in the way of Irishmen. And in the way of Irishmen, he was a romantic.

"Do you know what fate is?" he asked Mary now.

"That's when something is meant to be."

"Yes." A smile flickered at Dan's mouth. His eyes twinkled. "And it's when two people are meant to be. Do you know what I'm talking about, Mary Kilburne?"

Mary nodded. There was a lump in her throat, a wild fluttering in her heart. "Is it true, Dan?"

"It's true. Dear God knows it's true. Say my name again. It sounds special when you say it."

"Dan. Dan McShane. I feel like shouting it for everyone to hear." Mary clapped her hands in joy. She thought: Dan fancies me. I'm the luckiest girl ever born. "Dan McShane. What a grand name!"

"Ah." Dan laughed. "What a grand girl! Wait here a minute. Don't move." He ran a few steps to a man selling flowers from a pushcart. There was no haggling. He saw what he wanted and he bought it. He returned to Mary, putting the flowers in her hands. "For our first Christmas."

"Violets!" Mary pressed the tiny bouquet to her cheek. "I'll keep them forever."

The two young people reached the door of Mary's building. They gazed at each other, not speaking, hardly breathing. Dan pushed Mary's hood back. Gently, he stroked her long hair. He had no words for what he felt, nor were words necessary. Time passed and still they gazed at each other, a boy and a girl in love.

"I don't want to go upstairs," Mary said finally. "I don't want to, Dan, but I have to."

"I know. My family's waiting for me too." He drew

a violet from Mary's bouquet and wrapped it in his handkerchief. "To remember." He smiled. "I'll meet you here next Sunday at one. We'll have the day."

"Yes, Dan." Mary had forgotten about her Sunday walks with Harley. She had forgotten about Anna's warning. Dan was all she could think about, all she wanted to think about. "At one."

"There's some trouble between your cousin Bob and my da. I'm not sure what it is, but I'm sure of this . . . it's not our trouble. Let them have their quarrel. We're meant for better things."

"Yes, Dan."

"Here are your packages. Can you manage?"

"They're not heavy. Dan . . . when you first saw me walking with Anna, did you feel . . . I mean, did you . . . ? *Oh* . . ." Mary sighed, "I'm so clumsy. I can't get my thoughts untangled."

Dan laughed. He took Mary's face between his hands and stared into her eyes. "You're not clumsy. You're the beautiful girl I see in my dreams. And when I first saw you I knew you'd be my wife one day. It's true, Mary Kilburne. Never was anything truer. Never in all the world." He leaned closer to her. He kissed her lips lightly and then, in the next moment, he was gone.

Mary was trembling. She groped her way into the building, groped her way to the staircase. She sat on the stairs and tried to catch her breath. She closed her eyes. "Dan," she whispered. "Oh, Dan."

Slowly, the strength came back to Mary's legs. She climbed the stairs, wondering if she should tell Anna about Dan. Only then did she remember Anna's warning. She smiled, for all the warnings in the world would not keep her from Dan McShane.

Christmas dinner was over. The dishes had been washed and dried and put away. Now Bob heaped the kitchen table with wrapped and beribboned presents. He avoided Anna's eyes, looking instead at Harley and Jane. "They're for you," he said eagerly. "It's a real Christmas, just like we used to have. Well, open your presents. Go on, Harley. Jane, what are you waiting for? That big box there is for you. Go on. The box with the red bow, it's yours."

Neither Jane nor Harley moved. They were uncomfortable, remembering their parents' argument and what it meant. Jane was young, but still she understood the meaning of stealing. Harley certainly understood; several times in the last year he had looked for his own small savings, only to find them gone, taken by Bob. He had not mentioned the missing money to anyone. In his good-natured way he had let the thefts pass, hoping things would work out. Clearly, things had not worked out. He stared at the presents on the table, presents bought with Mary's money, and he was ashamed.

"What's going on?" Bob demanded. "I do my best to give you a fine Christmas and you turn up your noses. Is that the thanks I get? Well? Answer me!"

"Bob," Anna said, "this is no day to argue. The children will open their presents now. Go ahead." She nodded at Harley. "What's done is done."

Harley glanced at Mary. He saw that she was paying no attention and so he turned to his gifts. There was a shirt for him, and a fancy billfold of black leather. "Thank you, Pa. It's real nice."

126

"Is that all you've got to say? You didn't even look at the shirt. It's from a store, not a pushcart, and it's the best the store had. The billfold . . ." Bob sighed. He rubbed his sad, tired eyes. "Jane, it's your turn."

"Oh," Jane said as she opened a miniature tea set, and then a doll wearing a lace-trimmed red dress and tiny red slippers. She lifted the doll out of the box, patting its golden curls. A moment later she put the doll back. "They're wonderful presents, Papa. Thank you."

Bob sighed again. He looked from Jane to Harley, shaking his head. He looked at Anna and his mouth tightened. "You've turned my children against me," he said bitterly. "Don't deny it. I give them fine presents and they act as if I gave them dirt from the street. It's your doing."

"Bob, I never—"

"It's your doing," Bob shouted. "Damn you." He got his coat and cap and stormed to the door. "To hell with you. To hell with you all."

The door slammed. Anna sat down, staring at her hands. "Harley, take Jane and Rose to their room."

"Yes, Ma."

Jane went with Harley, but Rose refused to move. "I want my presents," she said. "Where are my presents?"

Mary, roused from her daydreams, took Rose by the shoulders and turned her to Harley. "Go along, lass. Please."

"*No.* I want my *presents.*" Rose stamped her foot. She beat her little fists on the table. "*Give me my presents.*"

"Stop it, Rose! Stop it!" Mary grabbed Rose's

hands. "That's no way to behave. And on Christmas."

"But my presents. I want—"

"That's enough. Georgy's wrapping a present for you in my room. Go fetch it."

Rose's tantrum ended abruptly. She smiled, sunny and sweet once more. "Thank you, Mary," she called, skipping away.

"I'm sorry about Rose," Mary said when the child had gone. "Anna, I'm sorry about everything. What happened with Bob . . . it's my fault. I should have kept still about the money. If only I'd kept still . . . I hope you can forgive me for the trouble I've brought."

"You didn't bring the trouble. It's been waiting for us all along. I suppose I knew. I didn't want to admit it." Anna shrugged. There was weariness in her voice and there was finality, one a part of the other. "I didn't want to admit what was happening. When Bob started drinking, I closed my eyes. When his drinking got worse, I closed my eyes. He lost himself somewhere along the way. And I closed my eyes."

"Things will be all right again. You and Bob love each other."

"It's bad to love too much. That kind of love . . . it blinds you to the truth. You think with your heart instead of your head. You make excuses. All this time I should have been helping Bob. But I didn't. I made excuses for him. Now it's too late."

"No, don't say that."

"Love is complicated, Mary. It's strong and fragile at the same time. It's . . . well, you'll find out for yourself soon enough. You'll fall in love and then you'll know." Anna looked at Mary. She looked again, for there was something different about her, something radiant. "Or are you already in love? My God, Mary. It's Dan

McShane, isn't it? You finally met up with him. That's why you were late getting home."

"Anna, I'm so happy."

"You're happy now. But it won't last. You must forget about him. . . . You and Dan McShane can only come to grief."

Five

Dan was the oldest of the eight McShane children. As the oldest, he had always been expected to set a good example for his brothers and sisters, to do what was right. "You owe it to the family," was his grandfather's favorite and frequent admonition. Dan accepted the responsibility, though he never forgot that he had a responsibility to himself as well. He had his own visions, his own plans, and these were often in conflict with the plans his family made for him.

There were arguments. The first serious argument occurred when Dan was fifteen, out of school and expected to join his father's small business, the Shamrock Pub. He had refused, choosing to work in construction instead. "I want to build things," he had told his irate father, "and that's what I'm going to do." The argument had raged for days, weeks, but in the end Dan had won. He was a construction worker, one of the best in Mr. Dwyer's crew.

Shortly after his sixteenth birthday, another argument bitterly divided the McShane family. It had concerned a young girl fresh off the boat from Ireland, a girl chosen by the elder McShanes to be Dan's wife. Again he had refused, and in the course of that argument his family had seen the full force of his temper. Marriage was no longer mentioned in the McShane household, for it was clear that Dan would choose his own wife, in his own time.

Dan thought that time was soon approaching. He had thought so ever since his first glimpse of Mary Kilburne. He had been drawn to her immediately. He had felt the pounding of his heart, the blood rushing to his face, and he had known. There was no single reason for his attraction. It was not Mary's smile or her walk or her beautiful long hair, though all of those gave him immense pleasure to behold. It was, rather, something indefinable, something that made him want to take her in his arms and keep her there. He wanted her in his bed, but he wanted more than that; he wanted her in his life.

Dan McShane was not given to doubt and he did not doubt that Mary would be his. He was aware of the obstacles that lay between them; he did not doubt they would be overcome. There could be no doubt, for he was young and strong and in love.

Now, whistling happily to himself, he turned the corner and saw Mary standing outside her door. It was a cloudy day, but she seemed cloaked in light. Her hair shone, and her eyes. Her skin, so fair and smooth, had the glow of polished ivory. "Mary McShane," Dan whispered to himself, loving the sound of it.

"Dan!" Mary cried. She ran to him, breathless. "I was afraid you weren't coming."

"Did you think anything could keep me away?" He gazed into her eyes, lost in their dark blue depths. He wanted to hold her, to press his lips on hers, but he knew he could not, not yet. "You take a feller's breath away, Mary Kilburne," he said. "Sure and it's a witch

132

you are."

Mary smiled, charmed by his playful brogue. "Would that be a compliment?"

"It would. And only the first of many. Do you mind?"

"I'll mind if you stop."

"I'll never stop. I'll be telling you pretty things 'til the day I die. All of them true." Dan stroked Mary's hair, then drew her hood around her face. "Mustn't catch a chill," he said softly.

Mary felt Dan's hand brush her cheek. She sighed. "I've been thinking about you all the week. Tripping over my own two feet. Elsie Jadnick says I need a tonic."

"I'll be your tonic," Dan laughed. "How's that?"

"Oh, that's grand."

"Come along then. I'm taking you to Chinatown."

"China!"

Dan shook his head, laughing again. "No, China-*town*. That's the neighborhood where all the Chinese people live. Haven't you heard about it?"

"I'm a greenhorn."

"Ah, but what a beautiful greenhorn. You do me proud, Mary Kilburne."

"I want to."

Mary's simple statement touched Dan's heart. He was warmed by her innocence, moved as he had never been moved before. "Mary," he said so softly it was a caress. "Mary. I love you, my darling girl."

"Oh, Dan, I love you." Tears stood in her eyes. She blinked them away, smiling. "Isn't it amazing what's happened to us?"

"You're amazing."

"The whole world's different now. I'm so happy. You

make me so happy. . . . It's like a dream."

"Ah, it's better than a dream. Dreams end. What we have will never end. Never in all the world. And that I promise you." Dan kissed Mary's lips. "Come," he said hoarsely. "I've a whole world to show you."

"Yes, Dan."

They took a streetcar to Chinatown. It was a long ride but to the two young people it seemed to last only moments. They talked and laughed and gazed at each other in wonder. There was no shyness between them. They accepted their feelings; they rejoiced in them. Other passengers watched and smiled. They could not help but smile, for Dan and Mary were a beautiful couple made more beautiful by love.

In Chinatown they strolled hand in hand through the narrow, winding streets. They saw joss houses, the shrines of Buddhist worship, and colorful shops and dozens of restaurants, some so small they had only four tables. "We'll eat later," Dan said, stopping at one of the shops. "First let's have a look inside here."

"Oh, can we?"

"Of course we can." He smiled at Mary. "We can do anything."

Hand in hand, they entered the shop. They looked at lovely fluted bowls, at paper flowers and paper fans, at graceful wooden flutes, and wonderful kites shaped like butterflies and dragons. Dan found a tiny silk butterfly in shades of blue and violet. "To match your eyes," he said, and bought it for Mary.

They continued their walk. Mary was fascinated by the sights of Chinatown, especially by the people. There were few women about but there were many men, most of them dressed in black, with little black caps and black pigtails. She thought the men very mysterious. She was enchanted by their quick, brilliant smiles. "I'm so glad you brought me here, Dan," she said. "It's like being in China. Mary Kilburne in China. Fancy that!"

"It's time Mary Kilburne had some Chinese food then. Are you willing?"

"Oh, yes."

Dan took her to a restaurant on Mott Street. There they feasted, though not on the chop suey always ordered by tourists. Dan ordered a spicy soup, spareribs in ginger sauce, fried dough cakes, and a dish made of shredded chicken and exotic Chinese vegetables. They ate course after course. They drank pots of tea. They talked for three hours. It was a heady time, intimate with discovery, with secrets shared.

"I love you," Dan said on the streetcar going home. "I love you," he said as they walked toward First Avenue. "I love you," he said when they reached Mary's building.

"I love you too," Mary replied each time, each time feeling such a surge of joy she thought her heart would burst.

Mary floated upstairs, lighter than air. Surely she spoke to Anna, to Rose and George; she could not remember. She lay on her bed and remembered only Dan, his smile, his voice, his touch. She slept and in her dreams Dan was there.

On their second Sunday together, Dan took Mary to Greenwich Village. They visited little galleries and quaint, dusty bookstores. They drank coffee in a candle-lit cafe. They talked and held hands and wished the day would last forever. Just before dusk, a sidewalk artist, bundled in greatcoat, fringed silk scarf, and beret, made sketches of Mary and Dan. *"Voilà!"* he cried, ripping the sketches from his pad. "The faces of *amour."*

On their third Sunday, Dan took Mary on a tour of Manhattan's skyscrapers. She was startled by the size of the buildings, but she was more startled by Dan's reaction to them. He stared, hypnotized, at their tall, sleek lines. There was pride in his gaze, and excitement. "I'm going to have my own construction company someday," he said finally. "I'll build buildings like this. I'll build whole cities!" He looked at Mary, looking deep into her eyes. "Do you think I'm foolish?"

"No, Dan. I think you'll do what you say. You'll have what you want from life. It's the way it is with you." Mary meant every word. In the last few weeks, she had gazed into Dan's heart, into his soul, and she knew he would not be denied what he wanted. She believed he could be anything, do anything; he was, after all, Dan McShane. "You're charmed," she smiled.

"Ah, I'm charmed all right. There's a spell on me and you cast it, Mary Kilburne. I'm not forgetting you're a witch." Dan laughed. His intense blue eyes twinkled. "I'm not forgetting you're *my* witch. Save all your magic for me."

"I promise."

"Do you?"

"Oh, I do."

"My darling girl." Dan looked at Mary for another moment, stroking her cheek, then looked back at the building. "I wish you could see one of these going up. We start with a hole in the ground and before we know it, we have forty stories. The frame," he went on, warming to his subject, "that's the most important thing, because it's the only thing that bears any weight. Once the foundation's laid, the frame's only a matter of bolting and riveting. We rivet beams, girders, cantilevers, brackets. . . . Listen to me," he said, shaking his red head, "talking about brackets when I've a beautiful girl at my side. Sure and it's a fool I am, Mary Kilburne. I'm begging your pardon."

"I could listen to you talk forever. Your voice is so grand. And your brogue."

"It's Granda's brogue. I borrow it on special occasions."

"When we're together, Dan. That's a special occasion."

Dan's handsome face became quiet, serious. He sighed. "Sometimes you say things and the breath stops in my chest. A word, a sentence, and I'm off in a fog."

"But that's love."

Dan drew Mary into his arms. He held her, his eyes closed, his heart beating wildly. When he released her, they were both trembling. "It's a fine day," he said, clearing his throat. "Let's walk awhile."

Hand in hand, they walked. They stopped for tea and cakes and then they walked some more. They said very little, for their minds and their bodies were stirred by feelings too powerful to speak. It was after six when they returned to Yorkville.

"I love you, Mary."

"I love you, Dan."

"Thank God for that," he said, kissing her lips. "Thank God."

Mary took a long time walking up the four flights of stairs. She entered the flat, so dazed and dreamy it was several minutes before she noticed the uproar in the kitchen.

Jane was screaming, great tears rolling down her cheeks. Her dress was ripped, one of her braids undone. Anna tried to comfort her, but to no avail. Rose, too, was screaming. She lunged at Jane, her little fists waving in the air. George had all he could do to restrain her. "It's bloody time you got home," he snapped at Mary. "Help me here."

"What is it? Georgy, what happened?"

"Ask Rose."

"Anna—"

"Take Rose into your room, Mary. *Please.*"

Mary ran to Rose. She took one of her arms, George the other, and together they dragged the enraged child into the bedroom. "Get over there," George said, trying to propel Rose to the bed. She screamed and kicked. Her face was red. It was terrible. *"Damn,"* George cried as Rose's foot crashed into his ankle. He lifted her up and threw her on the bed.

"Georgy!" Mary said, shocked by his roughness.

"Don't Georgy me. You don't know what's been going on here. You've been out having a grand time for yourself, while we've been here. All hell breaking loose . . . Rose, you stay there or I swear I'll slap you."

Rose's screams quieted from one breath to the other. She was astonished, for George had never spoken that way to her; no one had ever spoken that way to her. She glared at him, but quietly, her chest heaving up and down.

"Georgy, tell me what happened."

"As near as I can make out, it started at Frannie's birthday party. There were games, and prizes for the children who won the games. . . . Well, Jane won some little toy. Rose didn't win anything. She wanted the toy. Jane said no. And then all hell started."

"What? What started?"

"Our Rose chased Jane all over Frannie's place. She chased her up the stairs." George exhaled a deep breath. He wiped his wet forehead. "She chased Jane inside and backed her against the kitchen wall. She started pulling her hair, *hitting* her. Anna and me got her off, but by then she'd torn Jane's dress and everything."

"Rose did that?"

"Aye, she did. I saw it with my own eyes. I couldn't believe it. She was like a zany. Hitting and kicking and screaming."

"All that over a toy?"

"That's how it started." George looked at Rose. She was still glaring at him, the corners of her mouth drawn down in a pout. "But there was more to it. I saw. So did Anna . . . It was that Jane had something and she didn't. I mean . . . it wasn't the toy, it was the idea of the toy. What are you going to do, Mary?"

"I don't know. Rose, how could you hurt Jane like that? You'll have to be punished. You did a bad thing, a very bad thing. . . . Why?"

"It wasn't fair."

"What wasn't fair?"

"They gave her a toy. They didn't give me a toy."

"It was a game and Jane won."

"It wasn't *fair.*"

"You're not listening to me, Rose. It was a game. Some win at games and some lose. That's fair. But that's not what's important now. What's important is how you behaved to Jane. Going after her, hurting her. There's no excuse for it. You were bad. Very bad. Do you understand?"

"It wasn't my fault. You always blame me. You don't

love me anymore."

"Rose!"

"It's true. You always talk about *Jane*. You don't care about *me*."

Mary stared at Rose. She longed to hug her, to make things well again, but she knew things would never be well unless she could make her understand. "Listen to me," she said. "I love you. You're my own dear sister and I love you. But you did a bad thing."

"So did you. You lied to me."

"I never lied to you, Rose."

"You said when we came to America I'd have everything. But I don't have toys or pretty dresses. I don't have a kitten. You lied, Mary." Rose's eyes were hard, accusing. Her mouth was sullen. "And you're mean to me."

"Eh, she's no such thing," George said curtly. "You're the mean one. With your whining. With what you did to Jane and all. And not even sorry about it. I've never seen the like."

"Never mind, Georgy." Mary shook her head. "I'll see to the lass. You'd best see if you can help Anna. Go on."

"Aye, I'll go." George looked at Rose. An odd expression passed across his face. "I'll be glad to go."

Mary took off her coat. She draped it at the foot of the bed and then turned to Rose. "I know it hasn't been easy for you," she said. "It hasn't been easy for any of us. But we're trying. That's the important thing, to try. We're doing the best we can. . . . You'll have everything I promised."

"When?"

"I don't know when. It'll take time. But I promise you'll have all the toys and pretty dresses you want."

"And a kitten?"

"And a kitten. Only you must be patient. You must try to get along with Jane and—"

"I *hate* Jane."

"Don't talk like that. It's bad to hate."

"I *hate* her. She's mean. Everybody's mean to me."

Mary sat down next to Rose. Absently, she patted her golden curls. "How can I make you understand, lass? We can't go on this way. Anna has enough to worry about without your tempers. . . . It's not right for you to carry on so. If you'd only *try* to get along with Jane."

"*I hate Jane,*" Rose shrilled. "*Damn* Jane."

"Stop it! I won't have such talk! I won't!" Mary looked away. She closed her eyes, trying to put her troubled thoughts in order. She wanted to make excuses for Rose, but she could not. Seeing her this way, hearing her, she had to admit what she had long denied. "You're spoiled, lass," she said quietly. "You're thinking only of yourself, acting spiteful. I'll have to punish you."

"I didn't *do* anything."

"Yes, you did. And it wasn't the first time." Mary took Rose on her knee. She turned the child over and began to spank her. "I'm sorry, lass. I have to do this. It's for your own good."

Rose had never been spanked before. When she realized what was happening, she shrieked. She was furious, wriggling and kicking with all her might. Each light slap to her bottom brought a louder shriek of outrage.

Rose's cries pained Mary but they did not dissuade her. She did what she thought was necessary, stopping only when she decided her point had been made. "All right, lass." She sighed. "Now you know what happens when you're bad."

Rose rolled over on the bed. "I hate you," she said, fixing her pale blue eyes on Mary. "You're not my sister anymore."

"I'll always be your sister."

"You'll always be mean."

Mary stood up. She was tired, too tired to argue or explain. "One day you'll understand. We're all doing the best we can. That's all we can do." She went to the door, glancing back at Rose. "Stay in here. You'll be sleeping in here from now on, you'd best get used to it."

Rose, looking for a way to retaliate, kicked Mary's coat to the floor. She crossed her little arms over her chest and smiled.

"Pick the coat up."

"No!"

"Pick it up. Pick it up or I'll turn you over my knee again."

Grumbling, Rose picked the coat up and returned it to the bed. "Don't talk to me anymore," she said. "You're mean."

Mary walked out of the room and closed the door. She went into the kitchen. "Hello, Harley." She smiled wanly. "We've . . . had a bit of trouble."

"Ma told me. She's getting Jane to bed now."

"Is Jane all right?"

"She's fine."

"I don't know what got into Rose. I had to spank her."

"A little spanking never hurt anyone."

"It hurt Rose."

"Only her dignity, as Ma would say. Sit down, Mary. There's tea. You look like you need it. Go ahead, drink up. . . . I made it myself. Is it any good?"

"Oh, it's grand. Nice and strong." Mary sipped her tea. She was thinking about Rose, about the anger in her eyes, the pure spite. "I don't know what got into the lass. She never did anything like that in Hexter."

"Did anyone ever say no to her in Hexter?"

"I . . . suppose not. We gave her all we could."

"She'll get over it. Kids do." Harley stared at Mary. She was very pale and her shoulders seemed to sag. It bothered him to see her looking so unhappy. "Mary, all kids need a smack once in a while. I've had my share. It's not the end of the world, believe me."

"But Rose is . . . special. We came here to give her a better life. All I've given her so far is a spanking. I wonder what Pa would say."

"You couldn't let her get away with it, could you?"

"No."

"She has to learn. Isn't it best she learn from you?"

"I don't know. Maybe."

"Sure it is." Harley reached out. Shyly, he touched Mary's hand. To Mary it was a reassuring gesture, but to Harley it was much more. For months he had yearned to touch her, to hold her hand, to kiss her lips. He had not dared. "Let me cheer you up," he said. "It's not too late. We can have a walk. Twice around the block. How does that sound?"

"It's kind of you, Harley. But I'm tired."

"I've missed our walks."

"Oh?" Mary said in surprise. "I thought you'd be glad to have time to yourself for once. I've been such a burden."

"The best part of my week was Sunday, when we were together."

There was no mistaking the sincerity in Harley's

voice. Mary looked quickly at him. His eyes were bright with anticipation; his face was flushed. She realized he was waiting for her to say something, but she did not know what. "It's . . . kind of you, Harley. You're so nice to me."

Kind. Nice. Those were not the words Harley wanted to hear. He felt disappointment, but not defeat. She needs time, he said to himself, and I have time. "A walk would do you good."

"Another night."

Harley sat back. He clasped his hands behind his head and smiled slightly. "It won't work out with Dan. There's too much against it."

Now Mary flushed. She said nothing. She stared at the table and drank her tea.

"I know you've been walking out with Dan every Sunday. I've seen you together. . . . It's a mistake, Mary. You'll be hurt and that's the truth."

"Dan wouldn't hurt me."

"There's trouble between the Kilburnes and the McShanes. Do you know that?"

"I've heard."

"Pa will never allow it. He's . . . he's got his problems, but he's still head of the house. Ma's still his wife. She won't go against him in this."

Mary took a deep breath. She put her cup down and looked at Harley. "There's nothing to allow or not allow. It's just walks. It's nothing—"

"I've seen you together. It's more than walks. Dan has the look. So do you. You know what I mean."

"Yes," Mary whispered.

Harley nodded. He had not really expected a denial, for he knew Mary's honesty. He sensed her tenacity. She would not easily give up Dan McShane, he thought, but in the end she would have no choice. "I hope he's behaved himself. I hope he hasn't—"

"Hasn't what?" Mary frowned. When finally she understood Harley's words, she flushed an even deeper red. "Oh! No! No, Harley!"

"I'm just trying to warn you. I don't want you to be hurt. . . . People in the neighborhood say Dan can charm the birds from the trees. But it won't be enough. It won't get around Pa. Not the way he feels."

"How *does* he feel? What's the trouble, Harley? Do you know?"

"Sure I know. I was there."

"Will you tell me?"

"Well, it was after the fire. We'd been living in Yorkville for two months or so. Pa didn't have a job or money or anything. I guess old Pat McShane heard about what happened to us . . . because he came here. He sat right where you're sitting and offered Pa a job in his pub."

"What's wrong with that?"

"Nothing. Pat McShane's okay. Sentimental, like all the Irish. *Proud,* like all the Irish." Harley leaned forward. He gazed into the dark blue of Mary's eyes. "You probably like that in Dan. His stubborn pride."

"But what went wrong, Harley? Tell me."

"Well." Harley sighed. "Pa took the job. It killed him to do it, because he hates the Irish, but he took the job. Everything was fine . . . until Pa got drunk. It was a bad drunk, Mary. He was half out of his mind. He decided to tell Pat McShane what he thought about the Irish. And what he thought about Catholics and the Pope and everything else. There was a fight, a terrible fight. Pat was so mad he picked Pa up and threw him into the street. That's how he broke his ankle.' . . .

They're both proud men and there's bad blood between them now. They've hated each other ever since that night. That kind of hate never ends."

Mary pressed her hands together. She felt sick, cold. Her head throbbed. In Hexter she had heard about arguments that turned into feuds, feuds that generation after generation turned whole families against each other. "But . . . it has nothing to do with Dan and me," she said weakly.

"Pat will never let his son marry a Kilburne. Even if Dan talks him into it, Pa will never let you marry a McShane. That's the truth, Mary. Face it now, while you can."

"Marriage is a far way off."

"You'll be sixteen. Dan's almost seventeen. It's not far off. A year maybe."

"A lot can happen in a year. Things can change. People can change."

"Not Pa. And not Pat." Again, Harley took Mary's hand. "There's something else you have to think about. You and Dan aren't a secret. There's talk in the neighborhood. Not too much yet, but it's started. At first people thought you were a passing fancy with Dan. He's had a few. . . . Now they're not so sure."

"It's none of their account either way."

"Mary, most of the girls in the neighborhood have their caps set for Dan. If they see he's picked you, there'll be tongues wagging all over the place. And not kindly. There'll be nasty talk, a lot of it. Sooner or later, Pa will hear."

"What if he does? It's gossip. He won't listen to gossip."

"He'll kick you out, Mary. Ma won't be able to stop him."

146

"Harley!" Anna walked into the kitchen. "That's enough of that. You're being unfair."

"I'm only trying to tell Mary what to expect."

"You can't speak for your pa or for me." Anna looked sharply at her son though, as always, her look was softened by love. "But I can speak for *myself* and I'd like a few words with Mary. Will you leave us alone?"

"All right, Ma." Harley stood up. He walked away, then turned and walked back. Lightly, he touched Mary's hair. "If I was unfair, I'm sorry."

"Oh, Harley, I know you just want to help. You're such a good friend to me."

"Run along now," Anna said.

"I'm going." Harley went to the door. He took his coat from the hook, slinging it over his shoulder. "I'll find George. Maybe we'll have a soda."

Anna watched him go. She sat down. "What a day!" She sighed.

"I'm sorry about everything, Anna. About Rose . . . I gave her a spanking. I hope it helps. Is Jane all right?"

"She's sleeping. I don't think those two are ever going to be friends. If they learn to get along, I'll be happy."

"I know. It's a shame."

"Well, things don't always work out the way we want them to. You and Dan, for example. Are you serious about him, Mary?"

"Oh, yes."

"And he's serious about you?"

"Yes."

"I see."

"Don't be angry at me, Anna. I can't help how I feel."

"I'm not angry. I'm sorry. Harley was right about

one thing . . . Bob will never allow it. Nor will Pat. And it's more than the fight they had. It's religion. It's being English and Irish. It's being men and having the last word. . . . It's a man's world, Mary. Women can't fight it, they can only find their place in it."

"Dan will fight."

"Yes, he probably will. But he has seven brothers and sisters. He has a father and a grandfather. Will he fight them all? Can he?"

"Dan can do anything!"

Anna smiled despite herself. She remembered young love, the joy of it, the madness. She had only to think of her early years with Bob to know what Mary was feeling. "Well, a person can't be talked out of love. I'm not going to try. But there's trouble coming. You're in for grief, Mary. I wish I could make you see that."

"Dan said we'd find a way. I believe him."

"Dan doesn't know Bob. He doesn't know about hatreds and grudges. Why should he? He's young, at the beginning of life. Everything's always rosy at the beginning."

"Dan knows there's trouble. He said it's not *our* trouble."

"It will be, soon enough. When Bob hears you're seeing Dan . . ." Anna shook her head. Her green eyes were thoughtful. "He won't throw you out, I'll see to that. But he'll make it *hard* for you. So much harder than it is now. He'll make your life miserable. . . . Where will the joy be then? What will happen to the love?"

Tears filled Mary's eyes. She brushed them away. "I have to trust in Dan, Anna. I *have* to. He's in my heart now. I'll never get him out."

"Never is a very long time. And you're so young. . . .

There are other boys. Fine boys."

"Not for me."

Anna looked at her hands, lacing her fingers together. There was something more she wanted to say, though she was not certain she should. She considered for a moment. Finally she raised her eyes to Mary. "Do you know that Harley's sweet on you?"

"Harley?"

"Harley."

"He's my friend. He's kind to me, that's all."

"Harley *is* kind. But kindness has nothing to do with the way he feels about you. He's a boy in love."

Mary's eyes were wide, disbelieving. "In love? With me?"

"You told me boys didn't fancy you. Well, two boys fancy you now."

"I . . . don't know what to say."

"You don't have to say anything. Poor Mary, you have so much to think about already. Maybe I should have kept my mouth shut. . . . But that wouldn't solve any problems, would it? It's best to know where you stand. It's easier that way. People are less likely to get hurt."

"You mean Harley. I'd never hurt him, Anna."

"Someone's going to be hurt. You, Dan, Harley. Maybe all three of you. That's the sad part." Anna stood up. She gripped the back of the chair, staring at Mary. "You're like a daughter to me. I don't want to spoil your happiness. I just want you to know the problems ahead. They're there. Waiting." She leaned down and hugged Mary. "I'm sorry for being so blunt. I wish . . . I wish I believed in miracles."

Mary did not believe in miracles either, but she believed miraculous things sometimes happened.

Coming to America was one of those things, meeting Dan was another. The thought of Dan calmed her. She loved him and she trusted him and that was enough. "I'll talk to Dan," she said. "He'll find a way for us."

"Mary—"

"He'll find a way."

Six

"If you ask me," Elsie Jadnick said, looking up from the kitchen table, "the real problem is money. You need to put money aside. A nest egg. It's easier to thumb your nose when you've your own nest egg to fall back on."

"I don't want to thumb my nose," Mary said. "It's not that."

"What is it then? You're defying Bob, aren't you? Even though he doesn't know about it yet, it's the same thing. I'm not saying you don't have the right. Love is love. You're entitled. But love doesn't pay the rent or buy the food. That's where money comes in. You can call your own tune when you have money. It's like the Bible says . . . riches is a person's strong city."

"Riches! Oh, Elsie, I don't have a penny to myself. You know that. I give Anna two dollars and fifty cents each week. The other fifty cents I give to Bob. That's all my wages."

"I know. I know. But maybe we're overlooking some possibilities. Don't smile at me that way. I'm not crazy, not yet."

Mary went back to work. Starting at seven-thirty, she had scoured the floor, the hearth, the ovens, and the cupboards. She had baked the breakfast rolls, and cleared and washed the breakfast dishes. She had unpacked two cartons of groceries. In her fine hand, she had written out the dinner menu Elsie dictated. She had made a soufflé for Mrs. Sinclair's lunch. She had dressed the servants' lunch table and washed those dishes. Now she slipped a tray of tiny pastries into the oven and closed the door.

"How many are you making?" Elsie asked.

"Two dozen."

"That's about right. The ladies are always fussing about their figures, but you can't get them away from the tea table with a team of wild horses. Here, slice these cucumbers. They'll be wanting little sandwiches too."

Mary sat down across from Elsie. She took a knife and began cutting thin, almost translucent slices from the cucumbers. It was a simple task, but she gave it all her concentration, making each slice precisely the same size.

"You ought to have a tearoom," Elsie smiled. "You'd do well. There's money in tearooms."

"Oh, I've no head for business. My place is at a stove."

"We'll see about that." Elsie returned her attention to the kitchen budget. Squinting, she added a column of numbers, made a few notations, and then closed the ledger. "Mary, I want you to bake some of your honey cakes later."

"But there's coffee pie on the menu for tonight. Mrs. Sinclair—"

"They're not for the Sinclairs. They're for Mr. Basset. Tomorrow morning when he brings the groceries, we'll offer him a nice cup of tea and some of your cakes."

"I didn't think you liked Mr. Basset."

"Well, he's been good about prices. I can't say that for all the merchants. And he delivers on time every morning, no matter the weather."

"I'll be glad to make the cakes, Elsie."

"Good. . . . Did you ever add it up what they cost to make?"

"No."

"I did. About twenty-four cents a dozen, two cents apiece. You could sell them for four times that. Maybe more. The ladies in this neighborhood have money to burn. . . . Do you see what I'm getting at, Mary?"

Mary reached across the table and squeezed Elsie's hand. "Yes!" she said, her eyes brimming with sudden excitement. "Do you really think I could make pastries to sell? Do you think Mr. Basset would buy them? Oh, Elsie, it would be grand."

"It's just an idea. There's nothing definite."

"But it's a *grand* idea. It's . . . Elsie, what about Mrs. Sinclair? Will she let me? I can't afford to lose my job."

"First we'll see what Mr. Basset thinks. Then I'll put it to Mrs. Sinclair. We've been together a long time, her and me. I was with her when she was on the stage . . . seeing to her meals, to her clothes. She's a lady now, but she has a good heart. Not like some of them. I don't know what she'll say. I know she'll give it a fair hearing. There's a chance. A possibility. Never overlook a possibility, that's what *I* say."

Mary realized that it was more than a chance. It was *the* chance, the one she had prayed would come her way. There would not be much money in the beginning, but there would be some; she would save, penny by penny, nickel by nickel, and her savings would grow.

"Elsie, I don't know how to thank you."

"I haven't done anything yet. And maybe it won't work out, so don't get yourself in a tizzy."

"It will work out. It *will*. Dan says if you look hard enough there's a way. This is ours. I'll have money put by for when we're . . ." Mary paused, blushing. "For when we're married," she said softly.

"Listen to you. Not even sixteen and talking about marriage."

"I think about it all the time. Dan does too. Oh, Elsie, we love each other. With a little money put by, we can get married. We can make a home for Rose."

"Rose! Whatever conversation we have, it always comes back to Rose. It's not right."

"She's my responsibility. I promised Pa. I have to see to her. I *want* to." Mary smiled. Her eyes were alight with expectations, with dreams. "Rose is going to be a lady! She'll have everything she wants."

"And you paying the bills, I suppose. How does your Dan feel about that?"

Now Mary's smile wavered. Her face became still. "Rose has been out with Dan and me a couple of Sundays. They didn't get along too well. Oh, I don't blame Dan. Rose has her tempers and all. It's because she's unhappy. . . . But things will get better. Dan's so good with children." Mary's smile returned, brighter and wider than before. "I wish you could see him with children, Elsie. He's so sweet and funny."

"But Rose doesn't like him, eh?"

"She will. There's no resisting Dan McShane."

"I'll take your word for it." Elsie pushed her chair back. "Right now I have a roast to season. Make the tea sandwiches and set out the pastries. When you're finished, start peeling the vegetables for dinner."

"Yes, Elsie . . . Elsie? Thank you."

"Don't thank me yet. Let's see how we do with Mr. Basset. He's shrewd, that one. Dollar signs in his eyes." Elsie laughed. Her plump cheeks dimpled. "But there's two of us and only one of him. So maybe we'll do fine."

Mary could hardly wait for the day to be over. She did her chores, cooking and washing and fetching. She did them well, although her mind was elsewhere. It was on Dan, on Rose; above all it was on Mr. Basset, for he could, with a simple business decision, alter their lives.

Edwin Basset was a middle-aged man who had no wife, no children, no friends. He had a business, a thriving grocery store of good size, and his business was his life. He opened the store at six-thirty every morning and did not close until seven o'clock at night. Afterward, he went upstairs to his modest flat and worked on his account books. Profits brought a smile to his thin face. Losses, rare as they were, small as they were, brought a scowl.

He was a somewhat fussy man, the sort of man who saw a speck of lint at ten paces and rushed to brush it away. He was discreet and unfailingly polite. He was, by the standards of the day, honest. A few pennies might be added to the monthly bills of poorly run households, but never more than that. His weights and measures were accurate, or nearly so. He did not sell anything he knew to be stale.

Mr. Basset employed only one clerk, a harassed young man whom he did not trust. He would not have employed a clerk at all, but for his insistence on making his own deliveries. In that way, he reasoned, he could ingratiate himself with the cooks and housekeepers who were the source of his larger orders. To the more favored of those women, he occasionally brought a sweet or a packet of tea. They all received calendars at Christmas, "Basset's Fine Groceries" printed on each page.

Mr. Basset kept to a strict routine and the Sinclair house was always the fourth stop on his route. The Sinclair household, he knew, was not poorly run. Bills were checked and checked again, as were weights. Elsie Jadnick had been blunt. "If we're paying for a full pound of cheese, it's a full pound of cheese you'll give us," she had said. From that day on, all of her orders were filled to the exact ounce and delivered promptly. Edwin Basset, as he himself liked to say, was no fool.

Now, on this wintry, blustery March morning, he brought his delivery wagon to a halt and jumped down. He patted his horse, an old, gray swayback, and unloaded the two large cartons marked Sinclair. He looked inside each carton, matching the items to those on his list. When he was satisfied, he carried them down the stairs and rang the bell.

Mary opened the door. "Good morning, Mr. Basset." She smiled. "Please come in. It's a bitter day, isn't it?"

"March is like that." He nodded. "A moody month."

They walked through the corridor and turned into the kitchen. The Sinclair kitchen, unlike others he saw every day, was always spotlessly clean. He liked that. He liked the good, sweet smells that came from the ovens, and the sound of the tea kettle hissing on the stove. It reminded him of home, of the days when his mother was alive and doing for him.

"Good morning, Mrs. Jadnick," he said, putting the cartons on the table. He bowed slightly. "I have everything you ordered."

"That's fine. That's fine." She peered up at Mr. Basset. "Maybe you'd like a cup of tea? To take the chill off?"

"Thank you, Mrs. Jadnick. You're very kind. I would enjoy a cup of tea."

"Sit yourself down then. Mary, maybe you have some little cakes for us?"

"I'll get them."

Mr. Basset was pleased. Elsie Jadnick sometimes offered him tea or coffee; in warm weather, she sometimes offered him lemonade. But she had not gone so far as to offer him cake. He took it as a sign that she had forgiven him for his old "error" with the cheese. He was glad. He liked Elsie better than most of the other cooks in the neighborhood. Blunt though she was, and too sharp, he liked her homey ways.

Mary took two honey cakes from a warming pan in the oven and placed them on a gleaming white plate. She set the plate before Mr. Basset. "I hope you like them," she said.

"Honey cake! Why, I haven't had honey cake in years."

"It was a favorite back in Hexter."

"Yes. I'm English, you know. Or my parents were." Mr. Basset blinked behind his polished glasses. "I have a weakness for English cooking, I'm afraid. Do you make trifle?"

"The girl makes everything you can think of." Elsie smiled. She chuckled softly. "There's some who are born to cook. She's one of them. Well, go on, taste it. Eat it while it's warm. It's best that way, though it's good cold. There's some who prefer it cold."

Mr. Basset took a small bite. "My! It's excellent!

157

Excellent! There's something different about this cake. . . . You have a secret ingredient. Yes, my mother was the same way. She had her secrets in the kitchen." He took another, larger bite. "Excellent!"

Elsie and Mary exchanged glances. "Not like the sorry excuses for cake they sell in bakeries, is it, Mr. Basset?" Elsie asked.

"No, it certainly isn't. There isn't a really good bakery in the city. I've noticed that."

"And it's a shame. There's lots of people who like their sweets. Some are lucky. They have good cooks at home. But some have cooks who can't bake. And then there's some who don't have cooks at all. People like that are coming into the neighborhood now. Have you noticed? Into what they call apartment buildings."

"Oh, the character of the city is changing. There's no doubt of it, Mrs. Jadnick. Merchants like myself must be alert to such changes. We must anticipate. It's a trial, but what can we do?" Mr. Basset continued to eat. He finished the first cake, took a generous sip of tea, and put his fork to the second cake.

Elsie sat down. She sipped her tea slowly, peering thoughtfully at Mr. Basset. "It's not such a trial for a smart businessman like you. You're always ahead of everyone else. You had the dark chutney on your shelves before anyone else. And avocados! Before anyone else even knew what they were!"

"Well, a risk now and then." He shrugged his slight shoulders. "I'm a cautious man, but now and then I do take a risk."

"It's smart business."

Mr. Basset lowered his fork. He dabbed his mouth with his napkin and looked closely at Elsie. "I believe you are leading up to something, Mrs. Jadnick."

"Oh." Elsie laughed. "You're too smart for me. I thought I was being so clever. . . . Well, all right, now you know. It's about the cakes. Why don't you put a bakery counter in your store? Quality goods only. You'd make a pretty penny. And you have the room, what with the enlarging you did last spring."

"A bakery counter? But I sell groceries, not—"

"Selling's selling. If you can sell those funny-looking avocados, you can sell anything. Think of it like an extra service you're doing for your customers. Didn't you tell me you prided yourself on your service?"

"Yes, certainly. But a bakery counter? I know nothing about baked goods. I sell groceries, Mrs. Jadnick."

"You know what tastes good, don't you? You know people like sweets."

Mr. Basset removed his glasses. He rubbed the bridge of his nose, then put his glasses back. "You see, my father was a grocer. A greengrocer, actually. In England. I learned the business from him. The *grocery* business."

Elsie smiled cheerfully. "Well, I guess I made a mistake. It wouldn't be the first time. . . . I thought you were a man with a keen eye for profits. But there's no telling, is there? Mary, get another cake from the oven and wrap it nice. Mr. Basset will take it with him."

Mr. Basset knew he was being dismissed. He half rose from his chair, then, frowning, he sat down again. "Profits? Certainly I'm interested in profits. Fair profits," he added hastily. "But there would be an investment involved. Money out of pocket, Mrs. Jadnick. I would have to think about that very carefully. Yes, very carefully indeed."

"There's no investment. You have the space. You

have the counter. Say . . . just say you put in a selection of little cakes. Maybe cookies. And say Mary was willing to supply the cakes and cookies. Well, you pay Mary a fair price for what you sell. What you don't sell costs you nothing."

"Nothing?"

"Not a penny."

Mr. Basset grasped the soundness of the proposition. He would have to rearrange some stock, but that was a small matter. He would have to provide proper boxes; that, too, was a small matter. The important thing was that the venture would cost him nothing and bring him profits. He remembered the taste of the honey cakes. They will sell, he thought. And when word gets around. . . . "It's not out of the question," he said cautiously. "Perhaps something might be worked out."

Mary had been watching and listening, her fingernails digging into the palms of her hands. Elsie had warned her to remain silent, but now she gasped at Mr. Basset's encouraging words. "Oh, do you mean it?" she asked.

"What else do you make? What else do you make that I could handle in my store?"

"There's vanilla crumbles. And tarts. And I make Roly-Poly cakes."

"Roly-Poly cakes!" Mr. Basset remembered them from his childhood, for they had been his favorite sweet. They were not made in America; certainly they were not made for commercial sale. His store, alone, would have them. Suddenly he saw dimes and quarters and dollars accumulating in his cash box. "Yes!" he said. "We must have those. Children love them. Women will buy them for their children." Mr. Basset paused, removing his glasses, tapping them on the table. He had betrayed his eagerness and he cursed himself for it. He took a sip of tea, selecting his next words with care. "What price did you have in mind?"

"What price would you charge for, say, the honey cakes?"

"They are of reasonable size. I could charge . . . eight cents apiece."

"You could charge ten," Elsie said.

"Perhaps, Mrs. Jadnick. Of the ten cents, I would give you four cents, Mary. That's fair."

Mary saw Elsie nodding at her, urging her to accept. She hesitated. Many thoughts went through her mind, many numbers. "Thank you, Mr. Basset," she said finally. "But I want five cents. I want half."

"Half?"

"Yes, Mr. Basset."

"But it's my store. I'm offering you space in my store."

Mary shook her head. "Half is fair. I'm doing the work and paying for the ingredients. Half is fair."

Mr. Basset was annoyed by Mary's attitude. He considered it rude, unseemly. He considered forgetting the whole idea, but the thought of a full cashbox stopped him. He wiped his glasses and replaced them on his nose. "You drive a hard bargain. . . . Yes, all right. Half."

"Thank you, Mr. Basset."

Elsie was astonished at this turn of events. She had not expected Mary to argue over prices, or to hold firm once she had. This was a different side to Mary and she admired it far more than she did the side that was so often and so meekly sacrificed to her family. "Well," she said, standing, "there's some details to see to yet.

But if you ask me, it's a good bargain all around."

Mr. Basset rose. "Time will tell, Mrs. Jadnick. Speaking of time . . ." He took his watch from his pocket and frowned. "I'm late for my next delivery. I've never been late before."

"We won't keep you any longer," Elsie said, showing him to the door. "I'll let you know when Mary can begin. . . . Oh, Mr. Basset? I wouldn't mention this to anybody. Some other smart businessman might hear . . . might get the jump on you. You wouldn't want that, would you now?"

"No, Mrs. Jadnick, certainly not." He looked again at his watch. "Well, good morning. Good morning, Mary."

"Good morning."

He hurried off, practically running through the hall. The outer door opened and then closed. Elsie turned to Mary. "And you said you had no head for business! That was smart, what you did. And to Mr. Basset no less! I can't get over it, Mary. There you were, your chin set like stone, your shoulders squared. Haggling over a penny's difference."

"But it's more than a penny's difference. It's *lots* of pennies. I did some figuring in my head. Pennies add up."

"Sure they do. Sure they do. And they'll be adding up in your pocket."

"Elsie, there's still Mrs. Sinclair."

"I know. I'll have a talk with her now, if she has the time. Did you write out tonight's menu? Oh, there it is. I'll take it up to her. Keep your fingers crossed for luck."

"I will."

Elsie picked up the menu and read it. "That's fine.

I'm on my way. See to the broth, Mary. Keep stirring it."

"I'll see to it, but please hurry, Elsie. I can't stand the waiting."

Cynthia Sinclair sat at her graceful rosewood desk, reading the menu Elsie had presented for approval. She was dressed in a morning gown of bottle green trimmed with white lace. Her slippers were green also, and there was a tiny green bow in her upswept curls. She wore no jewelry save for a thin gold wedding ring and a huge diamond engagement ring. Those two pieces of jewelry she wore all the time, proudly. "The menu is very nice, Elsie. We haven't had saddle of lamb in a while. Since the last time the Whitfields were here. Or did you remember that?"

"Mrs. Whitfield said how much she liked it. I thought I'd make it for her again tonight."

"That's most considerate. She will be pleased, I'm sure. And Mary is making her special brandy pudding. Yes, that's very nice. It should be a lovely evening. . . . Was there something else?"

"I wanted to talk to you. If you have the time."

"I always have time for you, Elsie. What is it?"

"Well, it's kind of a long story. I'll tell it as straight as I can." Elsie began by mentioning Bob Kilburne and the money he had stolen from Mary. She mentioned Dan and little Rose. She mentioned Mr. Basset then, explaining in great detail the arrangements that had been suggested and agreed upon. "So you see, Mrs. Sinclair," she finished, "it's a real opportunity for Mary."

Cynthia Sinclair had been listening intently. Now

she folded her hands and stared at Elsie. "I regret this has gone as far as it has," she said. "It's quite impossible."

"You're always saying how you want to help Mary."

"Of course I want to help her. But there are limits. I cannot allow her to run a business from my home. It simply isn't done, Elsie. Surely you know that. How could you have gone ahead without speaking to me first?"

"I didn't know if it would come to anything. Before I bothered you, I thought I'd see what Mr. Basset had to say. I thought that was the sensible thing to do."

"You don't fool me, Elsie. What you thought was that I would have to accept the arrangements already made. You were wrong." Cynthia stood up. In a rustle of silken petticoats, she walked to the windows and drew the pale curtains aside. "I'm not happy about this. You put me in an extremely difficult position."

"I'm sorry, Mrs. Sinclair, but I didn't see any harm. It's a way for Mary to earn some extra money for herself. Lord knows she needs it. With that family of hers . . . all the responsibilities she has. It's hard for her. Not that she complains. She doesn't. She—"

"Elsie, I'm aware of Mary's problems. I resent you making them my problems. I resent it very much." Cynthia was seldom moved to anger, but she was angry now. She deemed Elsie's actions irresponsible and presumptuous. She would have fired any other servant for such presumption, though she knew she would not, could not, fire Elsie. There were too many years between them, good years and bad. Upset as she was, she could not forget them. "We will discuss your poor judgment another time. But you must cancel whatever arrangement you made with Mr. Basset."

"Mrs. Sinclair, I'm not one to harp on a subject—"

"Then please don't."

"But it's important. It's a chance for Mary. Maybe she won't get another. You wouldn't want to be the person spoiling her chance. I know you better than that. I've known you since you were a girl, not much older than Mary. All this," Elsie said, waving her hands at the expensive furnishings, "doesn't change what's inside you."

"I am sympathetic to Mary's predicament, Elsie. But I cannot allow her, or anyone, to run a business from here. Mr. Sinclair would be appalled, and rightly so."

"Well, maybe it doesn't have to be from here. She has her days off. She could do her baking at Anna's. . . . Deliver the pastries straight to Mr. Basset's store. It would have nothing to do with here."

"She is my employee. I expect my employees to work for me, not for others. Perhaps you find that unreasonable?"

"Now you're teasing me, Mrs. Sinclair." Elsie smiled, her small eyes crinkling at the corners. "You always did like a joke."

"I assure you there is no *joke* in any of this." Cynthia crossed the room. She stopped at a bowl of flowers and bent to inhale their scent. She straightened a seat cushion, moved a delicate crystal swan from one side of the table to the other. "You, Elsie, have put me in the extraordinary position of having to defend myself. And you have done it deliberately."

Elsie pretended not to understand. She furrowed her brow, looking up at Cynthia Sinclair. "I wouldn't do that."

"Do not forget I know you as well as you know me." Cynthia returned to her desk. She sat down, smiling faintly. "You are determined about this, I see. Why? I know you are fond of Mary . . . but there is more to it. Tell me."

"I'm thinking about the future. A person has a right to think about the future."

"Whose future?"

"Mary's. And mine too. I won't lie to you. I'm thinking about myself too."

"Why, Elsie," Cynthia said in surprise, "you will always be provided for. Surely you don't doubt that?"

"I know I'll always have a roof over my head and food on the table. That's more than most people can say. But this is a different thing. Mrs. Sinclair, I think Mary could have a tearoom someday. It's a good business. Maybe I could have a little piece of the business. Not much. I'm not greedy and never was. A little piece of a little business would suit me fine."

"I had no idea you were interested in business."

"I wasn't, not exactly. After all, there's only a few businesses a woman can have. A woman can have a boardinghouse, or a laundry. If she's educated she can have a school. The other business a woman can have is a tearoom. I'll tell you the truth, Mrs. Sinclair, I hate making those tiny little pastries. But Mary, now that's another story. She loves that work. And is there anybody who does it better? She's gifted that way."

"You would leave me, Elsie?"

"Oh, not right away. Not for a long time, probably. It's not that I want to leave. . . . It's that once before I die I want to have something that belongs to me. Like a bit of a tearoom. Do you see what I'm getting at?"

"I suppose I do. Of course it's easier said than done."

"I know. I know. Maybe it won't come to anything. But maybe it will."

Cynthia sat back in her chair. She took a flower from a vase on the desk and twirled it thoughtfully in her long fingers. "I would not wish to stand in your way," she said slowly. "Nor would Mr. Sinclair. But I must have some assurances. I must know that the duties of this household would not be neglected. Things run smoothly now. They must continue to do so."

"Mrs. Sinclair, I've never let you down before. I wouldn't do it now. Your house comes first, with me and with Mary. It's a promise and you know how I am about promises. If I make a promise, I keep it. That's how I was brought up and that's that."

"Very well, Elsie. I will take the position that what Mary does in her time away from this house is her own business. There are, however, a few conditions."

"Sure there are. That's only right."

"As I have already said, the duties of this household must not be neglected. In addition, Mary is not to use my kitchen for her project. No money is to change hands in my kitchen. Do you understand?"

"Yes, Mrs. Sinclair. And I agree. What's right is right."

"Lastly, Mary is to confine her outside baking to those things we do not serve here. I will not serve my husband or my guests what can be purchased at Mr. Basset's store. Is that quite clear?"

"It is." Elsie nodded.

"I will trust you to honor these agreements. . . . Don't give me any cause to regret my decision."

Elsie smiled, shaking her head. "I wouldn't do such a thing. I know what's right. I came to you, Mrs. Sinclair. There's some who'd go sneaking behind your back."

"Perhaps."

With some difficulty, Elsie pulled her bulk from the

narrow chair. "Thank you, Mrs. Sinclair," she said, smoothing her skirts. "I knew you had a good heart. I told Mary. Mrs. Sinclair has a good heart, that's what I told her."

"I'm glad I did not disappoint you," Cynthia said wryly.

"You never have. That's a fact. I can't say that for my own family, or for my husband who walked out on me, but I can say it about you."

Cynthia laughed suddenly, a great and raucous laugh that filled the room. She knew she had been manipulated; she did not really mind. Elsie was, in her way, an original, deferent and defiant at the same time. She knows her place, thought Cynthia, but that place is of absolutely no concern to her. "Really, Elsie, you are impossible!"

"Me?"

"I am curious about something. You are obviously hoping this project will finance a tearoom one day. But what if Mary marries her young man? There would be no tearoom then."

"Sure there would. Married or single, those two will always need money. Dan . . . that's his name, Dan McShane, he has seven brothers and sisters. He'll be helping them out 'til the day he dies. And Mary has her sister Rose. She wants Rose to be a *lady* . . . the English are strange that way. Always thinking who's a lady, who's not. They're taught like that, I guess. Anyway, it costs money to be a lady."

"Yes." Cynthia laughed again. "I have heard that."

"No disrespect meant."

"Oh, none taken."

"Well, I'll be getting back to the kitchen. I've lunch to make. And Mary's waiting. She's nervous as can be, waiting to hear about our talk."

"Was there any doubt as to how it would end?"

"Some." Elsie chuckled, walking out the door. "Some."

"How nice," Cynthia said to herself. "How nice there was at least *some* doubt."

Cynthia remained at her desk, shaking her coppery head and smiling. She would tell Preston about this fantastic conversation, she thought. He might not be entirely pleased, but he would be amused.

It was after midnight. The Whitfields had come and gone and now Preston Sinclair sat in his wife's boudoir, smiling as she told her story. He was a portly man, silver haired, attractive in late middle age. Like many of the Sinclair men he had flashing black eyes and a somewhat sardonic mouth.

Preston Sinclair had been born at Lucy's Court, the South Carolina plantation that had been home to his family for more than six generations. He had been twelve years old when the first shots were fired on Fort Sumter, beginning the Civil War. He had been sixteen years old, serving in the Confederate Army, when the war ended and Reconstruction began. Those terrible, tragic years had changed everyone who lived through them.

The Sinclairs had fared better than some. Lucy's Court had not been burned or even sacked. The family fortune, made in cotton and slaves and deposited, for the most part, in English banks, had not been diminished. But they had lost two sons. They had lost cousins. They had lost friends. Preston had returned home, cannon fire still ringing in his ears, to look upon the bloodied lands and hear the tales of death. He had been changed. The idealism he had felt as a boy he felt no longer. He became hard and cynical and, it was said, ruthless. These characteristics he tried to instill in his sons, Reeve and Burr.

Although Preston was firm with his sons he was indulgent with his wife. He cared for Cynthia more than he had ever cared for any woman. He enjoyed her, and that enjoyment was evident now. "Did Elsie really say that?" he asked.

"She certainly did! And much more. I was quite angry at first, but in the end I couldn't help laughing. Of course I gave her my permission. She knew I would. . . . You don't mind too terribly, do you, darling?"

"It's most unorthodox. In my day servants were content to be servants. They had no aspirations beyond a warm meal and a warm bed."

"Elsie is more than a servant."

"Yes, my dear," Preston said in his soft drawl, "I know. I remember how she hovered around when I was courting you. She was a mother hen, looking after her chick. Looking after me, to see I took no liberties."

"And you didn't." Cynthia smiled. "You were a perfect gentleman."

"I was not given any choice." Preston sipped his brandy, gazing around the blue-and-ivory room. The lights were low, the air scented with Cynthia's perfume. He leaned against the back of the silk chaise and sighed in contentment. "If you've given your permission to Elsie and Mary, I won't interfere."

"Thank you, darling."

"I can't deny you anything. As you well know."

"I know you're good to me, Preston. You're so ferocious when it comes to business, but you have always been good to me."

"A man must be ferocious in business. He must be without conscience. You wouldn't understand that, my dear, you are only a woman. A woman of tender sensibilities." Preston stroked Cynthia's smooth white hand. "If I had a daughter I would want her to be like you. But my sons, if they are to succeed, must be like me."

"Reeve is very like you."

"Yes . . . I had a letter from Reeve today. He wants to spend Easter at Lucy's Court. Burr wants to spend Easter here in New York. What do you think?"

"Well, Reeve almost always has his way. It might be nice to do what Burr wishes this once."

"Perhaps. Of course there are other considerations. If we went to Lucy's Court, I could visit the mills. The workers are more diligent when there's a Sinclair walking around Sinclair Mills." Preston looked into his wife's lovely hazel eyes. He smiled. "All right, my dear, we will stay here for Easter. The mills are at the top of production anyway."

"Burr will be pleased."

"So will you. Don't shake your head. I know you are not comfortable at Lucy's Court. . . . Foolishly, I keep hoping you will come to love it as I do. It's part of me. It's in my blood."

"I've tried, darling. Really I have."

"There is no more beautiful place. When I was a boy and thought about Heaven, I thought it would look just like Lucy's Court. I still think that."

Cynthia pictured Lucy's Court, a magnificent white-columned mansion set amidst acres of gardens and green lawns. She could see the beautiful old willows, their branches brushing the earth. She could see birds, hundreds of them in hundreds of different colors, singing at twilight. But such pretty images dissolved, as always, into shapeless, ghostly forms crying in the night. She, who was not at all superstitious, was convinced Lucy's Court was haunted. "Perhaps it is the idea that people were *owned* there," she said. Immediately she regretted her words, for the subject of slavery was a touchy one with Preston even now. "I'm sorry, darling," she said quickly. "I am being fanciful."

"Certainly you're being unrealistic. Do you think the Negras who work for me at Lucy's Court are any less owned than their ancestors? They are free, it is true. I pay them a wage, it is also true. But I own them as surely as my family owned their families. What would they do without the wage I pay, the roof I provide? Why, they would be lost, every one of them. Negras are incapable of caring for themselves. In their minds and hearts they are children. We in the South have always known that."

Cynthia turned her head away. She would not argue with Preston; she never argued with him. But she would not agree with him either. That was her one and only form of rebellion against her husband. If he noticed, he expressed no objection. "What a gloomy subject, darling!" she said. "I do hate gloomy subjects late at night!"

"Forgive me, my dear," Preston drawled. "We will speak no more about it." He leaned forward and kissed her cheek. "You are a delectable creature." He smiled.

Cynthia understood that her husband would not

return to his rooms this night. She rose. "I will change my gown. It is quite crushed by now."

She drifted off to her dressing room. Preston took a great swallow of brandy and then put the snifter down. He loosened his tie, removed his jacket. He was a gentleman in most things, but not in love-making. He imagined Cynthia coming to him and coarse color flared in his cheeks. He paced the room, waiting.

When Cynthia emerged from her dressing room she was wearing a robe and gown of thinnest ivory silk. She stopped before a lamp, letting light seep through the delicate fabric, and smiled at Preston. She knew he liked to be teased and so she teased him. All of her robes and nightgowns were of sheer or clinging materials; all had many tiny buttons and ribbons that had to be undone.

Slowly, Cynthia removed her robe. She stood in the half-light and opened the top buttons of her bodice. "It is a new gown," she said. "Do you like it?"

"Cynthia!" Preston cried out. He saw the lush curve of her breasts, the narrowing of her waist, and his black eyes glittered madly. "Cynthia!"

Cynthia took her time. She opened all the little buttons, untied all the ribbons. Her gown slipped from her shoulders and gathered about her hips. There were more buttons, more ribbons. Finally, her gown fell to the floor. She stood naked before Preston. "Will you take the pins from my hair, darling?"

Preston went to Cynthia. He pulled the pins away, burying his face in her coppery curls. His hands worked roughly at her breasts and when his mouth found hers it was insistent, demanding.

"Undress me," he said. It was an order. Cynthia

obeyed, removing his clothing even as his hands tore at her body.

Preston pushed Cynthia to the bed. He fell on top of her, murmuring obscenities and endearments both. Naked flesh pressed upon naked flesh. *"Now,"* he cried, his face red, crazed with lust. *"Now."*

Cynthia closed her eyes.

Seven

"Well, what's your big surprise?" Elsie asked Mary. "Can't you tell me yet? I'm dying from curiosity."

"Just another minute," Mary replied, moving closer to the kitchen table. "No, don't try to peek. I'm almost finished." She had heard about the Easter Parade from Dan. In newspapers she had seen sketches of elaborate Easter bonnets. Dan's descriptions and the newspaper sketches had given her an idea. It was to be a surprise, something special for Mrs. Sinclair, and she had spent countless hours getting it exactly right. "It's finished, Elsie," she said now. "You can look."

"Oh! My goodness, Mary, I never saw anything like it!"

"It's an Easter bonnet cake. For Mrs. Sinclair."

"My goodness, Mary!" Elsie stared in amazement at the glorious confection. It was rounded, shaped like a woman's bonnet, and festooned all over with birds and flowers of spun sugar. Around its wide brim was a delicate lattice of spun sugar for the veil. "So this is what you've been doing in the kitchen at all hours. You're a wonder and I don't mind saying so. Wait 'til Mrs. Sinclair sees."

"Do you think she'll like it?"

"That's a stupid question, isn't it? Of course she'll like it. Who wouldn't like it? It's beautiful. You must take it to her yourself."

"Oh no, Elsie. I couldn't do that. I'll just leave it for her and be on my way home. Dan's meeting me outside."

"You'll do as I say and that's that. All the work that went into this . . . you should hear what she says with your own ears. They're finishing breakfast now. Come along, I'll take you up myself. Nothing worse than false modesty, that's what I say."

It was not modesty, false or otherwise, that made Mary reluctant. It was the thought of the Sinclair family. She did not like Mr. Sinclair, for he seemed to her merely a younger version of Lord Worsham. She did not mind Burr, but Reeve Sinclair made her uneasy. She did not like the way he looked at her. There was familiarity in his flashing black eyes, and something else, something she could not read. "Elsie, I really ought to be going. Anna's expecting me to help with Easter dinner. I have the ham here in my basket."

"Will a few minutes make any difference? Is the ham walking away?"

"No, but—"

"Then you're coming with me. Pick up the cake and follow along."

Mary sighed. Carefully, she lifted the heavy silver cake platter and walked out of the kitchen with Elsie. "Go slow," she said. "It'd be a shame to drop it."

"See you don't."

The Sinclairs were finishing their coffee when Elsie knocked at the dining-room door. Flora, the young maid who served breakfast every morning, sprang to open it. "Oh, Elsie, it's you. They're not done yet."

"Never mind that. I want to see Mrs. Sinclair."

"What is it, Flora?" Preston asked impatiently.

"It's Elsie, sir. She wants to see Mrs. Sinclair."

"Well, don't stand there like a fool. Let her in."

"Yes, sir."

Cynthia looked up, smiling. "What is it, Elsie? Is there some trouble in the kitchen?"

"No trouble. Mary has a surprise for you. Wait 'til you see."

"A surprise! I love surprises. Do come in, Mary," Cynthia called.

Elsie opened the door wide. "Mrs. Sinclair says to come in. Hurry up, don't keep her waiting. But be careful . . . watch your step. Watch the carpet. That's it."

Mary carried her cake into the dining room. She felt all eyes turn in her direction and she blushed. "I'm sorry to bother you at breakfast," she said, her voice hardly more than a whisper.

Cynthia stood up, gazing at the creation coming her way. "Why, Mary, you've brought me a bonnet. . . . No," she said, taking a closer look, "you've *baked* me a bonnet. How exquisite! Preston, look at this. Isn't it wonderful?"

"It is indeed. Did you make this, Mary?"

"Yes, sir."

"All by yourself?"

"Yes, sir."

"Well, it's the prettiest thing I ever did see."

Everyone gathered around the cake, exclaiming over it. Only Reeve hung back. His eyes were fast on Mary.

177

They studied her face, her body. After a few moments, he sauntered to the table and glanced briefly at the cake. "Our Mary is an artist," he said in his soft drawl. "The flowers look real enough to pick."

"They do, Mary. It's simply charming! I have never had a nicer Easter present. Thank you so much."

"You're welcome, ma'am. I'll bring a knife and some plates, if you want."

"Heavens, no! I intend to show this off. The Spencers are coming for tea after the parade. They must see it. And Mrs. DuRoy is coming tomorrow. She must see it. You know"—Cynthia laughed—"I think my milliner should see it also. She is not half the designer you are, Mary."

"It's kind of you to say." Mary began edging toward the door, anxious to leave. "I'll be going now, Mrs. Sinclair."

"Certainly. But I would feel better if your beautiful cake were safe in the icebox. I don't want Burr getting to it before our guests arrive." Cynthia smiled at the younger of her stepsons. She had a deep fondness for him, a fondness she did not have for Reeve. "Will you take the cake back downstairs, Mary?"

"Yes, ma'am. I'll put it safe away."

"I'll carry it," Reeve said, lifting the platter from the table.

"Thank you, Master Reeve, but I can manage."

"Nonsense. After all your hard work, it is the least I can do. Isn't that right, Father?"

"Quite right. I am glad one of my sons is a gentleman. Burr, I hope you profit from your brother's example. There is nothing more important in a young man than good manners. The Sinclairs have always been known for their good manners."

"Yes, Father. So you say."

Preston did not like Burr's tone. He was about to reply sharply, but he remembered that servants were present and he changed his mind. "Help Mary with the cake, Reeve," he said. "Then see me in the library. We have things to discuss."

Reeve went to the door, Mary and Elsie following behind. They descended the stairs in silence. When they reached the kitchen, Mary took the platter from Reeve's hands. "Thank you, Master Reeve. It was kind of you."

"In addition to good manners, the Sinclairs have always been known for their kindness," Reeve said, sarcasm heavy in his voice. "Hadn't you heard?"

Neither Mary nor Elsie spoke. They were uncomfortable, unsure just how to respond to Reeve's presence in their kitchen. Elsie busied herself at the sink. Mary cut a length of cheesecloth and draped it over her cake.

"Well"—Reeve smiled slightly—"I see I am to be ignored. And by servants!"

Elsie turned away from the sink. She stared up at the dark-haired young man. "The kitchen's no place for you, Master Reeve, is it? Didn't I hear your father say he'd be waiting for you in the library? He doesn't like to be kept waiting. He doesn't like it at all. . . . You were kind to help the girl. Now it's best you go back upstairs."

"Are you dismissing me, Elsie?"

"I'm only sending you to your father, who's waiting for you."

"Yes, so he is. Dear Father." Reeve walked to the

179

door. "Happy Easter to you, Elsie, Mary."

"Happy Easter, Master Reeve."

Elsie listened to the footsteps fading away. She shook her head. "You never know what that one's thinking," she said. "A gentleman, his father calls him. I wonder about that. I wonder if he's such a gentleman underneath those fancy airs of his. . . . Here, Mary, I'll see to the cake. You be on your way now. And Mrs. Sinclair said to take these flowers for Anna."

Mary sniffed the pink roses and then put them in her basket. "I'm sorry to leave you with all the cooking today, Elsie. On a holiday and all."

"It's nothing to me. I have no place to go anyway. My sister's gone to Brooklyn. My cousins too. I'd rather be here. I'll take a few minutes and see a little of the parade later. You go along. Enjoy the day."

"I will, Elsie. See you tomorrow."

"Sharp at seven."

Mary carried her basket into the hall. She was at the closet, reaching for her coat, when she suddenly felt a hand on her breast. She screamed. Her basket fell to the floor as she struggled to turn around. She caught a glimpse of flashing black eyes, of a young, insolent smile. "Master Reeve!" she gasped. "Stop it! Stop it! *No!*" she screamed again.

Reeve cared nothing about Mary's screams. His hands clutched at her breasts. His mouth pressed hungrily on hers. He pushed her back, into the darkness of the closet. There was a loud thump then and, abruptly, Reeve fell away. He held up his hands, fending off the blows of the broom Elsie wielded. "Elsie, have you gone mad?" he demanded. *"Elsie,* what do you think you're doing?"

"What should have been done a long time ago. I'm giving you a thrashing."

Angry color rushed to Reeve's face. His eyes burned ebony fire. "How dare you? I will have your job, Elsie. I will have you dismissed at once."

"I hardly think so, Reeve." Cynthia Sinclair's voice was icy, as icy as the expression on her face. "I had second thoughts about your generous offer of help. I see I was not mistaken."

"It is not what you think, Mother."

"It is exactly what I think. You are to go upstairs immediately. I will deal with you in due time."

"She is only a *servant*," Reeve said, gesturing at Mary. "I am not the first man to—"

Cynthia slapped him. "You are no man at all. You are a bully. Only bullies attack those who cannot defend themselves. You are to go upstairs, Reeve. I will deal with you when I am ready."

Reeve rubbed the side of his face. He wanted to strike out at his stepmother, verbally if not physically, but he did not dare. He knew that she had more influence with his father than he did. He knew that a word from her would land him in the most serious trouble. "Father needn't hear of this. I . . . I will apologize to Mary."

"You will go upstairs. At once!"

Reeve bowed to his stepmother. He turned on his heel and hurried away. Cynthia watched him for a moment, then went to Mary. She took the sobbing girl in her arms and held her. "There now, it is all over, Mary. It will not happen again."

Mary was shaking. She could not stop crying. Reeve had terrified her and, now, the thought of losing her job terrified her anew. "I . . . didn't do anything," she sobbed.

"I know that. I do not blame you. Reeve is . . . at an unfortunate age. He is also headstrong." Cynthia took a lacy handkerchief from the sleeve of her gown and wiped Mary's eyes. "I will deal with him. He will not bother you again."

"My job, Mrs. Sinclair. I need my job."

"But you are not going to lose your job. You are not the one at fault. Please Mary, you must not cry anymore. You will make yourself quite ill."

"She'll be all right," Elsie said. "She just needs a minute or two. I'll see to her."

"Mary," Cynthia looked into her red, puffy eyes, "I will deal with this . . . matter. I want you to forget about it. Put it out of your mind."

"Yes, ma'am. As you say."

"I must ask you to be discreet. I would not want . . . talk to get around. Do you understand?"

"I won't say anything. I promise."

Cynthia nodded. "You're a good girl. Elsie, perhaps you should see Mary home."

"Her young man is waiting for her."

"Is he? Very well. Mary, you are certain you are all right? You do not feel faint?"

"I'm fine now. Thank you, about my job and all."

Cynthia bent and retrieved Mary's fallen basket. "You must not forget this," she said.

"Thank you."

"Well, if you're certain you are all right. . . ."

"Yes, ma'am."

"I will leave you then." Cynthia went to the stairs. She picked up her skirts, pausing to look back at Mary.

She seemed so young, so young and so vulnerable. "I hope the rest of your day is happier, Mary. Happy Easter."

"Happy Easter, Mrs. Sinclair."

"Come along, Mary," Elsie said, taking her arm. "You'd best wash your face before you meet Dan. You're liable to scare him, looking like you do now."

"No, he mustn't see me this way." Mary raised her hand to her tousled hair. The pins were loose, slipping from the braids coiled at the nape of her neck. One long lock of hair fell across her brow. "What would he think?"

"Don't ask stupid questions. Go fix yourself up."

Mary went into the small bathroom at the end of the hall. She washed her face and hands and scrubbed her mouth, trying to scrub away all memory of Reeve Sinclair's kiss. She undid her braids and brushed her long hair over her shoulders.

"That's much better," Elsie said when Mary emerged. "You look like a new girl. Pretty as can be. If you want to be smart too, you'll take Mrs. Sinclair's advice and forget about this morning. Master Reeve's not worth troubling about. Gentleman! Well, he'll catch the dickens from Mrs. Sinclair and that's that. . . . Here, here's your coat. And here's your basket. I know you're in a hurry, so run along."

"Thank you, Elsie. Thank you for your broom. It saved me."

"I wasn't born yesterday. I know a few things, including how to deal with the likes of Master Reeve. Now you go and have a good time. Go to your Dan McShane."

*   *   *

Dan stood on the corner, his hands in his pockets, his flaming red hair blowing about his face. Passers-by glanced at him and female passers-by smiled, for he was such a handsome figure, so filled with youth and vigor. He returned their smiles, inclining his head, though his eyes looked beyond them, searching for Mary. He could think of no one else. In his waking hours and even in his dreams she was with him. Disconcerting as it was, he did not want it any other way.

"Dan!"

He turned and saw Mary running toward him. He began to run too. They flew into each other's arms, smiling and sighing. "I was starting to worry about you, Mary Kilburne."

"I'm sorry. It was busy at the Sinclairs this morning."

"As long as you're here. Wait, let me look at you. . . . Your eyes are all red. Have you been crying?"

"Crying? No, it's . . . it's the pepper. I was grinding peppercorns and some of the powder got in my eyes." Mary did not want to lie to Dan. She wanted no secrets between them, but what happened with Reeve had to be a secret. She had promised Mrs. Sinclair; that was one reason. The other reason was Dan himself. She was afraid of what he might do if he knew the truth. "Pepper makes my eyes teary," she said.

"Is that all it is, Mary? I think you're working too hard. With your job and the baking you do for Basset's store, you've barely time to sleep. I don't want you to get sick."

"Oh, I'm healthy as a horse."

"There are horses and there are horses. Some drop in their tracks."

"Not me, Dan. Don't worry. I like to work. I have four dollars saved from Basset's store. It'd be twice as much if Anna had a bigger oven. Mr. Basset says my Roly-Poly cakes just fly off the shelves."

Dan laughed. He ruffled Mary's hair. "How can I argue with flying Roly-Poly cakes? How can I argue with you? You're always one step ahead of me, Mary Kilburne, and that's the truth."

"That's blarney."

"Blarney! Would you be accusing *me* of blarney?"

"Yes, and I love it."

"It's good you do. You're in for a lifetime of it . . . unless you get rich on Roly-Poly cakes and forget all about me. There you'll be, having tea with Mrs. Astor, while I—"

"Dan, don't talk that way. Even as a joke. It scares me."

Dan stopped walking. He took Mary's hands and stared into her eyes. "You're right, my darling girl. I shouldn't joke about us. I won't do it again . . . will you forgive me?"

"I need forgiving myself. I know I'm always talking about money . . . it's not that I want to be rich. I just want a life for us. For you and me, and Rose."

"I know. But you're not to worry, because I *will* be rich one day. Maybe sooner than anyone thinks. In the meanwhile, there are ways to get by. We'll manage. We may have to live on soup and tea in the beginning, but we'll manage." Dan winked at Mary. A great smile spread across his face. "Is it a bargain we have, Mary Kilburne? Sure and are you giving me your word on it?"

"Yes." Mary smiled back at him. "Not only my word,

my heart."

They continued their walk up Fifth Avenue. Strollers leaving church services or simply parading their finery, turned to admire the young and radiant couple. "Aren't they sweet?" a well-dressed matron murmured to her husband. He had to agree they were.

Dan and Mary parted two blocks away from her building. It was the only concession they were willing to make to neighborhood gossip. They made it reluctantly, for they had so little time together and each moment was precious to them. "I love you, Mary," Dan said. "I'll wish the days away 'til next Sunday." He kissed her. He held her briefly and then let her go. "Sunday."

"Sunday," Mary whispered.

She ran the two blocks home, her basket swinging on her arm. Without pausing for breath, she ran up the stairs to the flat on the top floor. Her hand was on the doorknob when she heard the sounds of an argument coming from within. No, she said to herself, not again; please not again.

Mary opened the door and walked inside. She saw Rose and Jane standing in opposite corners of the kitchen, glaring at each other. Harley stood between his mother and father, trying to quiet their shouts. Mary closed the door. Bob turned and, at the sight of her, his face reddened and his mouth shook. "So you're home, are you?" he thundered. "Well, I've something to say and I'm only going to say it once. Keep your brat away from my daughter or I'll give her a strapping she won't forget."

"But what—"

"Shut up. Don't talk to me. Just keep your brat away

from Jane. Or else." Bob grabbed his coat. He shot a scathing look at Anna and then marched to the door. "You've had fair warning, Mary. It's the only one you'll get." He left the flat, slamming the door behind him.

Mary could not bring herself to look at her cousins. She did not want to look at Rose. She put her basket on the table and took a deep breath. "I'm sorry," she said. "Rose will be punished . . . for whatever she did."

Rose stuck her tongue out at Mary. She stamped her foot. "I hate you!" she screamed, running off to her room.

"I don't know what we're going to do." Anna sighed. She went to Jane and picked her up. "I just don't know. There's never a moment's peace."

Anna carried Jane out of the kitchen. Mary sat down. She felt Harley's comforting hand on her shoulder. "What was it this time?" she asked.

"I guess it was my fault. I brought some Easter candy for the girls. Rose seemed to think I gave more candy to Jane than to her. She had quite a tantrum. George tried to calm her and she kicked him right in the. . . . She kicked him."

"My God, I don't know what's got into her. I swear I don't. Nothing pleases her anymore. Nothing satisfies her. Give her something and instead of being grateful, she screams it's not enough. I don't understand. It was never this way in Hexter."

"Mary, she didn't have to *share* in Hexter. Whatever you gave her was *just* for her."

"You make Rose sound so selfish. The worst part is I can't say you're wrong."

"Most kids are selfish. They grow out of it."

"Maybe."

"Rose has always been the center of attention. Beautiful little girls usually are. I hear Rose's teacher lets her get away with murder. And I hear the Goodmans are always giving her free candy from their store. I know Tommy Stoesel gives her all his pennies."

"What?"

"It's all right." Harley smiled. "Tommy's only seven. He follows Rose around like a puppy dog. He gives her his pennies, his jacks, his marbles. He'd give her his shirt if she asked for it . . . that's not the point. The point is, Rose has lots of admirers. But here, in this house, she's just one of two little girls. She's not the center of attention here." Harley sat down next to Mary. He turned her face to him. "Do you see what I mean?" he asked gently.

"Yes. I wish I didn't. Because if you're right, Rose will never be happy living here. She'll never be happy anywhere she's not the center of things. Harley, what am I doing to do? I can't let her go on making everyone miserable, including herself."

"If you had your own flat . . ."

"That's like saying if I had a million dollars. One's as impossible as the other. How could I afford my own flat? Where's the money to come from? Money! It always gets back to money."

"Listen to me, Mary. There's George's wages. And yours. And I know you're doing extra baking for someone or someplace. Don't worry, Pa hasn't figured that out yet. But I have. So there's money there. You could afford a small flat. Maybe it wouldn't be easy, but what's easy?"

"Who'd look after Rose?"

"You could hire a woman for a dollar a week and meals."

Mary's eyes became thoughtful. She pursed her lips, adding and subtracting numbers in her mind. "After rent and food and care for Rose, there'd be nothing left. Nothing. What happens when Rose needs shoes? Or if she gets sick? We'd be in terrible trouble."

"You have me to help. I can and I will." Harley brushed his sandy hair from his brow. He was smiling, for he had been waiting for this moment. It was his chance not only to help Mary, but to begin the winning of her. He could offer her a way out and that, in the end, would draw her to him. "Pa doesn't know about this—nobody does—but I have a second job. I work at the milk company stables every Saturday night. I've been saving that money for months. Look." He pulled a cloth pouch from a cord around his neck. "I have more than twenty dollars. It's for you."

"No, Harley!"

"Hear me out. . . . I'm not what's called an ambitious person. I only took this job so I could help you. I want to take care of you. Please let me."

"I can't, Harley. You're so kind to offer. I'll never forget your kindness . . . but I can't accept."

"Why not?"

"My family's my responsibility."

"Too much responsibility for one person."

"Maybe." Mary shrugged. "But that's the way it has to be."

Harley was not discouraged, for he knew Mary would have to turn to him sooner or later. He would be ready when the time came; in the meanwhile he would be patient. "Do what you think best," he said quietly.

"I'll keep saving my money, just in case." He stood up and went to the door, slipping into his coat. "I'm going to look for George."

"Did Georgy go out?"

"He *ran* out. Rose's tantrum really upset him. I never saw him that mad before."

"She's making everybody mad lately."

"Not you."

"Well . . . I'm trying to understand. It gets harder all the time. Poor Georgy. I guess it's worse for him. He's here, right in the middle."

"Don't worry. I'll calm him down and drag him home."

"Thank you, Harley. I'd be grateful." Mary smiled fondly at her cousin. "You're such a help to me."

It was a modest compliment, an unromantic compliment, but to Harley it meant a great deal. His heart was high when he left the flat. His step was light.

"Did Harley leave too?" Anna asked, walking into the kitchen. "This isn't turning out to be a very nice Easter."

"I'm sorry."

"*Rose* should be sorry. *She's* at fault, not you. You're always apologizing, while *she* . . ." Anna stopped. She grasped the back of a chair as if for support. "I didn't mean to speak so harshly. I'm just tired. I'm tired of all the tension in this house. Why can't people learn to get along? Arguments morning, noon, and night. They wear a person down. It's no way to live." Anna put her hand to her head. She brushed a strand of blond hair out of her eyes and looked at Mary. "I don't know what we're going to do."

"Harley thinks I could get a small flat. For Rose and

Georgy and me."

"Harley's wrong. You can't afford it. I've done some figuring. . . . Oh, not because I want you to leave, Mary. Or Georgy, for that matter. But because Rose can't go a day without picking on Jane. I hate to be so blunt, but I don't know how else to say it."

"I understand."

"You can't afford a flat of your own. That's not the answer. I don't know what is."

"When I marry Dan—"

"Marry Dan! That's a dream, nothing else. At your age you think love conquers all. It doesn't. It just causes more problems. We have enough of those as it is. We have Rose and Jane at each other all the time."

"Rose has a spanking coming to her. I'd best do it now."

"Mary . . . I really wish things were different."

"I know. We all wish that."

Rose did not look up when Mary entered the room. She sat on the bed, playing with her collection of marbles. She gazed at the rounds of colored glass and imagined they were splendid jewels fit for a princess.

"I want to talk to you, lass."

"No!"

Mary's patience was at an end. She took Rose by the shoulders and shook her. "You're going to listen to me! This time you're going to listen!"

Mary scolded Rose for twenty minutes. She spanked her, deflecting the child's kicks, ignoring her shrieks. "You have to learn your lesson," she said. "For all our sakes, you have to learn."

*   *   *

Easter dinner at the Kilburnes was a dismal affair. Rose and Jane sat as far away from each other as they could and only toyed with their food. Anna and Mary, watching the girls, feeling the antagonism between them, had little appetite. Bob came home too drunk to eat. George did not come home at all.

"I'll have another look around the neighborhood," Harley said as Mary cleared the dishes. "I'll find him."

"I hope so. When Georgy gets into one of his moods . . ."

"I'll find him."

But George was nowhere to be found. Harley searched streets, stoops, alleys, restaurants, and even bars, all to no avail. There was no sign of George; no one had seen him. Harley continued to look. Hours passed. As night fell and the street lamps were lit, he made one last tour of Yorkville. Finally he returned to the flat. "I don't know where George went," he said to Mary. "But he's bound to be back soon. He hasn't much money. And there's work in the morning."

"Georgy hates his work."

"Who doesn't? Mary, he'll be back any time now. He was mad, that's all. He's probably walking it off."

"You don't know Georgy's moods."

"I know he'll be back. He has no other place to go."

Mary knew that was true, but still she was uneasy. George had run off once before, in Hexter, and he had stayed away for three days and nights. He had reappeared without explanation or apology, retreating into a brooding silence that had lasted for weeks. "The lad's not like us," John had said at the time. "He hears his own tune and there's no changing it." Mary wondered what tune George was hearing now. She

192

wondered where it was taking him.

Later, lying in the bed she shared with Rose, Mary stared up at the ceiling and wondered some more. She did not sleep. Every noise, every random sound of night made her jump. "Please let Georgy come home," she whispered, praying. "Let it be all right."

Mary was up and dressed before dawn. When she walked into the kitchen, she found Harley at the table, a cup of tea in front of him but untouched. "Georgy didn't come home," she said.

"He will."

"What if something's happened to him?"

"Nothing's happened. We would have heard." Harley went to Mary. He saw the dark shadows about her eyes, the pinched look of her mouth, and his heart ached for her. "You mustn't worry. George will come back when he's ready. He's stubborn, like all the Kilburnes, but he can take care of himself."

"Oh, I'm not so sure."

"Of course he can. Anyway, we're getting ahead of ourselves. I'll bet he turns up at work this morning."

"I want to believe that, Harley. I can't. I have a funny feeling. Something's . . . not right."

Harley had the same feeling, though he did not say so to Mary. He made light of her apprehensions. He smiled and joked and insisted she drink a cup of tea. At six o'clock, Mary put on her coat and left for work. "I'll walk a ways with you," Harley said, running after her.

"You're kind to offer, but I'd like to be alone. . . . Will you get word to me if you hear anything? The Sinclairs have a telephone. You could leave word with Elsie Jadnick. She's allowed."

"Sure I will. Don't worry, Mary. He'll turn up."

"You never know with Georgy. He's . . . different."

The city was just coming to life when Mary began her walk to the Sinclair house. Other young girls, rushing to other kitchens, were all about. Stores were opening. Horse-drawn delivery wagons traveled the avenues alongside horse-drawn streetcars and, on Third Avenue, the El train rumbled overhead. Mary knew the sights and sounds of morning by heart. She paid no attention, walking rapidly, her head bent, lost in thought. It was six-thirty when she descended the few steps to the service entrance and let herself in. She went right to work, sweeping and mopping and scrubbing. She cooked the servants' breakfast, served it, and cleared the table. Over Elsie's protests, she cooked the Sinclairs' breakfast and helped Flora take it to the dining room.

"Rest a minute," Elsie said. "You'll wear yourself out."

Mary smiled but she did not rest. She could not, for to rest was to allow terrible thoughts to occupy her mind. She baked cheddar cheese bread for Mrs. Sinclair's lunch, and meringues for Reeve and Burr. She mixed a cream pudding that needed hours of careful attention to cook. Every time the telephone rang, or the bell, she started.

No messages came for Mary. She got through Monday and Tuesday, but by Wednesday the strain had begun to show. She was drawn, extremely pale. Her dark eyes, ringed with shadows, burned feverishly. Several times, baking pans slipped from her fingers and clattered to the floor.

"I've had enough of this," Elsie said finally. She sat Mary down and leaned over her, peering into her eyes.

"You have to pull yourself together. Do you want to get sick? What good will you be to anybody if you're sick?"

"If only I could talk to Dan."

"Well, you can't, so forget that. You'll have to talk to me. Though I don't know what there is to talk about. Boys George's age run away all the time. They come back all the time too. When they're hungry enough, tired enough. It's a stupid thing to run away, but he's not the first. He's not the last. I'm surprised at you, Mary. Where's your sense?"

"I can't help it. First Pa . . . now Georgy."

"Do you think he's dead? Is that it? What foolishness! Don't you know bad news comes fast? You can't keep bad news away with a stick. When you hear nothing, that's the time to rest easy."

"But where *is* he? Elsie, it's been three days."

"Off with his friends most likely. Getting into the kind of trouble boys his age get into."

"Georgy hasn't many friends."

"One or two's enough. Boys are boys. When they're in their teens they get into trouble. When they're in their twenties they break your heart. After that, it's anybody's guess."

"I'm frightened."

Elsie frowned, shaking her head impatiently. "All this fuss over a boy running away! Well, I'm not going to let you get sick over it." She went to a cupboard, returning with a bottle of green liquid and a spoon. "Here. I got this for you."

"What is it?"

"A tonic. I got it from the fishmonger's wife. She says she's Austrian. I say she's a gypsy. But gypsy women know their herbs . . . so you take two spoonfuls. You'll feel better right away."

Mary took the cap from the bottle and sniffed. "Oh, Elsie it smells awful."

"Sure it does. Sure it does. Medicine's supposed to smell awful. Drink it down. Two spoonfuls."

Mary swallowed the green liquid. It tasted every bit as vile as it smelled, but she dared not complain. "Thank you, Elsie," she said, trying to smile.

"You'll sleep tonight. And it's about time."

Mary did sleep, but when she awoke early Thursday morning all her fears returned. It was her day off and, hurriedly, she washed and dressed, running out of the Sinclair house just as the sun began to rise. She had gone only a few steps when she stopped suddenly, staring in disbelief. "Georgy!" She ran to her brother. "Oh, Georgy, I thought you were killed. Are you all right? Where have you been?"

"I had things to think about."

"What things? Georgy, I was so worried. I was scared. Promise me you won't run off again. *Promise.*"

"Let's go somewhere we can talk. Let's go to the park."

"What is it, Georgy? I'm feeling scared again."

"I told you I had things to think about. Well, I've done my thinking. Now I have to tell you what I decided. I came here special to see you, Mary. I want to tell you face to face."

"It's bad news then," Mary said flatly, looking away.

"Eh, it's what I have to do. You can call it bad news if you want, but it's what I have to do."

Mary made no reply. She walked across Fifth Avenue with George, walking with him into Central Park. They sat on a bench and for a while neither of them spoke. They looked at the trees coming into their full spring bloom, at the fresh green grass, at pigeons pecking after crumbs. "Tell me," Mary said at last.

George took a breath. He crossed his long legs and then uncrossed them. He clasped his hands so tightly his knuckles were white. "I'm leaving," he said. "Going away."

"I see."

"Mary, I never wanted to come to America. I never wanted to live in a city."

"We're here. There's no going back."

"Not to Hexter, but there's other places. Places away from the city. That's what I want. For a long time after . . . after Pa died, I was in a fog. I didn't know what I wanted. I thought it was best to do as you said. And it was only right, what with you carrying all the burden for us. . . . I took that bloody job. I tried to like it, Mary. Every time it got to be too much I told myself it wasn't forever. I told myself it was just a way to our future . . . I told myself all the things you told me. The trouble is those things don't work anymore. I can't stand it and that's the truth. Riding the El is a torture to me. The job is a torture. Living in that flat all squeezed together is the worst torture of all."

"Georgy, maybe I can get a flat of our own. With your wages and mine, and my baking, we'd manage."

George stared down at the ground. He laughed bitterly. "We'd manage like those birds there, scratching in the dirt for crumbs. Eh, it's not being poor I mind. It's all the rest of it. The El, the job, Bob with his hand out all the time. Rose."

"Rose?"

"You only see what you want to see."

"Speak plain, Georgy."

"Aye, I will. I've spent a lot of time around Rose since we came to America. I've seen things. . . . She's spoiled and she's mean. She'll never be anything else."

"Georgy! How can you say—"

"I'm home a lot more than you are. I know what I'm talking about. There was a time I'd have done anything for Rose. *Anything*. Now? Now I wouldn't lift a finger. You're worth ten of her, Mary, a hundred. I'll be sorry to say goodbye to you. But for the rest, for Rose, I'll be glad."

Mary heard the finality in George's voice. She looked into his eyes and saw that a door had closed, perhaps forever. "Where will you go?" she asked.

"There's a place called Long Island. It's full of farms. I'll get a job. Farm work's what I always wanted to do. . . . It's not so far away. We'll see each other."

"You'll need money."

"No. I've been saving what you gave me from your baking money. I have train fare and a little left over. It's enough. I have a strong back and two strong hands. I'll find work." George stood up. He walked a short distance away, kicking pebbles out of his path. After a few moments he returned to Mary. "I told Anna. She understands. I hope you do . . . 'cause I'm leaving today, this afternoon."

"Oh, Georgy." Mary dried her eyes. She took her brother's hand and pressed it to her cheek. "I'll miss you so much."

"Aye, I'll miss you. I'll send you some money when I get work. . . . Mary, I'm no one to give advice. I'm not smart that way. But I hope you'll make a life for yourself. Get out of that flat as soon as you can. If you stay, Bob will take every penny you have. And what he doesn't take, Rose will." George wrapped his arms around Mary. He hugged her. "Don't let them steal your life. Promise me."

"I promise, Georgy. I promise."

Eight

"For heaven's sake, Mary, sit and rest awhile. Look at you, you're exhausted."

Mary picked up a wooden spoon and began stirring yet another batch of batter. "Mr. Basset is expecting cakes tomorrow morning," she said. "They won't bake themselves."

"He can do without cakes one Friday."

"Maybe he can, but I can't. I need the money. It's just Rose and me now. If I don't provide, who will?" Mary arranged her baking pans on the table. Deftly, she spooned batter into each pan, then put the pans in the oven. "That makes two dozen." She nodded, turning back to the table to mix her special vanilla icing. "Maybe I can get in another dozen before bedtime."

Anna's gaze was steady on Mary. She was concerned about her, about her pallor, her driven restlessness. She wanted to help but she knew there was no help. Mary had received one blow after another and their effect, taken all together, could not be gauged. "You haven't said much about George."

"What's there to say? I didn't want him to go, but I couldn't stop him."

"Did you try?"

"There was no use in that. I saw how he was." Mary put the spoon down. She wiped her hands on her apron and then picked up the spoon again, stirring the icing vigorously. "I had time to think on the way home. I'll tell you something, Anna. The Kilburne men are good men but they're . . . not strong. That includes Pa. That includes them all. As far back as I can remember, it was always the women holding things together."

"Even if that's true, you're wrong to push yourself so hard. You're young, just a girl. You can't—"

"I can because I have to. I'm beginning to see how important money really is. When you have money you have choices. And that's what life's about, choices."

"Why, you're angry, aren't you?" Anna was truly surprised, for in all the many months she had known Mary, she had never seen her angry. "I'm glad you are. Sometimes anger can serve a purpose."

Mary was indeed angry. She was hurt and confused as well. It seemed to her that every time she got a step ahead, someone or something was there to push her back. She had never before questioned her life. She had accepted the teachings of her childhood, teachings in which there were two kinds of people, rich and poor, the latter existing to serve the former. She had accepted them because her father had accepted them, and his father, and his father's father, all the way back to the first Kilburne. Now she had begun to question. It did not seem fair, or even reasonable, that Lord Worsham should live idly and in splendor just because his bloodlines descended from Queen Anne. It did not seem fair that she should work sixteen hours a day and have nothing to show for it just because her bloodlines descended from mill hands. It was, in England, always a matter of blood. But this was America, and she would

not live in America as she had lived in England.
"Maybe you're right, Anna. Maybe anger has its
purpose. It's made me see something clear. In Hexter
there was always somebody's boot on my back,
keeping me down. That's not going to happen here. I
won't let it. The stars are out of my eyes now."

"Mary, what do you mean?"

"I've found a way to make money. Dan laughs at my
Roly-Poly cakes, but one day they'll get me my own
bakery shop."

"One day you'll get married."

"That has nothing to do with it. I can be married and
have a bakery shop too." Mary finished mixing the
icing. She tasted it, then set the big bowl aside. "Georgy
leaving that way taught me something. It's best to
depend on yourself, not other people. It's best all
around."

"Women don't have much say in such things.
Women have children to look after."

"Oh, I'll have children. I want children, Anna. When
they're young, they'll come to my shop with me. It'll be
like sitting in my kitchen."

"You've given this a lot of thought."

"I was sitting in the park after Georgy left . . . and I
started thinking. I thought about all that was right and
all that was wrong."

"George did what he felt he had to, Mary."

"I know. The same's true of me now. I'll do what I
have to." Mary opened the oven door and looked
inside, her practiced eye roaming over the baking pans.
She closed the door and went to the dozen cakes
already baked. Finished, they would be plump rounds
of chocolate cake with centers of jam and burnt sugar,
frosted with thick vanilla cream. As Mr. Basset had

predicted, they were his most popular items. "Would you like one, Anna?"

"No, thank you. I should be getting to bed. So should you." Anna glanced at the clock on a shelf above the sink. "Don't be too much longer. Bob could come in any time now. If he saw all this he might wonder. He might ask questions."

"I'm almost done."

"You're not almost done. I wish you'd let me help you. You never let anyone help."

"The work is mine to do. I'll do it."

"My God, you're stubborn." Anna smiled. "I suppose it's a good thing. I hope it is." She pushed her chair away from the table and stood up. "Good night, Mary."

"Good night."

Mary spent another hour at her chores. When all the cakes were filled and frosted and packed out of sight in Mr. Basset's boxes, she went to bed. She slept poorly that night and on the nights that followed. On Sunday, Dan took a long look at her and did not hide his alarm. The two young people talked, calmly at first, then heatedly. They almost had an argument, but when Dan realized he could not change Mary's thinking, he changed the subject. During the next weeks he planned their Sundays to be restful. Often he took Mary to the park. There he spread a blanket on the grass and held Mary's hand while she napped. He made her eat the thick meat sandwiches he brought from home. He made her drink milk. He told her funny stories and made her laugh.

"Well, you're looking better," Dan said one Sunday in June. "But you're still too pale. I'm going to fix that. I'm taking you to the beach. I'm taking you to

Coney Island."

"Coney Island?"

"You just come along with old Dan McShane. Sure and the roses will be blooming in your cheeks."

Dan and Mary took the train to Coney Island. It was, to Mary's eyes, the most wonderful place she had ever seen. She was awed by the miles and miles of beach. The ocean, which had seemed so threatening from the deck of the *Royal Star,* was a gentle white-capped blue, lapping gracefully, endlessly at the shore. She felt the sun, the salty breezes, and she clapped her hands together like a child.

"Catch me if you can," Dan dared her, starting to run along the beach.

"I'll catch you." Mary ran after him. Her hair streamed behind her, the wind blew in her face. She felt such a sense of freedom she wanted to shout. Suddenly all her cares were forgotten. "Come on, Dan," she called, passing him. "You can do better than that."

They ran faster, laughing, breathing in the good sea air. When they could run no more, they collapsed on the sand and built a sand castle. They ate cotton candy. They rode the Ferris wheel to dizzying heights. "Oh, Dan, it's been the best day of my life," she said when they were once again on the ground.

"It's not over yet. Let's have a stroll on the beach."

"Do we have time?"

"Ah, time stands still for us, Mary Kilburne. We're blessed."

Mary felt blessed. She felt young and happy and utterly free. If I live to be a hundred, she thought, I'll never forget this day. "I wish we could stay here forever," she said to Dan. "Just you and me in a little tent on the beach."

"A tent! You have to learn to dream grander dreams. We'll live by the ocean one day, but not in a tent. I'll build us a fine house . . . with windows as wide as the sky . . . and fireplaces . . . and our own private path to the ocean."

"I can see it, Dan. I can see it just the way you say."

"Can you see us there?"

"Oh, yes. We're holding hands, like now. There's a fire in the fireplace and we're sitting by it, listening to the ocean."

"So you've had a look at our future, Mary Kilburne. Would you be approving?"

"I wish it wasn't the future. I wish it was now."

Dan gazed at Mary. There was a light in the deep blue of his eyes, a light both loving and amused. He said nothing more. He led her to a deserted stretch of beach and there, beneath an outcropping of rocks, they sat down. "Are you comfortable?" he asked.

"I'm in the clouds."

"Are you?" Dan smiled. He stroked Mary's cheek. Gently, he traced the line of her mouth. "Not all of our dreams are for the future. Some are for now. . . . I love you so much, Mary. Will you marry me, my darling girl?"

"Dan . . ." Tears glistened in Mary's eyes. Her heart leaped. "Yes," she cried. "Yes, Dan, yes." She fell into his arms, sighing as he covered her face with kisses. "I love you. Oh, I love you, Dan."

Dan felt the beating of Mary's heart against his own. He felt her warm breath on his neck. He looked at her, and moment by moment his eyes became more intense. He lifted his hand and touched the hollow of her throat. It was a tentative gesture, questioning.

"Dan," Mary whispered.

Dan bent his head and kissed Mary's lips. She was murmuring against his mouth and clinging to him and he held her tighter. "I want to make love to you, Mary."

"Yes . . . yes."

Their clothes seemed to slip away. They lay naked on the sand, fire raging within them. Their bodies touched and their hands sought each other passionately. "You're so beautiful," Dan cried in rapture. "So beautiful." He caressed Mary's mouth, her throat, her breasts, the darkness between her legs.

Mary trembled, swept away by an ecstasy that was as sweet as it was fierce. "I love you, I love you," she said, again and again, until Dan could not remember when she had begun speaking, and their love was one with the crashing of the ocean and the blaze of the sun.

Dan and Mary said very little during the ride home; there was no need. They knew their love now. They knew their passion. The tender glances that passed between them, the touch of their hands, spoke what words could not. Mary settled her head on Dan's shoulder and closed her eyes, remembering. Dan smiled. My darling girl, he thought, my darling girl.

It was dark when they reached Yorkville. They were later than they had ever been before, but still they were reluctant to part. "We have so many plans to make." Dan smiled, nuzzling Mary's head. "Our wedding day. When will it be?" They stood in the shadows of the soft spring night and decided to marry on Mary's birthday, less than two months away. "We'll tell no one of our plans," Dan said. "It's best that way. Once we're married, there won't be anything they can do."

"But Anna . . . I should tell Anna."

"Not even Anna. It's our secret, Mary Kilburne. Once we're married we'll tell the world. We'll shout it from the rooftops, from every street in New York. Once we're married, not before."

Mary agreed, for she knew they dared not take the slightest chance. A wrong word, intentional or not, could ruin their plans. She shuddered at the thought. "You're right, Dan. You're always right."

"Ah, I wonder if you'll still think so when we're an old married couple."

"I'll always think so. Always."

Dan kissed her. "Go home, my darling girl," he said. "Go home now or I won't be able to let you go at all."

Mary did not remember walking home. She did not remember walking up the stairs. She found herself at the door of the flat and she laughed. She was still laughing when she entered the flat, a young woman now, pink with sun and wind and love. "Hello, Anna. I'm sorry to be . . ." Her voice trailed off, for Anna was crying. "What's wrong?" she asked. She looked around the kitchen and saw Bob. His face was pale, stony. His eyes were cold. "What's wrong, Cousin Bob? Has something happened? . . . is it Rose?"

"So you're home," Bob said, walking slowly toward Mary. "And you want to know what's wrong, do you? Well, it's not Rose this time. It's you."

"Me? I don't understand. What have I done?"

"You know what you've done. You know all right. It'll do you no good to play the innocent with me. Don't try."

Mary looked at Anna but Anna only continued to cry, her head in her hands. Anxiously, Mary looked again at Bob. "What is it, Cousin? *Tell* me."

"It's you! It's you sneaking around behind my back! Shaming me with that papist bastard McShane!"

Sudden fear stabbed Mary's heart. She felt as if her breath had been cut off, as if the floor beneath her feet had turned to quicksand. "I . . . don't know what you mean."

"So you're a liar as well as a sneak!" Bob roared, pounding the table. "God only knows what else you are!"

"It's not true," Mary cried. "Whatever you've heard, it's not true."

"Oh, it's true all right. I heard about it from Herman Busch, who heard about it from his daughter Myrna. I argued with him. I told him no Kilburne would mix with a McShane . . . he told me to ask around. Well, I asked. My own wife knew about it. . . . Now *I* know and I'm putting a stop to it. It's *over.* You're through shaming me. And yourself. It's *over."*

Mary pressed her hands together to keep them from shaking. Her throat was dry, aching. Tears stung her cheeks. "It's . . . not like that. There's no shame to it. Dan and me . . . we're going to get married."

Bob slapped Mary's face. The force of his blow spun her around. She lost her balance and fell against the edge of the sink. "There's more where that came from," Bob shouted. "Married! I'll see you dead before I'll see you married to a McShane!"

He raised his hand again but Anna was pulling him away. She clawed desperately at his arm, dragging him back step by step. "Bob, don't," she pleaded. "Don't. You'll hurt her."

"Why shouldn't I? And why should I listen to you? It's your fault in the first place. I didn't want them here.

It was your doing. You talked me into it. What did I get for my trouble? One runs off, one's a brat, and this one . . . this one shames me with a *papist*. With a *McShane*."

"Bob, she loves him."

"Don't tell me that again. I don't want to hear that." Bob slapped Anna's hand away. He turned on Mary, a terrible look in his eyes. "You and your dirty papist are finished. Do you hear me? It's over. Done."

"No." Mary put her fingers to her bruised lip. She stared at Bob. "It's not over," she said quietly. "You can beat me if you want, but it's not over. We're getting married. You can't keep us apart. Nobody can keep us apart."

Bob returned Mary's stare. A strange smile touched the corners of his mouth. "Nobody can keep you apart, eh? That'll be news to Pat McShane. That's right. I went to see him today. I asked him if he knew where his precious son was. He didn't. Oh, he knew his son had been seeing you. But he didn't know it was a regular thing. He didn't know it was turning serious. . . . He knows now. When he gets through with Dan—"

"Dan will fight his father. He'll fight anyone who tries to stand in our way."

"So he'll fight, will he?"

"Yes."

"And you'll fight?"

"Yes."

"I'll throw you out of here. I'll throw you out tonight, with nothing but the clothes on your back."

"Then we'll get married right away. Dan has a job. And I can bake cakes at home and sell them. We'll get by."

"Is that a fact?"

210

"Yes."

"Well, that puts a different color on it, doesn't it?" Bob sat down at the table. He was silent, drumming his fingers and smiling. "I see I can't stop you, so go ahead. Do what you want. I'll tell Rose you said goodbye."

Mary had begun to relax. She had begun to believe the argument was won. It took a moment for Bob's last sentence to break through her thoughts. *I'll tell Rose you said goodbye.* "What do you mean by that?" she asked. "I'm not leaving Rose. She'll go with Dan and me."

"Now there you're wrong."

"What do you mean? . . . Anna, what does he mean?"

Anna turned away, shaking her head. "I'm sorry, Mary."

"Oh, God," Mary cried. "Where's Rose? What have you done with her?" She started to run to the bedroom but Bob reached out and grabbed her arm. "Cousin Bob, I want to know where Rose is. Tell me where she is."

"There's no cause to worry. Harley took Rose and Jane downstairs to Frannie's. I couldn't have two little girls listening to a conversation like this, could I? Do you want them to know what a sneak you are? What a—"

"Is Rose all right?"

"She's fine."

"Then what are you *talking* about? Why did you say she couldn't go with Dan and me?"

"It's very simple. Rose isn't going anywhere with anyone. She's staying here, at least until I say different. You go. Go with your papist. But Rose stays here."

Mary paled, for she understood the seriousness of

211

Bob's threat. She was very still, forcing herself to think calmly, clearly. "She's my sister. She'll go where I say. I'm responsible for her, not you."

"You're wrong again."

"How am I wrong?"

Bob laughed. "You're a spunky one, aren't you? Standing there, your chin sticking out, trying to stare me down. Well, it'll do no good . . . *I'm* responsible for Rose. And I have it in writing from your own dead pa. He wrote to me before he left Hexter. He said if anything was to happen to him, *I* was to have charge of Rose. I was to look after her 'til you came of age."

"No! You're lying!"

"Am I?"

"You're lying!"

"Let's see about that." Bob put his hand in his pocket and removed a folded sheet of paper. He dropped it on the table, smiling. "This'll take the spunk out of you," he said.

Mary looked at the paper. Her mouth opened, closed, opened again. "That could be anything. How do I know—"

"Read it. It makes me what's called a guardian. Rose's guardian. Go on, read it." Bob unfolded the letter and gave it to Mary. "It's in your pa's hand, as you can see."

Mary took the letter in her trembling fingers. She recognized her father's plain handwriting, his signature at the bottom of the page. For a moment all the words blurred together. She blinked rapidly and, taking a breath, began to read. The last paragraph she read over and over, for that paragraph concerned Rose: "Rose is on my mind. If something was to happen to me then who would see to her? Georgys in his own world. Mary

212

is a fine lass. Shes fine and strong too like her mother. But shes young. What could she do for our Rose there in a new country? So Im asking you, Bob, if anything was to happen to me, to take charge of Rose til Mary is of proper age. Its the most important thing."

"Well?" Bob said smugly. "Do you see how it is?"

"Pa didn't know how things were when he wrote this."

"He wrote it. That's all that matters." Bob took the letter back, returning it to his pocket. "Rose stays here."

"But you don't even like Rose."

"Like her? I can't stand the sight of her!"

"Then why do you want to keep her here?"

Bob only smiled in reply. It was a nasty smile, full of malice, and Mary drew away in alarm. "I can't believe it," she said, for she was beginning to understand. "You . . . would do such a thing? You'd ask me to choose between my sister and Dan?"

"But it's a simple choice. If you want to see your sister again . . . you'll give up your papist."

"Anna," Mary said desperately, "you'll help me. You'll make Bob see he's doing wrong."

"I tried." Anna put her head in her hands. She was crying. "I can't help you in this, Mary. I'm so sorry."

"There!" Bob smiled. "It's up to you. It makes no difference to me one way or the other. Of course Rose's life won't be easy here with you gone. She'll be answering to me."

There was a great chill through Mary's body, and a terrible sickening. The room became cloudy. The walls and ceiling were pale mists coming closer. She felt faint. She reached for a chair, sinking into it, shuddering. And then a pit of blackness opened at her feet.

Mary fell to the floor with a thud. Anna ran to her, bending over her crumpled form. "Mary! . . . Mary!" She felt for her pulse, then opened the top buttons of her shirtwaist. "My God, Bob, look what you've done to her. She's fainted. . . . Help me carry her to her bed."

"She can lie where she is for all I care."

Anna looked up at her husband. Her eyes were like green stone. "I don't know what's happened to you. I don't know you anymore."

"Maybe I don't know you either. You take the papist's side against me. *McShane's* side. You do that, even knowing how I feel."

"Dan has no part of your quarrel. Mary has no part of it. Why must you hurt them? It's just meanness. You've become mean." Anna wet a cloth and pressed it to Mary's forehead. "And to your own kin."

Bob stood abruptly. "My own kin! My own kin that sneaks around behind my back with McShane. My own wife that does nothing to stop the sneaking around. You're supposed to be on my side, Anna." Bob went to the door and flung it open. "If you were any wife to me, you'd be on my side."

The door slammed. Anna continued to minister to Mary. She rolled some towels and put them beneath her head. She patted her face, her wrists. "Mary . . . Mary, can you hear me? Mary, open your eyes." Anna opened a cupboard and removed a bottle of ammonia. She waved it under Mary's nose. "Wake up," she said softly. "Wake up now."

Slowly, Mary's eyes opened. They fluttered shut, then opened again. "What happened?"

"You fainted. Here, let me help you up. Easy, don't try to get up too fast." Anna helped Mary to her feet.

"Are you all right? I'll get you a bit of that rum you use in your cakes."

"No . . . I have to . . . What time is it?"

"It's just after ten."

"I have to see Dan."

"Mary, you can't. You must rest. Besides, it's too late to—"

"I have to see Dan. There has to be a way to work this out. I have to see him."

"Sit down a minute and catch your breath." Anna pushed Mary into a chair. She leaned over her, taking both of her hands. "You're in no condition to go anywhere now. You . . . can write Dan a note. Harley will take it to him."

"I have to see Dan *myself*. We have to talk about this. . . . If we could take Rose and run away someplace . . ."

"Be sensible, Mary. Where would you run? Where would you live? How? There are too many problems. You must see that now."

"There's a way around problems. We'll find it. Dan will."

"I can't let you go. I don't know what would happen if Bob found out you went to Dan."

"He won't. He'll be drinking all the night." Mary stood. She pushed past Anna to the door. "I have to do this. I have to," she said, running into the hall. She lifted her skirts and ran down the stairs. She was passing through the vestibule when a hand touched her shoulder. She jumped. "Harley, you scared me. I thought it was Bob."

"Where are you going?"

"I have to see Dan."

"At this hour?"

"It's important. You don't know what happened."

"Of course I know. Listen to me, Mary. There's probably a terrible argument going on at the McShanes' right now. The same argument you had with Pa. You're the last person they'll want to see."

"I have to try."

Harley stared at Mary. Her face was white, her eyes two wide, feverish pools of anguish. Her breathing was rapid, too rapid, he thought to himself. She looked sick, on the point of collapse. "You can't go alone." He sighed. "I'll go with you. I'll see if I can get Dan to come downstairs."

"Hurry," Mary said, dragging Harley after her. "We've no time to waste."

Harley and Mary ran through the streets as if they were being chased. They bumped into a lone man taking an evening stroll, narrowly avoided an oncoming carriage as it turned a corner. Harley tried but could not slow Mary's pace. They were both out of breath when they reached Dan's building. "You stay here," Harley said firmly. "I'll go upstairs and see if I can get Dan."

"I should go with you."

"No, Mary. Pat would slam the door in your face. And if he doesn't, Mick will be after you with his cane. Mick's the grandfather and he has a temper worse than Pa. Stay here. It's best."

"All right, Harley. But hurry."

Harley went inside and began climbing the stairs. He knew he could wait a few minutes out of sight and then tell Mary that Dan refused to see her. He considered the possibility, rejected it. He wanted the matter settled once and for all, and without deceit. He continued up the stairs, following the sounds of a furious Irish argument to the McShane flat.

The ten McShanes lived together in six rooms. They lived peaceably for the most part, amidst a jumble of beds and schoolbooks and children's toys. They were not exactly poor; certainly they were not rich. The Shamrock was a flourishing tavern, but since Pat McShane gave away as many drinks as he sold, it seldom showed a profit. All the children worked after school, even the youngest ones, and Mick kept house. Thye ate well. Their clothes were clean and neatly pressed. Their shoes were always shined. They managed as well as anyone and better than most in Yorkville.

The McShanes were known as a happy family but, on this night, they were far from happy. They were crowded into the kitchen, all ten of them. Voices rising in argument, then fading away as other voices joined the battle. Mick saw it as a battle for his grandson's soul and he said as much over and over again. He banged his cane on the floor and railed at Dan in his thick brogue. He cursed the hated British, the Sassenach; he warned of eternal damnation. Pat was less dramatic but just as determined. The brothers and sisters made their own arguments, some deeply felt, others concocted to placate their enraged grandfather.

Dan listened to them all. He listened to them in silence, for he had no intention of making a bad situation worse. He had been angered, insulted, even amused, but he had not been moved. Never for a moment had he considered abandoning Mary. He loved her. He wanted her. He would have her for his wife. It was that simple and that complicated. He settled into his chair, prepared to endure a long night.

His brother Tim was holding forth when a knock

came at the door. There was a second knock, a third before anyone noticed. Pat threaded his way through the children and opened the door. "It's you, Harley," he said, frowning. "And what are you doing here?"

"I wonder if I could have a word with Dan, sir?" He shifted his cap from hand to hand and smiled. "Just a word. It's important."

Pat's frown deepened. Under the circumstances, he knew he should throw Harley out. But he liked the boy; Harley was half British and a Kilburne, but he liked him. "A word about what?"

"It's . . . kind of hard to explain."

"You can have your word. Be quick about it."

"Yes, sir. I will."

Mick was on his feet, pointing his cane at the door. "Would that be a Kilburne standing there?"

"Don't get excited, Granda." Dan sighed, standing. "It's only Harley. I'll see what he wants."

"Harley is it? I'm holding no grudges against Harley. But his father's the divil's own. You tell him that."

"I'll tell him, Granda." Dan walked around his grandfather, around his brothers and sisters, and went to the door. "Hello, Harley," he said. "Granda has a message for you."

"I bet he does. Could we step into the hall, Dan?"

"Sure." Dan followed Harley outside. He waited until the door closed, then looked over the banister. "Is Mary with you?"

"She's downstairs."

"I suppose Bob's laid down the law."

"He's done more than that. He's threatened to take Rose away from her if you two . . . go ahead with your plans."

"The bastard!"

"He loves you too. Look, Dan, this is serious. Mary is—"

"Tell me on the way," Dan said, rushing to the stairs.

Harley explained as much as he could. He was truthful, direct. "So you'll have to call a halt," he finished. "It would kill Mary to lose Rose."

"Call a halt? We're going to be married, Harley. Do you think I'd let Bob, or anyone, change that?"

"You have to."

"The hell I do!"

Dan threw the door open. Even in the shadowy streetlight he saw Mary's pallor, her feverish eyes. "My darling girl," he said gently, taking her in his arms. "Everything will be all right."

"How, Dan? How?"

"We'll be married sooner than we planned, as soon as we can get a license. We'll get a flat and move Rose into it."

"Where?"

"Anywhere. There's a building on Second Avenue—"

"No, we have to go away. Far away. If we stay around here, Bob will take Rose. He has the right. He has a paper from Pa."

"We'll get a flat downtown."

"That's not far enough. We have to leave the city."

"Calm yourself, Mary." Dan held her tighter, stroking her hair. "Don't be afraid. I won't let Bob take Rose from you."

"Then we'll leave the city? Go far away from Bob?"

Dan looked long into Mary's eyes. His hand was against her cheek, smoothing it. He tried to smile but, seeing her great distress, he could not. "Mary, my darling girl . . . you must trust me to handle Bob.

You'll have Rose. You'll have anything you want, but here. I have a job here. It's a good job. I won't find another like it outside the city . . . Mary, I want to make a future for us. The city is the place to do it. Can you understand? We're not children. We can't run away at the first sign of trouble. We must face it, whatever it is."

"I'm so scared, Dan."

"If we trust each other . . . if we trust our love, nothing can hurt us."

"You won't take Rose and me away? You won't think about it?"

"I can't, Mary. If we run from this, we'll run from everything. We'll be destroyed. . . . I can't let that happen to us."

"Then there's no hope."

"Mary—"

"There's no hope, Dan." Mary stared at him blindly, wildly. Tears splashed across her cheeks. "What can we do? There's no hope."

Dan was stunned, for he could not believe Mary would take Bob's threat so seriously. Bob was a weakling, a drunk. How, he wondered, could she fear a man like that? "Mary, listen to me. *Hear* me. I'll see to Bob. You have nothing to be afraid of. Nothing. Do you understand?"

"She's past understanding," Harley said.

Dan looked at her and he knew that was true. "You need sleep, my darling girl. I'll take—"

"Father Malone," Mary said suddenly. "We must go to Father Malone."

Dan sighed, cradling Mary's head on his shoulder. "It's too late to go anywhere now. We'll go tomorrow, after you've had some sleep. I'll take the day off and we'll go."

"We must go to Father Malone tonight. He's our last chance, Dan." She was pulling at him, scratching at his hands, his arms. *"Please.* He'll know what to do."

Dan glanced at Harley. He shrugged. They both saw Mary's condition; they knew she was close to hysteria. "All right," Dan said finally. "If that's what you want. Hush, my darling girl. We'll go to your Father Malone."

Father Malone, uncombed, hastily dressed, sat at his desk in the rectory of St. Brendan's Church. He had been asleep when the ancient housekeeper had knocked at his door, summoning him to the study. "It's a Mary Kilburne to see you, Father," she had said. "And two boyos. All of 'em in a state. You'd best hurry." Father Malone had hurried. He had thrown his clothes on and rushed down the stairs to the study. There he had seen Mary for the first time in eleven months.

He was shocked by what he saw, for Mary was deathly pale, trembling, her eyes burning as if with fever. Her hair was in disarray, her lip bruised. Horrible thoughts went through his mind but he forced them aside. He found seats for everyone. He called for tea, and ice for Mary's lip. He poured a small glass of brandy and made Mary drink it. He sat down at his desk, folding his hands. "Tell me what's happened," he said.

Dan spoke first and at length. He spared no details, nor did he pause for Father Malone to comment. Determination shone in the intense blue of his eyes. When he turned his eyes on Mary, they shone with love. A strong, brave boyo, thought Father Malone.

Mary spoke then. Words tumbled from her, but incoherently. She stammered and cried and clutched at Dan. Her voice broke. Her chest rose and fell with dry sobs. All the while her eyes burned sickly.

"Father Malone," Harley said quietly, "if this goes on much longer, it'll be the death of her."

"Yes, yes, I see that."

Father Malone saw many things. He saw three young people trapped in impossible situations, tied to families, to obligations, to prejudices, to poverty. Some of those things could be overcome, he thought, but not all. He could offer empty phrases of comfort. He could speak of the mystery of God's ways. He could quote the Bible, the saints. And when all the words have been spoken, he said to himself, these children will be no better off than they are now. They'll still have their pain. They'll still have their tragedy.

"Are you a religious boyo, Dan McShane?" he asked. "Do you believe?"

"Yes, Father. In my fashion."

"Then you know what I have to be telling you."

"It was Mary's idea to come here. Not mine."

"You'll help us, Father Malone?" Mary asked anxiously. "You'll tell us what to do? I knew . . . you were our last chance. That's why . . . That's . . . I told Dan you'd help us. . . . Our last chance . . . You'll tell us what to do?"

Father Malone left his desk. He went to Mary, kneeling at her side. "Child, you must listen to me. And you must be strong. There are things in life we don't always understand. We—"

"You'll help us, Father? Now? You'll help us?"

"God will help you. You must ask His help. He will give you strength to understand—"

"God? . . . Why are you talking about God? You must help us. Now."

"It's not in my power to help you, child." Father Malone took Mary's hand and held it. He talked to her softly, soothingly.

Mary did not hear him. She knew that hope was lost. Images of Rose came into her mind, and then images of Dan. Looming over them both was Bob, laughing louder and louder until she had to cover her ears. She swayed slightly. Father Malone caught her when she fell.

"Dr. O'Conner is two doors down. Number 619. Fetch him . . . tell him to hurry!"

Nine

Mary lay in the housekeeper's narrow bed at the rectory. She had been there for two days and nights, drifting in and out of consciousness. Dr. O'Conner came often but there was little he could do, for he had diagnosed exhaustion, exhaustion of mind and of body. There was only one cure and that was sleep. The tiny room was darkened, the curtains drawn, voices hushed. Mary slept, though not peacefully. Even in sleep her mouth trembled and her hands clenched so that the knuckles sprang out under the skin.

Mary awoke on the third day. The housekeeper, Mrs. Grogan, bathed her and braided her hair. She brought a tray with vegetable broth and a boiled egg, standing over her until she finished every bit of it. Father Malone came to sit with her. In the afternoon, Anna came. "Mary, thank God you're better. . . . Rose is fine," she said, anticipating Mary's question. "You needn't worry. And you needn't worry about your job. I had a nice talk with Elsie and Mrs. Sinclair. Mrs. Sinclair says you're to have a rest. With pay! Isn't that kind of her?"

"How is Dan?"

"He's been very worried about you, of course. Those

violets on the table are from him. It's not easy to find violets this time of year, but he found them."

"I can't marry Dan."

"I know, Mary. I'm sorry."

"Father Malone says it's for the best."

"Maybe it is."

Mary turned her head away. "I love him. I'll always love him."

"I know it hurts. But the pain will be a little less each week, each month. There's no medicine like time. You may not forget him, but in time it won't hurt so much. In time it won't hurt at all."

"Do you believe that?"

"Yes, I do."

"I don't."

Anna looked upon Mary's pale and haggard face. The feverish glint was gone from her eyes. Now they were flat, without spark or light. Her voice was flat too. It was not the voice of a girl, but of someone old, immensely tired. Dan had sounded the same way, she thought, her heart aching for them both. "Dr. O'Conner said you can go home tomorrow. You'll have to rest. At least you'll be resting at home, where I can take care of you."

"I want to go back to work."

"Not for a week. Dr. O'Conner was very firm about that. Elsie wouldn't let you in the kitchen before then anyway. She wants you to get well. We all do."

"Does Bob?"

The bitterness in Mary's voice was unmistakable. Anna looked down at her hands. She twisted her wedding ring around and around. "Bob did a terrible thing. There's no excusing it. I won't try. . . . But somehow we have to find a way to live together."

"I'll keep out of Bob's way. Will he keep out of mine?"

"Mary, you have every right to hate him. But you mustn't. For your own sake, you mustn't. Hate won't change anything. It will only harden your heart."

"What's wrong with that?"

"Everything. You have your whole life ahead of you. I know it's not the life you planned . . . but it can still be a good life. If you let it. If you let yourself feel again."

"There's too much pain."

"The worst pain is to feel nothing."

Mary was silent. She took Dan's violets from the table and held them to her cheek.

"Well, Harley," Father Malone said, "we've done all we can. The rest is up to you. I'm thinking it won't be easy."

"Mary's a sensible girl."

"She has a woman's heart. Don't be forgetting that."

"She gave Dan up."

"She had no choice."

"That's what I mean, Father Malone. In the end, Mary will always do the sensible thing. It's the way she is."

"The sensible thing isn't always the thing that brings happiness."

"I know. I agree with you. But that's another reason why I'll be good for Mary. She's *too* sensible. I can show her how to enjoy life. All she knows is work and work and more work. I can show her the fun in life."

"I'm hoping you're right. If you're wrong, you'll both pay dear."

"I'm not wrong."

"You're a good boyo and I'm wishing you well." Father Malone smiled, his sharply observant eyes fast on Harley. "But there's an old saying . . . Be careful what you wish for."

"Irish mysticism?" Harley asked with a laugh.

"Truth."

"I'll take my chances."

"That you will." Father Malone nodded. "Mary's in the study. Go have your talk."

"Thank you, Father. We'll see you before we leave." Harley turned and walked down the narrow corridor. When he reached the study he knocked once and went inside. "Hello, Mary." He smiled. "I've come to take you home."

"Oh, I was expecting Anna."

"She had some things to do. And I wanted to come. So I told my boss I was sick and here I am. You don't mind, do you?"

"No. But to lose a day's pay . . ."

"Just out of a sickbed and you're already worrying about money. Didn't Dr. O'Conner tell you worrying was bad?" Harley moved a chair next to Mary and sat down. He was, Mary noticed, wearing his one good suit. His tie was neatly folded and his hair was brushed off his brow. "It's a special day," he said, seeing her curious glance. "I thought I'd make myself presentable."

"Special day?"

"You're going home."

"Except for Rose, I'm not looking forward to it."

"Mary . . . did you know I'd had a promotion at work? I'm not a runner anymore. I'm a clerk now. It's a better job and a raise in pay."

"That's nice, Harley. I'm glad for you."

"And I still have my Sunday job. That's an extra dollar a week."

"Yes, that's nice."

"I'm trying to say something, Mary. I guess the best way is just to say it. You're not happy at home. You'll never be happy there. Pa won't let you. He'll take your money . . . he'll take the life out of you."

"That's what Georgy said."

"He was right. But it doesn't have to be that way . . . I've rented a flat. It's on Lexington Avenue. Four rooms. In front, so it gets the sun. Mary, I rented it for us . . . I want you to marry me. Please marry me."

"Are you playing a joke, Harley?"

"I've never been more serious. I love you. I want to marry you. I have a job, and savings. The flat's rented. Pa's given his permission. There's nothing to stop us."

Mary stared speechlessly at Harley. There was a long silence. Rain brushed against the windows and, somewhere in the distance, a clock chimed the hour, but in the study of St. Brendan's rectory there was silence. Harley studied Mary's face and saw only surprise. Her eyes were wide, her lips slightly parted. She was so still she did not seem to be breathing. "Please say something, Mary."

"I don't know what to say. I . . . I'm fond of you. I'm very fond of you, Harley, but I couldn't marry you. I couldn't."

"Why not? Because you don't love me? I know you don't. But *I* love *you* and that's enough for now."

"It isn't."

"You're fond of me, Mary. Love will follow. Meanwhile I have enough love for both of us. . . . Think about it. We'll have a nice flat, away from Pa. You'll be able to stay home and look after Rose. You can do your baking at home too. And whatever you earn from it you can save, because we'll live on my wages."

"You don't understand. I couldn't marry you feeling the way I feel about Dan."

"That's over. Or it will be soon. How long can you love a memory? Can a memory make a home for you and Rose? Even if you were willing to waste your life on a dream, there's Rose to think about. You won't be able to do much for her as long as you're living in Pa's house." Harley knew he was taking unfair advantage of Mary; he could not help himself. He was driven by his own emotions, his own wants, all of them pointing toward Mary. This was his opportunity and he had to seize it before it slipped away. "I'll make you happy," he said earnestly. "You and Rose and I will be a family."

"Harley . . . Oh, Harley, I can't think straight."

"I know I caught you by surprise. I just thought it would be best to settle this before we left here."

"There's something you don't know. There . . . might be a child. Dan's child. I'm not ashamed and I don't mean to hurt you. But that's the truth of it."

"Dan told me. It makes no difference. If there's a child, it'll be my child too. I like children. I'll make a good father. At least I'll show my children a good time."

"Any child would be lucky to have you for a father. There's such kindness in you, Harley . . . but maybe kindness is the wrong thing now. It's keeping you from looking at the truth."

"The truth is I love you. I wasn't being kind when I asked you to marry me. I wasn't feeling sorry for you or anything like that. I love you, Mary. I think we'll be happy together. You and Rose and I and whatever children come along. Tell me what's wrong with that."

"Nothing."

"You don't sound sure."

"I'm thinking about you, Harley. It wouldn't be fair to you."

"That's for me to decide. And I've decided. I want you to marry me. Will you?"

Mary looked away. She watched the rain misting the windows and quite suddenly she remembered the choking black mists of Hexter. She remembered their lives there, miserable lives, for they had been without hope. A person can live without love, she thought to herself now, but not without hope. And living in Bob's house is living without hope. "You're sure this is what you want, Harley?" she asked.

"I'm sure."

"Then I'll be pleased to marry you. I'll be a good wife. I promise I will."

Harley reached out to Mary and put his arms around her. "You'll never be sorry," he said softly. "What's past is past. We have all the rest of our lives, and they'll be happy lives, Mary. I'll see to that."

"Yes. We'll be happy." Mary's throat felt dry and parched, and her eyes also. Dan! she cried silently from the depths of her soul. Oh, Dan, forgive me!

"Let's go home and tell Ma the news. She's been worried. She'll be glad everything's settled."

"I hope so."

"Sure she will. She's already looking at material for our kitchen curtains." Harley helped Mary up. "Don't worry," he said, smiling into her eyes. "I'm a pretty lovable fella. You'll soon get used to me."

Mary smiled too. She took the hand he offered and

walked with him to the door. "Rose will be surprised."

"She'll have her own room when we move. She'll like that. And she'll *love* getting away from Jane."

"What about school? Will she have to change schools?"

"I'll see to all those details. You're not to trouble yourself. You're going to be pampered, like it or not."

"Ah, there you are," Father Malone called. He stood at the end of the corridor, looking from Harley to Mary. "I've been waiting for you two. Will you be joining me in a cup of tea before you go?"

"We'd like to, Father, but I've ordered a cab. It should be here any minute."

"A cab, Harley?"

"It's a special day. We're going to ride in style."

"But a cab . . ."

They reached Father Malone and Mary looked at him for a moment. "Harley and me are getting married," she said.

"Are you now? Well, my best wishes to you both." Father Malone shook Harley's hand. He turned and kissed Mary's cheek. "I'm hoping you'll be very happy, child. Sure and there's happiness due you."

"Thank you, Father."

"You've a good boyo here. I can see the love dancing in his eyes." That I can, thought Father Malone, but in your eyes, Mary, I see only resignation. "A family's a wonderful thing," he nodded. "It's the only thing that matters."

"Would you come to the wedding, Father?" Mary asked. "I'd like you to be there, wherever it is."

"Ah, you couldn't keep me away . . . providing it's all right with Mr. Kilburne," he added hastily. "I wouldn't want to be angering anyone on such a happy day."

"Bob won't be there."

Harley glanced at Mary in amazement. "But I can't keep Pa from—"

"That's the one thing I'll ask of you, Harley. You can make any plans you want. Except about Bob. I don't want him there."

"He'd never forgive me."

Mary did not speak. She stared at Harley, her eyes fixed, her chin thrust forward stubbornly.

Harley realized that Mary was not going to yield. Looking at her, he realized she would never make her peace with Bob. Nothing would be forgotten; nothing would be forgiven. If pressed, she would argue, and he dared not risk an argument. "I'll think of some way to handle Pa," he said. "If you don't want him at the wedding, he won't be there."

"Thank you, Harley."

Father Malone, observing the brief exchange, was troubled. He saw Harley's reluctance to disagree, but worse, he sensed his fear of doing so. What kind of marriage will it be, he wondered, if Harley's afraid to say what's on his mind.

"Father Malone?" Mrs. Grogan called from the hall. "There's a cab for the boyo."

"Yes, right away."

"We'll be going now," Harley said, shaking the priest's hand again. "Thank you for all your help."

"Not at all. It's what I'm here for. You take good care of Mary. Don't be disappointing me."

"You have my word."

"And you, Mary Kilburne. Don't be so hard on yourself. Work is all well and good but nobody should work all the time. Even God rested on the seventh day.

Remember that."

"Yes, Father. It'll be easier now . . . with Harley."

"Ah, it's glad I am you see it that way. A husband and wife should lean on each other. They should share the burdens of life. Share the bad, when it comes. And share the good. That's the strength in marriage."

"I wish you could marry us, Father."

"I can't, child. You know that. But I'll be giving you my blessing. And praying to God for His." Father Malone walked the two young people to the door. "Send word when you've set a date," he said. "Or better still, come and see me."

"You'll be at the wedding?" Mary asked. "That's definite?"

"I'll be there. One way or the other, I'll be there."

"Thank you, Father. We'll send word when it's going to be. And we'll send you something for all your trouble these last days. For my keep and all."

"There's no need of that. What was done was done in friendship. As for your keep, Mrs. Sinclair sent her carriage with great baskets of food. Vegetables and fruit, and a ham that could be feeding an army. Our priests will be eating well this week and into next. I've written her a note, but perhaps when you see her you'll tell her she's remembered in our prayers."

"I will, Father."

"Come along, Mary. The cab is waiting."

"Goodbye."

"Goodbye, child. Goodbye, Harley. God be with you."

Harley helped Mary into the horse-drawn cab. The driver, wearing a top hat and a shabby black coat, tapped his whip and they were on their way.

"Isn't this grand?" Harley smiled.

"Like gentry. But you shouldn't have. It costs dear."

"Mary, I'm bound and determined to show you how to enjoy yourself. And this is the first lesson. Sit back, put your head against the cushion there . . . and gaze out at the world as if you were Mrs. Astor and Mrs. Vanderbilt all rolled into one. That's it . . . but you have to look down your nose a little. You have to look right through people, as if they didn't exist."

"Like Lady Worsham."

"Exactly like that!"

Mary, despite the way she was feeling, enjoyed the little game. "One thing about you, Harley. You can always bring a smile."

"There'll be lots of smiles and lots of laughter. Leave it to me."

Mary settled back for the ride. Rain beat softly at the roof of the cab and it was a pleasant sound. It soothed her. Harley held her hand and that was soothing too. Once or twice she glanced at him. They were not loving glances but they were fond. Harley knew the difference. He told himself that someday he would see love in Mary's eyes, and passion.

The hansom cab came to a stop outside the tenement building on Eighty-first Street. Several surprised neighbors stared after Harley and Mary as they alighted. Harley enjoyed the moment. He bowed playfully to Mrs. Albers and to old Mr. Fermoy. To Mrs. Gulden, who was a gossip and a shrew, he tipped his cap. "This is fun," he said, smiling at Mary. But she was already rushing inside, her mind on Rose.

"Wait for me," Harley called. He paid the driver and then ran after Mary. "Slow down," he said, catching her halfway up the first flight of stairs. "You're supposed to be taking things easy. Besides, Rose isn't home from school yet."

"Oh, I forgot about school. I guess I'm still not thinking straight."

Anna was at the top of the stairs. She dropped her scrub brush and embraced Mary. "I'm so glad you're home. How do you feel? You look better. Do you feel better?"

"Anna, Harley and me are getting married."

Anna's eyes moved quickly to her son. They stayed on him for a long moment, unchanging, unreadable. "Is that so, Harley?"

"I proposed and Mary said yes. I told you she would, Ma. There's nothing to worry about now. We'll be happy."

"Of course you will. And I'm happy for you both."

"I'd like to have a word with Anna. Just the two of us. Would you mind, Harley?"

"No. I'll leave you to your talk. But if you talk about me, say nice things."

"Anna," Mary said when Harley had gone, "I want you to know I didn't lie. I told Harley I was fond of him . . . fond of him, not in love with him. But I also told him I'd be a good wife. And I will be."

"I know you'll try."

"Getting married was Harley's idea."

"I know that too. It's been his idea for quite a while. I admit I tried to talk him out of it. I couldn't. He loves you very much, Mary. All he wants is to make you happy. I hope he can. Marriage is hard enough without . . . old memories getting in the way. They can cause a lot of hurt."

"I'll see that doesn't happen. Harley's kind and good and I'll be a good wife to him."

"Well," Anna said, reaching into the pocket of her

apron, "first you'd better see this." She handed a sealed envelope to Mary. "I've been carrying it around for two days. It's from Dan."

Mary looked at the envelope. She turned it over several times. Finally she slid her finger beneath the flap and withdrew Dan's letter. He had written but a single line. Mary read it again and again. "I'll never stop loving you, my darling girl. Never in all the world."

"Are you still going to marry Harley?" Anna asked.

Mary was shaken, but she composed herself. She took a breath and clasped her hands behind her. She gazed into Anna's clear green eyes. "Yes," she said firmly. "Unless you tell me not to. It's your right. You're Harley's mother and you want to protect him. If you think it's wrong to marry, tell me. But tell me now. After this morning, there's no turning back."

"From the beginning, I'd hoped you'd marry Harley. Then you met Dan. That changed things. I want my son to be loved. Can you love him?"

"Harley says love will come in time."

"It may. If you let it. Then again it may not. You once said you'd never get Dan out of your heart. If that's true, you and Harley won't have much chance."

"That was before."

"Before what?"

"Anna, I see how life is now. We have to take what we're given and make the best. That means being a good wife to Harley. Maybe I won't feel the same as he does. Maybe sometimes I'll . . . remember things. But he'll never know it. I'll never hurt him and that I promise. If I promised more, I'd be lying. Marriage isn't all moonlight and poetry anyway. Is it?"

"It's nice to have romance, at least at the start."

"Lots of things are nice to have."

"You sound hard, not like yourself."

"I'm only saying how things are. I'll care for Harley. I won't let him down. Maybe that's better than a wife who's all romance at the start and then, after a while, doesn't give her husband any thought at all."

"Maybe it is." Anna put her arm around Mary's shoulder. She looked at her, smiling slightly. "I just want you to be sure. Very sure. So much has happened, how can you be sure of anything?"

"It's time to start making a life, Anna. I can't do it by myself. I don't think Harley could do it by himself either. But together we can. Isn't that what marriage really is? Making a life?"

"Making a life and *living* a life. There should be pleasure in it. There should be fun."

"Harley will see to that." Mary laughed for the first time in days. Light came into the darkness of her eyes. "Harley's going to show me how to have fun and I'm going to show him how to get rich."

"Rich!"

"Oh, I know it sounds foolish now. But wait and see." Mary bent, gathering up Anna'a pail and brushes. "I'm not going to spend my life on my knees. And neither are you."

"Well, you've got your spirit back. But don't start pushing yourself, Mary. Dr. O'Conner—"

"It'll be easier now. With Harley."

"I hope so. I certainly hope so."

Anna and Mary climbed the stairs to the flat. Not another word was said about the marriage. Mary had nothing to say; Anna, for her part, decided she had nothing worth saying. She would not interfere, now or later. There had been enough interference, she thought, and with questionable results. She herself had doubts, many of them. But Harley and Mary were grown, entitled to their own lives, even to their own mistakes. "I didn't tell Harley about Dan's letter," she said when they were inside. "Though I think he suspects."

"I'll tell him. There'll be no secrets between us."

"I'm glad."

Mary went into her bedroom. Harley was there, looking quietly out of the window. He turned when Mary came in. He smiled. "Did you and Ma have a good talk?"

"She gave me this note. It's from Dan. You can see it."

"It's not my note. It was written to you . . . I wondered if you'd mention it."

"Why shouldn't I? I'm not going to keep secrets from you, Harley. Maybe a surprise now and then, but surprises are different from secrets."

"One last thing about Dan and then I'll drop the subject. He's moved out of Pat's flat. He's living in a boardinghouse downtown. I have the address, if you want it. I told him . . . I promised him I'd give you a chance to change your mind. If you want to see him, I'll give you the address."

Mary hesitated only a split second before replying. "No, Harley. Nothing's changed," she said. She thought: Nothing's changed but everything's changed. I love Dan but I'm marrying Harley. I have to. There's no other way for us, for Rose and me. And I have to forget about Dan. I owe it to Harley to forget. Dan! Dan, it's true you're in my heart. You'll always be in my heart.

"Mary, are you sure?"

"What? Oh yes, I'm sure. I don't want the address. It was . . . good of you to offer, Harley."

"I want you to be happy, you know that, don't you?"

"I know. I will be."

Relief was visible in Harley's face. His eyes seemed to brighten, to shine. "Would you like to see the flat I rented?" he asked eagerly. "We could go now. I have the key."

"I'd like to wait for Rose, if you don't mind. I want to tell her about us. I don't know what she'll think about us getting married. I hope she's not upset."

Harley knew Rose would not be upset. He knew she would consider the situation, looking as always for any advantages she might gain. There were advantages and so she would be pleased. "Remember to tell her she'll have her own room," he said.

"Oh, I will. She'll be glad of that. . . . Could we see the flat later? After supper?"

"Sure." Harley shrugged. "But if you're going to be busy with Rose, I might as well go to work. I'll tell the boss my stomach suddenly got better." He smiled at Mary, running his finger along her cheek. "See what you've done to me? Engaged for an hour and already I'm worrying about work. Talking about being engaged . . ." He took a small box from his pocket. "This is for you."

Mary opened the box to see a tiny pearl set in a thin circle of gold. "Oh, it's grand. It's beautiful, Harley. I've never had anything so beautiful."

Harley took the ring and slipped it on her finger. "Now it's official. Happy engagement, Mary."

"It's beautiful," Mary said again, staring at the ring.

She was about to say he had spent too much money, but she stopped herself in time. "Thank you, Harley."

"I wish it were a diamond. The biggest diamond in the world."

"No, this is just right. It's perfect."

Harley gazed at her for some moments. He kissed her lightly and then strode across the room. "I'll see you later. Remember to get your rest."

"I will."

Mary sank down on the bed. She looked at the ring, holding it up to the window. The little pearl glowed in the gray and rainy light. The gold of its setting twinkled. Mary had never owned any jewelry before. She had not expected to own any jewelry beyond a wedding band, a wedding band given to her by Dan. Now, looking at the ring, touching it, she saw only Dan. She closed her eyes and he was there. He was smiling, holding out his hand to her. "I'm sorry, Dan," she whispered. "I'm so sorry."

Mary stayed in her room all morning. At noon Rose bounded in, waving a pink cambric handkerchief over her head. "Teacher gave it to me for being blackboard monitor," she said excitedly. "Just me. Jane didn't get anything."

"Rose . . . I'm home after four days away. Aren't you going to give me a hug?"

"Yes. All right."

Mary wrapped her arms around the child. She knew Rose had not really missed her, for Rose did not miss people. She did not miss Mrs. Warren, the woman who had cared for her in Hexter; she did not miss her father or her brother. Once in a while she spoke of them, though never with any sense of longing. "I've some-

241

thing to tell you, lass. I'm getting married. To Harley."

"Why?"

"Well . . . there's lots of reasons."

"Harley's *poor*. You said we'd have things in America. But Harley's poor."

"He won't always be poor. He has a little money put by already. We're going to move to our own flat, you and Harley and me. You won't have to share my room anymore. You'll have a room of your own."

"Jane isn't coming?"

"No. Jane will stay here with Anna and Bob."

"Oh, good! When can we go?"

"Soon. A month maybe. I'll be able to stay home and take care of you. I can cook your favorite food and make clothes for you. And we can play games. Would you like that?"

"Just me? Jane isn't coming?"

"No, Rose. Jane isn't coming."

Rose threw her arms about Mary's neck. "Thank you," she cried in delight. "Thank you, Mary. You're the best sister of all."

Mary smiled, happy to at last have done something that pleased Rose. She felt the child's soft cheek against her own, felt the tickle of silken curls, and she began to relax. If it pleases Rose this much, she thought, it's the right thing to do. "Go along and have your lunch now. We'll talk more later."

"We're really moving?"

"We are."

"Do you like Harley?"

"I like him very much. And I want you to be nice to him."

"Oh, I will." Rose's smile was sweet. Her golden

lashes fluttered. "I'll be the best lass in the world. You'll be proud of me."

Mary laughed as Rose skipped out of the room. She felt better. She hardly noticed the dull and hollow ache in her heart.

After supper, Harley took Mary to see their new flat. It was not in a tenement, but in a brownstone recently converted from a private residence to apartments. It was on the third floor and in the front, looking out on tree-shaded Lexington Avenue. The building was old, in poor repair, but there was an elegant look about it. To Mary's eyes it was grand indeed. "Harley, I wasn't expecting such a place as this."

"It's one step above a slum, no more."

"A high step. Can we afford it?"

"Do you like it?"

"Of course I do. But—"

"Then we can afford it."

"I'm serious."

"So am I. I'm not nearly as rash as you think I am, Mary. I've done some close figuring. If we're careful, we can afford twelve dollars a month."

"Twelve dollars!"

"It's not so bad. We'd be paying eight in Yorkville. And I'm sick of Yorkville. Everybody knows everybody's business there. Talk, talk, talk. It's a gossip mill. . . . Wouldn't you like to start out fresh? We could do that here. Nobody knows us. Nobody cares one way or the other."

Mary glanced away, considering. A fresh start was not worth four dollars a month to her, but it was worth it to Harley, for, more than talk, he wanted to escape Dan's memory. "All right." She nodded. "I won't complain about the rent. But maybe I could help with it. Maybe I could be janitress here."

"No. Not my wife." Harley took Mary's hands and raised them to his lips. "I couldn't stand that. Besides, I made a bargain with the landlord. I'm going to do handyman work in the building . . . fixing things. If he's satisfied with my work, he'll take two dollars a month off the rent. It's a good bargain. I did all the fixing at home anyway. I'm used to it."

"You wouldn't mind?"

"I like to tinker with things. I'm pretty good at it. Mary, I'll do whatever I have to to keep us out of the slums and out of Yorkville. Trust me."

"I do, Harley. It's just that you have two jobs already."

"I'll manage. I'm doing it for you and that's reason enough."

Mary was touched. She turned and kissed Harley's cheek. It was a spontaneous gesture, devoid of passion, though not of warmth. "You're so good to me," she said. "I'll try to be the wife you deserve."

They looked at each other. Mary's eyes betrayed the doubt she felt, the guilt. Harley's eyes were bright. "Come." He smiled. "I'll show you around."

The kitchen, to Mary's great relief, had a new stove, a new icebox, and spacious cupboards. The other rooms were small, but graced with lovely old woodwork and wide window seats. The larger of the two bedrooms she chose for Rose and, once that decision was made, she and Harley set about measuring and making lists of what they would need. The lists filled two pages, for there was not a stick of furniture in the flat. "I know a nice secondhand store," Harley reassured her. "We'll do it a little at a time. And once in a while we'll have a splurge."

"You and your splurges." Mary laughed.

"Well, what's life for?"

Ten

"I can't believe it!" Elsie said for the fifth or sixth time. "Marrying Harley! Changing your whole life around! And for what? Tell me that, Mary, if you can. For what?"

"I've told you. I want a life of my own. I won't have it as long as I'm living in the same house with Bob. I won't have peace or privacy, or money either. I can't stay there, Elsie. In a way it's worse than Abbeywood Manor. At least it's no better. I work and work and have nothing to show for it. Rose is still going about in rags."

"Rose! She's the real reason you're doing this."

"What if she is? She's my responsibility. There's no one else. Pa's gone, and Georgy's off on a farm somewhere. That leaves me. . . . Anyway, I'm not doing it *only* for Rose. I want a life for myself too. Harley's offered me a life. He's kind and good and it's the right thing to do."

"You could get Bob to change his mind about Dan. Nag a man long enough and he'll give in every time."

"No, he won't change his mind about Dan. I know that. I've . . . accepted it. And we can't talk about Dan anymore. It's not fair to Harley."

Elsie shook her head from side to side, her little eyes squinting at Mary. "Worry about yourself," she said. "Are you being fair to yourself?"

"I'm very fond of Harley."

"Like a brother, not like a husband."

"Please, Elsie. It's all decided. There's no going back. I don't want to argue with you. I've had my fill of arguing."

"All right, all right." Elsie sat back in her chair. She folded her arms over her ample bosom. "But are you sure it's so smart to quit your job? Mrs. Sinclair pays the best wages in New York. You won't get another job half as good as here."

"It's not a job I want. I want a business. I can bake at home for now. I'm going to talk to Mr. Basset about baking larger orders . . . when I've enough money saved, I'll open a bakery. Maybe, when the time comes, you'll open it with me. You'd like to be part of a business, Elsie. I know you would."

"A bakery? A bakery's not really a business for a woman. But a tearoom, that's different."

"That's silly. Women do most of the baking in the world. Why shouldn't they be able to make a profit from it if they want? Is there a rule? A law?"

"No." Elsie smiled. "But you'd raise a few eyebrows."

"I don't care about that. I just want to bake pastries and sell them at a profit. I want to make money, Elsie. Baking's the only way I know. You're the one who started the idea."

"I remember. And if that's what you want to do, I say you should do it. It'll be a lot of work, more work than a tearoom. But work never scared you."

"There's something else. I'll be working here another three weeks. I owe Mrs. Sinclair proper notice . . .

after that I was wondering if maybe she'd order her pastries from me. I could deliver anytime. Anything she wanted."

"Well, I don't see why not. We'll hire a new scullery maid, but I don't expect she'll do any baking . . . I don't see why Mrs. Sinclair couldn't order from you."

"Will you ask her?"

"It's best you do it. You're going to be in the selling business, after all. It's best you learn how. Don't be shy. Don't be timid. . . . Maybe it's true the meek will inherit the earth, but they won't go far in business."

"Oh, Elsie." Mary laughed. "You're a good friend. I'll take your advice."

"That's fine. That's fine. But now you'd best take yourself home. You're supposed to be resting this week, remember? Get your rest while you can. With all your grand plans, you'll need it."

"I'll have Harley to help."

"Well, you'll have him. Whether he'll help or not is a different question. Men want what they want. Then they're out the door. Or some of them are. Maybe you'll be lucky with your Harley. I hope so."

Mary stood up. She smoothed her skirts and then reached for her light cotton shawl. "I'll see you Monday, Elsie. Sharp at seven. Now I'm off to see Mr. Basset."

"Mind he doesn't think he has the upper hand. Let him think *you're* doing *him* the favor and everything will be fine."

"Maybe I am doing him the favor," Mary said, smiling.

Mr. Basset's store was as scrupulously clean and neat

as the man himself. The counter tops were polished. The shelves, even the highest ones, were dusted. Everything that should have been covered was covered; everything else was displayed in straight, tidy rows. The wood floor was swept and scrubbed almost white. Mr. Basset had been the first storekeeper in the neighborhood to have electric lights and they were pleasantly bright on all the glass and marble and wood. A pure white cat sat in his accustomed place in the corner, a warning to any mouse foolish enough to venture within.

Mr. Basset had a small room at the rear of the store where he took his lunch, and Mary sat in that room now. She sipped a cup of tea, waiting patiently for him to finish with a customer. She was calm, confident, for she realized that this was the beginning she had sought. From this beginning her savings would grow, and from her savings would come a business of her own.

"Mary," Mr. Basset said, returning, "I am sorry to have been so long, but it doesn't do to rush a customer. It's not good business, is it?"

"No, Mr. Basset."

"You were saying . . . you were saying you are to be married?"

"Yes, that's right. And I'll be leaving the Sinclairs in three weeks time."

"I see." Mr. Basset removed his glasses. He polished the lenses until they sparkled. "I am happy for you, Mary. I hope, however, this doesn't alter our business arrangement."

"In a way it does. I wanted to talk to you because I have a different arrangement in mind."

"Different? The one we have is most successful. I'm not inclined to tamper with success. I'm a cautious man, you know. In these changing times caution is essential."

"You don't understand, Mr. Basset. I didn't make myself clear. I want to go on supplying pastries to your store . . . but I want to supply larger orders. And I want to add a few things."

Mr. Basset sat down. He put his glasses back on, staring at Mary. "Did you say larger orders?"

"After I'm married I'll be home all day. I'll have more time to bake. I could supply, say, three dozen Roly-Poly cakes every day. And three dozen other little cakes or tarts."

"I have no doubt they would sell," Mr. Basset said thoughtfully. "The problem is counter space. I haven't enough counter space for six dozen pastries. I couldn't put another counter in. That would be an expense, money out of pocket."

"There's space. There's a whole counter going to waste. The sweets counter. All those toffees and hard candies wrapped in colored papers. They're pretty to look at, but nobody buys them. All they're good for is collecting dust."

Mr. Basset's eyes narrowed behind his glasses. He was deeply offended. "Dust!"

"I'm sorry. I know there's no dust in your store. But you know what I mean. The sweets don't sell. What good are they to you if they don't sell?"

"Why, they are prestige for the store. They are imported from England. No one else carries them."

"They don't sell. My cakes do. Would you rather have prestige or money in the cashbox?"

Mr. Basset frowned. His whole face seemed to draw together in concentration. "I have always carried sweets. It's . . . an amenity."

"A costly one. I want to try out a new line of cakes. Not little ones, but big ones you could sell for sixty cents. I'll need the space."

"Sixty cents is a high price."

"But worth it. There's a black velvet cake I used to make for Lady Worsham of Abbeywood Manor. And a crumble cake too. This is a rich neighborhood, Mr. Basset. . . . Think of the profits if I'm right."

Mr. Basset did not trust himself to reply immediately, for he was heady at the possibility of new and unanticipated profits suddenly filling his cashbox. The idea, he knew, was valid. He wondered why he had not thought of it himself. This girl, this Mary Kilburne, always seemed to be a step ahead of him. "Perhaps," he said after a great pause. "Of course it would be a financial sacrifice for me," he added, trying to gain an edge, any edge. "I have an investment in those sweets. If I do as you suggest, my investment will be lost."

"It's lost already."

"You would have to bear some of the loss."

Mary smiled. She shook her head once and firmly. "Mr. Basset, I'm offering you more profits to share between us. I'm doing my part. But if you want a way to use the sweets . . . I'd put them into a lot of little bags and give them away to the cooks and housekeepers in your customer book. As presents. I'd put a little note in each bag, saying to try our new cakes."

"Give the sweets away? Why, it isn't even Christmas!"

"Giving them away is better than throwing them away. It's up to you. I know you'll do what's best for your store." Mary looked closely at Mr. Basset's anxious face. She decided to gamble. "But you understand," she said quietly, "I have to do what's best too. So if you don't want my new cakes, I'll have to make a different arrangement. There's another store I've heard about. Wheeler's Fine Groceries?"

"Wheeler's! Wheeler's can't compare to my store. It's small, and none too clean. The quality is poor. The variety. . . . I could go on and on, Mary. Surely you would not want to be in such a store as that?"

"I want to make money, Mr. Basset. I'm grateful to be in your store. And why wouldn't I be? It's the best in New York. But still . . . Well"—she shrugged—"it's up to you to decide."

"You are shrewd," he said, both impressed and annoyed. "There is, however, something else to consider. If your cakes don't sell, then I will have lost my investment for nothing."

"If that happens, I'll pay you back. That's fair."

"You will sign a paper to that effect?"

Mary nodded. "To that effect only."

Once again, Mr. Basset removed his glasses and polished them. "It's unusual to see a young girl so sure of herself."

"I have to be sure, Mr. Basset. It's business."

"Yes, I suppose it is." He rose abruptly. "Very well. Come with me. We will look at the space you want."

They left the back room and went into the store. The clerk was unpacking a carton of cocoa tins. He did not turn around. Mr. Basset led Mary to the counter that would soon be hers. He gazed down at the sweets, many hundreds of them in bright and shiny papers. It had been his mother's idea to stock them. He was genuinely sorry to think of them gone.

"It's perfect," Mary said, checking the dimensions of the counter against a tape measure. "You'll be pleased, once we're done."

Mr. Basset said nothing, though he had the feeling that, bit by bit, Mary Kilburne was taking over his store. It was an uneasy feeling. Only the thought of profits made it tolerable. "When do you want the space?" he asked.

"In August. I'll be in my new flat by then. Mr. Basset, there's one more thing. I'll go on buying my ingredients from you. But they have to be at cost."

Mr. Basset's lips parted. A pulse began to throb in his neck. "That's quite impossible! I never sell anything at cost!"

Mary had been prepared for such a reaction. She had considered her own response very carefully. "I want to be fair, Mr. Basset," she said. "But I want to be fair to both of us."

"I have expenses. There is the ordering. And handling. My clerk doesn't come free. There is his salary."

"Well, I said I want to be fair. I'll buy my ingredients at cost, with half a cent added on top."

"Half a cent is hardly—"

"I'll be buying more from you than I did before. It's a good bargain."

"Who is putting these ideas into your head, Mary? Mrs. Jadnick?"

"It's not Elsie. I have ideas of my own."

"One cent on each item you buy. I won't take less."

Mary nodded, for that was the figure she had had in mind. "It's settled then. I'll start writing the notes about the new cakes."

"And charge me for the paper? No, Mary. I will write the notes myself."

"As you say, Mr. Basset. I must be going now, but I'll have your regular order of Roly-Poly cakes here on

254

Monday morning. Sharp at six-thirty."

"Very well."

"I want to thank you. I know you have your doubts about what we decided. You'll be pleased though, once it's done."

"Time will tell. The cashbox will tell."

"Good day to you, Mr. Basset."

"Good day, Mary."

Mary was smiling as she left the store, for she felt she had accomplished a great deal. She had been fair, certainly as fair as Mr. Basset would have been if their positions were reversed. He was not too proud to haggle over pennies; neither was she. She had held her ground and soon, very soon, dreams would become reality. I must tell Dan, she thought, then quickly corrected herself: I tell Harley.

Harley would not have been surprised by Mary's lapse. He would not have been concerned about it either. He was a happy young man, in love, guided by an unshakable trust in the future. His days were busy, for suddenly he was paying attention to his work. His new industriousness did not go unremarked. Brokers and secretaries and clerks at the firm of Rutherford & Day nodded approvingly at him. He had always been liked; now he was admired too.

In his spare moments, Harley haunted secondhand stores. Mary had left the furnishing of their flat to him and he wanted his choices to please her. Wisely, he bought the furniture for Rose's room first. He bought a new bed, a used dresser painted white with tiny pink flowers, and a used, child-sized table and chairs. He bought a big rag doll and sat it in one of the two chairs.

"A surprise for Rose," he told Mary, though in truth it was a bribe.

Harley bought a kitchen set, and a small sofa for the parlor. He took weeks shopping for their bedroom furniture, settling at last for a used brass bed with a new feather mattress. He polished the brass himself, working at his task until each post, each bit of fluted trim shone. The dresser he bought was also used, but he sanded and stained and oiled it. When he was finished, it looked as good as new.

"You should be very proud of yourself," Anna said to her son one day late in July. "You've worked wonders."

"It wasn't easy." Harley smiled. "Mary has me on a budget. She watches every penny."

"You can't blame her. Money's not easy to come by. And you have a high rent to worry about."

"I'm not worried, Ma. I'm enjoying myself."

"And Mary? She doesn't say much when she's at home."

"I wish I knew. The way things are, I don't see much of her. But it's only eleven days until she leaves the Sinclairs for good. Only fourteen days to our wedding." Harley poured a cup of tea for his mother. He poured a cup for himself and then sat down at his kitchen table. "Fourteen days," he said. "It's a short time, but it can seem forever."

"You're not having second thoughts, are you?"

"No." Harley laughed, shaking his head at Anna. "My mind was made up months ago."

"Harley . . . it's really a father's place to talk to his son, but Bob . . . you know how he's been lately. What I mean is . . . is there anything you . . . want to know?"

"Know?"

"Well, about . . ." Anna blushed bright red. She looked away, smoothing the knot of hair atop her head. "About the . . . wedding night."

"Ma!" Harley exclaimed, more amused than shocked.

"Oh, I know it's not my place. But your father's in a bad way, and there's no other man in the family."

"You're okay, Ma. You really are. You don't have to worry though. I know all I need to know." That was an exaggeration. There were, in fact, certain things about which he was curious, things that had not been made entirely clear in a visit to Dr. Parker. He himself had asked direct questions. Dr. Parker had answered some of them; others he had ignored or evaded. "Nature will take its course," he had said often during their conversation. Harley supposed that was true. "Thanks for asking, Ma. I can see from your face you didn't want to."

What Harley saw was relief. Anna had dreaded having an intimate discussion with her son. She felt only relief that it was not necessary. "The curtains are almost finished," she said, swiftly changing the subject. "I'll bring them tomorrow night."

"Ma, I've been thinking . . . if I gave you the money, could you buy some kind of pretty material and make a dress for Mary? Kind of a wedding dress?"

"It was going to be a surprise, but I guess I'll have to tell you. Mrs. Sinclair has already given me money to buy material. There's enough for new shoes, and a bonnet too."

"She did that?"

"She's a good woman, Harley. She treats her servants like human beings. And, as she said, a wedding happens only once."

"Does Mary know about the money?"

"No. Don't you tell her either. She was planning on wearing her skirt and shirtwaist to City Hall. Now she'll have a nice surprise."

"But there's a problem."

"What?"

"If Mary has a new dress, Rose will want one. Ma, I don't want any trouble on our wedding day. If Rose starts—"

"She won't. I'm making a little dress for her too. It'll even have a bit of lace at the collar. That should keep her quiet . . . at least for a while." Anna smiled.

"Good. Anything to keep her quiet."

"It's not going to be easy, living with Rose."

"I plan to bring her little presents from time to time. She's sweet as sugar when she gets presents."

"That's bribery."

"If Rose is happy then Mary will be happy. That's all I care about."

Mary and Harley were married at City Hall in August of 1906. The ceremony was perfunctory, witnessed only by Anna, Rose, and Father Malone. It could not be said that Mary was radiant, but she was lovely in a long dress of white lawn and lace. Her slippers were white kid. Her bonnet was pale straw, trimmed all over with tiny flowers made of silk. She carried a bouquet of summer daisies given to her by Harley.

The new bride and groom, wearing matching, plain gold wedding bands, rode to their flat in a hired cab. The small wedding party followed in another cab and, when they reached the flat, they found Elsie there, presiding over a table of food provided by Mrs. Sinclair. There was cold chicken and ham, potato salad with chives, ice cream, and strawberries. There was champagne, the first any of them had ever tasted. There was a two-tier wedding cake baked by Elsie.

There were presents, a handmade quilt from Anna, an Irish lace table cloth from Father Malone. Elsie's present was a handsome mantel clock of brass and dark oak. Mr. Basset had sent a pound of tea, a pound of cocoa, and three jars of preserves. Mrs. Sinclair had sent a complete set of bone china that was, Mary instantly declared, too good to use. While everyone was exclaiming over the presents, Harley reached into the pocket of his brand new suit and produced a miniature porcelain cat for Rose. She had not given much thought to Harley before but, in that moment, she decided she liked him.

The celebration continued until dark. Elsie was the first to leave, and then Father Malone. Anna gathered up her bonnet and purse and, with tears in her eyes, embraced her son. "You're a man now," she said. "My little boy, a man."

"I love you, Ma. . . . Tell Pa I'll come see him."

"I will. I'll tell him." Anna turned and embraced Mary. "You're really my daughter now. I'm so glad."

"I'm glad too, Anna. And don't worry. I'll take good care of Harley."

"Take care of each other," Anna said, looking from Mary to Harley. "Be kind to each other. That's the only advice I'm going to give you." She went to the door, opening it. "Good night."

"Good night," Harley and Mary called together.

The door closed and they were alone. It was an

uncertain moment, for neither of them knew what to say. They smiled. The silence grew deeper. Mary looked down at the floor.

"This is silly," Harley said finally. "We're acting like two kids on their first date."

"I know."

"Well, let's stop it. Let's relax and have a cup of tea."

"You go ahead, Harley. I want to look in on Rose. Her first night in a new room and all. She might feel out of place. I'll just tuck her in."

But Rose was already asleep, curled up in her bed with her big rag doll. Mary opened the window. She hung up Rose's dress and put her hair ribbon on the dresser. "Sleep well, lass," she whispered, leaving.

Mary went into her room, the room she would be sharing with Harley. The bed had been turned down. A new white nightgown lay across it. She closed her eyes, trying not to think about the hours ahead.

"Are you all right, Mary?" Harley stood in the doorway. His eyes were quiet, questioning. His lips smiled, though very slightly. "Mary?"

"Oh, I'm sorry, Harley. Don't mind me. It's all the excitement of the day, I suppose."

"Can I get you anything?"

"No. I'm fine."

"Well . . . I'll finish my tea while you change."

Harley left her. She undressed quickly, slipping into the new nightgown. She brushed her long hair and then sat at the edge of the bed. There was no air of joyful expectation about her, no air of excitement at becoming a bride. Sitting on the bed, her head bent, her hands clasped tightly in her lap, she seemed not a bride at all but a person condemned, waiting for sentence to be passed.

"Hello, Mrs. Kilburne." Harley smiled, walking into the bedroom. He was nervous, pulling at the belt of his robe. He looked very young. "I guess your name is Mary Kilburne Kilburne now," he said.

"One's enough."

Harley sat next to Mary. Her gown was not sheer, but he could see the curves of her body pressing against the cloth. His breath quickened. He touched her shoulder and, at his touch, she drew back. "Don't be afraid, Mary," he whispered. "I won't hurt you. I only want to love you. . . . Let me love you."

Harley opened the buttons of Mary's gown. He saw the sweet fullness of her breasts and his hands began to shake. Soon the gown lay on the floor. Harley gazed at Mary's naked body in a kind of wonder, for he had never beheld anything as beautiful, as perfect. His hands were on her, and his mouth. He threw off his robe and took her into his arms. He was murmuring incomprehensibly, moaning. His every action was gentle, though beneath the gentleness there was urgency.

Mary wanted to return Harley's passion. She could not. She pretended response, for she thought it her duty to do so. Hours later, when Harley again took her into his arms, she pretended again.

It was early morning when Harley sat up in bed and looked lovingly at his wife. He watched her for a long time, smiling, rejoicing in the memory of their night together. He thought of all the nights to come and he laughed softly. Mary stirred. He bent over her, brushing her hair from her brow. "I love you, Mrs. Kilburne," he whispered.

In sleep, Mary reached for his hand. "Dan," she said.

Dan became the third presence in their bedroom. Harley knew that when Mary dreamed, she dreamed of Dan. He knew that when she kissed him, it was Dan she kissed. If he was bitter, he gave no indication. Occasionally, hurt would dim the brown of his eyes, but never for very long. He smiled and laughed and made his little jokes. He was always kind, always gentle. Outwardly he was a happy young man; if, inside, he cried, no one knew.

Mary would not have called herself happy, but she was content. She cooked and cleaned and sewed. She took care of Rose. She did piles of washing and ironing. At night, when Harley had finished his handyman chores and she had finished her baking, they sat at the kitchen table and studied the stock market. They pored over the financial pages Harley brought from work, and the books Mary brought from the library. Harley was the teacher, but Mary was an apt pupil. By September she understood the workings of Wall Street. By November, having withdrawn three dollars from her savings, she owned her first share of stock. "We'll buy one share a month," she said to Harley. "If Mr. Basset agrees to carry my pies in his store, we'll buy two."

In December, Rutherford & Day promoted Harley from clerk to junior bookkeeper. He had been expecting the promotion. He had wanted it, for he wanted Mary to be proud of him. He returned home that night with flowers and chocolates and a bottle of wine. Mary calculated the cost of Harley's gifts but said nothing. She had other things on her mind. Smiling and pink with blushes, she told him they were going to have a baby.

Harley was euphoric. During the months that followed he went about in a daze. "A baby!" he said to himself at least ten times a day. *"My* baby." He felt the long shadow of Dan McShane receding at last. Whether it was true or not was of no importance; he felt it to be true and that was enough.

Mary was no less euphoric. She had always wanted children, but this child had special meaning to her. It meant closing the door on the turbulent past. It meant love, love she had been unable to give to Harley. She went to work making the parlor into a nursery. She bought a cradle and a chest of drawers, blankets and diapers and little shirts. For once, she did not count the cost.

Winter came and the winter of 1907 was severe. Wind-whipped rains drenched the city day after day. When the air turned sharply colder there was snow, eight inches of it during one storm, a foot of it during another. People struggled through the icy white streets with collars turned up and caps pulled low. Hands and eyes and noses were reddened by driving winds, numbed by cold. Through it all Mary made her deliveries to Mr. Basset's store. She left home thirty minutes earlier each morning because, in such fierce weather, the walk took thirty minutes longer. She arrived back home in time to see Rose off to school and Harley off to work.

"This has to stop," Harley said one morning in February. "You'll make yourself sick."

"Oh, I'm healthy as a horse. Now go on, you'll be late."

"I'm not going anywhere until we've talked. Mary,

think of the baby."

"Who do you suppose I'm thinking of, if not the baby? He'll need things. There'll be expenses. We need the money."

"Money isn't everything."

"Isn't it?"

"No!" Harley frowned, turning away. He had promised Mary that he would not interfere in her business activities. He had kept his word, remaining silent even when he wanted to scream. But now he was worried. Terrible thoughts haunted his mind. He knew women had miscarriages all the time. He knew that, sometimes, they died. "Look, Mary, money's important—"

"Important? Money's the only protection in life. Our baby's not going to grow up like Rose and Georgy and me. Hungry half the time, wearing rags. He'll have it better. I'll see to that . . . we'll see to that."

"I make a good salary. And you put more money in the bank every week than some men earn."

"Not lately. There were the things for the baby. There were the new winter clothes for Rose."

"And the sled."

"Well, she wanted it so much. A lot of the children have sleds. This is a richer neighborhood than Yorkville, Harley. The children have more here. It's not fair to deny Rose."

"I'm not asking you to deny Rose anything. I wouldn't want you to. But she has luxuries and you're *still* going around in rags. In all kinds of weather."

"I don't need new clothes. The clothes I have are clean and warm. And what difference does weather make? It was as bad in Hexter. I'm used to it."

"At least let me make your deliveries for you."

"No, Harley. It's kind of you to offer, but I like doing it myself. I've told you that before."

"In your condition . . . it's not right."

Mary sat down. She sipped her tea, staring at the plain white tablecloth. "I have a feeling that's what Mr. Basset thinks. He hasn't said anything, but he looks at me in a queer way."

"Let me make your deliveries for you."

"I can't put my work off on someone else."

"I'm not someone. I'm your husband. I want to do it. Let me."

"Maybe. We'll see."

Harley tilted Mary's face up to him. He smiled. "Say yes . . . please? For the baby's sake?"

"All right." She sighed. "But I'll have to explain to Mr. Basset first . . . and you'll have to get up earlier."

"I'll get up with the birds, if there are any birds left in New York. I don't mind."

Mary reached for Harley's hand, pressing it to her cheek. Suddenly she felt like crying.

Mr. Basset was greatly relieved by the new arrangement, for the sight of Mary's swollen stomach embarrassed him. He dealt with Harley and did so efficiently, counting out to the last penny Mary's share of each day's profits. Harley disliked these transactions. He disliked collecting money, money earned not by him but by his wife. And although Mary made it a point to refer to the money as "ours," he was acutely aware that it was, in fact, hers. If Mr. Basset had any thoughts on the subject, he prudently kept them to himself.

Weeks passed, months. The harsh winter gave way to a sweet and gentle spring. Trees that had been shivering with cold now came into brilliant green bloom.

Flower vendors returned to street corners. Children returned to stoops and sidewalks. Their laughter, as they rolled hoops, as they played jacks and marbles, rode the soft breezes of the season.

Mary liked to sit at her window and watch the children at play. At such times she would put her hand on her stomach and imagine her own child. She always imagined a boy, for she wanted a boy. She wanted him to look like Harley though, most of all, she wanted him to have his kindness.

Anna visited every afternoon. She did the chores Mary was unable to do, getting down on her hands and knees to scrub the floor, bending over the washboard to do the laundry. "Rose could make the beds for you, Mary," she said during one of her visits. "It's not hard. She's certainly old enough to help."

"Yes, but she's been upset lately . . . about the baby coming and all. I don't want to put more strain on her. Oh, I know what you're thinking, Anna. Rose is spoiled. I admit it. There's just nothing I can do about it, not now. . . . Don't worry, it's going to be different with the baby. He won't be spoiled. I'm not going to make the same mistakes with him I made with Rose."

"Are you so sure it's going to be a boy?" Anna asked, amused.

"I want to give Harley a son."

"He'd be quite happy with a daughter."

"He'd be happier with a son. I know how men are."

But in truth, Harley had no preference. His only wish was for a healthy child and that wish was granted on the evening of August 12, 1907. On that evening, after fifteen hours of labor, John Harley Kilburne was born. According to the kitchen scale, he weighed exactly eight pounds. He had a fluff of dark hair, pale blue eyes, and a lusty cry. Everyone agreed he had the stubborn Kilburne chin.

Mary and Harley were as delighted as they were proud. They gazed upon their son, touching his tiny fingers, stroking his downy cheeks. They exclaimed over his good looks. They made funny noises and were certain they saw him smile.

In her happiness, Mary invited Bob to see his grandson. He came to the Lexington Avenue flat with Anna and Jane and, for the time of their visit, the Kilburnes were a family again. It was to be the last time. At two o'clock in the morning, a very drunken Bob fell down a flight of stairs and broke his neck. He died instantly.

Book Two

Eleven

"Mary's Pastry Shop" was scripted in gold letters on the wide plate-glass window. In the window was a tempting display of cakes and pies and delicate little pastries arranged on lacy doilies. There were trays of cream buns and beribboned baskets of cookies. Passers-by could not help stopping. They gazed at the luscious confections and were drawn irresistibly into the shop. No matter how full the shelves were in the morning, they were empty at day's end.

Mary had rented the shop in 1909. Now, three years later, she owned it. The lessons she had learned from Mr. Basset she applied here. Her shop, like his, was immaculately clean. The glass display cases sparkled, as did the marble counters. The wood floor gleamed. Her one clerk, a young woman named Mabel, was neatly attired in a long-sleeved black dress over which was a starched white pinafore. A ruffled white cap covered her dark curls. Also like Mr. Basset, Mary kept lists of her customers, carefully noting their preferences. At Christmas time, the cooks and housekeepers with whom she dealt received plum puddings or boxes of gingerbread.

The shop was located in the Murray Hill area of the

city, though its reputation extended far beyond. Smartly dressed women came from all over to buy the unusual pastries. Some sent their servants. Livery identifying the houses of Vanderbilt or Gould or Astor was not an uncommon sight in Mary's shop. Mary did the baking, the ordering, the bookkeeping. She offered tea to her customers. She found time to chat with them. When the shop was very busy, she helped Mabel at the counter. All this she did with one or another of her three small children in tow.

"If you are to be successful, you must mind your manners and know your place." That was the advice given to Mary by Mr. Basset shortly before her shop had opened. She had heard such advice all of her life, though coming from Mr. Basset, a man she respected, it took on new importance. She had gone to the library and, in addition to books on accounting, she had borrowed books on grammar and etiquette. She had studied them, insisting that Harley test her. When the doors of her shop opened for business, she felt prepared.

Mary's shop was successful, often clearing more than a hundred dollars a week. It was a lot of money and she needed it, for she had a lot of expenses. She had Rose, now twelve years old and enrolled in Miss Beardsley's School for Young Ladies. The school was but one expense. There were also music lessons and art lessons. There were clothes. It seemed to Mary that they were always arguing about clothes, for when Rose had worn something four or five times, she considered it old.

Harley said little about the money so freely lavished on Rose. But Mary knew it bothered him. And for good reason. They had three growing children to support. They had a six-room floor-through flat on Lexington Avenue that was not inexpensive. They had obligations to Anna and Jane. Pondering the monthly bills, pondering Mary's dawn-to-dark work schedule, Harley would look at Rose and shake his head. Once in a while he would remark on the unfairness of it all.

Mary's response, partly out of guilt, partly out of need, was to work even harder. Against everyone's advice, she continued supplying pastries to Mr. Basset. It took nothing away from her store, she reasoned, for she had her own customers. It was an extra source of income. And it was a way of thanking the man who had given her her start. Mr. Basset, in turn, devoted fully a third of his store's space to her cakes and pies. Sometimes he was not certain if he was running a grocery or a bakery. He was certain, however, of the profits, which were sizable indeed.

Mary arrived at her shop every morning at five o'clock. She went directly to the kitchen in the rear and from five o'clock until the seven o'clock opening the four ovens were in constant use. Once the morning's baking was arranged on the shelves, she began all over again. Her oldest son, Johnnie, disliked the shop. He preferred to stay at home with Irene, the woman Mary had hired to look after the children during the day. But three-year-old Peter and two-year-old Oliver loved it. They loved the bright warm kitchen with all its wonderful aromas. They loved the cookies they gobbled when their mother was not looking. When they jumped up and down, pleading to be taken to the shop, Mary was only too happy to say yes.

This day, a crisp autumn day in October, Mary was alone in the kitchen. The morning's baking had been completed. Mr. Basset's order was boxed and tied, awaiting his wagon. By seven o'clock, when his wagon had still not appeared, Mary went outside to look for it. There were many delivery wagons about, but none of them his. Frowning, she went back into the shop. "I wonder where Mr. Basset is," she said to Mabel.

"Hasn't he been here yet?"

"No. I telephoned to his store and there was no answer. It's not like him to be late."

"You could set your watch by Mr. Basset."

"I know. That's what I was thinking."

Mary returned to her kitchen. She mixed batter and cut out three dozen cookies, putting them into the oven to bake. She dusted a tray of tea cakes with powdered sugar. She began chopping almonds, but when nine o'clock came with no sign of Mr. Basset, she took up her purse and shawl and left. "I'm going to Mr. Basset's store, Mabel. Something must be wrong. He's never been late a day in his life."

"Maybe his horse is sick."

"Maybe," Mary said thoughtfully. "But Mr. Basset would have telephoned me. He knows we have a telephone in the shop. . . . No, I'll feel better if I go over there. I hope there hasn't been an accident. The ceiling in his store has been leaking for a week. If it's fallen in, he'll be beside himself."

"Well, I'll look after things while you're gone."

"Thank you, Mabel. There are some cookies in the oven. See they don't burn."

Mary took the Third Avenue El uptown. As she walked from the El to Mr. Basset's store, she composed her thoughts. If the store had been flooded, she could stay to help clean it up. If it was anything else, the horse or the wagon, then there would not be much she could do. She was concerned, for she knew how Mr. Basset felt about his store. It was everything to him.

Carl, Mr. Basset's clerk, was standing outside the store when she got there. Crates of merchandise had been delivered and left at the door. There were no lights showing in the windows. "Carl," Mary said, "where is Mr. Basset?"

"I don't know. I was here at six-thirty this morning, same as usual. But no Mr. Basset. The door's locked."

"Don't you have a key?"

"Mr. Basset would never give no key to nobody. Anyways, he was always here to let me in. Except this morning. I didn't know what to do. I been waiting all this time."

Mary pressed her nose against the window and peered inside. The ceiling was still in one piece. The floor was dry. "Mr. Basset lives upstairs, doesn't he?"

"I think so. I never been there myself."

"We'd best go upstairs and knock on his door. Something's wrong."

"Upstairs? Are you sure we should? Nobody never goes up there."

"Which doorway is it?"

"That one," Carl said, pointing. "At least that's where I seen him go."

"Come along." Mary went to the right of the store, Carl trailing behind. In the vestibule of the building she looked at the row of mailboxes. "Basset. 2F . . . Come along, Carl. Hurry."

Mary started up the stairs. She had gone halfway up when she began to run, impelled by a sudden feeling of anxiety. She reached the door and pounded on it. "Mr. Basset?" she called loudly. "It's Mary, Mr. Basset. Open the door."

There was only silence and she pounded on the door

again. "Mr. Basset! It's Mary . . . can you hear me?"

"He ain't in there."

"Where else could he be?"

"He ain't answering you."

"Maybe he's ill. You saw Mr. Basset yesterday, Carl. How was he? Did he complain of anything?"

"Aw, he never says nothing to me."

"Well, how did he look?"

"Same as usual." Carl shrugged.

Mary tried the door. It was locked. She leaned into it with her shoulder, but it would not move. "Help me, Carl. We have to get the door open."

"How? There's no key."

"Mr. Basset may need our help. He may be ill. Influenza is going around, Carl."

"I know. But we'll never get this door open. Look how solid it is."

"Stay here. I'll be right back." Mary ran to the stairs. "Don't leave, Carl. Wait for me."

"Okay, Mary."

She ran down the stairs and into the street. A block away she found Officer O'Brien walking his beat. Whatever she said to him was persuasive, for he blew his whistle, summoning help. Another policeman came running and the three of them rushed back to Mr. Basset's flat.

Officer O'Brien and his partner managed to open the door. They went inside, looking around warily. "Mr. Basset, sir? Are you hereabouts? It's the police, Mr. Basset." There was no reply. Officer O'Brien turned to his partner. "That would be the bedroom," he said. "Let's be having a look inside."

Mary and Carl remained in the parlor. The room

was spotless, but without any furniture save for a desk, a chair, and a lamp. Mary peeked into the kitchen and saw it had only a small table and one straight-backed chair. Stacked neatly on the table was a single plate, a single cup and saucer. There seemed to be one of everything, never two, and that bespoke the solitary nature of Mr. Basset's life. Mary remembered all the times she had invited him to come to dinner. Each time he had politely declined. She had not pressed, but now she wished she had, for the thought of Mr. Basset sitting alone in his empty flat saddened her.

"Well, Mary," Officer O'Brien said, closing the bedroom door, "I'm afraid it's bad news I have for you. Mr. Basset has passed on, God rest his soul."

"He's *dead?*" Carl asked, whipping off his cap.

"That he is."

Mary was shaking her head stubbornly back and forth. "He can't be. There's a mistake. Mr. Basset was never sick a day in his life."

"Ah, but it goes that way sometimes. A feller can be blooming with health and then . . . I'm sorry, Mary."

"What . . . what happened to him?"

"I'm no doctor, but I'd say it was his heart. He passed on in his sleep and I'm thinking that's a blessing."

"May I see him?"

"You don't want to be going in there. It's no fit sight."

"I want to see Mr. Basset."

"And would Mr. Basset want you to see him? Ask yourself that."

No, thought Mary, he would not. The very idea of her entering his bedroom would have been offensive to him. He had been scrupulously private in life; she would not violate his privacy in death. "You're right, Officer O'Brien," she said softly. "But is there anything I can do?"

"Would you be knowing the next of kin? The relatives?"

"I don't think there are any relatives. . . . Carl, do you know of anyone?"

"No one never came around. The only one came around was the lawyer. Claymore the name is."

Mary nodded. "Philip Claymore is . . . was Mr. Basset's lawyer."

"We'll see he's notified then. There's nothing more you can do. Best to be on your way."

"But the arrangements," Mary said.

"We'll be notifying the morgue and the lawyer feller. Between them, they'll see to the arrangements. . . . Here, Mary, you're not looking well. Do you want to sit down awhile?"

"I'm fine. I just wish . . ."

"Well, when it's sudden like this it's twice the shock. But don't be forgetting it was peaceful."

Mary glanced at Carl. He seemed very confused, twisting his cap in his hands. "We should go, Carl. We'll only be in the way here."

"What about the store?"

"I don't know. I suppose that's up to Mr. Claymore to decide. Come along, the police have things to do here." Mary opened the door. Carl looked around the flat one last time and then walked into the hall. "I'll go with him," she said to Officer O'Brien. "Thank you for your help."

"I'm sorry the way it turned out."

"Yes. Yes, so am I."

Carl preceded Mary downstairs. When they were outside he looked at her. "Shouldn't I open the store?" he asked. "O'Brien could get the front door open."

"Oh, I don't think you should do that." Mary felt sorry for Carl, for he was as set in his ways as Mr. Basset had been. The store was like a home to him. For ten years he had arrived every morning at six-thirty, doing the same small tasks day after day, neither seeking nor receiving promotion. Clearly he had expected to spend his life unpacking crates and stocking shelves for Mr. Basset. "Carl," she said, "I'm sure Mr. Claymore will be in touch with you. He'll tell you what to do."

"What do I do in the meantime?"

"If you don't hear from Mr. Claymore in a few days, come see me at my shop. You know where it is."

"You don't think I should open the store?"

"No, I don't."

"I was supposed to wash the windows today too." Carl put his cap on. He sighed. "I guess you know what's the right thing. So I'll do what you say. I'll wait to hear from Claymore."

"That would be best."

"Well. . . . 'Bye, Mary."

"Goodbye, Carl."

Mary watched him walk away. For several minutes she just stood there, unsure herself of what she should do. Finally she walked to Third Avenue and took the El downtown. She went back to her shop. She told Mabel what had happened and then telephoned Elsie. She tried to work, but her heart was not in it. At two o'clock she went home.

Harley was at work. The children were taking their

279

naps. Mary sat at the kitchen table, thinking about Mr. Basset. After a while she put her head in her hands and cried.

"I'll take your books, Rose," Mary said. "Sit down, I'll get your tea."

Rose Kilburne, at twelve, was a startlingly beautiful child. Her hair, though drawn back with a ribbon, was a glorious mass of curls, still the color of polished gold. Her lashes were gold too, and very long. Her skin had the delicate glow of translucent porcelain. She was petite, with tiny hands and feet and a tiny waist. Dressed in the pleated skirt, middy blouse, and tie worn by the students of Miss Beardsley's school, she looked like a small and perfect doll. "Your eyes are so red, Mary," she said now. "And why are you home so early?"

"It's a sad day. Mr.—"

"I *hate* sad things. Don't tell me." Rose smiled, playfully covering her ears. "Anyway, you promised we'd talk about my new dress, the one for Melanie's birthday party. I want blue silk. With ruffles, but not too many."

"Rose," Mary said quietly. "Mr. Basset died."

"Oh? I'm sorry . . . but can I have blue silk? Amanda is going to wear green and I—"

"Rose! Didn't you hear what I said? Mr. Basset died. *Died*. And all you can think about is a new dress."

"I said I was sorry. He was old, wasn't he? Old people die."

Mary threw up her hands. She turned, slamming the tea kettle on the stove. "Is that what you're learning at

Miss Beardsley's school? To have no feelings? To care about nothing but clothes and parties?"

"Miss Beardsley says a lady must always look her best. Especially for a social engagement. Miss Beardsley says—"

"To hell with what Miss Beardsley says!" Mary looked at Rose, her eyes dark with anger. "I think I should have a talk with your Miss Beardsley. Someone should tell her life is more than one big . . . what does she call it? A social engagement? She's teaching you fancy talk, I see. Well, life is more than fancy talk too."

"She's a lady!"

"Oh, that makes everything all right. If you want my opinion, Agatha Beardsley is silly and pretentious."

"You wouldn't understand."

"Why? Because I'm not a lady? Because I'm in trade? Your Miss Beardsley, with all her airs and graces, doesn't mind taking my money . . . money earned, may I remind you, in trade. She takes it, and at every possible opportunity asks for more."

"It's not my fault Mr. Basset died."

"What?"

"You're angry at me because he died."

"No, I'm angry because you don't care. If it weren't for Mr. Basset we'd have nothing. You'd be scrubbing pots in somebody's kitchen . . . and I'm not so sure that would be a bad thing. If you knew what work was, you'd know what life was."

Rose began to cry. Tears slipped down her cheeks and her pretty mouth quivered. Mary could never stand to see Rose cry; she could not stand it now. She went to her sister, hugging her. "I'm sorry, lass. I was hard on you, I know. But you're so thoughtless sometimes. You're getting too . . . grand."

"I don't mean it, Mary," Rose said, fluttering her lashes.

"I won't have you turning into a Lady Worsham. Do you understand? I won't have it."

"I'll be good. I promise . . . but please don't say anything to Miss Beardsley. I'm so happy at her school. If I had to leave there I'd . . . I'd . . . wither away."

"Wither away!" Mary suppressed a smile. "I suppose you got that from those silly books you and your friends read."

"They're not silly. They're about *true love.*"

Sighing, Mary went back to the stove. She fixed tea, putting it on the table with a plate of sugar buns and a pot of jam. "Have your tea and then do your homework."

"Mary, about my dress . . ."

Mary's eyes flashed. "We'll talk about it later," she said very quietly.

"But Melanie's birthday party is in two weeks."

"Later. We'll talk about it later or we won't talk about it at all."

Mary left the kitchen. She went into her bedroom and closed the door. She slept for a while but, at four o'clock, when Irene brought the children in from play, she was there to greet them. She took Peter and Oliver on her lap, tickling them and making them laugh. Johnnie, reserved as always, stood a short distance away and watched. Mary sent Irene home early. She fed the children. She gave them their baths. She was reading them a bedtime story when Harley came in, beaming at the sight of his wife and children all together.

Mary fed Rose and then she and Harley sat down to

a leisurely dinner by themselves. Harley was genuinely sorry about Mr. Basset's death, but his reminiscences were fond and funny and they lifted Mary's spirits. Her spirits fell again when she told Harley about Rose. "So I don't think I'll let her have the dress. She had a new dress for Ellen's party. She can wear that."

"Of course she can. But if it's going to bother you . . ."

"It won't bother me. Why should it? Rose has a closet full of dresses."

"Well, she'll cry and carry on. There'll be a terrible row. If you're going to give in anyway, you might as well give in at the beginning and save yourself from trouble. You have enough on your mind, Mary. One dress more or less makes no difference."

"It's that school. I'm sorry I ever put her in that school. I should have listened to you. If I had, Rose wouldn't be trying to keep up with her rich classmates."

"It's not the school. Oh, Miss Beardsley's is making things worse. But Rose always wanted things. The problem is, the more you give her the more she wants."

"Yes, that's it exactly. . . . Rose isn't getting her way this time. And I'll be firm about it."

"Why? Why now?"

Mary looked down at the table, brushing crumbs into the palm of her hand. "I don't know. I . . . just have the feeling that if it's not now it'll be never."

Harley's reply was interrupted by a knock at the door. "I'll see who it is," he said, rising. "Are you expecting anyone?"

"Maybe it's Anna."

"Ma wouldn't come by so late."

"You get the door. I'll get the table cleared."

Mary stacked the dinner dishes in the sink. She

changed the tablecloth and set out clean cups and saucers. She was putting a chocolate pie on the table when Harley returned, followed by a white-haired man with bushy white mustaches. "Why, Mr. Claymore," Mary said, "this is a surprise."

"I apologize for intruding at such a late hour. I didn't know the name of your attorney, and when I tried to telephone you I found a business listing only."

"We don't have a telephone here. . . . Please sit down, Mr. Claymore. Have you met my husband?"

"Yes, indeed. We introduced ourselves at the door."

"Would you care for tea? A piece of chocolate pie?"

"In a moment perhaps. Now I must catch my breath. I'm afraid I have been rushing about all day. I am much too old to be rushing about."

Mary looked questioningly at Harley. He shrugged. "Mr. Claymore says there are some matters concerning Mr. Basset."

"That is quite correct. There are several matters which cannot wait."

Mary sat down at the table. "I'm very sorry about Mr. Basset," she said, pouring tea. "I'll miss him."

Mr. Claymore nodded thoughtfully, smoothing his mustaches. "I was his attorney for many years. He always seemed an odd sort of fellow. Pleasant enough, but removed. Of course he was entirely dedicated to his business. I admired his dedication." Mr. Claymore took a sip of tea. He sighed. "But you are no doubt wondering why I am here. I won't keep you in suspense. It is about Mr. Basset's will. It must be filed. That is the law. Between now and the filing, however, there are decisions to be made."

"We'll be glad to help in any way we can."

"If you need temporary help in the store—" Harley began.

"It is nothing like that. Please allow me to tell you about the will. There is only one bequest, in the amount of five hundred dollars. That is to . . ." Mr. Claymore opened his briefcase, removing a sheaf of papers. "That is to one Carl Jurgen, his clerk. The remainder of his estate goes to you, Mary."

"What?"

"Mr. Basset named you his heir. There is the bequest to Jurgen. There are a few other small expenses . . . but apart from those, the estate is yours." Mr. Claymore looked at the papers once more. "That includes the store and its contents, the building adjoining the store, one horse and wagon, one cat . . . and, of course, the bank accounts."

Mary reached for Harley's hand. She gripped it tightly. "There must be some mistake."

"I assure you there is no mistake. The will was duly drawn and signed. You are Mr. Basset's sole heir."

"But . . . I don't understand."

"Surely you know Mr. Basset had no family. You are as close as he came to having a friend. He respected you, Mary. He often spoke of your business abilities. Now you will have the opportunity to prove him correct. The bank accounts total in excess of twenty thousand dollars. It is a tidy sum."

"Twenty . . ." Mary's grip tightened on Harley's hand. She looked at him in utter amazement. "Harley . . ."

"Twenty thousand dollars?" Harley asked. "Twenty *thousand?*"

"Yes. That is the accounting as of this afternoon.

There are moneys still to be added, moneys owed by Mr. Basset's customers."

"But . . ." Mary leaned forward, staring intently at the lawyer. "I saw Mr. Basset's flat today. He had very little. He had . . . nothing. Yet you are saying he was a rich man."

"Indeed he was, by some standards."

"But the way he lived . . ."

"Well, one must understand the sort of fellow Mr. Basset was. He cared nothing for riches. He cared only for the *getting* of riches. There is a difference."

Mary and Harley stared at each other, dumbfounded. Mr. Claymore gave them a moment to consider their changed circumstances, then he cleared his throat. "Now to business," he said crisply. "Mr. Kilburne, I understand you are with Rutherford & Day."

"I'm a senior bookkeeper. And I'm in training to be a broker."

"Excellent! A financial background will serve you well in the management of your wife's inheritance. In addition to the cash assets, there is the property. The store and the rental apartments. It will be a full-time job."

"Perhaps. But it won't be my job."

"I beg your pardon?"

"Mr. Basset left his estate to Mary, not to me. It has nothing to do with me."

"My dear young man, you cannot expect your wife to manage such assets. She is a woman, after all. A woman has no place in a man's world."

Harley shook his head. "Mr. Basset had great faith in my wife's business abilities. You said so yourself."

"Of course. And I am certain Mary would do quite

well managing the store. But the other, the cash assets and the rental property, those are entirely different matters."

"Not to me."

"Nor to me," Mary said finally. "You're talking about me as if I weren't here, Mr. Claymore. Don't I have any say in this?"

"Certainly you do. If I seemed rude, I apologize. It is only that I assumed . . . Well, I will leave the details to you and your husband to discuss in private. I am here tonight because certain decisions must be made. It is proper to wait until a will is filed. But in this case, and because I anticipate no contest, I chose to move ahead. There is the matter of the store. You must decide when you want to reopen it. There is the clerk to consider. There are perishable goods to consider. There is the question of interrupting service to valued customers. There is even the matter of the cat."

"The cat?" Mary asked.

"Mr. Basset's will contains only one stipulation to your inheritance. It is that you provide care for the cat and the horse as long as they are alive. The horse is stabled. But as the cat is presently alone in the store, requiring food and water . . . you see what I mean."

"Yes," Mary smiled. She wondered if Mr. Basset's stipulation had been prompted by affection for the animals or merely by a desire to neatly tie up loose ends. She preferred to believe the former. "That was thoughtful of Mr. Basset, wasn't it, Harley?"

"We all have our soft spots," he replied quietly.

"In my opinion," Mr. Claymore said, "you would be advised to reopen the store tomorrow morning. At the latest, the morning after. It is never wise to interrupt business. Customers are too easily lost."

"I appreciate your advice, Mr. Claymore. But I have my own plans for the store. We're going to renovate it. When it reopens it will be a pastry shop, not a grocery. I'm not interested in the grocery business."

"A pastry shop?" Mr. Claymore returned the papers to his briefcase. He stroked his mustaches. "Yes," he said slowly, "as you already have one pastry shop, I see your point. Stay with what you know, eh? That's sensible enough. Of course a renovation will be costly. Funds will not be available to you until the will has been filed."

"I'll arrange the funds." Mary glanced quickly at Harley, sorry to have spoken without consulting him. "Do you agree, Harley?"

"It's your decision." His tone was light, though his eyes seemed troubled. His smile was forced. "Whatever you want."

"Mr. Claymore, I'll continue Carl's salary during the renovation. He's a good worker. I'd like him to work for me. I'll see to the cat too."

"Very well. There will be a great many papers to sign, after the will is filed. If you do not have an attorney, I must advise you to retain one."

"I'd like you to be my attorney, Mr. Claymore. Will you?"

"With pleasure. I am familiar with the estate. That will be helpful." Mr. Claymore permitted himself a small smile. "Most of my clients take my advice, Mary. But you have a mind of your own. It will be interesting indeed."

"I hope it will be profitable."

"Yes . . . Until the filing, rents and outstanding bills

will be collected by my office. You may begin the renovation, provided you do so out of your own funds. There is still the question of the merchandise. My office will begin an inventory tomorrow morning. Once inventoried, my office can sell it outright to another grocer, if you are willing."

"I'll look at the inventory when you're finished. But I think I've another use for it. We'll see."

"As you wish. Now I must be on my way."

"Won't you have some pie?"

"It is tempting, but I must decline. It is very late already."

Mary went to the cupboard and removed one of Mr. Basset's boxes. She put the pie in the box and gave it to Mr. Claymore. "You can have it with breakfast." She smiled. "It's especially good with coffee. And it's good to know the products you're representing."

"So it is. Thank you, Mary. Mr. Kilburne, it was a pleasure to meet you."

"I'll see you out."

"Good evening, Mary."

"Good evening, Mr. Claymore."

"Do call me Philip. We are going to be working closely together, after all. There's no need of formalities."

"Thank you, Philip."

Harley led the other man out of the kitchen. When he returned, moments later, he was very subdued. Mary ran to him. "What's wrong, Harley?" she asked. "You were so quiet all the time Mr. Claymore was here, and now you look like the world's come to an end."

"Maybe it has. Our world anyway."

"What do you mean? Harley, we were being buried

289

in bills. Now we're rich. Or almost . . . I'm sorry Mr. Basset died, you know I am. But I can't be sorry we've come into so much money."

"*You've* come into it."

"It's our money. It doesn't matter whose name is on the will. It's our money, yours and mine."

Harley sat down. He ran his hand through his sandy hair, staring into space. "How are you going to do it all, Mary? How are you going to manage two shops and a building and cash accounts? Do you know how much work that is? You're seldom home as it is. Will you ever be home once this starts?"

"Of course I will. I'm not going to do everything by myself. Elsie will manage the new shop. I'll give her a share of the business, the way I always planned. She'll be in charge of the new shop, not me. As for the building and the accounts, I was hoping you'd manage that end. You know finances. You can do whatever has to be done."

"Then neither of us will ever be home."

"Harley, you knew I wanted more shops."

"Sure. But I thought that was in the future. Not now. Not while the children are so young. They need their mother around."

"Peter and Oliver go to the shop with me all the time. They enjoy it."

"What about Johnnie? You certainly don't spend a lot of time with him." Harley sighed. "Or with me," he added quietly.

"That's not fair."

"Is it true?"

Mary was silent, for she knew it was. She was not as close to Johnnie as she was to her other children, in part because he did not seem to want closeness, in part because she found her oldest son difficult to understand. He was remote, an observer who kept himself at a distance, watching. Often she sensed his disapproval, though of what she could not say. She delighted in Peter and Oliver, but Johnnie was a puzzle. Mary turned her thoughts to Harley. She had not really neglected him, nor her duties to him, but it was true she had less time to share. Her hours at the shop were long. And at night she had books to do, supplies to order.

"Don't answer me now," Harley said. "Just think about it."

"I've been busy with the shop. You've been busy too, working during the day, studying at night. But once we're established things will be much better. We'll have time to do as we please."

"Will we?"

"Oh, yes. I promise. The money will help us, Harley, not hurt us. No more worries. And think what it will do for Anna and Jane. They'll have a decent life. The money means no more worries all around."

Harley was far from convinced, but he had said as much as he intended to say. He stood up, holding out a small chain on which were several keys. "The keys to Mr. Basset's store, storeroom, and flat. Claymore has one set. He left this set for us. I'll go over there now and see to the cat."

"You don't mind?"

"I could use a walk."

"Thank you, Harley. I'd be grateful."

Harley did not kiss her before he left. He got his coat and hat and hurried out. He walked rapidly through the streets, as if he were trying to leave his thoughts behind. *No more worries.* Mary's words echoed again and again in his mind. He did not believe them. He believed their worries were only beginning.

Harley fed the cat. He played with him for a while, but when he felt the walls of the store starting to close in, he took his leave. He paused at the corner, looking south, then north. He walked north, toward Yorkville.

Anna was still janitress of the building in Yorkville. She lived in the same flat, though the parlor was occupied by a boarder, a retired schoolteacher named Amy Brush. Such economy measures were necessary, for Anna had refused to take more than a couple of dollars from Harley and Mary each month. It was pride, foolish pride, she knew; it was also a desire to make things as easy as possible for her son. She knew the pressures of a young and growing family, the costs. She knew the pressures Rose brought to bear, with her fancy school, her fancy clothes, her fancy ideas.

Anna was about to go to bed when she heard the knock at the door. She pulled her robe close and went to answer it. "Who's there?"

"It's Harley, Ma."

"Harley!" Anna opened the door, alarm clear in her eyes. "What's wrong? Is it Mary? One of the boys?"

"No, Ma. Everything's all right. Can't a fella visit his mother without causing a panic?" Harley smiled. "Can't a fella come inside?"

"Oh, I'm sorry. Of course. Come in, come in. Make yourself comfortable. I'll put water on for tea."

Over tea, Harley told his mother about Mr. Basset. He told her about Mr. Basset's will. She was incredulous, hardly able to comprehend the startling turn of events. "But Harley," she said when he had finished, "you don't seem the least bit happy. I'd be in the clouds."

"It's a big change, Ma."

"It certainly is! My God, you're rich!"

"Mary's rich."

The excitement left Anna's face. She sat back, no longer smiling. "I see," she said. "You're afraid of what it might mean."

"Mary married me because she needed me. Even with her shop a success, she still needed me. Now . . ."

"What? Do you think Mary is going to leave you because she has lots of money? If you do, you don't know Mary."

"It's not that exactly. It's . . . it's so many things. I don't think Mary is going to pack up the boys and leave. She's not that way. But she may *want* to pack up and leave. That's just as bad. Damn it, it's worse."

"Mary has her reasons for wanting money, beyond the usual reasons. She's had awful experiences in her life. Along the way, she decided money could protect her from heartache. She decided money was a magic shield. For her and Rose, and now for the boys. She has many reasons, but leaving you isn't one of them."

Harley stared down at his teacup, turning it around and around. "I remember how Mary was when Pa died. The look in her eyes. She realized that if she'd only waited a year . . . she could have had Dan."

"Mary would never say such a thing."

"She didn't say it. She thought it. I know Mary very well, Ma. Believe me, she thought it."

"You're feeling sorry for yourself. I won't let you . . . I'll be blunt. You went into this marriage with your eyes open. You knew how Mary felt about Dan.

293

You knew those feelings might linger a long time. They probably did. . . . Now it's six years later. Mary may still think of Dan once in a while. But it's only a thought. It's unimportant. Compared to a marriage and children, it's nothing. You and Mary have a life together."

"Mary doesn't love me. I thought she would, in time. I was wrong."

"Mary doesn't love you in a romantic way. She *does* love you. There are many kinds of love, Harley. The moonlight kind doesn't last. What Mary feels for you will last a lifetime. Be grateful for it. It's rarer than you think."

"Is it enough?"

"Only you can answer that. You didn't seem to have any doubts before all this money fell into your lives."

"A few. They weren't very serious before. They weren't painful. Before."

"And now?"

"I don't know, Ma. I don't know."

According to his wishes, Edwin Basset was buried alongside his mother in a small cemetery on Staten Island. Also according to his wishes, no mourners were present. Mary and Harley visited his grave the next day. They placed a spray of red roses on the freshly turned earth and said goodbye.

Harley was uncharacteristically depressed during the ride home. He was pale. He looked tired. Mary noticed and took his hand. "Why don't you forget about work today?" she said. "Go home and have a rest."

"I will if you will. Or better still, let's go someplace,

just the two of us. Let's find a pretty restaurant and drink wine and eat oysters and . . . No?"

"I'd like to, Harley, really I would. But I have to go to the shop. I have six dozen Roly-Poly cakes to get in the oven. Then there are contractors to see, plans to look at. You understand, don't you? There's just too much to do."

Twelve

There was war in Europe but America was in peace and prosperous. Mary's second shop had opened early in 1913. By 1915, she had four shops and a central kitchen to supply them all. She had a growing number of employees, an accountant, an attorney. She had a growing stock portfolio, and investments in real estate. Money seemed to flow from all directions, though it hardly slowed Mary's pace. Watching her, Harley realized there would always be too much to do.

The Kilburnes moved again, this time to an airy light-filled apartment overlooking Central Park. There were ten rooms, large rooms with gleaming hardwood floors and high ceilings. Mary had spent the better part of a year furnishing their new apartment and she was proud of it. With its pale walls, its silken couches, its slender and polished tables, it looked not unlike the Sinclair residence. It was as serene, as graceful. Mary was proud of her home, but not foolish about it. When the children scattered their toys around or scraped their roller skates in the hall, she was not disturbed. She laughed, joining them as often as possible in their games.

Mary gave birth to her fourth son in 1916. Named

Edwin Basset Kilburne, he was blond and blue-eyed and very small. He lived only two weeks and his death, in the middle of a rainy, windswept night cast a terrible shadow over the Kilburnes. Peter and Oliver retreated into silence. Johnnie was disconsolate, for he had developed a fierce attachment to his youngest brother. Mary, putting her own grief aside, tried to comfort him but was rebuffed. She was rebuffed, too, by Harley. He refused to speak to her, refused even to look at her. When he slept at all, he slept on the couch in the study.

Mary understood Harley's reaction. She knew he blamed her for Edwin's frail health, for his death. In fact, she blamed herself. Throughout her pregnancy, Dr. Craig had urged her to slow down, to sleep eight hours at night and rest during the day. She had tried, but always work had interfered. Now there was grief, and guilt.

In the days following Edwin's funeral, Dr. Craig was called often to the Kilburne apartment. He was called for Johnnie, whose spells of hysteria were becoming alarming. He sedated the boy. He talked to him at some length. But as concerned as he was about him, he was more concerned about Mary and Harley. They were both haggard, both hollow-eyed with fatigue. The tension swirling around them was palpable. On his third visit, Dr. Craig decided he had seen enough. He ordered Mary and Harley into the study and closed the door. "You are both behaving like asses," he said without preamble. "The death of a child is a great tragedy. Grief is normal. It is even healthy. But not when you wallow in it. And that is what you are doing. You are destroying yourselves with grief and, I am afraid, guilt." Dr. Craig strode across the room. He sat down heavily, shaking his dark head. "There is no place for guilt here. It's inappropriate. As you know, Edwin died of a breathing problem. One of his lungs was obstructed, due to a malformation . . . a defect of birth, having nothing to do with the health of the mother or the father. Someday, there will be a cure for such problems. At present there is none. The thing to remember is that Edwin would have died in any case. There is absolutely no reason for guilt."

"I understand, Doctor."

"You say you understand, Harley, but do you? Mary, do you understand?"

"I'm trying. I'd like to think that's the truth."

"Certainly it's the truth! Talk to another doctor if it will ease your mind. Talk to a dozen doctors. They will all tell you the same thing."

"That's not necessary," Harley said.

"I want you to consider something else. Your behavior, and yours, Mary, is having a bad effect on Johnnie. He cannot be expected to recover from his grief while you two are behaving as you are. Children tend to mimic what they see. Children sense things, in this case the most awful tension." Dr. Craig rose. "That is a warning," he said sternly. "I advise you to heed it, lest you do harm to Johnnie. He is on the sensitive side, you know."

"We know, Doctor." Mary nodded. "We've been . . . thoughtless."

"Indeed you have. Now put the past behind you and start fresh. You have a lot for which to be thankful. Remember that."

"Thank you, Doctor. For taking the time to talk to us."

"I hope it wasn't time wasted."

Dr. Craig left the study. Mary and Harley looked at

each other. "He's right," Harley said wearily. "We have a lot to be thankful for. And *I* have a lot to apologize for. I've treated you so badly, Mary. I'm ashamed of myself. I wish—"

Mary went to Harley, covering his mouth with her fingers. "Don't. Don't apologize to me. We've both been half crazy. But now it's time to start fresh, just as Dr. Craig said."

Harley stood up. He circled the room once, twice. "Don't misunderstand me, Mary. It has nothing to do with you . . . but I need to be by myself. Just for a day or so. I'll call Ma to come stay with you."

"No, I'll be fine. . . . Where will you go?"

"I don't know. Anywhere. It doesn't matter. I just want to clear my mind. It has nothing to do with you, Mary, and that's the truth. I'm so damn tired."

"I understand." Mary nodded, swallowing hard. "Harley, you'll be coming back?"

"Of course." Harley draped his arm lightly about Mary's shoulder. "Of course I'll be coming back. I'll always come back."

Harley was gone two days and nights. He spent them in a hotel room, drinking heavily for the first and last time in his life. His mind was not cleared but clouded, and there was relief in that. When he returned home he was sober, clean-shaven, smiling once more. He spent a lot of time with his sons, especially Johnnie. The following Monday he went back to his broker's desk at Rutherford & Day. He and Mary resumed their life. They were careful with each other, immensely gentle. They were husband and wife again, though Mary knew they were not the same people they had been before.

While Harley went back to a full work schedule, Mary did not. Her twelve hour days became nine hour days. She left more details to Elsie, who was her partner and her assistant. She spent more time at home. Peter and Oliver were glad to have extra hours with their mother; Johnnie seemed annoyed by her presence. He found ways to fault whatever she did. He complained about his food, about his room, about the small presents she brought him. Dr. Craig counseled patience, but for Mary it was not an easy time. "What am I going to do about him?" she asked Harley over and over again. He sympathized, though he made no effort to intervene.

Indeed, as time passed, Harley took less and less interest in his home life. Outwardly he had not changed. He was still cheerful, smiling, ready with silly riddles and puns to amuse his boys. But often he was preoccupied. It was hard to get his attention, harder to keep it. Sometimes he was late coming home to dinner and, on a few occasions, he did not come home to dinner at all. "Clients," he said when Mary questioned him. He said no more, closing the subject with a smile.

There was a growing sense of disquiet in Mary. Their lives should have been happy, she often thought, yet they were not. They were neither happy nor unhappy, but in a kind of limbo somewhere in between the two. On a morning in the autumn of 1916, Mary looked into the mirror and frowned at what she saw. Her hair, though still thick and shining with golden lights, was without style. Her clothes were old, very plain, befitting the poor servant girl she had been, not the woman she had become.

That same morning, Mary visited Anna and the two women went shopping. Gone were Mary's staid shirtwaists and drab skirts. In their stead were silk dresses in vivid shades of blue and green and plum.

There were matching kid slippers and saucy veiled hats and little purses appliquéd with lace. For evening there were opulent gowns of rich satin, cut to enhance the curve of breast and hip. In the most extravagant gesture of all, there was a sable wrap. "I won't let myself think what all this cost," Mary said to Anna on the way home. "If I did, I'd faint dead away . . . I just hope Harley likes what I bought."

"How could he not? They're beautiful clothes and you look beautiful in them. It's such a pleasure to see you spend money on yourself, for a change. I'm curious though. What brought this spree on?"

"Oh, I don't know. I suppose it was for Harley."

"Harley?"

"I've been looking dowdy lately. Harley deserves better than that. He hasn't said anything, but still . . ."

"I'm sure he'll say quite a lot when he sees you. He'll be delighted!"

"I hope so. We're going to the theater on Saturday. I'm going to surprise him."

"You certainly are," Anna said, gazing thoughtfully at her daughter-in-law.

Mary waited impatiently for the days to pass. When Saturday finally came, she spent the whole afternoon getting ready. She took a long, scented bubble bath and then, wearing a robe over her new silk underclothes, she sat down at her dressing table. The latest fashion magazines were spread on the table. She studied each one in turn. "Ah," she cried when a particular sketch caught her fancy. She tore it from the magazine and fixed it to her mirror, smiling.

Mary's gown was of velvet and satin, in a deep blue the color of her eyes. Its bodice was cut low, daringly low, revealing the cleft between her full and pearly breasts. Once or twice she tugged at the fabric's edge in an effort to raise it to a more modest line, but, after glancing at herself in the mirror, she let it be. Her shining chestnut hair was swept atop her head and dressed with brilliant blue plumes. At her ears and throat sparkled the sapphires that Harley had given her for her last birthday.

Mary rose from her dressing table and glided to the full-length mirror. She pirouetted, her arms extended, the plumes in her hair swaying gracefully. It occurred to her, really for the first time, that she might be pretty.

"Is that you, Mary?" Rose stood in the doorway. Her mouth hung open. Her eyes were huge with disbelief. Jealousy seized her, for suddenly she felt her own beauty outshone by Mary's. "What have you done to yourself?" she asked.

"It's a new me . . . new clothes, new hair style. I even have a new perfume. Well, do you approve?"

"You don't look very dignified."

"Why must I always look dignified?" Mary smiled. "We're going to the theater, not to church." She spun around again. "Isn't it a lovely gown?"

"I suppose," Rose admitted grudgingly. "But what happened to the plain black gown you always wear when you go out?"

"I threw it away. It was so old and dull. I wanted something . . . special."

"Why?"

"You're a fine one to ask that question. You're forever asking for special dresses and outfits."

"I'm young."

Mary laughed. She bent, kissing the top of Rose's head. "I'm not exactly in my grave. I'm not that much older than you, lass."

"You're *years* older. Years and years. I'm only sixteen, but you're twenty-five. That's old."

"I'll remember to take my cane when I leave. . . . Why are you in such a bad mood tonight? What's wrong? Tell me."

"I was in a good mood until . . ."

"Until what?"

Rose turned away and as she did so she saw Mary's sable wrap lying on the bed. *"Sable,"* she exclaimed. "Is that *sable?"* She rushed to the bed and lifted the soft fur, holding it against her cheek. "When *I* asked for a fur you said no."

"Because you're too young. I'll get you a fur when you graduate from Miss Beardsley's school, not before. Anyway, it's not far off. Another year or so. Meanwhile you have your fur-trimmed coat and your fur muff."

"Amanda has an ermine cape."

"Amanda is not my concern."

"If you can have a fur, so can I. That's fair."

"Not really. As you yourself pointed out, I'm old. Old people are allowed certain things that young people aren't. I don't want to argue with you, Rose, not tonight. Can't we go one night without arguing?"

Rose sat down, tossing her golden curls. "I came in to ask you about the Christmas Cotillion. May I go? You have to decide, because I have to tell Amanda's mother."

"You know I'd rather you didn't. You don't belong at that cotillion, Rose. It's for society girls and boys. It's for very rich people. And no matter what you may think, we're not rich. We have some money, but it's not *that* kind of money. It will never be that kind of money."

"But Mrs. Wingate invited me."

"She invited you because you and Amanda are friends. Rose, it's not the cotillion I mind. It's much more than that. You're traveling in very rich circles. When the time comes, you're going to want to marry within those circles. It won't happen and you'll be hurt."

"I already know who I'm going to marry."

"What?"

"His name is Simon Ellsworth. He's from a wonderful family. His mother inherited millions. His father's wealthy too, and a congressman. The Ellsworths go way back. . . . They fought in the Revolutionary War."

"Oh? On whose side?"

"Mary!"

"I'm sorry." Mary sat next to Rose. She took her pretty little hand. "Do you have reason to think Simon wants to marry you?"

"All the boys want to marry me. I'm going to choose Simon."

"You're very sure of yourself, Rose. But you're forgetting that all those boys who want to marry you have parents. Parents who have their own plans for their sons. Money marries money. That's how great fortunes are made greater. You always have your nose in the society pages; you know how things are."

"Oh, pooh! Jeremy Van Linden married a waitress. A *waitress.*"

"And was disowned by his family. After that, he had second thoughts. His wife is now his former wife. Or so the newspapers say."

"That won't happen to me. Congressman Ellsworth thinks I'm wonderful. I heard him tell Mrs. Ellsworth

I'd be an asset to the family. I know what I'm doing, Mary. I'm going to marry Simon and be rich, rich, rich." Rose tilted her head to one side, smiling sweetly. "Please may I go to the cotillion?" she asked.

"I wish you wouldn't . . . but then my wishes don't mean anything, do they?" Mary stood up. She went to her dressing table and dabbed perfume behind her ears. "I won't stop you from going. I just hope you're not in for a disappointment. Wanting and having are two different things. Life can be . . . cruel."

"Not my life."

"No, because you've had me smoothing the way for you. I won't always be able to do that."

Rose was no longer listening. She had accomplished her purpose and, after stroking the sable wrap a last time, she went to the door. "Have a good time tonight, Mary," she said.

Harley passed Rose in the doorway. He patted her head absently and then walked into the room. "Am I late?" he asked, glancing at his watch. "I'll hurry getting dressed."

Mary turned around. She looked eagerly at Harley, color rushing to her cheeks as she realized how much she wanted his approval.

"Why, Mary . . ." Harley stood absolutely still, stunned by Mary's beauty, by the seductive splendor of her costume. "I don't know what to say."

"It's a new gown. Do you like it?"

Harley took a step forward. He saw the swell of Mary's ivory breasts, the voluptuous curve of her hips, and he was stirred almost to madness. He wanted to rip her clothes away, to press her naked body to his in passionate love that knew no bounds. A strangled cry escaped his lips. He struggled against the desire that burned in him. He fought it, reminding himself that passion had no place in his marriage. Mary did not want his passion, he reminded himself; she had never wanted it.

"Harley, don't you like my gown? I've done my hair too."

"Yes," he said quietly. "You look beautiful, Mary. More beautiful than I've ever seen you . . . I'll . . . I'll hurry and get dressed."

They went to the theater and after the theater they went to supper. Heads turned when they entered the restaurant, for Mary was dazzling, and Harley, with his charming smile and abundant sandy hair, made a handsome escort. They drank champagne, quite a lot of it, though it made small difference in their moods. Striving to be gay, Mary was merely edgy, troubled by Harley's inattention. His mind seemed to be elsewhere; when he looked at her, he seemed to be looking elsewhere. They talked, mostly about the children. Harley told a few modest jokes. Time passed, but very slowly.

During dessert, a client of Harley's came to their table. He was drunk, staring boldly down the front of Mary's gown. Twice, Harley asked him to leave. The waiter asked him to leave, and then the captain insisted he do so. But all urgings were in vain. There were more bold stares, several lewd remarks. The last of these remarks enraged Harley. He sprang to his feet, upsetting china and crystal in his haste. He lunged at the drunken man and knocked him to the floor with one punch.

Mary was in tears when they left the restaurant. Harley was grimly silent. There was no conversation during the ride home. Harley sat in his corner of the

307

taxi, Mary in hers. When they reached their apartment, Harley disappeared into the study. He stayed there all night. Mary lay awake, staring at the ceiling, thinking. She could not account for Harley's behavior, not this night, not any of the nights in the last months. She knew the incident in the restaurant was meaningless; in normal times, they would have laughed about it. But times were not normal. They had not been normal since Edwin's death, since Harley's two-day absence following Edwin's death. He had changed in those two days. He had left, she knew, seeking peace, perhaps seeking answers. Whatever answers he had found had changed him.

Early on Sunday morning, Peter and Oliver bounded into the bedroom. Their faces were aglow with excitement, for Sundays were special to them. "Good morning, Mama," they chorused.

"Good morning." Mary smiled, opening her arms to them.

"Where are we going today?" Oliver asked. "To the park?"

"It may be a little cold for the park."

"Then where?"

"Well, I have tickets to a puppet show. Will that do?"

The boys, one dark, one fair, jumped up and down happily. *"Puppets,"* Oliver cried. *"Puppets."*

"Now go have your baths and I'll start breakfast."

"Is Papa going with us?" Peter asked. "Where is he?"

"Papa's in the study. But you mustn't bother him. He's working."

Oliver put his finger to his lips. "Ssh," he whispered. "We must be very quiet, Peter. 'Specially you."

Peter began to chase his younger brother, making funny faces at him. Oliver squealed and ran from the room. "You'll never catch me," he called over his shoulder. "Try and catch me."

Harley did not join his family on their Sunday excursion. He went out, but Mary had no idea where. She debated with herself and decided not to ask.

Gradually, Mary resumed her old schedule. By the winter of 1917 she was working ten hours a day. By winter's end she was working twelve, sometimes thirteen hours. She added a line of breads to her shops and one of them, a hearty, rough-textured "Country Bread," became one of her most popular items, as popular as Roly-Poly cake and Black Velvet pie.

She had offices in the large westside building that housed her central kitchen. The offices consisted of three rooms, one for her, one for her secretary, and one for Elsie. They were Spartan rooms, furnished with office necessities only, though Mary had fresh flowers everywhere. On this warm and sunny April day, she was fussing over a vase of daffodils when Elsie burst in. "Here!" she said, waving a newspaper in Mary's face. "It's happened!"

"What's happened?" Mary asked, frowning. "Elsie, you're shaking." Mary took the newspaper. She paled, for the headline, black and six inches high, said *WAR*. "My God," Mary gasped. She fumbled for a chair and sat down. "My God."

"I told you it was coming! I told you! What else could Mr. Wilson do? . . . Oh, but think of it. Our poor boys going over there, fighting and dying." Elsie, too, sat down. She was gray-haired now, fat instead of plump. Steel-rimmed glasses perched on her nose. "It's a tragedy, Mary. There's no other word for it."

Mary's heart was pounding. Her hands were damp. She reached for the telephone and called Harley, but he was not in his office. She called Anna's apartment. There was no answer. "I must get home," she said, rising quickly. "I must find Harley." She snatched up her hat and purse and gloves and rushed to the door. "Do you think Harley will have to go to war?"

"Dear God, I hope not."

"I must get home. Take care of things, Elsie."

Mary ran down the stairs and into the street. She found a taxi cab at the corner and gave the driver her address. She sat back and then leaned forward, gripping the edge of the seat. "Please *hurry*," she said.

"I'll do my best, Missus. But look at it. Traffic's real bad."

Mary glanced out the window and knew it was going to be a long ride. The streets were clogged with motor cars and horse-drawn wagons, both fighting for space in which to maneuver. There were many people about as well, their anxious faces bespeaking the anxiety in their hearts. Newsboys shouted from every street corner, holding their black headlines aloft.

Mary thought about leaving the taxi and walking home, but the weakness in her legs convinced her otherwise. She sat rigidly, her lips pressed together. Every few minutes she put her handkerchief to her forehead. When the driver began to talk of the war, she silenced him with a cry.

"Sorry, Missus," he said and then said no more.

They had stopped for a traffic light when Mary heard a sudden commotion and turned her head to look. Half-a-dozen construction workers, shouting and gesturing, were gathering at the site of a building renovation. They seemed angry about something, shouting to one of their fellows atop a steel girder. Mary was about to turn away when she saw the large sign in front of the building. "McShane Construction Company" it said in bold green letters. She looked past the sign and there, rushing into the middle of the argument, was Dan McShane. "Dan," she said softly.

"What's that, Missus?" the driver asked. "Did you say something?"

"No . . . no, I didn't say anything."

Mary continued to stare at Dan. He was taller than she remembered, lean and hard muscled. His hair was still the color of flame. His eyes were that intense blue, startling even at a distance. It would have been a simple matter to call to him, or to leave the taxi and go to him. She did neither. She felt her chest tighten, but only for a moment. When the light changed and the taxi started to move again, she made no effort to stop it.

Mary had always wondered what her reaction would be if she chanced to come upon Dan. She knew it would happen sooner or later and she wondered if she would feel the old grief, the dull and hollow pain that was the worst pain of all, or if she would feel joy. Now that it had happened, she did not know what she felt. She asked herself why she had not called to Dan. Several answers occurred to her, though they did not seem to be the right answers. She was confused. When the taxi pulled to a stop in front of her building, she was relieved.

"Terrible about the war, isn't it, Mrs. Kilburne?" the elevator operator said to Mary as she rode upstairs. "Good thing I got this bum leg, or I'd be going."

"Have you seen my husband? Has he come home?"

"I didn't take him up. Maybe Sam took him up. It's a crazy day today, what with the war news."

"Yes. Thank you, Joe," Mary said, stepping out of the elevator. She crossed the carpeted hallway and let herself into the apartment. "Harley?" she called. "Harley, are you home?" She went from room to room, looking around. "Is anyone home?"

"I am the only one here, Mrs. Kilburne." The cook, a stout German woman with a crown of thick blond braids, poked her head out of the pantry. "The children are at their school. Irene is doing shopping."

"Has Mr. Kilburne telephoned?"

"No. There were some calls, but not from the mister. I wrote the messages for you. They are on the desk in the living room. I get them, *ja?*"

"That's all right, Greta. I'll get them."

"Mrs. Kilburne, you know that war is declared?"

"I know. It's very sad."

"Mrs. Kilburne, I am a good American. I am sorry for my country where I was born, but for the Kaiser I am not sorry. He will get what he deserves, *ja?* America will win this war."

"I wonder if there are any winners in war."

"America will win. This I know."

Mary went to the living room. She looked at the messages on the desk, none of them important, and tossed them into the wastebasket. She lifted the telephone receiver and called Harley again. He was still not in his office. Mary poured a sherry for herself. She drank it slowly and when she had finished she poured another.

Harley came home late in the afternoon. Mary had been pacing the hall and so was at the door to meet him. She took his coat, his hat and briefcase, and put them in the closet. She brought him a whisky and soda. "You look like you need this," she said.

"I do, thanks. Where are the boys?"

"In their rooms. I spent the afternoon trying to explain war to them. As if anyone can explain war."

"Well, I don't see how we could have stayed out of it any longer. God knows Wilson did his best to keep us out. But there's no dealing with the Kaiser." Harley sipped his drink. He sat back, stretching his legs in front of him. "I'm sorry I didn't return your calls, Mary. I was on the trading floor most of the day. The market was going wild. War means profits."

"I was worried about you."

"Worried? Why?"

"Harley, you won't have to go? You won't have to go to war?"

"I'm almost thirty. The army doesn't want me. War is for young men, and that's the pity of it. A lot of young men will die before they've really had a chance to live."

"Are you sure you won't have to go?"

"If the war lasts a long time, I suppose even we old guys will be called. But I don't expect it will last a long time. Now that we're . . ." Harley looked curiously at Mary. "Why are you so concerned?"

"Why? How can you ask that? I don't want you to go to war, Harley. You could be hurt. My God, you could be killed!"

Harley seemed amused by such a notion. He laughed. "Not a chance," he said. "I'm the sort who will live to a ripe old age . . . for whatever that's worth."

"It's worth quite a lot."

"You flatter me," Harley said, laughing again.

"I wish I understood you. There's nothing funny in this. I've been half out of my mind all day . . . worrying about you, about what might happen to you."

"But nothing's going to happen. I won't be involved in the war, not in the fighting anyway. I'm sorry if you were worried. I should have telephoned."

"Yes, you should have."

Harley stood up. He went to the windows, gazing down at Central Park. His face, in the fading light of day, was thoughtful. A frown creased his brow. He was thinking about Mary, for he had been surprised by her expressions of concern. He knew she loved him, though he also knew it was a love born of habit, of years shared. Now he wondered if it could be more than that. He wondered if he dared allow himself to hope again. He turned, about to speak, but Mary spoke first. "I saw Dan McShane today," she said.

Harley's face changed subtly. The smile that had begun to flicker in his eyes vanished. "Did you?"

"I was in a taxi on my way home. We passed a construction site. Dan was there. He apparently has his own construction company now."

"How is he?"

"I don't know. I didn't stop."

"Why not?"

"I don't know. I was in a hurry to get home. I was upset."

"Surely you could have stopped for a moment."

"I could have. I didn't."

Harley returned to his chair. He sat down and lit a cigarette. "Dan never married, you know."

"How would I know? How do you?"

"Dan's youngest brother works as a runner at Rutherford & Day. We talk from time to time. As a matter of fact, I've seen Dan himself a couple of times during the past few years."

"Seen him?" Mary asked, startled. "You never

mentioned that."

"I didn't think there was any point. There was no message to relay. Dan stopped by to see his brother and I happened to run into him. We talked. Once we went out for a drink." Harley's tone was casual, though his eyes were fixed intently on Mary, watching for her reaction. He saw only surprise. "Dan and I aren't exactly chums," he went on, "but I always liked him. I admire him, I suppose. He's everything I'm not."

"What do you mean?"

Harley shrugged. He leaned back, drawing on his cigarette. "He's always at the center of things. At center stage, so to speak, while the rest of us are background players. And his construction company . . . he built that up from nothing. It's still small, but it won't stay small."

"You've built a career from nothing. I don't see the difference."

"Oh, there's a big difference. I go to an office in someone else's company. Dan's built his own company, literally with his own two hands. In that"— Harley smiled—"you and he have a lot in common."

"I didn't know you wanted your own company."

"That's not the point."

"What is?"

"Accomplishment. He's accomplished something, just as you have. I admire that."

"Harley, you've had responsibilities Dan hasn't had. As for me, do you think I could have accomplished anything without you?" Mary stopped as she realized the truth of her words. She had not really thought about it before, but now, remembering back to the beginning, she realized how much she had relied on Harley. She sought his advice and, once given, she took it. It was almost always the correct advice, for his judgment was almost always flawless. What she knew of business, he had taught her. What profits she earned from business, he managed, doubling, even tripling them. "From the start it was you, Harley," she said. "Whether it was teaching me about business, or making deliveries to Mr. Basset's store when I couldn't, or finding the right places for my own shops, or investing the money . . . it was you. And all the other things. You helped with the children when I was busy. You even helped with the housework."

"Don't remind me." Harley laughed. "That part is our secret."

"I'm serious. You never give yourself enough credit."

"I'm not looking for credit."

"What are you looking for, Harley?"

Love, thought Harley to himself. I'm looking for wild, passionate, insane love. *I* want to be at center stage. "My youth," he replied finally. "I seem to have lost it."

America's entry into World War I did not end the fighting overnight, as some had confidently predicted. It raged on and on, filling the newspapers with statistics more grim than those of the day before. It was a time of great patriotism, though when the bands had stopped playing and the last songs had been sung, the horror remained. Sons and brothers and boyfriends returned home crippled or blinded or gassed or shellshocked. Some never returned.

The horror was particularly real in Yorkville, where suddenly all Germans were suspect. The bewildered immigrants sent their sons and brothers to fight against the country of their birth while, at home, they were harassed by their own neighbors. Mr. Schultz, the butcher, had bricks thrown through his window. After the third such incident, he draped his window with American flags and put up a new sign reading "Joe Smith's All American Butcher Shop." The attacks ceased. Sauerkraut was renamed "Liberty Cabbage" by German grocers who had had their own windows broken. Anna, still a Yorkville resident, had several times come to the defense of her neighbors, dispersing groups of stone-throwing children and chasing them with her broom.

But life returned to normal in November of 1918, when the war finally ended. Jubilant crowds took to the streets, cheering. In the Kilburne apartment, champagne corks popped and everyone, including the children, toasted the armistice. Anna joined them, though she was unusually subdued.

"It's a celebration, Ma," Harley said. "Smile, the war's over!"

"Yes, and thank God it is. But I was thinking about all the young men who died. . . . If you were a little younger, you might have been one of them, Harley."

At that, Mary drew closer to her husband, taking his arm.

Thirteen

One of the young men who returned from the war was
Simon Ellsworth. He returned a hero, having led a
charge on a German stronghold in the Argonne Forest.
Everyone agreed he was a most unlikely hero, for he
was, in word and deed, extremely gentle. He was shy
also, the inevitable result of a loud and blustering
father. Simon returned home in December. In January
of 1919, his engagement to Rose Kilburne was
announced in the pages of the *New York Times*.

Rose decided on an engagement of six months.
Those six months she spent shopping and going to
parties in her honor. There was an engagement party
given by Mary and Harley. There was a bridal shower
given by her best friend, Amanda Wingate. The
Ellsworths hosted a dinner for their future daughter-in-
law. Miss Beardsley was hostess at a formal tea. Rose
basked in all the attention. That Simon was often
relegated to the sidelines, forgotten, was of no concern
to her. She smiled radiantly, twinkling and blushing as
befitted a bride-to-be, charming everyone she met.

Mary was not charmed, nor was she deceived. "I
know why you're marrying Simon," she said to Rose
one day in April. "He's a young man you can control. A

319

rich young man. You certainly don't love him."

"What of it? You didn't love Harley. Did you?"

"I was very fond of Harley. We—"

"Oh, pooh! I'm fond of Simon. He's a lamb."

"A lamb who's about to be fleeced."

"That's nasty."

"Rose, you're going to make Simon miserable. You're going to make yourself miserable. It's not worth it, not for all the money in the world. I beg you to reconsider. There's still time."

"Reconsider!" Rose turned her beautiful pale blue eyes on Mary. Her smile was chilly. "I'll do no such thing. And I'd appreciate it if you'd mind your own business. I'm not a child anymore. I won't be bullied."

"When were you ever bullied?"

"All the time! You were always telling me what to do. You were always *blaming* me for something. Do you remember how often you took Jane's side against me?"

"Do you remember how often you attacked her? Kicking and screaming and pulling her hair?"

"If I did, she deserved it."

Mary sighed. She cleared a space among the many boxes on Rose's bed and sat down. "You have no need of money now. You don't have to marry for it. Marry a man you love. At least marry a man you like."

"I'm going to marry Simon," Rose said, tossing her golden curls. "You can't stop me, no matter how hard you try."

"I gave up trying to stop you a long time ago. There is no stopping you, Rose. You're inexorable."

Rose was not certain what that meant. She glanced at Mary and then glanced away, tossing her head again.

"Well, I can't put a stop to your marriage plans, Rose. But I can put a stop to your spending. Look at all

these boxes. Look at all the boxes in your closets . . .
dresses and shoes and coats by the dozens. You've
bought enough for ten brides. You're not to buy
anything more."

"Are you punishing me?"

"I've spent a small fortune on your new wardrobe. I
hardly call that punishment. I've been very generous,
but it can't go on. You're not to buy anything
more . . . I mean it."

"But I just need a few—"

"*No*. Not another thing. And to be sure you're not
tempted, I'll inform the stores that my accounts are
closed to you. Enough is enough, Rose."

"I don't suppose it makes any difference. I'll soon
have my own accounts. I'll have everything I want
when I'm Mrs. Simon Ellsworth."

Rose became Mrs. Simon Ellsworth in June. The
ceremony at St. James Episcopal Church was attended
by three hundred people, most of them family and
friends of the Ellsworths. The church was bedecked
with flowers. Large, white satin bows draped every
pew, and a white carpet stretched from the door to the
altar. White-gloved ushers were everywhere. Mary,
seated in the front pew, smiled at all the ostentation.
She recalled her own wedding at City Hall and she
shook her head.

The music began. Peter and Oliver, the ring bearers,
walked down the aisle first. They were followed by six
bridesmaids dressed in ruffled pink silk, and then by
Amanda Wingate, the maid of honor. Mary smiled at
her handsome young sons. Oliver winked at her and
she had to cover her mouth to suppress a laugh. Her
gaze settled next on Simon. He was slender and of
medium height. Brown, center-parted hair framed his

oval face. He had a gentle mouth and wide eyes of deep gray. Except for their gray color, his eyes might have been the eyes of an eager and devoted puppy. Simon was twenty-three years old, but despite his age, he was an innocent. Harvard had not changed him. War had not changed him. He had an uncomplicated attitude toward life and such an attitude, thought Mary, would not serve him well with Rose.

Mary turned as admiring murmurs filled the church. She saw Rose, on Harley's arm, walking down the aisle. Rose was the most beautiful bride anyone had ever seen. Her gown was a cloud of white peau de soie, with cascades of lace at the sleeves and hem and hundreds of tiny seed pearls embroidered on the full skirt. Her long, lace-bordered train was similarly embroidered with pearls. Atop her golden curls she wore a tiara of diamonds and pearls given to her by Mrs. Ellsworth. Secured by the tiara, her filmy veil appeared to float about her small and exquisite face. She carried white roses.

Tears came into Mary's eyes at the sight of her sister. All the bad times, the arguments and hurts were instantly forgotten. When Harley took his place next to her in the pew, she grasped his hand. "Isn't Rose *lovely?*" she whispered.

"She's lovely all right. Poor Simon."

The Kilburne apartment was not large enough to accommodate all the wedding guests and so the reception was held in a ballroom at the Plaza Hotel. Fifty tables, dressed with white cloths, candles, flowers, china, and crystal, were arranged as for a tea dance. An orchestra played discreetly at the far end of the room. Waiters passed among the guests, pouring champagne. Lunch was served, an elegant lunch of vichyssoise, cold lobster and veal, and then the wedding cake was brought in. It was a magnificent creation, five tiers high, all white save for a tumble of spun sugar primroses. Mary had baked the cake herself.

Harley made the traditional toast to the bride and groom. There was applause. More champagne was drunk. Then the dancing began. Simon, for all his shyness, was an excellent dancer and Rose looked like a small and delicate doll in his arms.

"Well," Harley said, leading Mary onto the floor, "that's that. Are you pleased?"

"I wish Pa could see Rose. His dream came true after all."

"Thanks to you."

"And to you, Harley. I know how hard it was at times. But you never said a word."

"Good old Harley." He smiled, waltzing his wife across the polished floor.

Anna, in a simple gown of sea green silk, was seated at one of the tables, sipping champagne. Her eyes followed Harley and Mary as they danced. In truth, many eyes followed them, for they were a splendid couple. Harley had not been handsome as a boy, but as he had grown older the contours of his face had become strong, almost rugged. His smile was more knowing. His sandy hair, once an unruly mop, was now meticulously barbered and brushed.

Mary, at twenty-eight, had a true beauty. Her eyes were still darkest blue, but they had a depth they had not had before. Her pale ivory skin glowed. Her figure was fuller, all deep, lush curves. Now, in a soft blue gown, her wonderful hair in gleaming rolls atop her head, she was the most radiant woman in the room.

"What are you staring at, Mama?" Jane asked, sitting down.

"Oh, here you are. I haven't seen much of you today. You're certainly the belle of the ball. Who was that you were dancing with?"

"A cousin of Simon's. He's sweet."

"Well, Harley said you could have a wedding just like this one, whenever you're ready."

"Goodness, I wouldn't want a wedding like this one. It's too much fuss. It's not . . . personal. Though I loved Rose's gown. It would be lovely to have a gown like that. When I'm ready." Jane smiled and it was Anna's smile. She looked very much like Anna, with the same bright blond hair, the same clear green eyes. She had classic features and a long, graceful neck. Her taste in clothes was similar to Anna's as well, leaning toward dresses of simple cut and design. They suited her, for she was tall, quite slim, with an elegant look. Today she wore a peach-colored gown gathered at the bodice and edged in satin. She wore the coral earrings Harley had given her for Christmas. In her upswept hair was a single coral comb. Jane was a schoolteacher. She had a first-grade class in the Yorkville school she herself had attended. And she had a beau, a laughing, black-haired Irishman who was also a schoolteacher. "What were you staring at, Mama? You looked so grim."

"I wasn't staring. I was *looking* at Mary and Harley. They make a fine couple."

"Do they?"

"What in the world do you mean by that, Jane?"

"I'm not sure. Harley seems awfully distant. Mary makes a great fuss over him, but he seems . . . distant."

"Nonsense," Anna said, though her tone was less

than convincing. She, too, had noticed the changes in Harley. They worried her. "Harley's been working very hard, that's all. Then there was all the bother of this wedding. He's tired, that's all it is."

"I think you know better than that. Why don't you have a talk with him?"

"If there's any talking to be done, and I'm not saying there is, Mary will do it. She's a capable woman, Jane. She's had a lot of trouble in her life. She's managed to rise above it."

"Speaking of trouble . . . look who's here."

Anna turned her head. "Oh, it's George. Well, coming to his sister's wedding is the least he could do. Rose won't care, but it will be nice for Mary."

Mary was beaming at George. She had seen him only a few times in all the years since he had left; she was delighted to see him now. He was heavier. His hands were callused and there was dirt beneath his fingernails. People looked at him curiously, for in his ill-fitting suit and clumsy shoes he was clearly out of place. Mary moved quickly to put him at ease. "I'm so glad you could come, Georgy," she said, linking her arm in his. "Have you seen Rose? Isn't she lovely?"

"I said hello to her. I said congratulations. If you want to know the truth, she couldn't wait to get rid of me. I guess my clothes aren't fancy enough for her, nor my manners."

"Don't be silly. It's just that there are all these guests. It's been a long day for her."

"She's got what she wants now. She's got the money. Does she care anything for the lad?"

"Of course she does!"

"It's me, Mary. You can speak the truth. Did she marry him or his money?"

"Simon is a *very* nice young man."

"I see. She married his money. I feel sorry for him. He's going to learn some hard lessons. . . . You, Mary, you still haven't learned. Spending all this money for a fancy wedding. You work for your money, you shouldn't throw it away."

"Rose will only have one wedding."

"Eh, I wouldn't be too sure of that. Not knowing our Rose the way we do."

"Georgy," Mary laughed, "you haven't changed a bit."

"Aye, I have. I'm getting older."

"But you look fine. Blooming with health!"

"It's the farm life, Mary. It's healthy on a farm. Anywhere away from the city is healthy. I have two hundred acres now."

"All you need is a wife."

George smiled. He shook his head and a lock of brown hair fell across his brow. "There's a widow nearby who's glad of my company. No strings attached, if you follow my meaning."

"Don't you want children?"

"Children! One of them might turn out to be like Rose. Or worse, like me . . . Where are your kids? I'd like to see them."

"Oh, Johnnie and Oliver were tired and Peter had a headache. I sent them home with Irene. You'll see them later."

"No, I'm getting the next train back."

"You can't, Georgy. I wanted us to have some time together. You never come to New York. Now that you're here, please stay awhile. There's plenty of room at our apartment. You can sleep late in the morning and I'll bring you breakfast in bed. How's that?"

George put his big hand on Mary's shoulder. "I'm a farmer," he said. "Early to bed and early to rise. Besides, who'll look after my animals if I stay here? I have to get back, Mary . . . but I'd like you to bring the boys up one weekend before school starts. There's a nice, gentle horse they can ride. There's swimming not far away. There's a hayloft. Eh, they'll have a grand time. So will you. The country air will be good for you. Put some color in your cheeks."

"I'll ask Harley."

"I'll ask him. I want to see him before I leave anyway. You know, I always liked Harley. He's done right by you."

"Yes."

"Well, I'll catch him before he starts dancing again." George bent and kissed Mary's cheek. "I'll see you before I go."

"Be sure you do, Georgy."

Mary circulated amongst the guests. She talked to people she had never seen before and would never see again. She talked to endless numbers of Ellsworths, smiling until her mouth felt stiff. Every few minutes she looked in Harley's direction, trying to catch his eye, but he was busy with his dancing partners and did not notice. Mary watched him gliding about the room. What an attractive man he is, she thought in surprise.

Rose and Simon departed the reception at six o'clock. They were to spend the night in an upstairs suite and then sail for Europe in the morning. To Simon, Europe meant war and death and things best forgotten; he had not wanted to go. Rose had insisted. Pouting, fluttering her long golden lashes, she had prevailed. Two huge first-class staterooms had been booked—one for the newlyweds and one for

Rose's luggage.

Mary and Harley remained to say goodbye to their guests. Once more Mary smiled and smiled, repeating empty phrases over and over again. She sighed with relief when the last of the guests had gone. "I thought it would never end," she said to Harley. "I'm exhausted."

"I'm not surprised. Come, I'll take you home."

"Take me home? Aren't you staying?"

"I have a few things to do. Clients."

Mary looked sharply at Harley but she said nothing. She took his arm and together they left the hotel.

Greta was waiting at the door for them when they returned. She was tearful, anxiously wringing her hands. "Mrs. Kilburne, Mr. Kilburne, it is good you are home."

"What's wrong?" Harley asked.

"The doctor, he is here. He said at first it was not serious. Now he has changed his mind. It is Peter. He—"

Mary and Harley raced down the hall to Peter's room. "Damn," Harley said, tugging at the doorknob. "It's locked . . . Dr. Craig, are you in there?"

Dr. Craig opened the door. He took a step into the hall. "I locked the door to keep the other boys out of Peter's room," he said quietly. "It is a necessary precaution."

"What's wrong with Peter?"

"I'm afraid he is very sick. In the beginning I suspected only influenza. Now the symptoms are quite clear. It is infantile paralysis."

"No," Mary gasped, clinging to Harley's arm. "It can't be. Peter was fine. He had a little headache,

that's all. Just a headache."

"Headache is an early symptom of many illnesses, most of them minor. In this case, it is very serious indeed."

"We're wasting time," Harley said. "We must get him to the hospital. My car is downstairs. Or I could call an ambulance."

"That is out of the question. The child is much too ill to be moved. I sent for the things I will need. There are two nurses on the way as well. For now there is nothing we can do."

Harley was very pale. His mouth shook. "There must be *something*. Medicines. Specialists. There must be specialists in this field."

"I have been in contact with Dr. Schyler. He is on his way also. But I'm afraid he agrees with my diagnosis. And because the symptoms developed so rapidly, we are forced to conclude it is a most severe form of the illness. Do you wish me to speak frankly?"

"Of course we do."

"Then I will not hold out false hope. The paralysis is already in Peter's legs. There is every likelihood it will spread to his lungs. If it does, he will die . . . I am very sorry."

"Die." Mary lifted her stricken eyes to Harley. She began to cry, shaking her head back and forth in denial. "I don't believe you, Doctor," she said through her tears. "Peter was fine. How could he be fine one moment and then . . ."

"We know so little about this illness, Mary. It strikes suddenly, usually in summer. Children seem particularly vulnerable to it. We don't know why. There is no prevention. There is no cure. Some survive it, but others—"

- "I want to see him. I want to see Peter right now."

"First you must compose yourself, Mary. Peter is naturally not aware of the seriousness of his condition. If he sees you this way, he will know."

"I won't—"

"Listen to me. The child is in pain and running a high temperature. That is bad enough. I don't want him upset. He will need all his strength if he is to have any chance of fighting his illness. As it is, it is only a tiny chance. Don't take it away from him. And that is true for you too, Harley. When you see your son you must be cheerful. I know I am asking the impossible, but for Peter's sake you must do it."

"I understand," Harley said. He took his handkerchief from his pocket and dried Mary's tears. "You heard Dr. Craig. We have to try."

"Yes. Harley. I will. I'll try."

They entered Peter's room. He was in bed, his young face flushed with fever. His right hand tried to push the blanket away. His left hand did not move at all. "Mama . . . Papa," he said hoarsely, "it hurts so much. Make it stop hurting."

Mary and Harley bent over their son. Mary smiled at him, brushing his hair from his fiery brow. "Do I hear you complaining about pain?" she asked lightly. "You who went around a whole day with a broken hand? Remember that, Harley? This scamp broke his hand playing baseball and didn't tell us for a whole day. Remember?"

"I remember. Dr. Craig said you were very brave, Peter. You must be brave now. Don't think about the pain. Try and think about something else. Would you like me to tell you a story?"

"Yes, Papa. Would you?"

"Sure. A book story or a made up one?"

"Made up."

Harley brought a chair to Peter's bedside and sat down. "Let's see." He smiled. "What would be a good story? I know. I'll tell you about the baseball player who was really a big sheepdog."

Peter tried to laugh. A sound came, a hoarse and raspy sound from the back of his throat. "Yes, Papa," he said. "Tell that one."

Harley began his long, elaborate story, adding unlikely details as he went along. Mary sat in a chair at the other side of the bed. Her eyes never left Peter's face. She did not hear Harley's story; she heard only the urgent words of the prayers that formed in her mind.

"And that's how Shag O'Reily became the best baseball player in all of America," Harley finished. "That's the true story."

"And a wonderful story it was," Dr. Craig said, coming to the bed. He felt Peter's forehead. He felt his neck. "But I think Peter should rest now. Are you tired, Peter?"

"I don't know. It hurts. . . . Where's Oliver?"

"He's resting," Dr. Craig replied quickly. "Johnnie is resting too."

"I want Oliver."

"Later. Let him have his rest." Dr. Craig took a thermometer from a glass on the table and shook it down. "Open your mouth, Peter. That's a good boy."

The next hour saw a continual stream of people in and out of Peter's bedroom. Two crisply uniformed nurses arrived. Dr. Craig conferred with them briefly and then sent them out of the room to wait until they were needed. Attendants arrived carrying oxygen equipment. They placed the equipment according to

Dr. Craig's direction and left quietly. Dr. Schyler, short and bearded, trailed by his young assistant, was the last to arrive. He and Dr. Craig went to a corner of the room and spoke at some length.

Peter noticed the comings and goings but he was too sick now to wonder or care. His face was red, burning with fever. There was a terrible and unseeing glint in his eyes. He moaned and Mary's heart twisted at each sad sound. When Dr. Schyler approached the bed, she looked up. "Help him," she said desperately. *"You must help him."*

"I promise you we will do all we can, Mrs. Kilburne. I cannot promise more than that."

"It's not enough!"

"Please, Mrs. Kilburne—"

"It's not enough! You must . . ." But Mary had no chance to finish, for Harley was at her side, dragging her away from the bed. "What are you doing?" she cried. "I have to stay here, Harley. What are you doing? Let me go."

"Dr. Schyler has to examine Peter," he said gently. "We'll wait outside until he's finished."

"No. No, I'm not going. I have to stay here."

"Mary, get hold of yourself. This isn't doing Peter any good."

"I don't want to leave him," she said, though her voice was quieter.

"We'll be right outside. Come along. Come, Mary, take my hand."

Harley led her into the hall. He searched his mind for words to comfort her, but he knew there was no comfort, not in words, not in gestures. There was only waiting, and the waiting seemed to go on forever. He paced. He smoked a cigarette. He glanced often at

Mary, for he was as worried about her as he was about his son.

They were still in the hall when suddenly Oliver darted out of his room, running to Mary. "Is Peter sick?" he asked. "Why can't I see Peter?"

"The doctor is in there now."

"Can I see Peter when the doctor leaves?"

Mary looked at Harley. He swept Oliver into his arms. "It's late, you know," he said, trying to smile. "Why aren't you in bed?"

"Everybody said Peter was sick. I wanted to see him but they wouldn't let me. Can I see Peter?"

"No." Harley ruffled Oliver's dark blond hair. "I want you to go back to bed."

"I'm scared, Papa."

"There's nothing to be scared about. Papa's here. And Mama and Irene and Greta. But I tell you what . . . just for tonight you can sleep in Johnnie's room. Would you like that?"

"I asked him and he told me to go away."

"Well, you tell him I said you could sleep in his room tonight."

"Okay. I'll tell him Papa *said.*"

"That's my boy." Harley put him down, patting his little rear. "Don't let Johnnie bully you."

"I won't, Papa. Good night. Good night, Mama."

"Good night, darling." Mary waited until he had gone, then turned to Harley. "What will we tell him if . . ."

"I don't know." Harley passed his hand across his pale and haggard face. "I just don't know."

When they were allowed back in Peter's room, they found a very somber Dr. Craig. "It is as I feared," he said.

333

Peter's condition worsened as the night wore on. Despite the doctors' efforts, his fever continued to rise. His breathing became labored. An oxygen tent was placed over him, but it did no good. He lapsed into coma and an hour later he died.

"Peter," Mary screamed. She threw herself on the bed, sobbing, clutching her son's small, still hand. "Oh, Peter."

Harley pulled her away. "Come, Mary," he said, blinking back his own tears.

Mary cried for days. She cried all through the funeral and all through the ride home. When she arrived home, she took a bottle of brandy into the bedroom and closed the door. She refused to eat, refused to see the people who came to comfort her. She drank, though the oblivion she sought eluded her.

It was early in the morning when Mary looked up to see Johnnie standing at the foot of her bed. "You shouldn't be in here, darling. Mama doesn't feel well."

"I know . . . I know something else."

"What, Johnnie?"

"You wish I'd been the one to die instead of Peter."

Mary's eyes widened. She sat up very straight, staring in shock at her son. "Johnnie! That's not true!"

"It's true." Without another word, he turned and walked out of the room.

Mary chased after Johnnie but he would not speak to her. He crossed his arms over his chest, set his jaw, and said not a word. Mary's questions went unanswered, as did her pleas. "I'm sorry, Mrs. Kilburne," Irene said, embarrassed, as she often was, by the defiance of her charge. "I don't know what gets into him sometimes."

"Johnnie, won't you *please* talk to me?" Mary asked

again. "Why are you behaving this way? What have I done? Tell me."

"He's in one of his moods, Mrs. Kilburne. . . . Johnnie, answer your mother."

"No! I won't! I hate her!"

Mary slapped her son. Instantly, she regretted her action. She stared at her hand as if she had never seen it before. Her eyes, when she looked at Johnnie, were filled with surprise, with hurt.

But Johnnie only smiled. In his smile was triumph.

It was July and Elsie sat in the spacious, sunny living room high above Central Park. She sipped a glass of sherry, squinting questioningly at Mary. "When are you coming back to work? That's what I want to know. All the rest is talk."

"Soon."

"When is soon?"

"Did Harley send you here to prod me?" Mary adjusted the sash of her ruby silk dressing gown. She folded her hands in her lap, though her fingers moved restlessly. "He's been at me and at me to go back to work."

"He's right. He's only thinking of what's best for you, Mary. You're not one to sit at home brooding. That's not your way. Harley knows you very well."

"And I know Harley. He thinks if I'm busy with my work I won't notice how little he's home."

"What in the world are you talking about?"

"Oh, Elsie, it's clear enough. Harley's seldom home anymore. Even when he's home, he's not here. He spends time with the children, but as for me . . . I might as well be on the moon. It's quite clear. There's . . .

another woman."

"Shame on you for thinking such a thing! There's men like that. I know from my own experience. But Harley's not one of them. I never saw a man so devoted. You're not yourself yet, Mary. That's why you're having crazy thoughts."

"Harley's away for dinner five nights out of seven. He's away most weekends. When I ask him about it, he says 'clients.' That's all he ever says. After Peter . . . after Peter died, he stayed home for two weeks. I thought maybe . . . But then he went back to work and it started all over again. We live in the same house but we're strangers. That's the truth."

"A man has to work."

"What work do you suppose Harley is doing at night, Elsie?"

"If he says he's with clients, then that's where he is."

"I wish I believed that." Mary stood up. She went to the windows. In the park below, children played games and dogs romped, their tails wagging as they raced after balls and sticks. Jaunty little boats sailed on the pond. Cloths were spread for picnics. The sight depressed Mary, for she remembered the picnics she and Harley had had there. She remembered sailing boats there with the children, before Peter had died and Johnnie had, at least in spirit, been lost to her. They had been good times, she thought, yet she had not realized they were good times. She had always been preoccupied, first with Dan McShane, and then with her business. She wondered if she could really blame Harley for turning to someone else. "It's too late," she said, more to herself than to Elsie.

Elsie's eyes narrowed. "What kind of foolishness is that?" she asked. "Your trouble is you've shut yourself away brooding. Brooding always leads to crazy thoughts. Come over here and sit down, Mary. Come on. You need someone to talk sense to you and I'm just the person to do it. *Too late.* I never heard such foolishness."

Mary returned to her chair. She took up her teacup, then put it down again. Her fingers drummed at the arms of her chair. "There's nothing you can say."

"There's plenty! While you're sitting here feeling sorry for yourself, your business is going down the drain. The business you built from nothing, from a few Roly-Poly cakes. You've always been a smart girl, Mary, but there's times you let your feelings get in the way. This is one of those times. Leaving me in charge! That's stupid! I can run a store, maybe a few stores. But a whole business? When all I ever wanted anyway was a tearoom?"

"I've seen the statements, Elsie. You're doing fine."

"Wait 'til you see the next set of statements. Listen, Mary, times have changed. Maybe you haven't noticed, up here in your ivory tower. Maybe you haven't heard, but there's hard times out there. There are a lot of people out of work. There's inflation. *That's* the truth."

Mary nodded. She was aware of conditions; she could not help but be aware, for the newspapers wrote of little else. Prosperity had died with the signing of the armistice. The country was in a postwar Depression, with some three million people out of work and long range estimates going as high as five million. There was, she knew, no hope for a quick recovery, for factories were overexpanded, shelves glutted, foreign markets devastated by the years of havoc and destruction. There were twenty thousand millionaires

337

in the country, but most people were having trouble making ends meet, for postwar inflation meant the dollar was worth approximately forty-five cents.

And those were only some of the problems facing the country. Organized labor was beginning to flex its muscles, protesting the low wages of prewar years, the Open Shop. Strikes were epidemic, hitting steel, the railroad, the garment trades, coal mines, and even vaudeville houses. Some of the strikes were bloody, as private police forces, armed with clubs and worse, moved in on strikers. Businessmen were, for the most part, unsympathetic; in their view, unions were tools of socialism. They were "foreign," to be despised.

In Chicago and Washington, there were race riots. In the south, there was the rebirth of the Ku Klux Klan.

"I'm aware of the problems." Mary sighed.

"What are you doing about them? Sitting here all dainty and delicate isn't solving anything. Some of your stores are losing money for the first time. Some of your employees are talking about a union. There's decisions to make, Mary. I'm not going to make them. Who is?"

"I have the reports here. I'll read them and—"

"That's not good enough. You have to decide and decide now. . . . Do you want a business or not? You could sell out and get a good price . . . if that's what you want. If it isn't, you'd best be in your office tomorrow morning."

"Sell? I have no intention of selling. The business will go to the boys, when they're old enough. They may want to sell, but until then—"

"Fine. If that's your decision, fine. I'm glad of it, 'cause I'm not ready to retire yet. But you're going to run the business. You're going to be in your office first thing in the morning, ready to work. It's settled."

Mary smiled fondly at Elsie. "Don't I have any say in the matter?" she asked.

"You'll have all the say you want, once you're back at work. This sitting around all day, drinking tea, it's not for you, Mary. It suits some women, maybe most, but not you. You've worked all your life. Work's a part of you. And don't forget, work *means* something. There's pride in it. There's the knowing that you earned your way." Elsie nodded, shaking her finger at Mary. "Once you're back in your office you'll see I'm right. You won't have time for moaning and groaning and being dramatic."

Mary returned to work the next morning. She was reluctant at first, but as time passed her zest for business was rekindled. She put in long, hard hours six days a week and often took work home with her at night. It was solace, solace for a distant husband, for a hostile son. In those last months of 1919, Kilburne Bakeries Incorporated was born. Mary reorganized the company, cutting here, adding there. She had seven shops, a huge central bakery, and plans to package and distribute Roly-Poly cakes as far west as Ohio.

The employees of Kilburne Bakeries, bakers and clerks alike, were unionized. They had Mary's blessing. "I wish I'd had a union when I worked for Lady Worsham," she said to the organizer who came to take the vote. That she had succeeded without a union was, to her mind, beside the point. Times were changing and she was determined to change with them.

Fourteen

Keeping up with the changing times was often easier said than done. It was a new world, perhaps best exemplified by what the newspapers called the "New Woman." The New Woman wore lipstick and bobbed her hair. She shortened her skirt a full six inches and displayed her legs in sheer stockings, sometimes rolled below the knee. She danced the fox trot and the Charleston and the black bottom. She even smoked cigarettes.

But more than fashions and manners changed. Attitudes changed too. It was said that America lost its innocence during the war; certainly men and women seemed less innocent. They were ready to enjoy themselves and, as the old conventions gave way to the new, they were freer to do so. In such an atmosphere the era of the speakeasy began.

Prohibition became law in July of 1920. In Virginia, the Reverend Billy Sunday gleefully eulogized the demise of John Barleycorn: "Goodbye, John. You were God's worst enemy. You were Hell's best friend. The reign of tears is over." In New York, the Anti-Saloon League urged everyone to "Shake hands with Uncle Sam and board the water wagon." Such stirring words were heard all the time, but for every ten people who were willing to heed them, a hundred were not.

"It's a bad law," Harley said to Mary one night in 1922. "And bad laws will always be broken. Nobody's forcing the Drys to drink. Why must the Drys force their views on others? It's a stupid law, too. Do you know that people who never drank before are drinking now?"

"That's human nature." Mary sat at her dressing table, brushing her long hair. She had refused to cut it, though she had accepted other changes in the styles of the times. She wore her clothes fashionably short now and she wore lipstick. "That's also because of the speakeasys. The ones we've been to were great fun. They were like parties, but without all the stuffy formalities."

"I'm glad you feel that way."

"Oh? Why?"

Harley sat down. He stared at Mary's reflection in the mirror. "Well, I have something to tell you. I'm not sure you're going to like it."

"Don't keep me in suspense." She smiled. "Tell me."

"All right. I resigned from Rutherford & Day this morning. I'm going into business for myself."

"Why, Harley, that's wonderful!"

"Let me finish. It's not the brokerage business. I'm opening a club . . . a speakeasy, if you will."

The brush dropped from Mary's hand. She turned around, gaping at Harley. "Is this one of your jokes? You can't be serious."

"I'm very serious, Mary. I bought the building six months ago. It's a nice old brownstone on Forty-ninth Street . . . the renovations have already begun. We should be open in time for New Year's."

"Harley . . . I don't believe it. You gave up a career for . . . for a *speakeasy?* How could you? What were you thinking of?"

"Myself, I suppose. I'm tired of working for other people. I'm tired of working at a job I never really liked."

Mary was shaking her head in disbelief. Her hands rose and fell in her lap. "But it was more than a job," she said. "It was a career, a wonderful career. In another year or two it would have been Rutherford & Day & Kilburne. You said so yourself. Was that a lie?"

"That was the truth. And it played a large part in my decision. Mary, I didn't *want* it to be Rutherford & Day & Kilburne. I've spent half my life there. That's enough. Now I'd like to do something I'll enjoy. Is that so hard to understand?"

"No."

"It wasn't a hasty decision. I thought it through very carefully. If the club's a failure, I'll take a substantial loss, though not a fatal loss. There are my bank accounts, my stocks, a few other investments. My assets aren't as impressive as yours, Mary, but I'm not a poor man. Johnnie and Oliver will be provided for, as always."

"Still, it's a risk."

"A small risk. I may lose some money. And," Harley shrugged, smiling, "my standing in the community may go down . . . but then I never cared about that."

"Johnnie cares a great deal about that."

"I know." Harley rose abruptly. He began to pace, his head bent, his hands clasped behind his back. "Johnnie's my son and I love him. That doesn't mean I'm blind to his more unpleasant traits. He has Rose's avarice. He has Pa's obstinacy. But worst of all, he's a snob. I hoped it was only a phase he was going through. It isn't."

"Then you must know what he'll think about your club."

"Of course I do. Let him. I'll be damned if I'll make apologies for my life. Next month, when he's home from school, I'll tell him my plans. But I'm through trying to please him."

"At least you *do* please him from time to time. As far as Johnnie's concerned, I can't do anything right."

"He has a lot to learn. Sooner or later, someone's going to knock him off that high horse of his. When that happens, it's my guess Mama and Papa will look pretty good to him. Even if we do work for our living."

"He rather liked your being a broker."

"*I* didn't like it. Don't you see . . . it's my turn now? I intend to have fun with my club, Mary. It will be a party every night."

"An illegal party."

"That doesn't bother me."

"You'll be dealing with bootleggers. With gangsters."

Harley laughed. He sat down again, shaking his head at Mary. "We have liquor right here in this apartment. Our friends have liquor in their apartments. Where do you think it comes from? Do you think the Good Fairy leaves it on the doorstep? It comes from bootleggers and gangsters, Mary. The scotch you drank just last week at a speakeasy came from bootleggers and gangsters. I didn't hear you complain."

"You could be arrested."

"That's not at all likely. It's true that government agents make a few raids here and there. They make a few arrests. But they're not really interested in people like me. They want the bootleggers. They're trying to cut off the source and that they will *never* be able to do. There's too much money involved. Millions! Even the government is helpless against the force of such money. Prohibition is a bad law. It will surely be repealed. Until then . . . Mary, there's a party out there. The biggest party New York has ever seen. Enjoy it."

Mary turned back to her dressing table. She brushed her hair vigorously, avoiding Harley's gaze in the mirror.

"Are you angry?" he asked.

"I don't know. I'm not very happy."

"I told you you needn't worry about the money. I'll—"

"It's not the money, Harley."

"I don't see what else it could be."

"No, you wouldn't."

Mary's mind was not on money or morality or the law. It was on her marriage, for she realized the strain Harley's new business would put on it. It was already strained, fraught with silences, and absences too often unexplained. "Why didn't you tell me about this when you bought the building?" she asked. "Why did you wait until it was a fact to tell me?"

"I didn't want to be talked out of it."

"And you thought I could?" Mary's smile was rueful, as was the look in her dark eyes. "You give me credit I don't deserve, Harley. Whatever I've had to say hasn't mattered to you in a long time."

"That's not true."

"Has it occurred to you that we'll never see each other now? You'll be working all night and I'll be working all day. We'll be lucky if we manage to pass each other in the hall."

Harley became very still. "I remember saying those same words to you once." He nodded. "It was years ago, when you were starting your business. My words didn't stop you."

"That was different."

"Why?"

"We were poor then."

"Hardly. I had my job. You had your first shop and you had just come into Mr. Basset's money. We were far from poor. We could have been quite comfortable, just as we were. But it wasn't enough for you. Do you remember?"

"I had responsibilities."

"Yes, you had Rose. And she was a costly responsibility indeed. But that wasn't the whole story. It didn't explain working eighteen hours a day, seven days a week. You were passionate about your work to the exclusion of all else. I knew why. It wasn't hard to figure out. All the passion you couldn't give to Dan McShane, you gave to your work."

Mary gasped. She whirled around, the sleeve of her dressing gown sweeping combs and bottles and jars to the floor. "That's a filthy thing to say! It's a lie!"

"I don't think so. I'm not blaming you, Mary. You couldn't help yourself. It was a need . . . now I have a need. I need to do something on my own. And to have fun at it." Harley stood up. He took a cigarette from a silver box on the table and lit it. He inhaled deeply, watching the gray smoke curl away. "It would be nice to have your approval."

"My approval isn't important now. What you said about Dan is important. Because it isn't true."

"I don't want to talk about it."

"You never want to talk, Harley. As soon as a subject turns serious you make a joke, or change the subject entirely."

"Serious subjects have a way of turning into arguments. And arguments are dangerous." Harley drew again on his cigarette. He looked at Mary for a moment, then looked beyond her. "Arguments can end marriages," he said quietly.

"Is that a threat?"

"A threat? From me? From good old Harley? No, I don't make threats. I was merely stating a fact."

Mary went to him. She put her hand on his arm, staring into his eyes. "I want you to know you're wrong. I want you to believe me."

"It doesn't matter now. It was such a long time ago."

"Too long for a terrible misunderstanding to go on. You must believe me, Harley. You *must.*"

"If I was wrong, I apologize. Now please, let's drop it. Anyway, I wanted to show you the plans for my club. They're in the study. I'll get them."

Harley rushed from the room, closing the door behind him. Mary stumbled back to her dressing table. She groped for the chair and sat down, putting her head in her hands. She felt the sting of tears as she thought about Harley. Had he been brooding over Dan all these years, she wondered. Had she given him reason to brood? Images from the past flooded her mind. She saw Bob Kilburne; she actually felt his big hand slap her face. She saw Dan, tall and flame-haired and splendid Dan McShane. She saw Harley, not as he was today but as he had been years ago, smiling, tender, his hair flopping across his brow. "Harley," she said, and suddenly she did not know if she was crying for Harley or for herself or for Dan.

Harley was slouching tiredly in his deep, black leather chair. Before him on the desk were the architects' plans for his new club. He glanced at them but did not really see them. He was angry with himself for having spoken so bluntly. He had not intended it. The words had come from nowhere, surprising him as much as they had surprised Mary. They were true words, he thought, but like many true words, best left unsaid. He wondered at the effect they would have on Mary, on what remained of their marriage.

Harley reached for a silver-framed picture of Mary. He stared at it, sadness filling his brown eyes. Then, from his pocket, he took another picture. It was smaller, unframed, and it showed a young blond woman with dimpled cheeks and a vivacious smile. He stared at it also, sadness deepening in his eyes. He sighed. "What a fine mess I've made of things, Sally," he said.

Club Harley opened in January of 1923. It was a gala event, attended by some of the city's best people. Elegantly gowned and coiffed women waited while their elegantly dressed escorts spoke a password into a filigreed peephole. Once inside, they had their choice of entertainments. The ground floor had a showroom complete with musicians and a tiny stage on which long-legged chorus girls danced. Tables were packed tightly around the stage and front tables were particularly desired by male patrons, for there they were only scant inches away from chorus girls clad in feathers and spangles and not much else. The second floor offered a far more sedate showroom. In it a single musician, a piano player, accompanied a lovely dark-haired woman as she sang sad songs of love gone wrong.

The third floor was Harley's favorite. It had, on one side, a stylish restaurant glittering with china and crystal and lit by a magnificent crystal chandelier. The walls were thick panels of carved wood. The tables were covered with snowy linen cloths and the chairs had deep cushions of dusty rose. Opposite the restaurant was a saloon resembling the turn-of-the-century saloon his father had owned. It had fittings of wood and brass, checked table cloths, and globes of frosted glass covering the lamps. There were big brass spittoons, though they were filled now with sand and used for cigarette butts.

None of the rooms were inexpensive, nor were they expected to be. Scotch and champagne sold for twenty dollars a bottle, rye for fifteen. Those people who brought their own liquor paid two dollars for a pitcher of water. The newly invented "couvert" charge ranged as high as twenty-five dollars in some speakeasies; at Club Harley it was ten dollars, pure profit.

On opening night, Harley reserved numerous tables for friends and family. A dozen of his former Rutherford & Day colleagues were seated near the stage in the downstairs showroom. His lawyer and banker and their wives were in the second floor showroom, as were Jane and her new husband, Tim Malloy. In the restaurant, the largest table was reserved for Mary, Anna, Elsie, Rose, and Simon.

Rose's arrival at Club Harley had caused quite a stir, for even in the midst of a moneyed crowd, her furs and jewels were spectacular. She wore a hooded cape of sable, lavishly trimmed with silver fox. She wore a headband encrusted with diamonds, diamond earrings, and diamond bracelets on both wrists. A diamond solitaire the size of a walnut sparkled on her finger. She wore pearls too, four ropes of them reaching almost to the loose waist of her ivory satin gown. There were pearl buckles on her tiny satin slippers.

"My God, Rose"—Harley laughed when he saw her—"did you rob a jewelry store on your way here?"

"I suppose that's one of your jokes, Harley. I'll have you know these are all gifts from Simon. He's *such* a good husband. You would do well to follow his example."

"I would be bankrupt if I followed his example." Harley smiled warmly at his brother-in-law. "How are you, Simon?"

"He's fine," Rose said. "Can't you tell just by looking at him?"

"As a matter of fact, he looks a little tired to me."

"Well, he's not. Are you, Simon dear?"

"Rose," Simon replied quietly, "I was hoping to have a few words with Harley. That is if you don't mind. Do you mind?"

"No, I wouldn't dream of interfering. You take all the time you want." Rose tilted her head, smiling radiantly at her husband. "But don't be *too* long. You know I'm absolutely lost without you."

"Go on, Rose," Harley said. "Mary and the others are waiting. I promise I'll return Simon to you safe and sound."

Rose left them, smiling, waving regally as all around heads turned to stare at her.

"Come this way," Harley said, leading Simon to a small table at the back of the room. He ordered scotch and the waiter brought it in china coffee cups. "To

Rose." Harley smiled, raising his cup. "I didn't know she'd married a Rockefeller."

"A Rockefeller?"

"All those jewels she's wearing, Simon."

"Oh, those. Yes. Yes, I see what you mean." Simon lit a cigarette. After one puff, he stubbed it out. "Those are only some of her jewels. She has many more."

"Well, I must say that's very generous of you." Harley looked closely at Simon. His four years with Rose had aged him. The eager sparkle was gone from his eyes. His face was thinner, his forehead lined. He hardly seemed to smile at all anymore. "I apologize for being personal, but can you afford such generosity?"

"I'm not certain I can. That's what I wanted to talk to you about, Harley. I have only the income from my trust fund, you see. I can't touch the principal, except for what the executors call 'compelling' reasons."

"You should never touch principal."

"Yes. Yes, that's true. But my expenses . . ." Simon lit another cigarette. Again he took one puff and then put it out. "As you know, our Gramercy Park house is rather large. It requires many servants. And Rose entertains a great deal. It is expensive to entertain on that scale. And then there are the cars. . . ."

"Your trust income is sufficient to cover those expenses. With quite a lot left over."

"Those expenses, yes. It's the other expenses . . . Rose's clothes and furs and jewels. The things she buys for the house . . . Why, she bought a French porcelain last week that cost five thousand dollars. Now she is talking about buying a summer house. I don't know how I can manage that."

"For heaven's sake, Simon, you must put a stop to her wild sprees. She's bleeding you dry."

Simon stared into his coffee cup. He seemed to be debating with himself. When he spoke, his voice was very quiet. "I'm afraid of losing her," he said. "I love her. I'm such an ordinary kind of fellow. But she's *beautiful*. Rose is the most beautiful girl in the world!"

"And the most extravagant. Look here, I'm not telling you to stop buying her gifts. You must make the gifts more . . . modest."

"Yes. Yes, I've thought of that myself. It's hard. Her friend Amanda has so much. It's hard to deny Rose."

"Where have I heard those words before?" Harley sat back, sipping his drink. "Well, how can I help you?" he asked. "I'll be happy to lend you money if—"

"Oh no, Harley." Simon shook his head earnestly. He blushed. "I couldn't possibly take money from you. It's kind of you to offer, but I couldn't do that. I was wondering about the stock market. I have my trust income, and Mother is willing to advance me money for investment purposes . . . I hear that fortunes are being made in the market these days."

"It's true the market is rising. It's a good time to go in, provided you're careful. Some brokers disagree, but I have never believed in risking more than you can afford to lose. It's gambling, after all."

"Could you . . . perhaps tell me the names of a few stocks I might buy? I know it is a lot to ask. . . ."

Harley looked into Simon's wide, puppy dog eyes and he smiled. "Not at all," he said. "But there's a better way of going about this. You should have a broker assess your situation and then make recommendations. I'm out of that business, as you know. Your executors might want to put you in touch with a reliable broker."

"I'm afraid my executors don't think much of my business sense. They treat me like a child, Harley. I asked them about brokers and they put me off. I would prefer not to use Father's brokers."

"Well, it's easily solved. I'll have my broker telephone you in the morning. He's with Rutherford & Day, my old company. He's a good man. Careful but not too careful."

"I would be very grateful. Thank you."

"Then it's settled. Although I must warn you again, Simon . . . even if you do well in the market, you can't hope to keep up with Rose's sprees. You can't go on spending more money than you have in income. It will never balance out."

Simon nodded. "I shall try to be firm," he said. He turned his head and stared across the room at Rose. "But she is so *beautiful.*"

The opening night party at Club Harley continued into the wee hours. All the rooms were filled to capacity and departing guests were quickly replaced by new arrivals. "You got yourself a good speak, kid," Harley's bootlegger said to him late that evening. "You got the right crowd. All the swells. For them, the best booze only."

"I'll remember that." Harley laughed, going back to his table. Mary was alone at the table, drinking a cup of tea. "Had enough champagne?" he asked.

"Quite enough."

"I saw Ma before she left, but what happened to Elsie?"

"Oh, she had to go too. Her train leaves for South Carolina in just a few hours."

"I forgot about that. Preston Sinclair's funeral."

"Yes. She's going to stay with Mrs. Sinclair for a while. There's apparently a lot to be done. And you know Elsie."

"It's nice of her to take the time and trouble."

"Well, that's Elsie." Mary's tone was light, though inside she ached. Has it come to this, she wondered tiredly. Are we reduced to mumbling inanities at each other? My God, what's happened to our marriage! "Harley, are you going to be here much longer?"

"I don't know. Until closing."

"When is closing?"

"There's no definite time. Are you in a hurry?"

"It's very late. Or very early"—Mary smiled—"depending on how you look at it. Don't these people have homes to go to?"

"A night on the town isn't going to hurt anyone, Mary. It might even do some good. You enjoyed yourself tonight. Admit it. I saw you laughing and chattering away. Isn't it nice just to have fun once in a while? The one thing I can say for Rose, perhaps the only thing, is that she knows how to have fun."

A sharp rejoinder came to Mary's lips. It died there, for she knew she had to be careful with Harley. With the tensions between them as real as they were, a wrong word could lead to other wrong words, *divorce* among them. She could not bear the thought of that. "You're right, Harley," she said. "I suppose I'm a little tired. I'm not as young as I used to be."

Harley looked at Mary, really looked at her, and his eyes softened. "But you're more beautiful now than you ever were. Years ago there was the promise of beauty. Now . . ." He fumbled for a cigarette. He lit it with the gold lighter Mary had given him and then leaned back, smiling. "You had the eye of every man here."

"They were looking at Rose. I just happened to be in the way."

"Of course they looked at Rose. Anyone wearing the crown jewels is going to be looked at. The looks you got were different. They were quite naughty."

"Is that so?" Mary laughed, though she was delighted by Harley's unexpected compliment. Her cheeks were pink and her eyes glowed. "I'm flattered," she said.

Harley reached his hand toward hers but, suddenly, as if he had changed his mind, he pulled it back. He stood. "I have some things to do downstairs," he shrugged. "The last show is about to start. Would you like to see it?"

"All right," Mary sighed. "Why not?"

"I apologize for being late," Mary said, sitting in a chair across from her attorney, young Philip Claymore, Jr. "As you know, I had rather a late night."

"Yes, indeed. It was past one when my wife and I arrived home. We had a most wonderful time at Club Harley. We were seated just next to Judge Drew. A charming man, I'm happy to say. Not at all the same man he is in a courtroom."

"I'm sorry your father wasn't there, Philip."

"He wanted to be. His doctors are very strict with him, however. He must get his rest and avoid all alcohol. That would probably be good advice for all of us . . . although I confess Father doesn't like it one bit."

Mary opened her purse. She took out a small leather-bound book and consulted her notes. "Have you had a chance to review the purchase agreement on the Madison Avenue property?"

"It's in order. It carries a heavy tax assessment,

Mary. Are you aware of that?"

"I am. It doesn't change my mind. That property will cost me money for a while, but eventually it will be worth a fortune. It's not for me, Philip. It's for my sons."

"Yes, as a long term investment it's sound. There are papers for you to sign. And while you're here, you might as well sign the papers on the new delivery trucks." Philip picked up one of several file folders on his desk. He looked at the tab and then gave it to Mary. "Those are the property agreements. My secretary has the truck agreements. Excuse me," he said, rising. "I won't be a moment."

"No hurry."

The room in which Mary sat was large and wood-paneled, with tufted leather chairs and English hunting prints on the walls. The lamps were polished brass. An antique carpet decorated the floor. It was a comfortable room and Mary liked it. She relaxed, settling back as she opened the file. She signed the first two documents, but when she came to the third, she frowned. It was, she saw, a list of properties belonging to Harley. She recognized all the addresses save one.

"Here we are," Philip said, returning to the room. He held out a sheaf of papers. "I need your signature on each copy."

"Just a minute, Philip. I found this list . . . but what is this address on Forty-eighth Street? That's a residential street, isn't it? When did Harley buy a residential property?"

Philip took the list from Mary. "Obviously this was misfiled," he sighed. "I apologize. You have my word such a mistake will not happen again."

"But what is that property, Philip?"

"It's not familiar to me. Perhaps it's something my father handled. No doubt the property has already been resold." He sat down, putting the list in the top drawer of his desk. "I know you're anxious to return to your office. If you will sign those papers, we will be finished for today."

Mary looked at Philip. He was a calm, pleasant man of twenty-seven, a Yale graduate known for his brilliance in contract law. She had never seen him flustered, in or out of a courtroom, yet he was flustered now. There was a faint blush of color in his cheeks. His hands moved too quickly across his desk. His glance was too carefully averted. Mary said nothing more about the property. She signed each paper and when she was done, she closed the file. "Is that all?" she asked.

"For now. Although I advise you to keep your pen handy. Next week we will have the distribution agreements for you to sign."

"So soon?"

"There is no reason to delay. The stores in New Jersey and Pennsylvania are anxious to stock your Roly-Poly cakes. And all the arrangements have been made. Why delay?"

"You're right, of course." Mary stood up. Philip stood also. He came around the side of his desk and helped Mary into her coat. "Thank you." She smiled. "I will see you next week. . . . Oh, I will be bringing Jane Malloy with me. Elsie has been training her in company procedures, but I think it's time she had some first-hand experience with contracts."

"Then I take it you are still planning to make her your assistant?"

"When Elsie retires, yes. I take it you still object

to that?"

"I'm afraid I must. I'm your attorney, Mary. I am obligated to give you the best counsel I can. It's not personal. I consider Jane to be a fine young woman. Kilburne Bakeries, however, is no longer a small family company. Once the distribution plans are completed, it will be a national company. You will need a well-trained business mind to assist you."

"By that, you mean a man?"

"Men are surely more reliable. They don't leave to . . . raise families."

"Philip." Mary laughed. "May I remind you that Kilburne Bakeries was built by a woman?"

"You are exceptional. But let us put gender aside for a moment. Let us consider business only. Because business is vastly more complicated now than it was even five years ago. It's becoming more complicated every day. If Kilburne Bakeries is to grow it must have sound business thinking behind it. Certainly if you propose to make a stock offering—"

"No! That I will never do! I didn't work day and night to wind up beholden to a group of stockholders. Kilburne Bakeries will remain a privately owned company. I began the business for my family, Philip. It will remain in family hands."

"Well, we have had this argument before."

"As many times as we may have it in the future, the outcome will be the same. It's a *family* company."

"Consider the position of the banks. You will be facing major expansion in a few years. You will need funds. Do you suppose banks will lend money to a company run entirely by women? It is out of the question!"

Again, Mary laughed. "I am only too aware of the

problems in that regard," she said. "I'll deal with them when the time comes. Don't misunderstand me, Philip. I'm not closing the company to outsiders. Quite the contrary. Now that we're going into distribution, I intend to begin an executive training program. There will be a great many men in important positions."

"I hope that includes the position of your assistant."

"No. I know exactly what I want in an assistant. Someone smart and practical and hard-working. Above all, I want someone I can trust. That person is Jane."

"There are any number of trustworthy young men around."

"Any one of whom would, sooner or later, try to maneuver me out and take over. No thank you, Philip. . . . I learned a few things from Mr. Basset. I learned to protect what's mine."

"I can't quarrel with that. But you put it in the wrong light."

"I don't think so. I've made up my mind. You know how I am when I've made up my mind."

"And you know I'll continue to urge you to change your mind."

"That's fair." Mary smiled. "Now I really must be going. Goodbye, Philip. Don't bother to see me out."

Mary walked through the paneled outer offices to the elevator. The ride downstairs was brief and, once outside, she immediately hailed a taxi. She gave the driver the address of her office. Moments later she leaned forward, giving him an address on Forty-eighth Street instead. She tried to tell herself it was simple curiosity; in her heart she knew it was more than that.

Fifteen

"Here it is, lady," the driver said, bringing his taxi to a halt outside a handsome old brownstone building.

"Thank you." Mary stared at the building. It appeared to be a private residence, neat and well kept, with pleated silk curtains at the tall windows. There was nothing unusual about it, nothing out of the ordinary. "Thank you. But you can take me to the other address now."

"You're not getting out?"

"No. I would like the other address please."

"Okay." The driver shrugged, tugging his cap lower on his forehead. "It's your money."

The taxi began to move again. Mary sat back. She looked at her watch. She tried to concentrate on work, on the day's appointment schedule, but her mind was irresistibly drawn to the brownstone. "Wait!" she cried. "I've . . . I've changed my mind. I'll get out here."

Amidst a screeching of brakes, the driver stopped his taxi once more. "You're wearing down my tires, lady."

"I'm sorry." Mary opened her purse. She found a ten-dollar bill and thrust it at the glowering driver. "I'm sorry," she said again, stepping onto the curb.

Mary took a few steps in the direction of the

brownstone and then stopped. She gave herself many reasons to turn away. They were good reasons, for they had to do with trust and loyalty and seventeen years of marriage. But even as she considered them, her legs were carrying her forward. She felt the sudden racing of her heart, the quickening of her breath.

There was an unmarked mail slot in the door. The bell was also unmarked. Mary lifted her hand to the bell. She hesitated, wondering what she might say to the person who answered. She hesitated a while longer and then pressed the bell.

"Good morning, ma'am." A young maid, wearing a plain black uniform and white cap, stood in the doorway. She smiled politely at Mary. "May I help you, ma'am?"

"I . . . I was wondering if you could tell me the . . ." Mary did not finish, for she was staring at a small boy of four or five. He had run into the hallway, clutching a teddy bear under his arm, and Mary gasped as he came closer. There was no mistake; the child was the very image of Harley. "My God," she said.

"What is it, ma'am?" the maid asked. "Can I help you? Are you here to see someone? . . . Maybe you have the wrong house. They look a lot alike on this street. Maybe you want the house next door."

Mary fought her mounting anxiety. She searched desperately for an answer, any answer but the obvious one. She stared so hard at the child that he stepped back in alarm, hiding behind the maid.

"Ma'am, I have my work to do. I'll have to ask you to leave . . . Ma'am? Did you hear me?"

Mary was staring past the maid to a young blond woman at the end of the hall. She recognized her right away, for the young woman was Sally Hanson, Harley's former secretary. "Hello, Sally," Mary said when she was able to speak. "I think we had better talk."

Sally Hanson was twenty-four years old, the daughter of a Kansas wheat farmer. She had come to New York to be an actress, but so had many other girls, girls prettier and more talented than she. It had not taken her long to realize how poor her chances were. She found work as a secretary, first at an insurance company, then at Rutherford & Day.

Now Sally took a deep breath and walked toward Mary. She was tense, the color gone from her face. When she turned to speak to the maid, her voice was barely above a whisper. "Take Spencer to his room, Helen," she said. "See he stays there. We won't want to be disturbed."

"Yes, ma'am. Come on, Spencer. Let's go upstairs and look at your new picture book."

Mary watched the child as he walked away. When he reached the stairs he paused, staring at her over his shoulder. After a moment he smiled. It was a charming smile, Harley's smile. "I . . . would like to sit down," Mary said to Sally.

"Yes, of course." Sally opened the door to the parlor. She stepped back, allowing Mary to pass. "May I take your coat?"

"No, I feel a bit chilly." Mary sat down. She put her purse and gloves in her lap and looked at Sally. "Spencer is a fine boy."

"Thank you."

"He's the picture of his father."

Sally sank into a chair. Her narrow shoulders rose

and fell in a sigh. "I don't know what to say, Mrs. Kilburne. I'm sorry you had to . . . This is a painful situation for both of us."

"How old is Spencer?"

"He'll be four next month."

"Four. You and my husband have been . . . close . . . for a long time."

"I love Harley. I can't apologize for that."

"You have no *right* to love Harley. *No right.*" Mary put her hand to her forehead. She closed her eyes, struggling against the pain she felt, the horror. She began to shiver and she pulled the collar of her coat up about her neck. "How dare you speak of love?"

"It's true, Mrs. Kilburne . . . I didn't plan it. I never wanted anyone to get hurt."

"It's a little late to think about that now, isn't it?"

"I think about that all the time," Sally replied quietly. "Please try to understand. He was always so kind, so funny. I was all alone in New York. I was lonely. And I guess Harley was lonely too, in a way. . . . It just happened."

Mary studied the young woman who sat across from her. She was not beautiful, nor even very pretty. Her features were plain. Her wavy blond hair was cut short, in the new fashion, and ill became her square face. Yet there was a sweetness about her. It was in her soft blue eyes, in the set of her mouth. She wore a simple dress of navy blue wool. A cameo brooch was her only jewelry. "I suppose you expected to marry Harley," Mary said.

"No. I knew from the beginning that was impossible. Harley told me he would never leave his wife and children."

"But surely when Spencer was born . . ."

364

"Harley told me he would never leave you, Mrs. Kilburne. I accepted that. Spencer sees his father often. He doesn't know the difference. He's a happy child. He's loved. It's enough."

Mary's hands were icy. She rubbed them together, glancing around the room. It was small and cozy with a fireplace and overstuffed armchairs and footstools and little porcelain ornaments upon the tables. A lop-eared toy rabbit perched on the window seat and when Mary saw it her heart contracted. "So you are content to live in the shadows," she said, as much in pity as in anger.

"I make no demands on Harley."

"A child is a demand. Spencer is a demand."

Color stained Sally's fair skin. Her mouth quivered slightly but her gaze was steady. "I make no apologies for my son, Mrs. Kilburne. He's a wonderful little boy and I love him. I don't use him to hold on to Harley."

"The result is the same."

"When Harley's here, he's here by choice. It hurts you, but that's the truth."

"What do you know of truth?" Mary cried. "Harley is *my* husband. *That's* the truth."

"I have only a small part of Harley's life, the part he is willing to give me. I accept what he is willing to give, Mrs. Kilburne. I live from day to day. I expect no more than what I have."

"Very noble talk . . . coming from an adulteress."

"Mary, don't."

Mary turned and saw Harley framed in the doorway. His face was ashen, his eyes filled with pain. "What brings you here?" she asked. "Or have you been here all along?"

"Philip telephoned me. He said you . . . I'm sorry,

Mary. I'm truly sorry. I never wanted to hurt you. You must believe that."

"Must I?" Tears streaked her face. She was crying, then sobbing, beating her clenched hands against her knees. Harley went to comfort her, but she turned away. "Don't touch me," she sobbed.

Harley looked at Sally. She was sitting at the edge of her chair. Her body was rigid, unmoving. She had brightened at the sight of Harley, a wholly unexpected radiance coming into her expression. Her lips had parted in a great and shining smile but then, remembering the circumstances, her smile had disappeared. "Sally . . . please leave us," he said softly.

She rose. She stared at Harley for a long moment and then ran out of the room.

Harley knelt at Mary's side. "Please listen to me. Let me explain."

"There's nothing to explain," Mary said through her tears. "It's clear . . . it's finally clear. I suspected . . . but I never wanted to believe. . . . Oh, God. Oh, God."

"Mary, you must—"

"Don't talk to me. There's nothing . . . to say." Mary's head throbbed. Her heart was beating so fast she thought it would explode. Worst of all was the cold, a terrible cold she felt in every part of her body. "So many years, Harley. So many years and you threw them away. *Why?*"

"I . . . just wanted to be loved."

"Loved? I loved you."

"In your way, yes. As a friend, a companion . . . you never loved me as a man. I waited. I hoped. My God, Mary, I prayed you would love me one day. But you never did. And every day I died a little more. I couldn't stand it. You're the only woman I ever really wanted. I *ached* for you. I still ache. I know what it is to have you in my arms, but I don't know what it is to have your love. I'll never know that."

"You're wrong, Harley. I tried to tell you—"

"I'm not wrong." Harley stood up. He walked across the room, shaking his head. "There are many ways to commit adultery, Mary. The thought's as bad as the act. Maybe it's worse."

"I never—"

"Mary, do you remember our wedding night?"

"Of course I remember."

"That was the happiest night of my life. I woke up early the next morning just to look at you, to watch you sleep. In your sleep you spoke Dan's name. His name, nothing more. But in all the years of our marriage I've never heard you speak my name that way."

Mary's sobs began again. They were quieter now and infinitely sadder, for they came from the depths of her soul. "I'm sorry, Harley. I'm sorry. But that was so long ago. It was a lifetime ago."

"I remember a day in 1916. War had been declared that day. You seemed so worried that I might be drafted. I remember being surprised. I began to think maybe you *did* love me. For one glorious moment I let myself believe it . . . then you told me you had seen Dan at his construction site."

"Yes. But I didn't stop to talk to him. I went on my way. I don't understand," Mary said, her stricken eyes searching Harley's face. "I don't understand."

"I know you, Mary. You didn't stop because you were afraid to stop. You were afraid of what might happen if the two of you met again. You can't deny it."

Mary did not try to deny it, for in fact she had never understood her behavior on that day. She had not wanted to think about it and so had put it out of her mind. She had put a lot of things out of her mind during the course of her marriage. Now she realized she had been wrong.

"I see you have no answer," Harley said.

Mary dried her eyes. Wearily, she leaned her head against the back of the chair. "What's the use? It doesn't matter anymore. There are too many misunderstandings between us, too many hurts. And now there's Sally. . . . Do you love her?"

"She loves me."

"That's not what I asked."

"Mary, I needed someone."

"Do you love her?"

"I care for her. I care about her. In a strange kind of way, I think she saved my life."

"I saw your son. He's a fine boy."

"Yes, he really is. I have many regrets, but Spencer isn't among them. He's a joy, very like Oliver in nature."

"What are you doing for him?"

"Doing?"

"You can't let him go through life a bastard."

"Mary!"

"I didn't invent the word. Nor did I invent the world that takes such glee in using it. He'll be scorned, Harley. At the very least he'll be excluded from circles that are rightfully his. Have you thought about that?"

"Certainly I have. The situation is far from ideal . . . but times are changing. And he's a sturdy little fellow. He'll make a good life for himself, regardless of his parents' mistakes."

"Will he forgive his parents' mistakes?"

"I can only hope he will."

"You must do more than that, Harley."

"I've taken steps to secure Spencer's future. I established a trust fund for him, just as I did for our boys. He'll have good schools. He'll have everything he needs and—"

"He *needs* your name."

"That's the one thing I can't give him."

"But you can."

A shadow fell across Harley's face. He sat down, for suddenly his legs were weak. "What are you saying, Mary?"

"I'm going to file for divorce."

There was a wild roaring in Harley's ears, a sharp and searing pain in his chest. He held out his hand, as if in supplication, then dropped it limply to his side. The room seemed to darken, to tilt. "Well," he said after long moments had passed, "I suppose that's what you always wanted."

"No," Mary cried. "You're wrong, so wrong. I wish I could . . ." She left her chair, walking aimlessly about the room, stopping finally at the fireplace. She ran her hands over the smooth, hard stone. "There's no point in going on with this, Harley. What's past is past. It's done. We have to go on from here, from today. . . . The only way I know is to get a divorce."

"Divorce," Harley murmured. The word was like a knife, ripping at him and making him bleed. He pressed the palms of his hands together. The roaring in his ears grew worse. "Divorce," he murmured again.

"I'll . . . I'll have your things packed and sent here."

"Yes."

Mary was shivering with cold. She had never felt such cold before and she knew it came not from the room but from within herself. She huddled miserably inside her coat, cursing the twist of fate that had brought her to this house.

Harley watched her. When he could watch no longer, he went to a window and clenched his hands on the sill, staring blindly at the street beyond. Tears rolled down his face unchecked.

"You are sick, Mrs. Kilburne?" Greta asked when Mary arrived home. "It is the weather. So changing from day to day. Everybody is sick."

"I'm fine. A little tired, that's all. I decided to give myself the afternoon off."

Greta was not convinced. She saw Mary's red and swollen eyes, her trembling hands, and she frowned. "Let me help you with your things," she said, taking Mary's hat and coat and gloves. "Then I will get you a cup of hot tea."

"No, thank you. I'm going to lie down for a while. If anyone telephones, I'm not here."

"Wait, Mrs. Kilburne. There is a surprise. Johnnie is home. I came in from the shopping and he was here. He brought with him all his luggage."

"Where is he now?" Mary asked.

"In his room. He has not eaten. I asked him, but he says no. He says 'go away, Greta.' So I go away."

Mary sighed. "That sounds like Johnnie. I'd better go see what's happened. Thank you, Greta." Mary hurried through the hall to Johnnie's room. She knocked on the door. "Johnnie? It's Mother. May I come in?"

"Sure." Johnnie stood as Mary entered the room. "Hello, Mother," he said. "I didn't expect to see you so soon again."

"Why aren't you at school? What's happened?"

"I've been booted out," Johnnie replied calmly.

Mary stared at her son. He was sixteen years old, tall for his age, with dark brown hair and odd blue-green eyes. He had the stubborn Kilburne chin. "Why were you booted out?" she asked.

Johnnie shrugged his broad shoulders. "My behavior displeased Dr. Purdy. As a matter of fact, he called me a barbarian." Johnnie turned to his desk and took from it a white envelope engraved with the Greenvale School emblem. "Dr. Purdy wrote this letter to you and Father. Would you like to see it?"

Mary took the letter, though she did not open it. "I would like to hear your explanation first. What did you do?"

"Why do you assume I did anything? Why do you assume I'm always in the wrong?" Johnnie's voice was calm, tinged with the impertinence that was, by now, familiar. "It's hardly fair."

"I asked for your explanation. You must have done something to make Dr. Purdy call you a barbarian."

"Dr. Purdy is an old fool."

"Mind your tongue, Johnnie."

"But it's true. They should have retired him long ago. He's useless. Everyone knows he is. Parents like him for his fine manners. But the fellows—"

"Never mind that. I've had a very bad day, Johnnie. Let's get to the point. What did you do?"

"There was a fight. I won it. Dr. Purdy didn't care for my . . . methods. I'm sure it's all in the letter, along with my many other sins."

Mary sat in a chair by the window. She opened the letter, scanning the first two paragraphs, reading the third: "I regret to say that Johnnie displayed neither compassion nor sportsmanship. Even as his opponent lay on the ground, soundly defeated, Johnnie continued to beat him about the head and shoulders. Greenvale School cannot tolerate such barbarous actions." There was more, but Mary knew all she had to know. She looked at Johnnie. "Is this true?"

"That I thrashed Ronnie Fenwick? Yes."

"Why?"

"He said he was going to invite Elizabeth Bradford to the Snow Carnival."

"And?"

"*I* was going to invite her to the Carnival."

"And?"

"I told Fenwick to forget about her. I told him to invite someone else. He refused. I gave him a second chance. He refused again. So I punched him on the nose."

"*And?* Johnnie, get to the point."

"Well, he's no fighter. I had him down in no time at all. But he kept getting up. So when he went down again, I made sure he stayed down. Old Fenwick's going to need a new nose."

"You are proud of that?"

Johnnie smiled slightly. "I gave him fair warning. He persisted. He got only what he deserved."

"I see." Mary was quiet for a moment. She looked out of the window, rubbing her tired eyes. "You might have seriously hurt that boy. Did you give any thought at all to the possibility?"

"I'm good with my hands, Mother. I know what I'm doing. It wasn't my first fight."

"How well I know . . . I'm going to do everything I can to see it's your last. Starting with your punishment. It won't be a token punishment this time, Johnnie. Sit down."

"I'll stand, thank you."

"Sit down!"

"As you wish."

"Your monthly allowance is going to be reduced by a third. There will be no trip during the spring vacation. And there will be no car for your birthday. Is that all quite clear?"

"It's clear." Johnnie crossed his long legs. He examined the tips of his polished shoes with great interest and then looked at his mother. "It's clear, but I don't accept it. We'll see what Father has to say. He's a man. He understands these things. You are only a woman."

"I'm your mother and you will accept whatever I say."

"I'm sorry, but I won't. When Father comes home—"

"He's not coming home!" Mary winced. She glanced away, silently berating herself for speaking so hastily. She had not meant to discuss this with Johnnie, not yet. Now, she realized, she would have no choice. "You will accept the punishments I named. That's the end of it."

"Why isn't Father coming home? Where is he?"

"Very well, Johnnie. You'll have to know sooner or later. The truth is . . . your father and I have decided to . . . separate. He isn't going to live here anymore."

"Really?" Johnnie sat up straight. His mouth seemed to tighten, but only for a second. "Well, I'm not surprised," he said. "You never had time for Father, or for us. You made time for Rose . . . and for your precious business. But not for us."

Mary was not hurt by Johnnie's accusations: she had heard them too often before, usually when he was in trouble and searching for excuses. "You're very young, Johnnie," she said quietly. "There are many things you don't understand. Nor do you try to understand. You make yourself judge and juror of the world. Time will cure that. You'll learn that nothing is as simple as you think."

"You were never home."

"That's only half the story. You conveniently forget the other half, which is that I always took my children with me to the shops. I took you too, in the beginning. Until you suddenly decided you didn't want to go. *You* decided you'd rather stay home. That wasn't my fault."

"Actually, it was Rose's fault."

"What has Rose to do with it?"

"Did you know that Rose never liked me, Mother?"

"I knew the two of you didn't get along . . . I still don't see what she has to do with anything."

Johnnie's eyes flashed angrily. His mouth became very pale and for an instant he looked like Bob Kilburne. "Rose was always threatening me."

"Why didn't you tell me, Johnnie? I would have put a stop to it."

"I couldn't tell you. I was afraid of you."

"Afraid? But why?"

"Rose said you didn't want me around. She said if I

was bad you'd bake me in a pie."

"*What?*"

"That's what she said. I was little, three or four. I believed her."

Mary did not know what to think. She looked hard at Johnnie, looking for any trace of a smile. "Are you joking?"

"No. It's the truth. She said it all the time."

"I . . . I'm so sorry, Johnnie. I had no idea. I suppose she was jealous of you. Rose was the center of attention until you came along. She hated the fuss we made over you. But I never dreamed . . . How awful for you, Johnnie."

"My whole childhood was awful. I blame you."

Johnnie had spoken flatly, without any emotion at all, and that made his words the more horrible. It was as if he had said them many times in the past, not aloud but to himself.

A great coldness came upon Mary again. She shivered, staring at her son. "I'm sorry you felt that way, Johnnie. I know I wasn't a perfect mother, but I did my best. Perhaps when you're older you will be more forgiving."

"What's so wonderful about being older? You're older, Mother. It hasn't done you much good. You don't even have a husband anymore."

"That's enough! I warn you, not another word!" Mary stood, turning her back on Johnnie as she paced his room. His suitcases were stacked neatly in the corner. The few papers on his desk were neatly arranged, as were all the books on the shelves. There was not a single wrinkle in his bedspread and she knew, if she opened his closets, she would find not a single wrinkle in anything he owned. That was Johnnie, she thought, a young man of neat and solitary habits. While Oliver had been out, playing baseball and football and getting dirty, Johnnie had been alone in this room, working on his stamp collection. Oliver had dozens of friends; Johnnie had his stamps and his coins and his books. "You must go back to Greenvale," Mary said finally. "We sent you there for a reason. We hoped the school would broaden your outlook. We hoped you would learn to enjoy the company of other young people. You were starting to make some progress, Johnnie . . . you must go back."

"Are you forgetting about Dr. Purdy?"

"I'll handle Dr. Purdy. As for you, you're to write two letters of apology. Right now."

"To whom, Mother? If I may ask."

"To Dr. Purdy and the Fenwick boy, of course. You shouldn't have any difficulty writing the letters. They're deserved."

"I won't grovel, Mother."

"Apologizing is not groveling."

"It's a waste of time. There are other schools. I don't need Greenvale."

"You don't need a black mark against your name either. That's what expulsion will mean. It won't help when the time comes for college."

Johnnie's mouth curved upward in a small smile. "Is college so important, Mother? After all, I am heir to Club Harley. I'm heir to Roly-Poly cakes. Why, I could be king of Roly-Poly cakes."

"I'm in no mood for your sarcasm, Johnnie. Begin those letters *now*. I'll telephone Dr. Purdy."

It took Mary more than an hour to reach Dr. Purdy,

but less than fifteen minutes to convince him to change his mind. Once convinced, he became the gracious headmaster again, discussing Johnnie as he would an errant son. He promised to pay closer attention to him, to help him "find his way." Mary was properly grateful. She listened to Dr. Purdy drone on and on. When the conversation came to an end, she was relieved.

"Well," she said, returning to Johnnie's room, "the Fenwick boy is all right, thank God. And you may take the morning train back to Greenvale."

"Just like that?"

"Not quite. I'm donating a new chemistry lab to the school. Dr. Purdy is not the fool you think he is . . . have you finished the letters?"

"Here they are, Mother."

Mary read the letters carefully. She tore them up and threw the pieces into the wastebasket. "Do them again," she said. "This time without the patronizing tone."

"That's in your imagination."

"Johnnie, you'd best get over the idea that you're superior to everyone else. You're not. You have a quick mind. You have intelligence. But so do many other boys. Don't be smug."

"I'm sorry if I offend you, Mother."

"You're not sorry in the least. It's never *occurred* to you to be sorry about anything."

"What good does it do?"

Mary frowned. "That's a strange question," she said. "Have you an answer?"

"Several. But I'm afraid you must find your own answers. There are standards of right and wrong, Johnnie. You must find them. Use them as a measure."

"That's too oblique for me."

"Oh, I don't think so. It's a convenient excuse. You're good at convenient excuses." Mary looked away. She thought: In that way, you're like Rose. You take no responsibility for yourself. You take no blame. Poor Johnnie, you're smarter than Rose, but no wiser. "Finish those letters," she said. "I want to see them before dinner."

"Mother? The punishments you mentioned . . . if I am to return to Greenvale, I see no reason for them."

"But I do. The punishments weren't for being expelled. They were for fighting, for hitting a boy when he was unable to defend himself. My God, don't you understand that's *wrong?*"

"It's a subject for men. I still want to speak to Father."

"You will, don't worry. I'll telephone him later. I'm sure he'll want to read Dr. Purdy's letter for himself. The punishments, however, stand. *If* you behave yourself for the remainder of the school term, I'll consider restoring your full allowance. But no trip and no car. That's final."

"That's not fair."

"*Life's* not fair. If you learn nothing else, learn that."

Mary left Johnnie's room and went to her own. A fire crackled by the hearth and she sat by it, trying to warm her icy hands. She watched the flames dance behind the screen, vivid streaks of gold and red and blue. She reached to a side table and poured a brandy, drinking it quickly. It burned but did not warm.

Mary put a sweater on over her wool dress. She tucked her arms into the sleeves and sat again by the fire. As a small child, she had always been able to imagine pictures, shapes and forms and faces, in the leaping of the flames. She did so now, though the pictures she saw were not the pretty and fanciful images of childhood, but the images of a life in ruins, her life.

There was a knock at the door and Mary started. "Yes?" she called.

"It is Greta, Mrs. Kilburne."

"Yes, Greta. Come in."

The door opened. Greta poked her head inside. "There is Mrs. Sinclair on the telephone. It is the long distance."

"Mrs. Sinclair?" Mary jumped up. Anxiety swept over her, clutching at her heart, for she knew it must be bad news. She ran past Greta into the hall. She ran to the study and with shaking hands lifted the receiver. She heard Cynthia Sinclair's voice. "I'm so sorry to tell you this, Mary," she was saying, "but Elsie is dead. . . . She collapsed on the train. There was nothing anyone could do . . . I'm so sorry, Mary."

The funeral was in a beautiful old cemetery fifty miles outside of New York City. Many people were in attendance, including all the employees of Kilburne Bakeries. Flowers were everywhere, in wreaths and sprays and baskets. A blanket of red roses covered Elsie's bronze casket. Chairs had been set out and Mary sat in the front row, Harley on one side, Anna on the other. A minister was speaking, but Mary did not hear him. She sat and stared at the casket, dry-eyed, for she had no more tears left to shed.

When the minister finished speaking, Father Malone stood up to read from the Bible. His voice lifted and soared. It was a kind of music, music Mary remembered from a day so many years before, the day her father's body had been dropped into the sea. Where has all the time gone, she asked herself, wringing her cold hands. She looked at Father Malone and saw the gray at his temples, the lines bracketing his eyes. For the first time she noticed that he was not young anymore. The thought oppressed her like a great weight.

"Elsie is with God," Father Malone said to Mary when the service was over. He put his arm around her shoulder, just as he had on that long ago day, and smiled kindly. "I'm thinking she'll have her own ideas about the way Heaven should be run. Can't you hear her now?"

Mary smiled back at the priest. "I believe I can."

Father Malone stared into Mary's sad dark eyes. "Harley told me about your troubles," he said. "It's sorry I am. I'm praying for you. And if I can be helping you, if you need to talk, you know where I am."

"Thank you, Father." Mary's smile faded. She shook her head. "There's no help for me anywhere . . . I've made too many mistakes."

"Ah, but we've all made mistakes. That's what life's all about. God forgives us our mistakes, Mary. If He can forgive us, you can forgive yourself. It's not so hard. Search your heart. The answers are there."

"Perhaps."

"I'll be on my way now, Mary. There's a dance in the parish hall later and I'm chaperone. Come see me. We'll have a good talk."

"Yes, Father. Thank you. Have you a ride back?"

"Ah, Mrs. Sinclair sent a car for me and the Reverend Matthews. We're riding in fine style." Father

Malone kissed Mary's cheek. "Goodbye, child."

"Goodbye."

Harley came forward then. Simon was with him, pale and drawn, his wide gray eyes misty. "My sympathies," he said. "We will all miss Elsie."

"It was kind of you to come, Simon. I see Rose did not bother."

"Funerals upset her so . . . and there was the baby to consider. The doctor said Rose would not have an easy time. She thought it would be best to stay at home. For the baby's sake," he added quickly.

"Yes, I'm sure." Mary looked at Harley. She longed for the comfort of his arms, his broad shoulders. The thought of being forever without that comfort brought a tightness to her throat. "I'm sorry for the way Jane treated you before, Harley," she said. "It's just that she was so surprised to hear about . . . us. She'll get over it. She loves you."

Harley laughed shortly. "I doubt anyone will get over it. God knows I won't."

"I must go. I'm riding back with Mrs. Sinclair. She's waiting for me."

"I'd hoped you would ride with me."

"No, I can't." Mary touched Harley's hand. "Goodbye," she said. "Goodbye, Simon."

She hurried away, stopping to take two roses from the blanket covering the casket, then proceeding to Cynthia Sinclair's limousine. The driver opened the door. Mary got in. "I thought you might like to have this," she said, holding out one of the roses.

"Thank you, Mary." Cynthia sat in the far corner of her limousine. She wore a simple black suit, a strand of pearls, and a black hat with a short, spotted black veil.

A jacket of dark sable was folded at her side. She had insisted on making the arrangements for the funeral and on paying for it though, at the last, she had not joined the other mourners. She had remained in the car, watching the service through the window. "You must think me a terrible coward." She sighed now. "But I have had enough of death and funerals."

"I understand. I was sorry to hear about Mr. Sinclair."

"Preston's illness was long and painful. Death, when it came, was a blessing to him . . . still, it was hard. And so soon after our other tragedy. Only last month, Reeve lost his wife and child in an automobile accident." Cynthia put a cigarette in an ivory holder and lit it. "I just couldn't stand another funeral, you see."

"Of course."

"I'm glad. I value your good opinion." Cynthia signaled her driver that she was ready to leave. The car pulled out and she settled back against the upholstered seat. There were signs of strain in her face, but her beauty was unchanged. Her hair, though shorter and sleeker now, was the same magnificent coppery color. Her complexion was as fresh and smooth as a girl's. "Elsie valued your opinion also. She wrote me such wonderful things about you. She was so proud of your success."

"I wouldn't have had any success without her. Or without you, for that matter."

"Well, we never know how things will work out. In your case, they worked out splendidly."

"Thank you, Mrs. Sinclair."

"After all these years you still insist on calling me

Mrs. Sinclair. Please call me Cynthia. I much prefer it."

Mary smiled, shaking her head. "I can't. I know it's foolish, but I can't. Old habits . . ."

"We're no longer servant and mistress. We're friends. I certainly hope we're friends. . . . There was always something special about you, Mary. In the beginning, I thought it was merely that your ways were different. After all, you had just arrived from England. But as time passed, I realized it was more than that, much more. You have kindness and courage both. It is a rare combination. One I admire." Cynthia stared straight ahead. Her face, in profile, was as still as marble. "I envy you your courage, Mary. Does that sound strange? I never had courage, you see. I often wondered what my life would have been like if . . . Heavens, I am rambling on and on! I apologize."

"There's no need. Sometimes it's helpful to talk. And I'm a good listener."

"Yes." Cynthia sighed. She turned very slightly, fixing her glance not on Mary, but on the car window. "I've spent most of the last six years at Lucy's Court," she said. "They were not . . . easy years. Now, that part of my life is over. I'm going away, to Europe. I've leased a house in London."

"But that's wonderful. A holiday!"

"It will be a long holiday. I don't know how long . . . that is what worries me. That is why I am going to ask your help."

"Anything at all."

"Well, it is the New York house. I love that house, Mary. It means a great deal to me. I plan to live in it when I return from London . . . but I must be certain that nothing . . . happens to it in my absence."

"Perhaps a caretaker—"

"I've engaged a caretaker. The problem is . . . well, Reeve is most anxious to have that property. He was furious when he learned Preston had left it to me. Reeve is an influential man. He has power. In my absence, he may be able to find some way to take possession. I can't bear the thought of that. . . . It's not the house, it's what the house means. It's all I have left of the old days."

"How can I help?"

"It is a lot to ask, Mary, but I will ask nevertheless. I would like you to . . . keep an eye on the house, as it were. If you could stop by each week . . . you need not stay long. Just long enough to make certain nothing *unusual* is happening."

"I'd be glad to do it, Mrs. Sinclair. I'm fond of that house myself."

Cynthia's relief was visible. She looked at Mary and smiled. "I was hoping you would say that. I have a set of keys for you. There are only two other sets. My attorneys have one, and the caretaker the other. Reeve may have his own keys. He swears not, but I'm unwilling to take his word. Should you see him there . . . should you see anyone there, you must wire me immediately."

"Of course."

"I'm so grateful to you, Mary. I know it seems mad to carry on about a house. But it's important to me."

"Don't worry. I'll see there is no . . . interference. Though I'm not anxious to run into Reeve."

"The caretaker is quite capable of handling Reeve. And I pay him well. You have no worry on that account." Cynthia opened her purse and removed a gold flask. "Very old, very good brandy," she explained. "May I offer you some?"

"I shouldn't. I'm going back to work."

Cynthia nodded. She took not a sip but a slug of brandy, then returned the flask to her purse. "Are you happy?" she asked suddenly, staring at Mary. "I am not making polite conversation. I would really like to know. I would like to know that someone is happy in this . . . odd world."

Mary did not even consider telling her troubles to Cynthia Sinclair. She rubbed her cold hands together and smiled. "Yes, I'm happy," she said.

Sixteen

It was an especially hot and humid August in New York. Each day rain was prophesied for the morrow, but rain did not come. The air became heavier, the sky duller, the heat more intense.

The terrible heat was a particular trial to Rose, for she was in her tenth hour of labor, struggling to give birth to the child she had never really wanted. Dr. Craig's nurse applied cold cloths to her streaming forehead, but angrily she flung them away. She thrashed about in her bed, staring wildly around the great pink and white bedroom and shrieking at every pain. She had never felt such pain before. Her lips were bitten bloody and the bed sheets, where she had clawed them, were in shreds. Curses spilled from her mouth. Her screams shook the house.

Downstairs, Simon paced the drawing room. His face was white, his eyes frantic with fear. When the doorbell rang he dashed into the hall, pushing past the butler to open the door. "Thank God you're here, Harley," he cried, nearly falling into his arms. "It's *horrible*. Rose has been screaming for *hours.*"

"Come, Simon," Harley said gently. "Let's get you a drink." He took Simon's arm and led him back to the drawing room. He poured two very large drinks. "Here, drink this. And try to calm down. Everything will be all right. Dr. Craig has delivered hundreds of babies."

"But Rose is so delicate. Dr. Craig said it wouldn't be easy for her. Oh, *God,*" he cried again as another earsplitting scream came from upstairs. "If she dies—"

"No one is going to die, Simon. Drink up. I insist."

Simon put the glass to his lips and drank. The scotch brought color to his face but it did not calm him. He continued to pace, stopping every few seconds to stare beseechingly at Harley. "What can I do?" he asked. "What can I do?"

"All you can do is wait. Babies come in their own time."

"I shall go mad! Rose is my whole life, Harley. If anything happens to her . . . I wanted to stay with her, but Dr. Craig wouldn't let me stay. He threw me out. He did. Threw me right out."

"That's not surprising," Harley smiled. "He has his hands full with Rose. Come now, sit down. That's a good fellow. Take a deep breath and try to relax. You'll need a doctor yourself, the way you're going."

"I can't help it. I have never been so afraid . . . not even in the war!"

"Tell me about the war, Simon. You've never spoken about it. You must have war stories. They will take your mind off other things."

"No, I never speak of it." Simon stared down at the floor, poking at the fringed carpet with his shoe. "It was an awful time. I killed people, you know. Germans. I had to do it. They had their guns trained on my men. But it was awful. I still have nightmares. . . ."

"You came through the war, Simon. You will come

through this."

"At least I was able to be of some help then. I was able to take action. Now I can only sit here and wait . . . while poor Rose is suffering so."

"Kilburne women are stronger than you think. Take my word for it."

"Oh," Simon looked up sharply. "Did you reach Mary? Rose will want her."

"I telephoned her in Chicago. She's taking the next train back. She wouldn't have gone, but Dr. Craig said the baby was two weeks off. She'll be here as soon as she can."

"Chicago? Did you say Chicago?"

"That's right." Harley laughed. He tipped his glass back and finished his drink. "Roly-Poly cakes are sweeping the country. Haven't you heard?"

"Yes, I remember now. Forgive me, Harley, but my mind isn't working tonight."

An agonized shriek came from the upstairs bedroom and Harley winced. He put his hand on Simon's shoulder, steadying him. "I'll freshen our drinks," he said.

Upstairs, Rose dug her fingers into the mattress and shrieked again, for she felt as if her body were being ripped in two. Her face was red, drenched in perspiration. Her hair was a tangled and wet mass of gold. *"Help me,"* she screamed over and over again.

"Push, Rose," Dr. Craig said. "I can see the baby's head. You must push . . . harder . . . bear down."

Rose's curses filled the room. Neither Dr. Craig nor his nurse paid any attention, for they had heard them all before.

But Harley was shaken by the sounds coming from upstairs. He glanced quickly at Simon. "She'll be all right," he said.

"I begged Rose to have the baby in a hospital. I *begged* her. But she refused. Amanda had all her children at home and Rose was determined to do the same. *God.*" Simon covered his face with his hands. "I shouldn't have allowed it. It's my fault. *God,* what have I done?"

"Stop that! Babies have been born at home for thousands of years. It's no easier in a hospital . . . everything is going to be all right, Simon. You must believe that."

"It's been so long. What's taking so long?"

"It won't be much longer." Harley spoke with more confidence than he felt. He remembered that Johnnie's birth had taken fifteen hours. Mary had not had a doctor or a nurse, only a midwife. Peter had been delivered by a midwife too, though Dr. Craig had delivered both Oliver and Edwin. They had been home births. Spencer, alone amongst his sons, had been born in a hospital. But, thought Harley, no matter where they were born and no matter who delivered them, it always took a long time. "Simon," he said now, hoping to distract him, "would you like a game of chess? Cards perhaps?"

"I couldn't concentrate. . . . I am just glad you're here, Harley. I am so grateful. You . . . are always helping me. At my age, I shouldn't need anyone's help. Should I?"

"Nonsense. We all need help from time to time. You stood by me through all . . . my trouble. You were one of the very few. And apart from Ma, you are the only one who treats Sally decently."

"Are you going to marry her?" Simon asked shyly.

"Yes, when the divorce is final. It's best for Spencer."

"He's such a nice little chap. . . . Did he take a very long time to be born?"

"About twelve hours."

"Twelve hours! It has already been ten hours for Rose. I hope she doesn't have to go through another two."

Harley picked up the scotch decanter and carried it across the room. It was a large room, though its graceful proportions were obscured by the expensive clutter with which Rose had filled it. There were silk couches, too narrow and formal to be comfortable, and antique chests, chairs, and tables. Every table was crowded with objects: French porcelains, enameled music boxes, ancient Chinese puzzle boxes. Bouquets of silk flowers sat in the many crystal vases. Harley cleared a space and put the decanter down. "There's no telling about these things," he said, "but I would guess we haven't much longer to wait."

They had, as it turned out, less than an hour to wait. Shortly before midnight, Rose's screams ceased and an exhausted Dr. Craig appeared at the door of the drawing room. "Congratulations, Simon," he smiled. "You have a healthy daughter."

"Rose? How is Rose?"

"She had some difficult moments, but she's fine."

"Well, Papa"—Harley grinned, shaking Simon's hand—"congratulations!"

"Rose is really all right, Dr. Craig?"

"Yes, she's fine."

"Thank God." Simon allowed himself to relax and, as he did, an enormous smile spread across his face. His color returned. His eyes lost their crazed gleam. "May I see her?" he asked.

"Certainly. You may come too, Harley, if you wish."

"Are you sure? It's so soon."

"I think Rose is ready for compliments, the more lavish the better. After all, she worked very hard indeed."

They found Rose sitting up in bed, her head resting on half-a-dozen ruffled pink pillows. She looked dazed but quite lovely, for her face had been bathed and her curls brushed into a golden halo atop her head. She wore a clean pink gown and, over it, a lacy bed jacket trimmed with pink ribbons.

"My darling," Simon cried, rushing to her.

Rose turned her head. She pulled the silk coverlet close about her sore and aching body. "A girl," she said, almost inaudibly. "Rosemary."

"That's a perfect name. Rosemary it is." Simon beamed, staring down at the woman he adored. "How do you feel, my darling? Was it . . . very bad?"

"Dreadful," Rose answered, memory fresh in her mind. "The most dreadful pain." She yawned. She saw Harley and she smiled vaguely. "Where is Mary?"

"She'll be here soon. Congratulations, Rose. You must be so happy."

Rose moved her head on the pillows. She did not reply. Simon followed her glance to the other side of the bed and there, in a ruffled and flounced bassinet, he saw his daughter.

"Miss Rosemary Ellsworth," the nurse announced, smiling. "Come meet your daughter, Mr. Ellsworth."

"Go on," Harley said when he saw Simon hesitate. "She won't bite. . . . Well, go on."

Simon took a few tentative steps and then ran around the side of the bed. He bent over the bassinet, peeking at his daughter. She was tiny and pink and wrinkled, with a wisp of fair hair and a sweet upturned mouth. "Why, she's beautiful," Simon gasped. "Beautiful. Look at her, Harley. She's beautiful."

Harley took his place at the bassinet. He smiled at the tiny baby girl. "Hello, Rosie," he said. And from that moment on she was Rosie, not Rosemary or Ro or Rose, just Rosie.

Hours later, Simon and Harley sat in the library drinking hundred-year-old brandy. Many toasts were made. There was much laughter, for suddenly everything seemed very funny. There was, in more mellow moments, an occasional tear. "It's been grand," Harley said as the first light of morning streaked the windows, "but now it's time I made my way home." He stretched his arms above his head. He stood. "Look at that, we went through a whole bottle of brandy."

"I think I'm drunk. Am I drunk?"

"Perhaps a little. When a man becomes a father he's entitled to get a little drunk."

"A father," Simon said, still awed by the idea. "I'm a *father*. I can't believe it."

"You'll believe it when the bills start rolling in. Children are the greatest joy of all, but keep your checkbook nearby. You'll need it."

"That's all right. I don't mind. I have my own money tree now. People say money doesn't grow on trees. They are wrong, Harley. It does grow on trees. And I have a tree of my own. The stock market, that's my tree. I need only shake the branches and money rains down. Piles and piles of money."

"You *are* drunk, Simon." Harley laughed.

"Do you think so? Yes, I suppose I am. I have never been drunk before. Never in my whole life. It's no wonder my executors treat me like a child . . . but that's all right too. I don't care. I have a beautiful wife and a beautiful child and a beautiful money tree."

Harley looked thoughtfully at Simon. "I hope that's just the brandy talking," he said. "Because there is *no* money tree, least of all in the stock market."

"But there is." Simon nodded. His wide gray eyes were earnest. "Truly there is. My investments have doubled in value. My monthly income has doubled. And that's only the beginning."

"Simon, I have the terrible feeling you actually believe what you're saying. *Don't*. Oh, there's money to be made in the market. Quite a lot, in certain circumstances. But don't expect the market will solve your financial problems. As long as your expenses exceed your income, you will have problems."

"I have a plan."

"What plan?"

"Well, to make more money, I must invest more money. That's my plan. I have thought it through very carefully."

Harley sighed, for Simon's innocence, appealing as it was, was sometimes infuriating. "You are overinvested as it is. You're buying on margin, don't forget. If your margins are ever called—"

"That's why I need more investment capital. I have arranged a bank loan. It's a substantial loan, Harley. I'm putting it all into the market."

"A loan! Are you mad? The last thing you need is more debt. Banks charge *interest* on loans. Do you *understand* that? You're only getting deeper and deeper and deeper in debt."

Simon looked hurt. He dropped his eyes, his long lashes shadowing his cheeks. Harley regretted his outburst. He was ashamed of himself, for he felt as if he had kicked a small and defenseless animal. There was a long silence in the library. "I'm sorry, Simon," Harley said after a while. "Perhaps we'd best discuss this when our heads are clearer."

"Are you angry with me?"

"No, not with you. I would gladly strangle your executors though. If they'd given you the slightest bit of guidance early on ... Well, never mind. We'll talk about this another time." Harley took his jacket from a chair and slung it over his shoulder. "Don't worry, Simon. Things will work out."

Simon brightened. "Oh, I know they will." He smiled eagerly. "Everyone says the market is going to soar. I shall make a killing!"

"A killing, eh?" Harley shook his head, though he could not help but be amused. "I certainly hope so, Simon. I certainly hope so."

Harley was to remember Simon's words as the 1920s roared ahead. They were giddy times, strange times indeed for a country once guided by the Puritan ethic. There were Hollywood scandals and society scandals, all extravagantly detailed in the daily newspapers. There were murders on the streets of Chicago and New York as rival gangsters turned their machine guns on each other. There was jazz and bathtub gin and the bold smile of the flapper. Most of all, there was prosperity.

The coming of 1924 saw the stock market growing richer and richer each day. True, there were occasional setbacks, but for the most part, stocks went in only one direction and that was upward. There was, according to informed opinion, no reason it should not go on forever. It was Coolidge Prosperity. It was, in the words of a General Motors vice-president, a time when "everybody ought to be rich."

Wall Street had long been the province of the mighty, but no more. Clerks and shopgirls and taxi drivers now rushed to join the game. They had good reason, for success stories abounded. Everyone had heard of fortunes being made overnight, of modest sums turning into stacks of thousand dollar bills. It was not gambling, went the refrain; it was investing.

The distinction was lost on Harley. He considered the market wildly inflated and, in 1928, began to sell. His broker's protests were strenuous, but to no avail. "I'm rich enough," Harley said, and that was true, for his speakeasy had been earning some three thousand dollars a week and his investments easily as much. When all his stocks had been sold, he found himself a millionaire two times over.

Harley and Sally had been married for almost five years. It was not a happy marriage. Whatever need they had once felt for each other, whatever passion, was long in the past. They were friendly and they were considerate, but they were not husband and wife. They led separate lives. Sally divided her time between her son and an amateur theatrical company in Greenwich Village. Harley had his business and his afternoons with Spencer and occasional weekend visits with Oliver and Johnnie. He played squash with his old friends from Rutherford & Day. Two or three times a month he played chess with Father Malone. He went to football games with Simon. There were women in his life, but they were dalliances, always brief and always discreet. The only woman he really wanted was Mary.

Harley had seen little of Mary since their divorce. They met at Johnnie's graduation from Greenvale and, the following autumn, at a reception for the parents of incoming Harvard freshmen. The next year they met at a gala birthday party for Anna, the year after that at Oliver's graduation. Now, on a cold October day in 1929, they were meeting again.

Harley was nervous. Waiting in the living room of the Central Park apartment he once had called home, he lit cigarette after cigarette. He changed chairs several times. He paced. He was standing by the windows, tapping his fingers on the sill, when Mary entered.

"Hello, Harley," she said. "I didn't mean to keep you waiting, but I had a telephone call. I'm sorry."

"That's quite all right." Harley smiled. "You're worth waiting for."

"Flattery?"

"Truth." Harley could not take his eyes from Mary, for she seemed to grow more lovely and more stylish with each year. "You make me dizzy," he said.

"Then you must sit down. I wouldn't want you to fall and hurt yourself." Mary spoke lightly, but in fact she found it very difficult to be around Harley. She had to steel herself against the pain she felt, the yearning for things to be as they had been before. There was a great emptiness in her. Work did not fill it, nor did the attentions of several of New York's most eligible men. She needed Harley, but Harley was lost to her. "Sit by that little table there." She gestured. "Greta's fixed a nice lunch for us."

"Thank you. I appreciate your seeing me, Mary. I know how busy you are."

"I can take time off now and then. Besides, you said it was important."

"It is." Harley spread his napkin on his lap. He took

a sip of sherry. "It's about Simon. He worries me. I'm afraid he's headed for serious trouble."

"The stock market again?"

"Still. He's obsessed."

"Well, who isn't these days?"

"Very true. But you don't realize the depth of Simon's problems. To begin with, he's a margin player."

"Harley, almost everyone in the market today is in on margin."

"Let me finish. There have been a few nasty slides in the market recently. One in September, two or three earlier this month. Margin calls went out . . . Simon couldn't cover his margins."

"My God, did he lose—"

"He didn't lose a thing. I covered his margins for him. But that doesn't solve anything. Cracks are appearing in the market now. *Big* cracks. I'm afraid the whole damn thing is going to come crashing down. You follow the market. You must see what I mean."

Mary nodded. She remembered the slide of October 4, when stocks dipped from two to thirty points. She remembered the wave of selling on October 21, when stocks dipped again. Near panic had set in on October 24, for yet another wave of selling had sent values plunging by five billion dollars. The tickers had run an hour late that morning and dire predictions had been heard. But then the nation's bankers had stepped in, pouring nearly a quarter of a billion dollars into the faltering market. It had been a masterful stroke, and effective, for optimism had been restored. President Hoover himself had declared business to be on a "sound and prosperous basis."

"Are you listening to me, Mary?" Harley asked.

"I was thinking about what Mr. Hoover said."

"Presidents don't always speak the truth. They don't always know the truth. Some know only what they're told. Right now the bankers are telling Hoover everything's wonderful. Perhaps it is . . . perhaps it isn't. If it isn't, Simon's in a dangerous position."

"How dangerous?"

"First of all, he's running heavy margins. Secondly, he has large bank loans outstanding. Thirdly, he has tax problems. I want to get him out of the market and on financial course again. I've done some figuring. It will take approximately half a million dollars."

"What?" Mary's eyes were wide, staring. *"Half a million dollars?"*

"Approximately. That's the total of Simon's debt, give or take. I'd be willing to cover most of it, but I want certain assurances. That's where you come in."

"Half a million dollars?" Mary left the table. She wandered around the room, shaking her head. "I don't understand," she said. "How could he be that deeply in debt? How could that have happened?"

"It happened the way it always happens. Simon's expenses were running ahead of his income and he started looking for some magical solution. A money tree, to use his own words. The market was beginning its climb, remember. He made a little money, then a *lot* of money. Before long, he fancied himself a Wall Street wizard."

"Harley, Simon has an income of fifty thousand a year!"

"If he defaults on his loans, he won't have a penny."

"But with that kind of income, why did he go into debt at all?" Mary threw up her hands, for she knew the answer to her question: Rose. "God, I've been so *stupid.* I knew Rose was knee-deep in jewels and furs and servants . . . but I never stopped to add the cost. I suppose I didn't want to. . . . Poor Simon."

"If steps aren't taken, that may literally be true."

"What steps?" Mary returned to the table. She sat down, staring at Harley. "Are you really willing to put up all that money?"

"I'm a wealthy man," Harley shrugged. "All I ever wanted out of life was fun. And love. I got wealth instead. . . . Yes, I'm willing to put up the money. I'm *not* willing to throw it away. So you must convince Simon to get out of the market and stay out. Because he simply can't handle it. And you must convince him to hire a financial manager."

"You're his best friend. Surely you can convince him."

"I've tried. He won't listen to me. He may listen to you. He respects your business success."

"What about your business success?"

"A speakeasy?" Harley laughed. "That's no great trick. There are more than thirty thousand speaks in New York. All of them awash in money. I'm talking about business success that will last beyond Prohibition. Kilburne Bakeries will last." Harley lit a cigarette. He smiled. "I see your red and white wrappers all over town. And there are Roly-Poly cakes in every lunchbox from here to Michigan. Kilburne Bakeries will last, Mary. Even Simon has to be impressed by that."

"I don't think so. I tried to get him to sell when I did. He refused. He had the last laugh too. I sold General Electric at 128. Last month it was 396. Why should he listen to me?"

"You still made a tidy profit."

"I made a fortune. But I have a feeling Simon will find that to be beside the point. In a way, it *is* beside the point. The real problem is Rose."

"Of course. The other thing you must do is have a talk with Rose. Explain to her that she could lose everything. Simon's at the brink. One more step and it's all over."

"What about the Ellsworths? Can't they help?"

"The Ellsworth money is really *Mrs.* Ellsworth's money. Simon already owes her quite a lot. He owes everyone, except his father. He won't go to his father. And his executors are useless. There aren't many choices, Mary. God knows there's not much time."

"Yes, I see." Mary drank her sherry. She was quiet, considering what to do. Her own wealth had grown substantially during the last five years, in part from the stock market, but mostly from the distribution of Kilburne Bakeries products to stores in the east and midwest. On paper she was a millionaire. But her money, unlike Harley's, was not readily accessible, for the bulk of it was tied up in her company. "Well," she said finally, "I can't let you do this all by yourself. I'll put up some of the money. I'll talk to Philip, and Jane, and see what we can raise."

"No. I didn't come here for that, Mary. I have the money. I'll handle that part of it. You handle Simon and Rose. That's your part. The hardest part."

Again, Mary was silent. She rolled her napkin into a ball and threw it on the table. "It's *my fault,* Harley," she cried. "Don't you see? I should have done something about Rose years ago. I didn't have the heart to. I didn't have the nerve. This whole miserable situation is my fault."

"It's easy to look back and see what we should have

done. It's also a waste of time. What's done can't be undone." Harley put his hand on Mary's. "We learned that bitter lesson ourselves," he said softly.

Harley's touch, unexpected as it was, startled her. She felt her heart jump. She felt a sudden warmth and she drew her hand away. "Nevertheless, I have some responsibility in this. You can't expect me to ignore it." She stood up, avoiding Harley's glance. "I'll telephone Simon. Perhaps I can see him tonight. Excuse me, Harley. I won't be long."

Harley watched her walk off. She wore a plum-colored silk dress and its spare lines seemed to emphasize the full, luscious lines of her figure. Its short skirt displayed her long, long legs. Harley wanted to run after her, to take her in his arms and crush her to him. It was desire but it was need too, and he had to force himself to stay in his chair. He gripped the arms of the chair until his knuckles were white. The expression on his face was terrible.

"You are sick, Mr. Kilburne?" Greta asked, pushing a serving cart into the room. "Pardon, but I see you scowl. A headache, *ja?*"

"Yes. It's nothing. . . . How are you, Greta? It's good to see you again."

"Thank you, Mr. Kilburne. It has been a long time. But I remembered. See," she said, lifting the cover of a silver serving dish. "Poached salmon. The way you like it, with dill."

"How thoughtful of you." Harley smiled. "And all I was expecting was a ham sandwich!"

"You are teasing me. I know you, Mr. Kilburne." She smiled back at him. "You like to have jokes."

"Well, life is a joke. Don't you think?"

"*Ja,* sometimes I think that. In America everything

is, how do they say, free and easy."

"Easy, anyway."

Mary returned then. She inspected the lunch trays and nodded at Greta. "That's very nice. Thank you." She sat down, waiting until Greta had gone before speaking. "They're going to the Follies tonight. We made a date for tomorrow night instead."

"Probably just as well. You'll have time to think about what to say. You'll have to scare the hell out of them."

"Oh, don't worry. That's exactly what I intend to do. They'll hear a speech they won't soon forget, and *that* I promise."

But Mary never had the chance to make her speech. That Monday, thirteen million shares of stock were sold and losses exceeded ten billion dollars. Even the bankers, with their vast pool of money, were unable to stem the tidal wave of selling. The next day, a day which was forever to be known as Black Tuesday, the market crashed.

There was bedlam on the trading floor as desperate men shouted and screamed and wept. There was bedlam in the streets outside of the Exchange as desperate crowds gathered to witness the disaster. The toll was stupendous. The selling off of twenty-three million shares let loose a panic that would destroy thirty billion dollars in market values. Great corporations were struck a mortal blow, as were the investment trusts. And now the market's big men went down along with the clerks and shopgirls and taxi drivers who had put their last dollars in the golden dreams of Wall Street.

Simon received the news in a late morning call from his broker. He had been calm when he answered the telephone but, when he hung up, he was white, shaking so badly he could hardly manage the few steps to his chair. He was ruined and he knew it. There would be no reprieve. He knew he would lose his trust—if indeed anything remained in his trust—to the banks. He would lose his house. Almost certainly, he would lose Rose. An anguished cry came from his throat. He put his head in his hands and sobbed.

It was an hour later when Rose found him sitting at his desk. He stood as she entered the room, then sank back into his chair. "I must . . . talk to you," he said, his voice hoarse, muffled.

"There's no time, Simon dear. Amanda is coming for lunch and I have to dress. Are you joining us?"

"Please, Rose. Sit down. We . . . must talk."

"If you insist. But I . . . Simon, you look dreadful. What is it?"

Simon stared at his wife, at the woman he loved with his whole heart and soul. Tears pricked his wide gray eyes. His head throbbed. "There is very bad news, Rose."

"I *hate* bad news. Don't tell me."

"I must. . . . The stock market has crashed, you see. Great fortunes have been lost."

"Oh? Well, I'm sorry. But it has nothing to do with me, and Amanda will be here soon."

"I telephoned Mother. She's lost everything. She's wiped out."

"No! I *am* sorry, Simon. Will you have to help her?"

"You don't understand. I can't help her . . . I can't help anyone."

Rose's expression changed suddenly. Her eyes

became cold. Her mouth tightened. "You haven't lost your money, have you? You wouldn't be that foolish."

"Foolish, Rose?"

"I can't think of anything more foolish than losing all one's money. You haven't done that, Simon dear? Have you?"

Simon passed his hand across his face. "I've tried to give you a good life," he said, swallowing hard. "I've tried . . . to make you happy."

"And you have. I'm very happy . . . I'll go on being happy, won't I, Simon? There is no reason anything should change . . . is there?"

"I love you, Rose."

Rose folded her hands in her lap and stared back at her husband. "Have you lost your money?"

Simon could not reply. He saw the look in Rose's eyes and he knew there was no hope. "I . . . was only worried about Mother."

"Is *that* all?" Rose sighed. "For a moment, I was afraid it was serious. You mustn't scare me like that, Simon dear."

"Forgive me."

"Don't worry about your mother. She has resources, I'm sure. And your father is an important congressman, after all. He knows all sorts of rich people."

"Yes, you are right."

Rose stood up. "Now let me see you smile," she said. "You can do better than that. . . . That's better. You look *much* better." She went to Simon and kissed his cheek. "I do hate it when you're sad."

"Forgive me."

"What a goose you are! Of course I forgive you. I *love* you, Simon dear."

And then, with a toss of her silken curls, Rose was

gone. Simon sat there, staring into space. After some minutes he took pen in hand and wrote four letters, to his mother, to his young daughter Rosie, to Harley, and lastly to Rose. He sealed the letters, propping them against the telephone. He opened the top drawer of his desk. The revolver was small, jet black. Simon put it to his temple and pulled the trigger.

Seventeen

Mary sat in Rose's cluttered and airless drawing room. She had been there for an hour, having arrived just as Simon's body was being carried out, but she still had not seen Rose. Servants tiptoed back and forth, speaking in whispers. Newpaper reporters came to the door, protesting as they were turned away. The telephone seemed to ring and ring and ring. Through it all, Rose remained upstairs talking to the police.

Mary was alone with her thoughts, and they were grim thoughts indeed. Darkly, she pondered the ways of men and women, of the world, and of God. Father Malone had often told her that there were reasons for everything that happened, God's reasons. But there are no reasons, she thought now, only random acts. One act leads to another and then another, until the inevitable conclusion is reached.

"Mary?" Rose was poised uncertainly at the threshold of the drawing room. She looked confused, very small and very vulnerable. "It's so awful," she said, her hands fluttering at her sides.

Mary did not know what to say, for she considered Rose both victim and culprit in this grotesque tragedy. "I'm sorry, lass. Simon was such a sweet man."

"The police said there were many . . . suicides today. can you imagine?"

Rose had not moved from the threshold and so Mary went to her, taking her arm. "Come and sit down. I'll get you a brandy."

"There's blood . . . all over the library. On the floor, the desk."

"Don't, Rose. Don't think about it now. Where is Rosie?"

"Nanny took her to stay at Harley's. I . . . didn't tell her anything. Rosie, I mean. I didn't tell Rosie anything."

"Don't worry about that. She's too young to understand."

"But I'll have to tell her something. She'll wonder where her . . . daddy is."

Mary sat Rose down. She poured a brandy and gave it to her. "Drink it. It will help."

"Yes. All right."

Mary watched Rose. She saw the confusion in her eyes, the shock, but she saw no signs of grief. She recalled the day of their father's death, for Rose had been confused then too, but untouched by grief. She has no feelings, Mary thought, anger rising in her. "Do you want to talk about anything?" she asked.

Rose lifted her head to her sister. "He shot himself, you know."

"I know. The policeman outside told me. I came here as soon as I heard about the market . . . I'm sorry I was too late. I might have been able to . . . I'm sorry."

Rose finished her brandy. She put the glass down and Mary noticed how careful she was not to disturb the dozens of little porcelains on the table. "How could Simon do it? I don't understand. He left this," she said, taking his letter from her pocket. "If it's supposed to help, it doesn't."

Mary read the letter. It was heartbreaking, filled as it was with expressions of love and apology both. Innocence colored every line. "Poor Simon." She sighed. "He blamed himself."

"Of course he blamed himself. It was his fault."

"Rose!"

"It's true. You know it's true." Rose left her chair. She walked across the room, stopping to rearrange a bouquet of silk flowers. "He lost all our money, didn't he?"

"Money! Always money! Simon's *dead,* Rose. He's dead by his own hand, and all you can think about is money." Mary grasped Rose's shoulders, turning her around. "Simon killed himself because he thought he'd failed you. Doesn't that mean anything to you? Don't you *care?*"

"Certainly I care. I have my own ways of caring."

"I'd like to know what they are."

"They're none of your business. You're so quick to judge me, Mary. You're so high and mighty . . . you can afford to be. You've always had it easy. You had Harley to take care of you. And then Mr. Basset left you all his money. I had to fight to get the things *I* wanted."

"What?"

"You heard me. Everything always worked out for you, Mary. But not for me. It hasn't been easy for me. Did you care? I wonder if you ever cared. I wonder if you ever gave a damn."

Mary slapped Rose's face. She slapped her again, harder. Then Harley's arms were around her, pulling her away. "Stop it, Mary! Stop it!"

Mary slumped against him. She took a deep breath, staring in amazement at Rose. "All the sacrifices I made for you," she said quietly. "I must have been mad."

"Get out of my house," Rose shouted, rubbing her stinging cheek. "Get out now!"

"With pleasure. I'm all right, Harley. You can let me go."

"I don't think I should."

"I'm all right, really I am."

"Where are you going?"

"Away from here. Anywhere away from here. I've had all I can stand."

"Rose will need you."

"That's unfortunate, because I'm leaving." Mary glanced at Rose. She shook her head and then walked to the door. "Goodbye, Harley," she said, walking into the hall.

The butler, a solemn gray-haired man, gave Mary her coat and hat. He opened the door and she stepped into the fading afternoon light. Gramercy Park was quiet once again, for the police cars that had clogged its pretty streets were gone now. The few passers-by who had stopped to watch the unusual comings and goings were gone too. Mary's car was parked at the curb, but she waved her driver away. "You can go on back to the office, Carl," she called. "I feel like walking."

Mary walked for two hours. She had no particular destination in mind, nor did she even notice the buildings and stores and people she passed. The city was abuzz with talk of the Wall Street debacle. Mary heard snatches of conversations. She heard the surprise in peoples' voices, the fear. She heard one man declare the country to be "flat broke" now, and she thought that was probably close to the truth.

It was late afternoon when Mary found herself in front of Cynthia Sinclair's house. She did not hesitate. She climbed the stairs and used her keys to let herself inside. "Jack?" she called, looking around for the caretaker employed by Cynthia. "Are you here, Jack?" There was no response and Mary took the stairs to the second floor. She walked through the silent and polished hall to the morning room. There she sank gratefully into a chair.

Cynthia Sinclair traveled to America three times a year; the rest of the time she spent in Europe. She kept a townhouse in London and a villa just outside of Rome. She professed to be happy. Mary did not pry. She continued to visit the house and to write Cynthia once a month. It was no hardship, for here, away from ringing telephones and insistent secretaries and more insistent accountants, she found tranquillity. The pale silk walls and delicate rosewood furnishings were exactly as they had been years ago. The single table ornament, a long-necked crystal swan, still sparkled in the lamplight. It was, thought Mary, as if time had not passed at all, as if the bad things had not yet happened.

Mary turned when she heard a noise at the door. A man was standing there, a man with flashing black eyes. "Don't be alarmed," he said in a soft drawl. "I'm Reeve Sinclair. My stepmother owns this house . . . but who are you?"

"Mary Kilburne."

"Well, I never would have recognized you. You were a lovely girl, but you have become a beautiful woman."

"Thank you."

Reeve Sinclair laughed. "You really mustn't be alarmed," he said. "I'm not the impetuous youth I once was. . . . Yes," he nodded, "I remember taking liberties. Allow me to offer my sincere apologies, late though they are."

"What are you doing here?"

"Why, I grew up here. This was my boyhood home." Reeve sat down. He was unruffled, completely at ease, and Mary sensed that he would be at ease wherever he was. He was a handsome man. His features were slender, patrician. His hair was very black. There was about him a casual grace, the grace of someone who took wealth and privilege and charm for granted. "May I call you Mary?" he asked.

"Of course. But I still don't know what you're doing here. You're not supposed to be here."

"Are you?" He smiled.

"Yes. Mrs. Sinclair asked me to keep an eye on things."

"Cynthia was always very fond of this house. I am fond of it too. I expected to inherit it, as a matter of fact, but my late father had other ideas. . . . Whenever I'm in New York I stop by. I wander through the rooms and relive old times. Does that sound foolish?"

"I often feel nostalgic myself."

"It's more than nostalgia, Mary. I come here because this house is a part of my past. I have a great respect for the past, for heritage. Particularly the Sinclair heritage. Cynthia doesn't understand that, I regret to say."

"You put me in a difficult position. Mrs. Sinclair trusts me to see that her house is . . . not disturbed."

"And my presence is disturbing?"

"It would be to Mrs. Sinclair. How did you get in?

Where is Jack?"

Reeve smiled. His black eyes seemed to study Mary. "As to your first question—I have always had my own keys. As to your second question—Jack is no doubt in his room, enjoying the rye whiskey I brought him. Jack is an excellent caretaker, but he does have a weakness for rye whiskey. It's so hard to come by these days."

"I see. You bribe him."

"It's entirely harmless. Contrary to what Cynthia may think, there is no dastardly plot against her. I like being in this old house. Today, after all the frightful happenings, I needed to be here. I badly needed some peace and quiet."

"I can appreciate that. But I'll still have to wire Mrs. Sinclair in Europe."

"As you wish." Reeve smiled again, unconcerned. "I had occasion to wire her myself, shortly after the market crashed. Sinclair Mills dropped sixty points today."

"You're very calm, considering."

"Well," Reeve laughed, "Sinclairs have survived boll weevils, Civil War, Yankee armies, and even Reconstruction. I imagine we'll survive this. One way or another."

"I admire your confidence."

"Do you? Many Northerners find me arrogant. Cynthia finds me arrogant. I expect she told you that."

"She said only that you were a powerful man."

"I am."

And comfortable with your power, thought Mary. She was intrigued by Reeve Sinclair, for he was unlike any other man she had known. There was something compelling about him, something dangerous. His black gaze was unsettling, yet she could not look away from it.

"What is your verdict?" he asked, a smile playing at the edges of his handsome mouth.

"Verdict?"

"You have been inspecting me ever since I came in. Do I pass?"

Mary felt herself blushing. "It . . . was the surprise of seeing you again after so many years," she said.

"Is that all?"

"Of course. It *was* a surprise."

"So it was. . . . Tell me, Mary, why are you still doing Cynthia's bidding? You're a successful woman in your own right. What is the tie between the two of you?"

"I owe her a great deal. If I can do a favor from time to time . . . Why do you ask?"

"Curiosity is the obvious answer, but not the true one. Cynthia doesn't like me and that is a fact. I hope her attitude won't stand in our way."

"Our way?"

"I am going to invite you to dine with me tonight. I hope you will accept."

"No." Mary rose abruptly. She walked across the room, far away from Reeve Sinclair. "No, I couldn't. Thank you for asking, but I couldn't."

Reeve was not dismayed. He leaned back in his chair and smiled. "I am unaccustomed to rejection," he said easily. "Will you tell me your reason?"

"There are several reasons. It's been an awful day and I'm really quite tired. My brother-in-law . . ." Mary found herself telling Reeve about Simon. She talked at some length and then, to her astonishment, she found herself telling him about her quarrel with Rose. Reeve's eyes never left her face. "So you see," she finished, "I really need to be alone."

"What you need is a sympathetic ear and a shoulder to lean on. I offer mine."

"No, I couldn't burden you. I don't even know why I told you as much as I did. We're strangers."

Reeve's smile broadened. He shook his dark head. "Hardly strangers," he drawled. "You were the fantasy of my boyhood. I know you better than you think."

It was a suggestive remark and Mary was unsure how to respond. She looked at Reeve. She felt herself drawn to him, though in the back of her mind warnings stirred. "That's not an unusual fantasy," she replied finally. "The scullery maid and the young lord of the manor."

"You are no longer the scullery maid."

"But you are still the young lord."

Reeve stared silently at Mary. Light flashed in the blackness of his eyes. "I have met my match in you, Mary," he said quietly.

Mary saw him rise. She saw him walking toward her, a tall man, graceful, yet exuding strength and power. She did not move.

"And you have met your match in me." He smiled.

Reeve swept Mary into his arms, pressing his lips on hers. She tried to push away. She struggled, but only for a moment. In the next moment her arms went around him and, all caution gone, her lips returned his kiss. She was dizzy, lost in the fervor of his embrace. Neither of them heard the footsteps coming up the stairs.

"Oh! Excuse me!" It was Jack's voice, loud with surprise. He moved quickly to leave, too quickly, for he bumped into the door frame.

Reeve let Mary go. He turned around and now his eyes were hard. "What do you want?" he demanded.

"I came to ask if you needed anything, sir. But I see—"

"You see nothing. Is that clear, Jack?"

"Yes, sir. Clear," he nodded, backing out of the room. "It's clear, sir."

Mary was deeply embarrassed. Jack's sudden intrusion had caused her to see herself as he had seen her. It was a disturbing picture, for she could not explain her behavior. That she was lonely, that she had been lonely for a long time, did not occur to her. That she was depressed and therefore vulnerable did not occur to her either.

"Don't be troubled by Jack," Reeve said. "His entrance was ill-timed, but unimportant."

"I don't care about Jack. But what . . . happened between you and me was a mistake. I'm sorry."

"You're not sorry and neither am I. It surely wasn't a mistake. You have passion, Mary. There is nothing more exciting to a man than a passionate woman." Reeve's gaze lingered on Mary's face; slowly, it moved over her body. "Put passion with beauty"—he smiled—"and the combination is irresistible. It fires the imagination."

"You are as bold now as you ever were."

"Does that offend you? Or please you?"

"I must go."

"Certainly. We'll go to dinner now. I know a charming restaurant not far from here."

"No, I can't."

"Of course you can. Of course you will." Reeve leaned against the edge of the desk. He crossed his arms, staring in amusement at Mary. "Don't look so surprised," he said. "I am going to court you, Miss Mary. And I am going to win you. Sinclairs are not known for losing. Not anything. Not ever."

"I'm beginning to see why Northerners find you arrogant."

"But you're not a Northerner. You're English by birth. I am English by ancestry. We have that in common too."

"Too? It's the *only* thing we have in common."

"No, you're wrong. . . . There is something missing in my life. There is something missing in your life. I know there is, don't deny it. We go along day to day and we tell ourselves it doesn't matter. It matters very much."

"Perhaps. But you're presuming—"

"I never presume, Mary. That is a waste of time, and I do not waste my time. There are so many other . . . interesting things to do with it."

"Oh, I'm sure."

"Come." Reeve laughed. "We'll get our coats and be off. You will like the restaurant," he said, settling the matter.

"Do you always have your way, Reeve?"

"Always."

It was said there were many different Reeve Sinclairs, businessman, sportsman, ladies' man, squire of Lucy's Court. In business he was known to be ruthless and unforgiving, without scruple. Away from business his male friends saw him in another light. To them, he was the smiling host of hunting parties, an expert horseman and crack shot. Women saw only his charm and elegant good looks. The field hands and sharecroppers of Lucy's Court saw a tyrant who ruled as absolute master of his lands. Reeve would not have disagreed with any of those descriptions.

Mary sensed the darkness in Reeve's character. She chose not to think about it. Whenever the warnings in her mind grew too loud, she turned her mind to other things. Questions continued to nag at her, questions about Reeve and about herself, but resolutely she put them off.

It had been a week since their chance meeting at Cynthia's house, a week marked by the attentions of Reeve's courtship. He wined her and dined her and showered her with romantic presents. He sent flowers to her office every day, calling for her at day's end in his sleek black limousine. He took her dancing, and to the theater, and on moonlit carriage rides through the park. Mary felt like a young girl again. She dared not use the word love, though secretly she admitted to infatuation.

Mary's business associates did not know what to make of the change in her. Grim signs of the Depression were already apparent, but she seemed oblivious to them. She was late for meetings, uncharacteristically impatient. She canceled appointments at the last minute. Decisions were postponed. Reports went unread. She gave only one order—that no one was to be fired; everything else she left to Jane.

"You're ruining my business," she said to Reeve on an evening in November. "I can't concentrate. People are beginning to talk."

"And what are they saying?"

"I'd rather not know."

Reeve and Mary were in the suite he kept at the Savoy. It was a large suite, decorated to his tastes with Aubusson carpets on the polished floors and family portraits on the walls. The chairs and sofas were deep, covered in English chintz. His desk, by the windows overlooking Fifth Avenue, was a magnificent old Hepplewhite from Lucy's Court. Lucy's Court crystal lined the top shelves of his private liquor cabinet. Reeve opened that cabinet now. He selected a bottle of wine and uncorked it, carrying bottle and glasses to the sofa on which Mary sat. "I never discuss business after sundown," he drawled. "It's a rule."

"Not my rule. I really must get my mind back on business. Poor Jane has been doing her work and mine too."

"Does she object?"

"I don't know. Probably. She should. These aren't easy times."

"Why, I think they're wonderful times. We're together. And we are alone. I do like having you to myself." Reeve poured the wine. He gave a glass to Mary and then sat down beside her. "A toast." He smiled. "To Miss Mary, the fairest in the land."

"But I'm serious, Reeve."

"So am I. No more business talk tonight. I may be a simple country boy—"

"A simple country boy!" Mary laughed. *"You?"*

"At your service, ma'am."

Mary had to look away from Reeve's dazzling smile, his black-eyed gaze. She felt quite breathless. Sitting so close to him, she felt weak. "You're impossible." She sighed. "I wonder how many hearts you've broken

419

along the way."

"I?"

"Such innocence! You have something of a reputation, you know."

Reeve leaned back. His hand stroked the nape of Mary's neck. "I'm a man. Should I sit in my rooms night after night, doing needlepoint? Or should I take what life has to offer? I leave it to you, Miss Mary."

Mary drank her wine. She glanced toward the windows, watching the silken curtains ruffle in the breeze. "I don't want my heart broken," she said quietly. "Once is enough. Twice . . ."

Reeve's eyes narrowed, and the line of his mouth also. In silence he studied Mary. His look was not pleasant. It was the look that adversaries had learned, too late, to fear. "You are no doubt referring to Mr. Dan McShane."

"Oh, that was a long time ago."

"You could have married him, after your divorce."

"No."

"Why not?"

Mary did not notice the edge in Reeve's voice. She stared into her wineglass, a small and wistful smile lifting the corners of her mouth. "Amongst other reasons, Dan was already married. He married just a month before my divorce . . . Harley told me. He kept in touch with Dan through the years."

"How very odd."

"You would have to know Harley to understand. He's not the type of man to dislike anyone. Certainly no one dislikes him. I don't think he's ever had an enemy."

Mary had told Reeve a great deal about her past and

Reeve, in turn, had drawn certain conclusions. First and foremost, he had concluded that Harley was a fool. A man without enemies was, to his mind, a weakling, no man at all. Perhaps, he thought now, Harley was willing to abide ghosts in his bed, but I am not. "Look at me, Mary," he said. "Are you still in love with Dan?"

"Harley thinks I am."

"Answer me!"

But Mary could not answer, for Reeve's hands had begun to move over her body. She felt her breath quicken. She felt her breasts become warm and full. "Reeve," she whispered, looking into the fierce blackness of his eyes. "Reeve."

"I'll drive Dan from your mind," Reeve said. "I'll love you as you should be loved." He caught Mary in his arms, crushing his hot mouth upon hers, seeking, demanding. He pulled the pins from her hair. He tore her clothes away, and then his own. Roughly, he pressed his mouth to her naked breasts. His hands were like fire burning into her flesh.

Shadows of night closed about the room and, in the darkness, the lovers knew the depths of their turbulent passion. A clock chimed. A telephone rang. A chambermaid knocked at the door. Reeve and Mary heard nothing but their own cries.

The next morning, they drove to Connecticut and were married by a justice of the peace. Reeve returned immediately to Lucy's Court. Mary returned home to face her family.

"I really believe the old girl's lost her senses," Johnnie Kilburne said to his brother Oliver.

"Old girl? If you ask me, that *old girl* has more vitality in her little finger than your Elizabeth has in her whole body."

"I didn't ask you. And mind what you say about Elizabeth. She is to be my wife. We have an understanding. Soon, as soon as I have a better position in the company, we will marry."

"Aren't you getting ahead of yourself, Johnnie? You've only been in the executive training program for a few months. Advancement takes time, after all. It could take years."

"Bah! I intend to move up very quickly. I have ideas, plans for Kilburne Bakeries. No one is going to stand in my way."

"Well, you've never lacked confidence." Oliver smiled. He was seated across from his brother in the living room of the Central Park apartment that had been their home. Johnnie had his own apartment now. Oliver had his own rooms at Harvard, where he was a sophomore. He was a handsome young man with features that were usually described as clean-cut, and a mane of straw-colored hair. His eyes were large, soft blue. He resembled both his parents, though his temperament and disposition were Harley's. "But I do remember a time when you had no use for Ma's company. What changed your mind, Johnnie?"

"The company's changed. It's worth something now."

"It certainly is. Millions, if this Depression doesn't do us all in."

Johnnie regarded Oliver coolly. "You shouldn't believe everything you read in the newspapers," he said. "America's economy is sound. It's true there has been a setback. But it's only temporary."

"Tell that to the poor devils who have been thrown out of work. I'm sure they'll be delighted to know it's only temporary."

"There is no use discussing this with you, Oliver. You don't understand economics."

"No? I understand the economics of a paycheck . . . and what happens when that paycheck is taken away."

"Nevertheless, Kilburne Bakeries will continue to prosper. We are a strong company. We have no debt, no long-term obligations. Best of all, we sell and distribute inexpensive products."

"We?" Oliver laughed. "Is that the royal we or are you being wishful? It is still Ma's company. And don't forget Reeve Sinclair. He's Ma's husband now. He may have a thing or two to say about the company."

Johnnie's eyes darkened at the mention of Reeve Sinclair. He had nothing against the man himself, for he knew him to be of a wealthy and aristocratic family. In other circumstances, he would have welcomed Reeve's marriage to Mary. But now, in these circumstances, he viewed it as a threat. Johnnie intended to have control of Kilburne Bakeries and its assets one day. He was not foolish enough to suppose that control would come quickly or easily, but he had planned to keep himself within striking distance. Reeve Sinclair might complicate his plan; Reeve Sinclair might have plans of his own. "Mother was a fool to marry again," he said with disdain. "That is the trouble with women, especially women of a certain age. They are too emotional."

Oliver's laugh was loud. He shook his fair head, his eyes crinkling in mirth. "To hear you tell it, Ma is a doddering old lady with cane and shawl. Have you looked at her, Johnnie? Really looked at her? The fellows at school think she's the cat's meow. They think she's swell."

"For heaven's sake, she's almost forty."

"Forty!" Oliver teased, clutching his chest. "At death's door!"

"You're very frivolous."

"And you're very funny. I know you don't mean to be, but you're a howl, Johnnie."

Johnnie said nothing, though he wondered yet again how two people as different as he and Oliver could be brothers. They were three years apart in age, worlds apart in attitudes. Everything seemed to amuse Oliver. He sailed through life, a smile on his lips, a joke at the ready. He was, without any effort at all, an *A* student. He had been captain of the tennis team at Greenvale and president of his class. He had legions of friends. Strangest of all to Johnnie, his brother showed no interest in money and even less interest in power.

"You're smarter than I am, Johnnie," Oliver said now. "But you take yourself too seriously."

"Life is serious."

"Is it? I'm not convinced. We all wind up in the same place, in the end. So what's the difference? Why not have some fun along the way?"

"You and Father are two of a kind. Always going on and on about fun. Where would the world be if everyone thought like that?"

"Look where the world is now. Look where serious thinking has got us."

"The world's been pretty damn good to you," Johnnie said shortly.

"And to you."

"It will be. I'll have the world in the palm of my hand before I'm through. See if I don't."

Oliver nodded. He thought: And you still won't be happy. You'll still have your secrets and your schemes and your demons. "I believe you," he said.

"You pity me."

"What?"

"I have seen that look in your eyes before, Oliver. You think I am . . . misguided. Do you deny it?"

"I wish you had some friends, some interests beyond Ma's company. What good is money if . . ." Oliver did not finish, for he saw Johnnie's blue-green gaze harden. He had no wish to argue with his brother. There had been too many arguments over the years, some of them merely silly, some of them wounding. It was true that he pitied Johnnie, but pity would not change the man Johnnie was. "I shouldn't stick my nose in your business." Oliver smiled. "Call it brotherly concern."

"What you fail to understand is that I have no need of friends. I have my work. I have my hobbies . . . my stamp collection grows more valuable each year. And when I marry Elizabeth I will have a family. That is enough."

Oliver glanced at his watch. "I wonder what's keeping Ma," he said.

"Are you so anxious to congratulate her?"

"Of course I am. She hasn't had an easy life, Johnnie. I hope this marriage will make her happy."

"What sentimental nonsense! Who is ever happy?"

"Don't you expect to be happy with Elizabeth?"

"I expect to be content. That is all any of us should expect."

Mary had been just outside the door, listening to her sons. Now she took a breath and walked into the room.

"Hello, boys." She smiled uncertainly.

Johnnie stood. "Hello, Mother," he said, inclining his dark head.

"Ma!" Oliver ran to Mary, throwing his arms around her. "May I kiss the bride?"

"I wish you would."

Oliver kissed his mother, then stepped back to look at her. She was lovely in a slim dress of brilliant jade silk. Her eyes sparkled and there was a becoming blush on her cheeks. "You look swell, Ma. Just swell. I'm so happy for you. Congratulations."

"Thank you, Oliver. I hope you weren't shocked. It was a very sudden decision."

"No, I think it's romantic."

Mary saw Johnnie's mouth tighten. She went to her eldest son, gazing into his eyes. "I know you were shocked, Johnnie."

"Oh, I wouldn't say that, Mother. Not shocked, exactly. It's your life, after all. You're entitled to do as you please. Reeve Sinclair is an excellent catch, I hear."

"Do you?"

"Everyone has heard of Sinclair Mills."

"I didn't marry Reeve for Sinclair Mills."

"I know." Johnnie smiled slightly, coolly. "That is not your style, Mother."

"Ma," Oliver said, taking Mary's arm, "when are we going to meet him? Is he joining us for lunch?"

"Reeve had to return to South Carolina. The stock market crash has created many problems, as you can imagine . . . but you'll meet him at Christmas. We'll have a big family party. I promise."

426

"Good! I love parties!"

Mary looked lovingly at Oliver. He was a joy to her, kind, light-hearted, yet shrewd. She did not worry about him the way she did Johnnie. "You two run along to the dining room now. Greta has a nice lunch prepared."

"Aren't you lunching with us, Ma?"

"I must see Jane first. She's waiting in the study. We have several business matters to discuss."

"I should like to sit in on your meeting," Johnnie said. "It concerns me also."

Mary shook her head. "No, these are matters of policy. We are making changes to accommodate changed economic times."

"Very well. But those changes concern me."

"They don't, Johnnie. You're a long way from policy decisions. If I let you participate, I would have to let the other trainees participate. I have no intention of doing that. You tend to your job and let me tend to mine."

"You're wrong to exclude me, Mother. The company will be mine someday—"

"*Someday* is not now. And if I were you, I would not be so quick to make assumptions about the future. We don't know the future."

Johnnie's eyes were hard, fixed on Mary. "I know the future," he said.

Mary thought she heard a threat in Johnnie's voice. She turned, frowning, and left the room.

Jane sat at the desk in the study, her blond head bent over a stack of reports. She was twenty-nine years old, still married to Tim Malloy, still childless. Tim was child enough, she often thought, for he was rash and romantic and irresponsible. He was a schoolteacher

427

who thought of himself as a poet, and indeed he had filled dozens of notebooks with his efforts. Jane knew nothing would come of his poetry but she said not a word. She loved her husband and indulged his dreams. Sometimes she shared his dreams and those were the best times of all.

"I'm sorry to have kept you waiting," Mary said, entering the study. "I was with the boys. I'm afraid I didn't handle Johnnie very well at all."

"Does he disapprove of your marriage?"

"Oh, I'm sure. He disapproves of everything I do. This is no exception." Mary took her place at the desk. She sipped the tea that had been brought for her, smiling at Jane. "I will *never* be able to please Johnnie."

"Your company certainly pleases him. He can't wait to get his hands on it."

Jane's bluntness was typical of her. In business situations she was all business, clear-eyed and direct. Mary had come to value those qualities. When others around her rationalized or offered excuses, she turned to Jane for the truth. "Has he been causing trouble?"

"Johnnie's very good at seizing opportunities. You've been away from the company more than usual lately and so he started throwing his weight around. It caused some problems. He's the boss's son, after all. People aren't certain how to react. I told him to stop it, but he pays no attention to me."

"I'll talk to him before he leaves today. I will remind him that you are empowered to hire *and* fire. That may help." Mary opened her desk drawer and removed a file folder. "I've made a few decisions," she said. "First of all, I want prices cut by twenty percent at all the stores."

"Right."

"I'm expecting the stores to hold their own. They did during the Depression after the war. Of course this Depression will be much worse . . . but in hard times people like to treat themselves, even if only to a sugar bun. I think we'll be all right there. It's the distribution that worries me. A lot of the stores throughout the country that carry our products are going to be closing. If times get as bad as I think they will, we could lose one third of our outlets. Perhaps more. That means we would have to close the Pennsylvania plant. . . . Needless to say, I'll do anything to prevent that. I simply won't put three hundred people out of work."

"What do you have in mind?"

"Well, I think we have to give our customers more for their money. Let's sell three Roly-Poly cakes to a package instead of two. And instead of a fifteen-ounce Country Bread, let's package eighteen ounces." Mary sat back in her chair. She nodded at Jane. "I know what that will do to profits. But the important thing is to hold on to our customers. If we don't, hundreds of jobs will be lost."

"Philip has already recommended cutting back on personnel."

"Philip has never had to worry about paying the rent or feeding his family. I have. I know that fear. . . . You can start working on a contingency plan. We may eventually have to put our employees on half shifts. But only if absolutely necessary. And only to save jobs."

"I understand, Mary. I'll see to it."

"Here's a list of some other things. Executive salaries are to be lowered by ten percent. Executive travel is to be strictly monitored."

"I've sent a memorandum around stating that my

office must approve all trips and expense vouchers."

"Fine." Mary closed the folder. "Put the new prices and weights into effect right away. Let's see how we do . . . Why are you smiling?"

"I'm smiling because it's good to have you taking charge again. I was beginning to think you'd lost interest in the company."

"No, never. I admit I was distracted . . . Reeve is very distracting."

"That's love."

"I hope it is." Mary turned her latticed gold wedding ring around and around. "There's a great . . . attraction between us," she said quietly. "I hope it's love."

"Why, Mary, don't you know?"

"Reeve is a complicated man. I'm not uncomplicated myself. All I know, *really* know, is that suddenly I don't feel lonely." Mary looked at Jane. Her eyes were oddly thoughtful. "Am I making any sense?"

"Nobody wants to be lonely."

Mary rose. She walked to the windows and drew the curtain aside, staring at the street below. "I'm leaving for South Carolina in the morning, Jane. I'm going to join Reeve at Lucy's Court."

"Will you be away long?"

"A month. I'm going to have a real honeymoon. I've never had a honeymoon . . . or a vacation, for that matter. I realize it's a bad time, but that can't be helped. I promise to stay in close touch. I'll telephone every day."

"Just enjoy yourself. And remember to come back." Jane gathered her reports together. She put them into her briefcase and snapped it shut. "You will remember to come back?"

"Of course I will." Once again, Mary fidgeted with her wedding ring. She looked at Jane, then looked away. "Did . . . Harley have anything to say about . . . my marriage?"

"He was upset," Jane answered truthfully. "But this is no time to worry about Harley. You're going off on your honeymoon. Enjoy it."

Eighteen

Lucy's Court was one of the largest plantations in South Carolina, its fertile lands stretching for miles in all directions as far as the eye could see. The main house rose from the earth in classic, pure white majesty, all tall columns and wide verandas and graceful balconies. The broad double doors of the porticoed entrance were hand carved and had center panels of burnished bronze. The polished windows, draped in velvet and lace, gleamed. It was a house of astonishing beauty, timeless, unchanging.

Lush flower beds bordered the house. Beyond, the grounds were immaculately landscaped and very green, dewy grasses shimmering in the warm November sunlight. Weeping willows, splendid with years, sighed in the lazy breeze. Yellow honeysuckle blossoms scented the air.

Mary had been at Lucy's Court for a week but still she had not seen it all. There were stables and kennels and glass-walled conservatories in which bloomed exotic orchids. There were charming, whitewashed gazebos and summer houses. At the far end of the property, a narrow brook flowed, its banks dappled with wildflowers. Birds were everywhere and their sweet song fell upon the land as if in benediction.

Mary, who had known only the bleakness of Hexter and the concrete of Manhattan, was enchanted. She wandered the land so vibrant with life and thought she had found paradise. Reeve did not disagree. He had a passion for Lucy's Court, a passion that had begun in the days of his boyhood and grown stronger as years passed. He was, at Lucy's Court, a different man. His drawl became more languorous, his manners more elaborate, his posture more regal. He dressed differently too. By day he strode his lands in riding breeches and high, polished boots, a riding crop in his hands. At night he wore custom-tailored white suits and pale silk ties.

The changes in Reeve were vaguely disquieting to Mary, for they seemed to suggest a drifting into the past, into a time and a way of life that had vanished with the Civil War. Mary's observations were more accurate than she knew. In his mind and heart and soul, Reeve was a creature of the past, not the past of his own experience but the past of his ancestors. He had been brought up on their legends. The tales he had heard as a small child were of dashing and gallant men who ruled their vast plantations with iron hands, their every wish and whim instantly granted. Matters of discipline had been settled with whips, matters of honor with dueling pistols at twenty paces. All the men had been handsome; all the women had been flowers of the South. Reeve longed for such times, but only at Lucy's Court could he live them.

The house to which Mary had been brought had thirty-six rooms, untold passageways, and two huge attics. A virtual army of servants maintained the estate, all of them Negroes, all of them badly paid. Their ties to

Lucy's Court went back as far as Reeve's; indeed, many of them were the children and grandchildren of slaves. Reeve had mentioned that fact in passing, much as he might have mentioned the origin of a chair or a piece of silver. But Mary had been shaken. It reminded her that Lucy's Court had been built on human misery and degradation. It reminded her that Reeve did not care.

The old slave quarters still stood on the lands of Lucy's Court, though Mary had been forbidden to visit them. She had been forbidden to visit the cotton fields too, and the acreage tended by sharecroppers. "Those are not fit places for the mistress of Lucy's Court," Reeve had said, startling Mary with the hard and sudden glint in his eyes.

Mary saw little of Reeve during the days. He was up and out early for a morning ride, going then to the fields to confer with his foreman or the county agricultural agent. Part of every day he spent at Sinclair Mills where, it was said, he terrorized his employees. He was utterly intolerant of error, no matter how inconsequential. When errors occurred, his anger became cold and deadly. At best, the offending employees were humiliated; at worst, they were fired. They had no recourse, no union to which they could turn, and Reeve was determined to keep it that way. He had personally delivered a rousing speech to his fellow businessmen on the evils of unions. And he had personally carried one of the guns that had chased a union organizer from the gates of Sinclair Mills to the outer edges of Sinclair County.

"At one time," Burr Sinclair was saying now, "the North and South were considered different countries. There's something in that, even in these times." Burr smiled at Mary. They were seated on the shaded veranda, drinking juleps from tall, frosted glasses. Perfumed breezes came and went. Crickets chirped on the green lawns. The serenity of twilight was everywhere about, though Burr seemed less than serene. His dark eyes looked often to the graveled paths, seeking Reeve. If it was not exactly true to say he disliked his older brother, it was certainly true to say he feared him. "The thinking is different, you see."

"I'm not sure I do."

"Change is not welcomed here. It's suspect. It's denounced. Why, Lucy's Court hasn't changed in a hundred years. If some old Sinclair came back from his grave he would find Lucy's Court just as he had left it. And he would be glad."

"You exaggerate." Mary smiled. She had grown fond of Burr, of his quiet, thoughtful ways. He looked a great deal like Reeve, though his features were softer, his hair and eyes not quite as black. Burr and his family lived at Lucy's Court the year round and Mary sensed that caused him no small amount of inner turmoil. She had the feeling he loved Lucy's Court and hated it too. "I suppose a few of the old traditions have been preserved."

"All of the old traditions have been preserved."

"Surely not, Burr. A hundred years ago and less there was . . ." Mary decided not to finish her sentence, for it was an uneasy subject. She lifted her glass to her lips and sipped the julep. "Many things have changed."

"You are reluctant to use the word slavery. I don't blame you. It's the great stain on our land."

"It *was*. It's in the past."

Burr stared out across the lawns. He seemed to sigh. "Ask our field hands and sharecroppers if their lives are any better than the lives of slaves . . . it is the same,

Mary. Reeve owns them just as his ancestors owned their ancestors."

"Burr!"

"Forgive me," he said quickly, genuine regret in his voice. "Please forgive me. I shouldn't speak so of my brother. I . . . forget myself."

"Do you believe what you said?"

"It's not important."

"Of course it's important. It's a *terrible* thing to believe. And if it were true of Reeve it would be true of you too. You're a Sinclair. Lucy's Court is yours as well as Reeve's."

"No, it isn't. Father left Lucy's Court to Reeve. There were provisions in his will entitling me and my heirs to live here forever. But Reeve owns it. He owns the majority interest in Sinclair Mills also. I have the minority interest. Do you think my words were inspired by jealousy?" Burr asked, smiling slightly, sadly. "They weren't. I am no businessman. I could never run the mills and Father knew it. As for Lucy's Court . . ."

"Yes?"

"Well, if I owned it, I would make changes. Father knew that too. Father knew everything."

Mary remembered Preston Sinclair only dimly. He had been a decent employer, yet she had not liked him. In some way she could not explain, he had reminded her of Lord Worsham. Slowly, Mary turned her thoughts back to the present. She stared at Burr. "Why do you live here if you find it so unpleasant?"

"I love the land. It's what the land *means* that—"

"And what does the land mean, Burr?" Reeve strode onto the veranda, nodding at his brother. "You're the philosopher in the family," he said coolly. "Do tell us the deep meaning of the land."

Burr was pale. Mary saw his hands jump nervously in his lap. "I didn't hear you come in, Reeve," he said. "I'm afraid I've been boring poor Mary."

"But you're never boring. I would say you're positively fanciful at times. Isn't that right? Don't you agree?"

"I haven't given it much thought."

"Oh?" Reeve bent and kissed Mary's cheek. There was no warmth in his kiss. He hardly seemed to notice her, for his eyes were hard on Burr. "That would be the *only* thing you haven't given much thought."

Burr stood up. "I'll be going inside now." He smiled. "Emily and I are dining at the Cantrells' tonight. I must dress. . . . Good evening, Mary, Reeve."

"Good evening," Mary said. She waited until Burr had closed the French doors and then looked up at Reeve. "Is there some trouble between the two of you?"

"My brother is a goddamn fool," Reeve said shortly, sitting down. "That is the only trouble. Forgive my language, Mary, but he *is* a fool."

"I think he's sweet."

"A man is not supposed to be sweet. A man is supposed to be a *man*. Without tender sensibilities. Without . . . I swear his ways are positively womanly sometimes!"

"Reeve, that's not true."

"Burr is weak. I cannot abide weakness in a man." Reeve reached to the table and took a julep from a heavy silver tray. "What was he saying when I came in?"

"Nothing important."

"He never says anything important. That doesn't answer my question."

Mary stirred uneasily in her chair, wondering why she hesitated. She had no desire to be evasive, no reason, but something was warning her not to repeat Burr's conversation. She should repeat it, she thought, if only out of loyalty to her husband. Still, the words would not come. "Burr seems afraid of you," she said finally.

"Oh? What makes you think so?"

"He seems nervous in your presence."

"Perhaps, in my presence, he is reminded of his inadequacies." Reeve raised his glass and drank. He gazed at Mary for some moments, a smile edging his handsome mouth. "But we shouldn't waste this fine evening discussing Burr . . . I have a surprise for you, Miss Mary."

"But you're always surprising me."

"This is special. I have decided to give a fancy-dress ball in your honor. It will be in two weeks. The servants will begin tomorrow to prepare the ballroom."

"A ball! Reeve, what a charming thought."

"For a charming lady." Reeve raised his glass to Mary. "For you, my dear." He rose, going to the far end of the veranda and gazing out at his lands. His eyes glittered. They flashed. "My great-great grandfather, Ashly Sinclair, gave the first formal ball at Lucy's Court," he said. "It was in honor of his new wife, Lady Lucinda. . . . Those were glorious times."

Reeve could see those times in his mind—carriages arriving by the score, pickaninnies rushing to assist the splendid ladies and gentlemen; inside, great silver punchbowls and banks of flowers and hundreds of candles shining in crystal chandeliers. He could hear the musicians playing the Lucy's Court Waltz. He could hear the rustle of silk and lace as beautiful young

439

women glided across the marble floor in the arms of dashing young men.

Mary was troubled by Reeve's expression. She went to him, lightly touching his arm. "Reeve? You're a million miles away."

"No." He smiled. He took Mary's hands and kissed them. "I have just had a most wonderful idea. We will have a Confederate Ball. Ladies will come in the gowns and petticoats their grandmothers wore seventy years ago. And gentlemen will come in Confederate uniforms."

"Why?"

"Because those were glorious times. They had grace and beauty. They had magic."

"Some people would disagree with you," Mary said, more sharply than she had intended.

"Indeed they would. But I know the truth."

"You couldn't possibly, Reeve. You were not even born then."

He smiled again. It was an indulgent smile, the kind he might have given to a confused child. "The truth is in my blood, in my heart. It's here at Lucy's Court."

"Time passes and things change. Thank God they do."

"I don't expect you to understand, my dear. Not yet. When you have come to know Lucy's Court . . . and my friends and their plantations, then you will feel as we feel."

Reeve had meant his words to be reassuring; they were, to Mary, chilling. She did not want to feel as Reeve felt, for to do so was to accept without question the brutal history of Lucy's Court. She had put such thoughts out of her mind but now, after Burr's conversation, after talk of a Confederate Ball, she could not do that. Her life, at its worst, had never been as cruel and mean as the lives of those who had worked these lands, yet she felt a kinship with them. She knew what it was to be powerless, to live in constant fear.

"What is it, Mary?" Reeve asked. "What is troubling you?"

You are troubling me, thought Mary. I married you but I don't know you. All the doubts I forced aside are haunting me now. "Perhaps I'm tired," she said quietly to Reeve. "A lot has happened in a very short time." That's true, she said to herself; there was Simon's suicide, and my estrangement from Rose. There was this impetuous marriage. And now I am here, in a place of beauty but also of ugliness. "Perhaps too much has happened."

"I do believe Burr has upset you. . . . Well, I have the cure for that. There is a surprise awaiting you in your bedroom. Come." He smiled, holding out his hand. "Let me show you."

Mary slipped her hand into Reeve's, walking with him through the French doors into the house. In silence, they walked into the tall and stately hall, going to the curved staircase. Family portraits covered the wall at the side of the stair. Mary had often paused to study the portraits, but now she did not look at them. She stared straight ahead and tried to quell her wildly racing thoughts.

"Be careful, my dear," Reeve said as they reached the second floor. "You almost tripped."

"I'm sorry."

Reeve and Mary had adjoining suites in the east wing of the house. Reeve's rooms were large, decorated with antique furnishings and carpets and wainscoting of dark, hand-carved oak. A portrait of his father adorned one wall. The windows were curtained in dark velvet and sashed with gold cords. Mary's rooms were only slightly smaller. The walls were pale blue silk, as were the chairs and settees. A blue and gold Axminster carpet sat upon the floor. There was a lacy canopy bed piled with lace-edged pillows and comforters. The dressing table was oval, strewn with silver-backed brushes and combs and delicate crystal bottles and silver-framed hand mirrors.

"I hope you will be pleased," Reeve said now.

"Pleased?" Mary followed his gaze to the bed. There, atop all the pillows and comforters lay an exquisite antique ball gown. It was of silk and lace, aged to a pale tea color. The bodice was fitted, decolleté, with the merest suggestion of off-the-shoulder sleeves. The waist was tiny and from it flowed a voluminous skirt overlaid with lace. Next to the gown were half a dozen taffeta and lace petticoats in the same tea color. A jewel box lay open, displaying the famed Sinclair pearls.

"It was my great-grandmother's gown," Reeve explained. "I had the servants take it from the trunk in the attic. I want you to wear it at our ball. It is especially appropriate, now that it is to be a Confederate Ball."

"I'd be afraid to wear it, Reeve. It's magnificent, but so fragile."

"Nonsense. There are many wonderful evenings left in that gown. You will give it new life. And the pearls too." He smiled, lifting the jewel box. "Look how they glow."

Mary had never seen the Sinclair pearls before. She was properly impressed, for they were remarkable—the size of bird's eggs and perfectly matched, with a deep, rosy luster. Gently, Mary removed them from the box and held them against her hand. "No," she said, returning them. "They are too splendid to wear. They should be in a vault."

Reeve laughed. He tilted Mary's face to him. "Beauty is not meant to be locked away in a vault . . . you will wear the pearls."

"I would be uncomfortable, Reeve. I would rather wear my own pearls, the double strand Harley gave me."

"Harley! I am sick to death of hearing about Harley. Not a day goes by without your mentioning him in one way or another. I have had enough of it, Mary. Do you understand?"

"I'm sorry. I didn't realize—"

"Now you do. And now I hope I have heard the last of him." Reeve went to a chair and sat down. He pressed the tips of his fingers together, staring at his wife. "Try the gown on, Mary. I would like to see you in it."

"It seems a little small."

"Try it on. At once!"

Mary's eyes darkened in anger. She looked quickly at Reeve, about to speak, then changed her mind. She gathered gown and petticoats into her arms and walked off to her dressing room. Inside, she leaned her head against the wall and brushed a tear from her cheek. Reeve had, she remembered, snapped at her a few times before. They had been small outbursts, tiny compared to his outbursts with the servants. On those occasions she had seen a cold and deadly fury in him. She had heard the coldness in his voice. She had said nothing, refusing to think about it. Now she was forced to think about it; now she was forced to think about the nature of the man she had married.

"Hurry, my dear," Reeve called from the bedroom.

"I cannot wait to see you."

Sighing, Mary stepped out of her own simple dress and into the masses of petticoats. She slipped the gown over her head, struggling to make it fit. It was at least a size too small; she dared not look at herself in the mirror.

"Are you hurrying, Miss Mary?" Reeve called again, more urgently.

Mary picked up her skirts and returned slowly to the bedroom. Reeve had changed into a dark silk robe. He stood when she entered and, at the sight of her, his face colored with pleasure.

"I can't wear this," Mary said, tugging at the gown. "It's much too small . . . it's indecent."

Reeve was not listening. His eyes roamed over Mary's bare shoulders, over her creamy breasts spilling from their lacy restraint, over the abrupt curve of her waist. "Come here," he said, and it was an order.

Mary took several halting steps. It was hard for her to walk in the gown and even harder for her to breathe. "Reeve, this is foolish."

"Come here."

Mary risked another few steps, stopping just in front of Reeve. His eyes were very black. His mouth, twisted with lust, was no longer handsome. Roughly, he pulled at her breasts, pressing his hot mouth to her neck. He felt her flinch and that excited his lust to madness.

"Don't," Mary pleaded, frightened by the look in his eyes. She tried to break his iron grip. She fought, but to no avail. "Please don't."

Mary's resistance was thrilling to Reeve, for it was the stuff of his fantasies. He stripped away her gown and petticoats and threw her to the floor. He fell on top of her naked body, groaning, his breath coming in short bursts, his hands boring into her flesh. He bit and clawed. He took her violently, oblivious to her tears.

Long after Reeve had gone, Mary lay sobbing in her bed. She rose only once and only to lock her door.

The next day was warm but Mary wore a long-sleeved dress and a scarf about her neck to cover her bruises. She was pale, drawn. There were dark circles about her eyes, for she had not slept. All through the night she had thought about Reeve, about the man she had married so hastily. She did not deny the attraction she had felt for him, though she realized, as others had realized, that there were two Reeves; the passionate man she had known, if briefly, in New York, and the brutal man she knew, if briefly, at Lucy's Court. One was the true Reeve, she concluded, the other false.

Mary's first inclination had been to pack her bags and leave Lucy's Court. She had been on the verge of doing just that when she decided it was wrong to run away. She decided to stay, to discover the real Reeve Sinclair and thus the fate of her marriage. With those thoughts in mind, Mary went looking for Burr.

She found him in the music room, seated at a gleaming grand piano. His hands rested on the keys. His dark head was bent over an old, hand-written music sheet. "I'm sorry to interrupt you," she said softly. "I can come back, if you're busy."

"Not at all." Burr stood. He smiled at Mary. "I'm not doing anything important. This room is my hiding place. It always has been . . . once it was used for Sunday musicales. But that was many years ago. I'm the only one who uses it now."

"That's a beautiful piano. Do you play?"

"Yes. Poorly, I'm afraid. Musical talent doesn't run in our family. Years ago, musicians were brought from Charleston and Atlanta to play here. They wrote a lot of their own music. Quite lovely music." Burr opened a large leather folio in which were dozens of yellowing music sheets. "Look," he said. "The ink is faded and the paper is beginning to crumble, but these are all original compositions. I always wanted to have them copied and published in a book."

"Why don't you?"

"It's Lucy's Court music. Reeve won't allow it out of the house. Pity. Soon it will be dust. . . . But you didn't come here to listen to me rambling on. May I do something for you, Mary?"

"I have a favor to ask. I want to see where the sharecroppers live. Will you take me?"

"I can't." Burr turned away. He closed the folio and walked to the windows, leaning against the cushioned seat. "I don't know what your reason is, but I can't oblige. I am sorry, Mary."

"Is it a question of time? If you and Emily have plans, or if you're going to your office—"

"No. I seldom go to my office when Reeve is in residence. I'm only in his way. And Emily is lunching in Charleston today."

"Then?"

"Reeve has made it clear that you are not to visit certain areas. They're not pleasant areas, Mary. I would be happy to take you for a drive, but not there."

"I'm putting you in a difficult position. I don't mean to. You're a nice man, Burr. The last thing I want to do is cause you trouble. I'll go by myself."

"Wait." Burr walked swiftly across the room. He took Mary's hand, turning her away from the door.

"You mustn't," he said earnestly. "Reeve would be furious."

"I've seen something of Reeve's temper. I don't like it, but I'm not afraid of it anymore. Burr, try to understand. I have to know how the sharecroppers live. There are too many questions in my mind. I have to *know.*"

"Knowing won't change anything."

"It may."

"The sharecroppers live in shacks, Mary. Small, crowded shacks with no amenities at all. *I* think it's terrible. Other people think it's what they deserve. More than they deserve."

"Reeve thinks that?"

"Not only Reeve. Conditions here are not much worse than conditions at other plantations. Share-cropping is a hard, miserable life. That's no secret. But it comes as a surprise to some people. Cynthia visited the sharecroppers once. She returned to Lucy's Court with fire in her eye and shame in her heart, shame for the Sinclairs. That visit changed her attitude toward . . . everything."

"Yes, I can imagine." Mary glanced away, thinking about Cynthia Sinclair. Her thoughts were filled with sadness, for she knew that in marrying Reeve she had lost Cynthia's friendship. Her cable to Cynthia had gone unanswered, as had her letter. She had tried to telephone, but to no avail. "Cynthia is a woman of strong convictions."

"You have that in common."

"Sometimes I allow myself to be swayed. Not this time."

"Then you are determined to go?" Burr studied the resolute set of Mary's chin, the dark blue of her eyes.

447

He nodded. "Yes, I see you are. . . . You can't go alone. I'll drive you."

"That's not necessary."

"I'm afraid it is, Mary. The sharecroppers are Negroes. It would be a scandal if you went there unescorted. Excuse me, I'll have a car brought round."

Burr telephoned the garage and within minutes a low-slung Pierce Arrow was driven to the doors of Lucy's Court. Burr dismissed the driver. He held the door for Mary and then got behind the wheel. "You had better start preparing an explanation for Reeve," he said quietly, turning the car into the driveway.

They rode in silence. It was beautiful country, lush and undisturbed, all trees and birds and heavy, scented air. The roads were unpaved but they were smooth, posted every few miles with signs warning against trespassing and poaching. Mary smiled, suddenly reminded of Abbeywood Manor, where poaching had been a serious criminal offense. "Do you get many poachers?" she asked, amused.

"No. We're isolated here. Miles and miles from civilization."

"So I've noticed. It's a private kingdom, isn't it?"

"Reeve chooses to think of it that way. He has a feudal turn of mind. Father was the same. And Grandfather."

"But not you."

"I don't know why." Burr shrugged, his eyes fast on the road. "As a boy I heard the same stories Reeve heard. All the gloriously romantic stories of our ancestors and their daring deeds. . . . It's strange, really. Those stories made a great impression on Reeve. They meant nothing to me. I grew tired of hearing them. Reeve couldn't hear them often enough. Father always maintained that I lacked family spirit. In that, he was correct."

"What of your own sons?"

Now Burr's expression softened. He glanced side-long at Mary, smiling. "The twins are the joy of my life," he said. "They don't take anything too seriously, not Lucy's Court, not the family fortune, not the family legends." Burr's smile dimmed when he thought about his youngest son Beau. "Beau, on the other hand, is a true Sinclair. He's Reeve's protégé. Ever since Reeve lost his own son . . . But I am talking out of turn again. Forgive me, Mary."

"Reeve never discusses the accident."

"No."

"It must have been terrible for him. Sometimes tragedies change people."

"Sometimes."

"Burr, it's not my intention to pry. I just want to know about Reeve. I know so little."

"Emily says women know things by intuition."

"Are you trying to change the subject?"

"It's not a good subject, Mary. I have no answers, if it's answers you are looking for."

"But you know Reeve very well. You understand him."

Yes, thought Burr, I understand him. And it's to my sorrow that I do. "We are not close," he said.

"Still—"

"I can't help you, Mary. I am sorry." Burr turned the car onto a back road. Here the landscape changed abruptly. It was barer, browner, the trees choked with tangled and thorny vines. "We're almost there," he said. "Another five miles."

449

Burr and Mary stopped finally at a stretch of land on which huddled the miserable dwellings of the sharecroppers. They were, as Burr had warned, nothing more than shacks, unpainted wooden shacks with tin roofs. They were very old, the doorframes rotting away, the tiny front windows cracked, and had neither electricity nor plumbing. The land around the shacks was rock hard, covered not with grass but with a thick layer of brown dust which rose in clouds when the breeze stirred. Huge black flies swarmed about the reeking outhouses.

"Well," Burr sighed. "Are you ready to go back now?"

Mary turned. She raised sad, surprised eyes to her brother-in-law. "It's worse than Hexter," she said.

"I beg your pardon?"

"I was born in Hexter, a mill village in England. There a few men lived in splendor and everyone else lived in poverty. The worst poverty I have ever seen, until now . . . When we first came to America, we lived in a slum. Even that was luxury compared to this. The horses in Reeve's stables live better than this."

"Horses have value to him."

"And people don't."

Burr crossed his hands on the wheel. He stared through the windshield at the mean little shacks, the patches of bare and dusty earth. He looked weary.

"I apologize, Burr," Mary said. "I shouldn't press you this way. Some things speak for themselves."

"Shall we go now?"

"Please."

Burr was relieved. He started the car and drove off, keeping his gaze on the road, away from Mary. "Why did you want to come here?" he asked.

"This is part of Lucy's Court. Lucy's Court is part of Reeve. . . . You were right, Burr. I was looking for answers. Unfortunately, I found them."

"I think you knew what you would find."

"I wasn't certain." Mary put her hand to her bruised neck. Ugly memories rushed to her mind and she felt a chill. "I knew Reeve only a very short time before I married him. He swept me off my feet. But my feet are back on the ground now, where they belong."

"I urge you not to be hasty."

"Hasty? There's an old expression . . . Marry in haste, repent in leisure."

"You need time to get used—"

"No! I've been making excuses for Reeve ever since I arrived at Lucy's Court. I can't make excuses for his . . . shantytown. I won't. Those men and women live in misery. I lived in misery myself, years ago. I haven't forgotten what it was like. I'll never forget. And I have no wish to forgive."

Burr's hands tightened on the wheel. Nervously, his tongue flicked at his lips. "You mustn't defy Reeve," he said. "You mustn't." Burr was alarmed, and for good reason. Reeve's first wife had tried to defy him and had only come to grief; Cynthia had tried and she, too, had come to grief. "I don't often give advice, Mary. But in this case I advise you to think carefully before you say or do anything."

Mary did not reply. She looked out at the countryside, beautiful once more, for they were on the road to Lucy's Court. She thought about facing Reeve and the thought was daunting. Again, she touched her bruised neck; again, she remembered. Her heart was pounding by the time they reached the house. Her mouth was as dry as dust.

"Mary, please consider my advice," Burr said, opening the car door.

"I will. Thank you, Burr. You've been kind to me and I appreciate it. I'm only sorry I made things difficult for you."

Mary looked at him for a moment. She smiled, turning then and walking up the sparkling stone steps to the house. She let herself inside, her heels clicking on the marble floor as she went to the staircase. Mary did not see the shadow at the top of the stairs for her mind was on Reeve, on what she must say to him.

The second-floor hallway was cool, absolutely still. Porcelain vases filled with flowers sat atop slender marble pedestals. Sinclair aunts and uncles and cousins stared serenely from gilt-framed portraits. The servants had finished their chores and were nowhere in sight. Mary walked to her bedroom. She opened the door. Her desk was antique rosewood and from it she took pen and paper, beginning to write in her quick, clear hand.

"Did you have a nice time, my dear?"

The pen fell from Mary's fingers. She spun around to see Reeve sitting in a chair by the windows. His face was impassive, though his eyes burned. "I . . . didn't know you were home. It's early."

"Indeed . . . Well, did you have a nice time?"

"I went for a drive."

"It's a lovely day for a drive. And there is so much to see. Was Burr a satisfactory guide? Did he show you all the points of interest?"

Mary heard the mocking tone in Reeve's voice. She sighed. "We needn't play games," she said tiredly. "It's obvious you know where I went. But Burr had nothing to do with it. He tried to discourage me . . . I insisted."

"What spirit you have, my dear. Or did you forget that I had specifically forbidden you to go near the sharecroppers?"

"I'm not a child, Reeve. I won't be told where I can and cannot go. I wanted to see how they lived. I saw. That's all there was to it."

"I think not. You have that look in your eye. That reformer's look. One part righteous indignation, one part zeal . . . You imagine I do the sharecroppers an injustice. Is that correct?"

"I don't imagine. I know."

Reeve smiled. It was a nasty smile and Mary looked away. "You are new to Lucy's Court," he said slowly, "and so I cannot expect you to understand all our ways. But understand this . . . those are *my* negras and *my* lands. I stand no interference. Not even from you, Miss Mary. In future, you will kindly stay out of my affairs."

"I didn't intend to interfere. It would be useless. We don't see things the same way."

"It is not necessary that we do. You are a woman of mind and spirit, but I didn't marry you for mind and spirit." Reeve's black eyes traveled the length of Mary's body. He stood, crossing the room to where she sat. "You know why I married you." He smiled.

"Yes. I do now."

"And you married me for the same reason. In my arms you came alive. You knew passion you had not known before . . . perhaps that is troubling you. Perhaps that is why you locked your door last night." Reeve put his hands on Mary's shoulders, staring into her eyes. "Never . . . *never* lock your door to me again." He drew his hands back. He walked a short distance away. "For one thing, it is an empty gesture. I have keys to all the locks at Lucy's Court. For another thing, I am perfectly capable of breaking down any door in this house."

Mary did not doubt him. She felt fear rise in her, a cold and terrible fear tightening about her heart. She knew she could not spend another night at Lucy's Court. She knew, too, that she must find a way to leave without arousing Reeve's anger. Desperately, she searched her mind for an excuse, any excuse. "Reeve . . . I'd hoped we would be able to talk calmly . . . I had a telephone call from New York, you see. There are business problems. I promised I would return at once."

Reeve's eyes narrowed. "You are a poor liar," he said. "You had no telephone call. I am informed of all calls and all mail. *Why* are you lying, Mary?"

"I was . . . merely trying to be tactful. The truth is I need time to think. Time away from here. I'm very confused, Reeve. A lot has happened. I want to go back to New York for a while. It's best for both of us."

"I disagree. You are not going anywhere."

"I'm going back to New York. You certainly can't keep me here if I don't wish to stay."

"Can't I? Do you think I would allow you to embarrass me? Think again. You are staying here, as we planned . . . unless, of course, you want to walk to Charleston."

"I'll take one of the cars."

"No. The garage and the stables will be closed to you. And don't suppose Burr will intervene. He hasn't the courage to defy me. No one at Lucy's Court would dare defy my orders."

Slowly, very slowly, Mary grasped the meaning of Reeve's words. She was horrified. "Do you realize what you're saying?" she cried. "You can't keep me here against my will. Surely you wouldn't try."

"Wouldn't I?"

"The law will have something to say about it."

"The law? I am the only law at Lucy's Court. The only law in Sinclair County, for that matter. The sheriff takes his orders from me. . . . But all that aside, I'm not really keeping you here against your will. You are free to leave at any time. Providing you are willing to walk to Charleston. It is a fair distance."

"You're despicable!"

Reeve laughed. "I remember Cynthia sitting in this very room and saying the very same thing."

"It's no wonder she dislikes you so."

"But it's not me she dislikes. It's herself."

"Why should she dislike herself?"

"An interesting story, that." Reeve sat down. His earlier anger had passed. Now he was amused, enjoying himself, his hands resting lightly on the arms of the chair. "It was some years ago. I became suspicious of Cynthia's many trips to Charleston. So I had her watched—no, don't turn away, my dear. I am just getting to the interesting part—and I discovered that Cynthia, proper and honorable Cynthia, was having *quite* a romance with a Charleston artist. When I confronted her, she called me despicable and slapped my face."

"Poor Cynthia. I can imagine what you did in return."

"I did only what she had wanted me to do for a long time," Reeve drawled, smiling. "I undressed her and threw her on the bed and—"

"My God, no." Mary felt sick. She put her head in her hands and closed her eyes. "My God, how could you? You're . . . you're—"

"I am a man." Reeve stood. He walked halfway to the door and then stopped. "I will not disturb you tonight, my dear," he said. "You need rest after your . . . busy day. We'll have breakfast together in the morning. Things always look better in the morning . . . all this foolishness will be forgotten."

Nineteen

It was after midnight and all the windows of the sharecroppers' shacks were dark. A great stillness cloaked the land, broken only by the occasional sounds of crickets. There was a full moon, silvery against the pitch black sky. Reeve looked up at the moon as he stepped from his roadster. In the shadowy, silvery light his eyes seemed filled with menace.

Reeve had been drinking since eight o'clock. He was not drunk but neither was he sober, for he had consumed half a bottle of bourbon. Now he took a flask from the car, uncapped it, and drank again. He felt the fire of the bourbon race through him. He felt strong, invincible. He strode to one of the shacks and pounded on the door. When no answer came, he flung the door open.

Ezra Clay, a middle-aged Negro sharecropper stood in a corner of the one-room shack, shielding his young wife. "No, Mr. Reeve," he said, "not again. I'm begging you, Mr. Reeve. Leave us be."

"Now, Ezra, you know why I am here. Don't make a fuss. Claudine likes it . . . don't you, Claudine?" Reeve lit a lamp. He stared at the sharecropper's wife and smiled lewdly. "You can go, Ezra. Or you can stay and watch. But Claudine is going to make me happy tonight."

Tears wet Claudine's cheeks. She clung to Ezra, though she knew he could not protect her; she knew there was no protection from Reeve Sinclair.

"Please, Mr. Reeve," Ezra pleaded. "This be wrong. I'm begging you—"

Reeve struck Ezra with his riding crop. "One more word and I'll throw your nigger ass off my lands. Now get the hell out of my way." Reeve grabbed Claudine's arm, pulling her toward him. "You know what I want, girl. Get rid of that ugly nightgown and we'll have our fun."

Claudine looked helplessly at Ezra. In an agony of shame and fear, she began to undress. Ezra could stand no more. He ran from the shack, his despairing cries shattering the stillness of the night. Reeve heard nothing, so intent was he on Claudine's naked young body. He sat at the edge of the bed, motioning her forward.

Claudine knew what was expected. She sank to her knees before Reeve, removing his boots and then his trousers. She was crying, moaning piteously. When he forced her to look at him, there was only loathing in her eyes.

Reeve smiled. He reached for Claudine but, at that moment, the door crashed open and Ezra burst into the room, a rifle in his hands. "Go 'way from him, Claudine," he said. "This be between him and me."

"*Ezra,*" she cried, "they put the rope around your neck for this."

"Claudine is right," Reeve said calmly. "You don't want to hang, Ezra. Put the gun down and we will forget this ever happened."

"I ain't forgetting, Mr. Reeve. It be too late. Now you be getting what you deserve. The Bible say—"

"Put that gun down and stop talking like a fool." Reeve's voice was impatient but utterly without fear. He had never feared his sharecroppers, for he had never thought of them as men with angers and passions of their own. They were, to him, merely children, lazy and slow-witted children at that. "This is your last chance, Ezra. If you do not put that gun down at once, I will have the sheriff on you. Do you hear me, Ezra?"

"I hear you, Mr. Reeve."

"Well?"

"This be my answer," Ezra said, pulling the trigger.

The rifle blast caught Reeve squarely in the center of his chest. It jerked him upward, then threw him back on the bed. Blood poured from his gaping wound, soaking his shirt, trickling down his bare legs. His head fell to one side and the last signs of life went from his black eyes.

Claudine was screaming, running crazily around the room. Ezra put the rifle down. He snatched his wife's nightgown from the floor and gave it to her. "Get dressed," he said quietly. "Folks be coming by any time."

"Ezra," Claudine sobbed, "you done put the rope around your neck."

"I ain't sorry. It be damn time someone take a gun to Mr. Reeve. Damn time." Ezra heard footsteps, shouts coming from outside. He turned and walked to the doorway. "It be over now," he called to the crowd of sharecroppers. "It be all over."

The butler had awakened Burr from a deep sleep. He

had been groggy, hardly able to follow the older man's anxious pleadings for him to come downstairs. He had heard Reeve's name mentioned, and Ezra Clay's, but it had been several moments before he made any connection between the two. When finally he did, a terrible dread assailed him. He said only a few words to Emily and then, in robe and slippers, rushed downstairs.

Now, Burr stood with Ezra in the moonlit driveway of Lucy's Court. The great willows rustled in the breeze and crickets called. The air was heavy, scented with honeysuckle. It was a night like any other except that Reeve lay dead, wrapped in a blanket in the flatbed of Ezra's wagon. "That be the whole story, Mr. Burr," Ezra was saying. "I begged Mr. Reeve to leave us be. I begged him. But he jes' go his way. I done got Tucker's old gun. Mr. Reeve say, 'Put it down, put it down.' I done shot him dead."

Burr had heard Ezra's story three times and three times he had gone to the wagon to look upon the face of his dead brother. He had looked at him with pity, for he thought Reeve's violent death the inevitable result of his violent life. He knew his brother had abused the sharecroppers and assaulted their wives, doing so without the slightest scruple or concern. "I . . . understand, Ezra. We must think what to do now. . . . It will go hard for you." Burr knew just how hard. He knew Ezra would never make it to the courthouse, for the sheriff would notify the Klansmen of Sinclair County and Ezra would be hanged from the nearest tree. "We must think."

"I ain't running, Mr. Burr. You call the sheriff. I be here when he come."

Burr sighed. He rubbed his pale face, glancing

toward the wagon. "Yes, you stay here," he said slowly.
"I must speak with Mrs. Sinclair. . . . Is Claudine all
right? Was she harmed?"

"She be scared, Mr. Burr."

"Yes, I see. . . . Wait here, Ezra. I'll be back." Burr
hurried off to the house. He opened the door and
walked into the hall, startled to see Mary standing
there. "Mary . . . I'm afraid there's been . . . an accident."

"Reeve?"

"Yes, I'm afraid so."

"Has he been hurt?"

"There was . . . a shooting. Come with me, Mary.
We must talk."

Mary looked closely at Burr's pale face. She saw the
distress in his eyes, the thin, tight line of his mouth. "Is
Reeve dead?" she asked.

Burr lowered his gaze to the floor. Moments passed
in silence. When he looked again at Mary, his eyes were
moist. "I'm sorry," he said. "There was a shooting . . .
Reeve is dead. I'm sorry, Mary."

"My God!"

Burr took Mary's arm, leading her to a delicate gilt
chair. "Are you all right? I'll fetch the brandy."

"No . . . Wait, Burr. Tell me what happened."

Burr glanced quickly about the hall, for he did not
want to be overheard by the servants. He did not want
to start a panic amongst them, though he realized it was
probably unavoidable. They knew the Klansmen as
well as he did, and the Klansmen of Sinclair County
believed that when one Negro was guilty all Negroes
were guilty. Ezra had acted alone but, in one way or
another, Negroes for miles around would be made to
share his guilt. "We must talk, Mary. Not here. Let's go

into the library."

Mary rose unsteadily. She said nothing as they walked to the library; her thoughts were too confused, too disorderly to put into words. She felt no grief and that troubled her. Whatever else Reeve had been, he had also been her husband.

Burr opened the heavy double doors of the library and seated Mary in a deep leather chair. He went back to close the doors, then poured two brandies. "Please drink it, Mary," he urged. "It will help."

"Thank you. What . . . what happened?"

Burr repeated Ezra's story. He spared no details, apologizing often for his candor. But Mary was not surprised by what she heard. She recalled Reeve's attack on her so many years ago; she recalled his attack on her only last night. The danger she had sensed in him had been real. It had described his life and, finally, it had taken his life.

"That's as much as I know," Burr finished. "I believe Ezra. Even if I had any doubts, Reeve's past behavior confirms Ezra's account of things."

"Yes, of course. It's so sad all around. He'll spend years in prison, won't he? His life is over too."

"Ezra's life is over, but not the way you think. . . . Have you ever heard of the Ku Klux Klan?"

"I've read stories in the newspapers. My God, was Reeve a part of that?"

"No. Others in Sinclair County *are* a part of it, however. Ezra will never see a court or a prison. He will be lynched. There's—"

"Lynched?" Mary jumped out of her chair. She stared in astonishment at Burr. *"Lynched?"*

Burr took a swallow of brandy. He took another and then refilled his glass. "Most people in Sinclair County have nothing to do with the Klan," he said. "Most people just . . . mind their own business."

"Allowing the Klan to flourish!"

"Nobody challenges the Klan. They're vicious, illiterate trash . . . but they're deadly. One of the Cantrells tried to drive them out. He failed. Meanwhile his house was burned to the ground and a gasoline bomb was thrown through the window of his store. Klansmen always strike at night, in groups, concealed in hoods and sheets. They are cowards, you see. But *deadly*. They will lynch Ezra and no one will stop them."

"The sheriff?"

"He's also a coward. He fears the Sinclairs and the Klan equally."

"Then there's nothing we can do?"

"Well, there may be something. But we would have to agree, Mary. It would mean lying to practically everyone."

"Lying is the least of the sins around here."

"Yes." Burr passed his hand across his face. He sat down. "This is very hard," he said. "Reeve was my brother. I have certain duties to him, even now. Yet I cannot hand Ezra over to a lynch mob."

"If you have a plan, I'm listening."

"It's simply this: I will tell the sheriff that Reeve shot himself while cleaning his gun. Such accidents happen all the time. He would not question my word."

"Won't there be an inquest?"

Burr shook his head. "My word would be sufficient. And yours, of course, should you agree."

"I don't know." Mary sighed, pacing the vast book-lined room. "I don't know if Reeve deserved to die. Only God knows that. . . . I do know I can't cooperate

463

in a lynching, no matter the circumstances." She turned, looking at Burr. "All right. Tell the sheriff it was an accident."

"You must be absolutely sure."

"There are only two choices and both of them grate on my conscience. . . . What a nightmare this is, Burr! I keep thinking I'll wake up and none of this will have happened."

"I wish that were true. I would give anything to make it true. Unfortunately, that's not possible." Burr looked at his watch. He stood. "There is a great deal to do and not much time. If you have any second thoughts, tell me now."

"No second thoughts."

"It won't be easy, Mary. It was a circus after Father died. It will be the same now . . . people coming and going. Questions. Newspapers wanting stories and interviews. Telephone calls from all over. Arrangements to be made . . . Are you up to it?"

"I have to be up to it."

Burr walked to the door. "I'll deal with Ezra," he said. "And collect Reeve's car. Then I'll be back. Shall I get Emily to sit with you while I am gone?"

"Let's not drag anyone else into this, Burr. It's bad enough as it is."

"I know. I'm sorry."

Burr left the library. The hall was silent, empty, yet he could almost feel the presence of his Sinclair ancestors. He could feel their condemnation, for he knew his actions on this night betrayed the customs and beliefs by which they had lived. With a chill, he recalled the motto on the Sinclair family crest; "To serve our friends and vanquish our enemies." I am their enemy now, he thought.

Burr's face was somber as he walked again into the moonlit night. There was a dull ache behind his eyes. He saw Ezra standing in the shadows and he went to him. "Ezra, you must listen to me very carefully," he said.

"The sheriff be on his way, Mr. Burr?"

"Forget the sheriff for a moment. Just listen to me. Pay attention. This is important."

"Yassir, Mr. Burr."

"What you did was very bad. It was wrong. I can't condone what you did, Ezra . . . still, I have tried to understand. I understand your wanting to protect your wife."

"Mr. Reeve be using Claudine four times since he be back."

"Just listen to me, Ezra. What you did was *wrong,* but I understand why you did it. And I have decided not to tell the sheriff. . . . You shouldn't be hanged for wanting to protect Claudine."

Ezra gaped at Burr, for he could not comprehend what he was hearing. He had spent all of his forty-five years in a sharecropper's shack at Lucy's Court and not once in all those years had he known any kindness, however small, from the Sinclairs. They had been his masters, first Preston and then Reeve, brutally seizing what they wanted, brutally punishing resistance. Ezra had come to believe all white men were like that. Now, looking at Burr Sinclair, he did not know what to believe. "But . . . Mr. Reeve be dead," he said in confusion.

"I am going to tell the sheriff that Mr. Reeve shot himself while cleaning his gun. The matter will end there. Without lynch mobs."

Suddenly Ezra was crying, great tears rolling down

his lined black cheeks. "Thank you, Mr. Burr," he said, sniffing loudly. "You done saved my life. The Lord bless you, Mr. Burr."

"I'm not finished, Ezra. Listen to me carefully . . . what you did was *wrong* and nothing like that must ever happen again. If anyone else is ever harmed, white or Negro, I will personally deliver all the sharecroppers to the sheriff and let him sort it out. He will, too, with the help of his white-robed friends. There will be no second chances."

"I understand, Mr. Burr. I understand."

"Be sure you do. And be sure you tell the others. This is my first and only warning."

"Yassir, Mr. Burr. I understand."

"Very well." Burr walked to the wagon, climbing onto the high front seat. "Come along, Ezra," he called. "I need you to drive."

They drove beyond the stables, beyond the kennels, to a handsome one-story building known at Lucy's Court as The Armory. It had been built to Reeve's specifications some ten years before and had immediately become the starting point for weekend hunting trips. Its racks and cases contained every manner of weapon: sharp-bladed knives, bows and arrows, pistols, shotguns, and rifles. Reeve had been exceedingly proud of his armory.

Now Burr and Ezra carried Reeve's body inside. It was dark and they stumbled a couple of times, but finally they managed to lower Reeve into a leather club chair. "Wait for me outside, Ezra," Burr said. The door closed and Burr turned on the lights. He could not bring himself to look at Reeve. He knelt at his side and held his hand, a hand already cold. "Forgive me, Reeve," he whispered. "I wish there were another way.

I wish . . ."

Slowly, Burr rose to his feet. He took a rifle from the rack and loaded it. He closed his eyes then, for his head was pounding. It was no longer a dull ache but a screaming pain and he had to steady himself against the wall. "Forgive me, Reeve," he whispered again, picking up the rifle. He placed it at an angle on the floor and placed Reeve's finger upon the trigger. The shot echoed for several moments, surely the worst moments in Burr's life. He fled, running a jagged line to Ezra's wagon. "Take me to Mr. Reeve's car," he said, panting and gasping for breath. "Hurry!"

Ezra helped Burr into the wagon. He lifted the reins and drove off, barely able to see the road through the tears in his eyes.

"Thank you, Sheriff." Burr nodded, opening the front door. "You've been most kind."

The sheriff, a tall and brawny man dressed in the tan uniform of Sinclair County, twisted his hat nervously in his hands. "It's a sad day," he said. "A mighty sad day for all of us. Mr. Reeve was just about the greatest man we ever knew. After your daddy, that is. I reckon they was two of a kind."

"Yes."

"Anything I can do for you, Mr. Burr? Or for Miz Sinclair? Must of been a powerful shock to her, this happening on her honeymoon and all. Poor thing looked wore out."

"Thank you, but there's nothing anyone can do now."

"I reckon not. . . . I sure am sorry, Mr. Burr. Life's a bastard sometimes."

"Yes, Sheriff. I know."

"Well, I'll be on my way. If there's anything I can do—"

"Thank you."

Burr watched the sheriff walk down the path toward his car. He closed the door and leaned against it, sighing. He was exhausted. He wanted only to crawl into his bed and stay there, the covers drawn over his head.

"Burr?" Mary called from the far end of the hall. "Has the sheriff gone?"

"Yes, he's gone." Burr straightened up. He tied the belt of his robe and crossed the wide hall to his sister-in-law. Mary had been remarkably calm through their whole ordeal, calmest of all when Reeve's body had been taken away, but now he saw the awful strain in her face. She looked haggard, as if she had not slept in days. Her mouth was white and pinched. "I'm sorry," he said once again. "Why don't you go upstairs and rest? I can handle the arrangements."

"No, I'd rather keep busy. Was the sheriff satisfied?"

"His report says accidental shooting."

"Thank God it's over."

"That part is over. There's still the funeral. . . . I hardly know where to begin. So many people must be notified. And a statement must be issued to the press." Burr rubbed his tired eyes. His shoulders seemed to sag. "Sinclair Mills will be affected most of all."

Mary opened the door to the library. "We'd best get started," she said. "The sooner we start, the sooner this nightmare will be over."

"Yes." Burr nodded, following Mary into the library. "Why, Emily"—he stared at his wife, startled—"what are you doing in here?"

"Right now I'm pouring coffee. After we've had our coffee I'm going to help you all make your telephone calls." Emily Sinclair smiled. She was a small, pretty woman with curling reddish hair and dimpled cheeks. Her eyes, when she looked at Burr, sparkled. "Mary told me what happened," she said. "I'm proud of you, darling. I'm proud of Ezra too."

"Emily, you musn't speak that way."

"I'm not sorry about Reeve. No one is really sorry, so let's stop being maudlin and do what we have to do."

"Emily—"

"No, Burr. You know I'm right." Emily went to her husband and kissed him. She put her small hands on his shoulders, gazing into his eyes. "You're free of him now," she said quietly. "We're all free of him now."

A deep silence fell upon the room. No one spoke, no one moved, yet the atmosphere changed. The tensions of the past hours lessened as both Mary and Burr recognized the truth in Emily's words. Reeve was no longer a threat. He could not hurt them now; he could never hurt them again.

"Drink your coffee," Emily said, opening the drapes to the first rays of daylight. "Then we will do what has to be done."

There was a great deal to be done and it was Emily who organized the tasks. She made lists, pages and pages of lists, giving some to Mary and Burr, keeping some for herself. Relatives were notified first, and then the board members and executives of Sinclair Mills. Sinclair attorneys in Charleston and New York were notified. Wires were sent to European associates. Calls were placed to the state capital and to Washington and to family friends around the country. A statement was written and released to the press. The servants were

instructed to open and clean the guest bedrooms in the
west wing of the house. Black wreaths were ordered for
all the outer doors. Gardeners were dispatched to the
family cemetery to prepare the ground.

At noon, Mary and Burr and Emily went to their
bedrooms to bathe and dress. They did not stop for
lunch but returned immediately to their tasks. They
were busy throughout the afternoon and most of the
night, making calls and taking calls, spending a few
minutes with each of the many people who came to
offer sympathy. Flowers began arriving; the Western
Union office in Charleston brought in extra staff to
handle the deluge of telegrams. It was, as Reeve had
predicted, a circus. Late that night two cables arrived
from Cynthia Sinclair, one addressed to Burr, the other
to Mary. Neither cable mentioned Reeve but both
offered words of comfort and affection. The words
were important to Mary; when she tossed and turned in
her bed, unable to sleep, she called them gratefully to
mind.

During the next days Mary busied herself playing
hostess to scores of Sinclair relatives and friends, to
Reeve's business associates and hunting companions.
By the morning of the funeral, the great house at Lucy's
Court was filled to overflowing. Last to arrive were the
governor and the state's two senators.

Reeve's funeral was long, marked with all the pomp
and ceremony usually reserved for royalty. There were
hundreds of mourners and four lengthy eulogies, each
one more sonorous than the one before. There were
hymns sung by the uniformed chorus of the Southland
Military Academy. There were pipers. An old Confederate cannon was fired in salute and a Confederate
flag draped the ornate bronze casket. Mary watched

impassively from behind her black veil. She felt nothing.

There was a luncheon after the funeral and again Mary was hostess. She moved gracefully amongst the guests, leading them into the large and splendid dining room, seeing that their food was properly served, their glasses refilled. When, hours later, the luncheon ended, she saw the guests to their cars. "My compliments," Burr said as the last car pulled away. "You charmed them all, even the governor. And he is not overly fond of Northerners."

"Thank you." Mary smiled faintly. "I did it for Reeve. Appearances meant so much to him."

"Now you must rest."

"I'm going back to New York, Burr."

"Of course you are. But not yet. It will be days before the will is read. You must be here for that."

"I'm leaving on the evening train."

Burr frowned. He took Mary's arm and led her up the steps to the shaded veranda. "We can talk quietly here," he said. "We *do* have to talk. You haven't thought this through, Mary. You simply can't leave before the will is read. . . . All this may be yours now. Lucy's Court, the mills. Everything."

"No." Mary shook her head, sinking into a chair. "I was a Sinclair for less than a month. None of this is mine. I don't want it."

"You may have no choice."

Mary looked at Burr. Her smile was warm, filled with the fondness she felt for him. "You're a nice man, Burr Sinclair. I know I've told you that before, but it's worth saying again . . . these are your lands. The mills are yours. Yet you would not stand in my way if Reeve's will made them mine."

"I would not want to stand in your way. I have all the money I will ever need. I have the right to live here. That will not change. I don't care about ownership, you see. It's true I would make changes if Lucy's Court passed to me. But you would make changes also. Nothing is lost."

"You will continue to live here, Burr?"

"It's my home. New York is too . . . fast for me. Europe too far away. I will always live here."

"I'm glad. The South needs men like you. You have courage."

"Courage!" Burr's dark eyes widened in surprise. "I am the family coward."

"You defied the Klan. Quietly, in your own way, you defied them. And you saved a man's life. That's not a small thing, Burr. That's not the act of a coward. . . . When the time is right to move openly against the Klan, you will be there."

"I would like to believe that."

"Take my word for it. I haven't known you long . . . but after all we've been through together, I know you well. I'm very glad Lucy's Court is yours now."

"Reeve's will—"

"Reeve's will doesn't matter. If there's an inheritance, I'll refuse it. This isn't my world, Burr. The evening train will take me back to my world." Mary's gaze swept the broad lawns of Lucy's Court, the aged and magnificent willows. She breathed deeply of the honeysuckle air. "I admit I'll miss the beauty of these lands," she sighed.

"Then stay. At least for a while. New York will still be there."

"I'm counting on that." Mary laughed. "My life is

somewhere in New York. Exactly where remains to be seen."

It was cold and snowy when Mary arrived back in New York. There were traffic snarls and throngs of rushing people and the rude rumblings of subways. Mary felt oddly out of place. She stared at the tall buildings as if she had never seen them before. She strained to catch the rapidly spoken words of passers-by. She bumped into a lamppost and only narrowly avoided the path of a speeding fire engine. When finally she settled into the back seat of a taxi, it was several moments before she could remember her address.

Mary was amused. She felt as if she were fourteen years old again, a greenhorn discovering New York for the first time. It was exciting, no less exciting than it had been all those years ago. The city's energy was a joyous force unto itself. The city's noise was a kind of music, all crashing cymbals and blaring trumpets. Mary grinned foolishly, delighted to be back.

She was still grinning when Greta opened the door of the Central Park apartment. "Surprise!" she said, laughing at Greta's startled expression. "I know I should have called, but I was in such a hurry to get here."

"It is wonderful you are here, Mrs. Kilburne." Greta smiled. "Excuse me, I forget you are Mrs. Sinclair now. Excuse me, I will take your bags."

"You were right the first time. I'm Mrs. Kilburne."

"I hear about your husband. I am sorry."

"Thank you, Greta. . . . Leave the bags for now. I'd love a cup of tea. I haven't had a decent cup of tea in weeks. Would you mind?"

"I will fix it right away. There is cold chicken for sandwiches. And strudel I make myself. I can warm the soup from last night. Noodle soup."

"I'm not hungry, Greta. I just want to look around." Mary removed her coat and hat, throwing them on a chair. "You don't know how good it is to be home."

"*Ja,* I know. People go away but always they like to come home. All people are the same." Greta frowned, troubled by Mary's appearance, for she was thinner than she had been, paler. "You lose weight, Mrs. Kilburne," she said. "I will fix you a nice lunch. You must get your strength back."

Greta hurried off to the kitchen. Mary stood in the hallway for a moment and then walked into the living room. Eagerly, she touched the chairs, the polished tables. She ran her hand over the smooth marble of the mantelpiece. She went to the windows and stared at the snowy outlines of Central Park. *Home,* she thought; I'm really home.

Mary discovered that she was hungry after all. She sat in front of the crackling fire in her bedroom and ate all the food Greta brought. She drank three cups of tea. Indeed, she felt her strength returning. She felt strong enough to face the great mass of mail awaiting her attention. There were dozens and dozens of condolence cards. There were stacks of telegrams and letters. One of the letters was from Rose; Mary ripped it in two and tossed the pieces away. The longest letter was from Harley. His wording was careful, but immensely tender and tears sprang to Mary's eyes. She longed to go to him, to feel the comfort of his arms. She knew she could not and her tears flowed anew.

"Excuse me, Mrs. Kilburne"—Greta hesitated at the door—"I do not mean to interrupt. I wanted to take the tray."

Mary looked up, wiping her eyes. "That's all right," she said. "Come in, Greta. I was only . . . There are so many letters of sympathy."

"Maybe it is too soon to read those letters."

"Yes, maybe."

Greta lifted the tray from the small table and carried it to the door. "Is there anything else I can fix for you? A toddy is nice on such a cold day."

"I'm fine."

"Try to sleep, Mrs. Kilburne. Sleep is the best thing."

Greta closed the door behind her. Mary pushed all the letters aside, all but Harley's. She read it a second time and a third. When she had committed his words to heart, she threw the letter into the fire. The flames leaped, spitting bright golden sparks. Mary watched the changing colors. They were calming. Soon her tears ceased.

Mary spent most of the afternoon in her bedroom. She did some work, telephoning her office for the latest sales figures and matching them to her projections. She spoke with her attorney, then with her banker. She called her major distributors, soliciting their views on the deepening Depression. The pictures they painted were far worse than she expected. She realized how insulated she had been at Lucy's Court, how removed from the real world.

Mary read four newspapers beginning to end and they only confirmed her fears. Rising unemployment was a foregone conclusion, affecting every field, every business, no matter the size. The jobless had already begun to lose their houses and apartments. Farmers, just barely recovered from the postwar Depression, were once again facing bankruptcy. In the cities, rescue

475

societies and missions were enlarging their soup kitchens and organizing bread lines.

President Hoover continued to declare the soundness of American business. Almost no one believed him. Mary, on this day late in 1929, did not believe him either.

Twenty

Mary found no cause for optimism as the years passed. Fourteen million men were unemployed in 1932, one out of ever four American workers. Millions more had only part-time jobs to sustain them and their families. Factories were closing by the hundreds and bank failures were not uncommon. Beggars were seen in the streets. Bread lines were everywhere, for people were literally starving.

Mary was once again working sixteen-hour days. She was the first to arrive at her office each morning and the last to leave, taking work home with her at night. She worked on weekends. She worked on holidays. Often she arose before dawn, spending hours at her desk before going to her office. It was a killing schedule, dictated not by choice but by necessity, for Mary was fighting to save her company. She had had to close three of her New York shops; a fourth was in jeopardy. Nationwide orders for Roly-Poly cakes and Country Bread had fallen by twenty percent. She accepted those losses, though there she drew the line. "We've been going backward for three years," she said to Jane on a May afternoon in 1932. "It's time to start going forward again."

"No one's going forward these days, Mary. We're not doing so badly, everything considered. Our profits are way off, but at least we're showing profits. Most companies are running in the red. We would be too, except we have so little debt. You were right not to borrow. Philip was wrong."

"Philip has only one theory of business . . . borrow and expand. That's his theory. Or it was before the crash. Now he's urging more cutbacks. The hell with that. We're keeping both the Brooklyn and Pennsylvania plants open on full shifts."

Jane sat back. She lit a cigarette, staring at Mary through a haze of gray smoke. "Great." She smiled. "But sales don't warrant keeping two plants running at capacity. You've seen the figures."

"I see them in my sleep."

"Do you mean you actually sleep? That's news to me. It would also be news to your many harried employees."

"All right." Mary laughed. "I know I've been pushing everybody very hard. It can't be helped. We have to hold on to our share of the market. Bad times or good, we have to hold on."

"That's easier said than done. Ask General Motors."

"It's not the same thing. Cars are expensive. We're selling food, inexpensive food at that."

"Well, people are counting every penny these days."

"Exactly! People are looking for bargains." Mary leaned across her desk. Her dark blue eyes sparkled. "I sneaked out to the movies the other night," she smiled. "They were giving away dishes. That gave me an idea. . . . Don't frown, Jane. It's not going to cost us very much at all. It's a matter of packaging."

"You've lost me."

Mary opened a file folder. "Look," she said excitedly, "here are the wrappers for Country Bread and Roly-Poly cakes. Look at all that empty space. Let's *use* that space. Let's have recipes printed on the bread wrappers. Here . . . I have a dozen inexpensive recipes here, bread a main ingredient in all of them."

"Yes, of course. I see what you mean."

"It's not as good as free dishes. But it's something extra. Something housewives will find helpful. What do you think?"

"I think it's perfect. I'll take your recipes to the test kitchens and have them work up maybe a hundred of their own."

"I have something different in mind for Roly-Poly cakes. Something for the kids. There's enough space inside the wrappers for cartoons or riddles or puzzles. Get the advertising department on it right away. I want to see their proposals next week."

"A surprise in every package. They'll like that. The salesmen will like it too." Jane stubbed out her cigarette. She shook her blond head, smiling. "I suppose we should all be grateful you went to the movies."

"I got a free sugar bowl too!"

"Just what you needed."

"It's fun getting something for nothing. Those movie people know what they're doing. It costs them some money, but they get it back and more. That's what we have to do. And soon, before the American Baking Company beats us to it. They're an aggressive company. They're fast catching up to us."

"Never. You're always one step ahead." Jane looked at her watch, checking it against the clock on the mantel. "Oh, I didn't realize it was so late. Is there anything else, Mary?"

"That's all. I'm sorry to bring you back here after work. But I'll be away from the office for a few days and I wanted you to have the recipes."

"Congratulate Oliver for me . . . I remember him in his cradle. Now he's graduating from college. Where does the time go?"

"I try not to think about it." Mary stood, leaving her desk. "I'll walk you out," she said.

"Why don't you come with me? Tim and I are taking Ma out to dinner tonight. It will be quiet, just family."

"I wish I could. I haven't seen Anna in two weeks."

"Then come along."

"I can't."

"Why not?"

Mary closed the door to her study, walking into the hall with Jane. "I'm expecting someone," she said. "Rose is coming over in a little while."

"Rose? Did I hear you correctly? Did you say Rose?"

"Yes. It wasn't my idea. I put Rose out of my life a long time ago. I've kept her out too."

"Out of your life, not your heart. She's still your sister."

"That meant something to me once. It meant everything. . . . No more."

"Why are you seeing her?"

"Harley telephoned and asked me to see her. He said it was important. I'm sure it is. I'm sure it's about money. What did Rose ever care about but money?" Mary sighed. There was no sparkle in her eyes now, no smile. "Anyway, it was Harley's idea. He talked me into it. He can be very persuasive."

They reached the foyer. Jane took her hat and purse from the closet. She went to the door, stopping then to look at Mary. "Personally I'm glad you're seeing her again. Settle your old arguments. It's time."

"How can you say that? You know what Rose is. She certainly made your life miserable."

"She was the terror of my childhood." Jane smiled. "I admit it. In a way, she terrorized us all. But we're not children anymore, are we?"

"Rose will *always* be a child."

"If that's true it's really quite sad." Jane opened the door. She smiled at Mary, tapping her briefcase. "I'll visit the test kitchens first thing in the morning. And I'll meet with our geniuses in advertising. Don't worry, Mary . . . don't worry about Rose either. You'll do the right thing."

Whatever the right thing is, thought Mary, walking into the living room. She had not seen or spoken to Rose in three years, refusing her telephone calls, tearing up her letters. She had thought about her often, but always with anger, always with hurt. The memory of their last argument was sharp. Other memories were sharp too, for she could not forget that she had sacrificed a life with Dan to make a life for Rose. There had been so many sacrifices over the years. And what good did they do, Mary asked herself now. Rose is not happy, nor am I.

The doorbell rang. Greta went to answer it. Mary remained seated though her face was suddenly tense, her hands clenching at her sides. She heard voices and then footsteps coming closer. She looked up to see Rose standing at the edge of the room. "Come in, Rose," she said.

"Thank you for seeing me."

"It was Harley's idea. . . . Well, come in and sit down."

"Thank you."

Mary watched Rose walk across the room. She wore a spring dress of pale blue linen with ruffled lace collar and short, ruffled sleeves. There were pearls at her ears and wrists. A dazzling square-cut diamond adorned her finger. Rose was thirty-two years old, but she hardly seemed to have aged at all. Her hair was still golden and curly, her skin still perfect. She was slim, as fragile as a porcelain doll. "It's been a long time, Rose," Mary said slowly. "How are you?"

"Oh, it's been so terribly hard for me . . . I'm alone, after all. It's hard raising a child alone . . . Rosie will be nine soon. She's very different from me. Sometimes I can scarcely believe she's my own child."

"Harley says she's a wonderful little girl."

"Oh, she is. She's just . . . different. She doesn't seem to like the friends I choose for her. She has no interest in pretty clothes. We argue about that. But once she makes up her mind . . ."

"That sounds exactly like you, Rose. Once you made up your mind there was no changing it. Have you forgotten?"

"It was long ago."

"So it was."

"Mary . . . I want to apologize to you for what I said . . . last time. I was upset. I really wasn't thinking. I didn't mean it, Mary. Goodness knows I've tried to apologize. I wrote to you. I telephoned."

"Do you suppose saying you're sorry rights the wrongs?"

Rose lowered her eyes. She was obviously nervous, twisting a corner of her lacy handkerchief, moving about in her chair. She was unusually pale. "It's not easy for me to apologize."

"You haven't had any practice. People let you get away with things. No questions asked, no apologies expected."

"Is that my fault?"

"I don't know. According to you, nothing was *ever* your fault."

"I'm sorry I treated you badly. I really am."

Mary went to the sideboard and poured drinks. She gave one to Rose, then sat down again. She sipped her drink but her eyes remained on her sister, for she had never seen her so agitated before, so unsure of herself. "Very well," she nodded. "I accept your apology. But that's not why you're here. I understand you have some problems. Money problems?"

"Yes."

"Tell me. And tell me the truth, Rose. No fairy tales."

"I'm almost poor. That's the truth."

"Poor?" Mary looked at the enormous diamond on Rose's finger. She laughed. "You have more jewels than Tiffany. You have furs and cars and a porcelain collection worth thousands. You have a house on Gramercy Park . . . is that what you call *poor?"*

"I'm going to lose the house, Mary. It's mortgaged and I can't make the payments. Even if I found a way to make the payments, there are other expenses. There are debts. I owe everyone. I owe the servants back wages."

"Why in God's name did you mortgage the house? That house was your security for the future. Surely there were other ways to raise money. How could you have been so *foolish?"*

"Wait, Mary. I didn't mortgage the house. Simon did. He borrowed against it to buy more stocks. He was always buying stocks. Everybody was, in those days." Rose dabbed her handkerchief to her lovely blue eyes.

She was sniffling, her lower lip quivering. "You're so quick to blame me for things," she said. "But that wasn't my doing. It was Simon. I didn't even know about it until after . . . after he died."

Mary felt guilty. She had jumped to conclusions, unfair conclusions as it turned out, and she was sorry. She looked away, for the sight of Rose's tears still pulled at her heart. "Forgive me," she sighed. "I just naturally assumed—"

"You're always assuming things. Always putting me in the wrong. You must think I'm some sort of . . . *monster.*"

"That's not true, Rose."

"Yes, it is." Rose's sniffles were louder now. Tears splashed her pale cheeks. "You *hate* me," she said.

Mary left her chair and went to Rose. Gently, she stroked her golden curls. "Don't cry, Rose . . . I didn't mean to make you cry." Mary's voice was contrite. All the anger she had felt toward her sister began to fade. She wanted only to comfort her, to see her smile again. "Please don't cry, Rose."

"I can't help it. I have so many worries."

"We'll work things out."

"How?"

"First of all, we'll go over your finances and see where you stand. I'm sure it's not as bad as you think. You still have the income from Simon's trust, don't forget."

"Half his trust was lost in the crash. Wiped out. There's only a very small income," Rose sobbed, "and a mountain of bills. You don't know how . . . hard it's been."

Concern deepened in Mary's eyes. She frowned. "I'll help you. I promise. But please stop crying. You'll make yourself sick. . . . Please, Rose."

"I'm scared."

"Don't be."

"You'll help me, Mary?"

"Of course I will. Now wipe your eyes and blow your nose."

"All right."

Mary returned to her chair. She sat down heavily, reaching for her drink. She needed it, for these few minutes with Rose had shaken her. Her easy susceptibility to Rose's tears was troubling, as was her willingness to again become involved in Rose's problems. It was as if time had not passed, as if nothing had changed.

"I feel better now, Mary." Rose smiled sweetly. "Knowing you are on my side makes me feel better. Amanda's been such a good friend to me, and Harley's been wonderful. But there's only so much they can do."

"Harley? Have you been borrowing money from Harley?"

"I had no choice. The Ellsworths haven't spoken to me since Simon . . . And you wouldn't speak to me. I had nowhere else to turn."

"What about the income from Simon's trust?"

"It's less than twenty thousand a year. I can't live on that. The house alone costs almost that much to run. There are all my other expenses too. That's why I'm in debt."

"Just what is the amount of your debt? Do you know?"

Rose began to fidget again, plucking at the lace edge of her handkerchief. "Well," she said, avoiding Mary's sharp gaze. "It's . . . a lot."

"How much is a lot?"

"Not counting the mortgage on the house . . . over a hundred thousand."

Mary's gasp was the only sound in the room. She stared at Rose, astonished. "A hundred thousand? How can that be? It's impossible. . . . Rose, the average workingman in this country is earning sixteen dollars a week now. Sixteen dollars! Yet you manage to *owe* a hundred thousand?"

"I have expenses. There's Rosie—"

"If you fed Rosie diamonds for breakfast, that still wouldn't explain it." Mary stood up. She paced about the room, shaking her head. "I can't imagine how you managed to spend so much money," she said. "But it must stop. At once. This is insanity. Sheer insanity."

"I have *expenses,* Mary."

"You also have an income. You are supposed to balance one against the other. Don't look at me that way, Rose. Twenty thousand a year is a substantial income, especially in these times. You will have to learn to live on it. As for your debts . . . I'll help you with them, provided you help too."

"How can I help? I have nothing."

"Nothing? What about your jewels? Your furs and cars?"

"What about them?"

"They must be sold."

"*No.*" Rose wailed, new tears rushing to her eyes. "I'll sell the cars, but that's all."

"Then there's no reason to continue this discussion. You haven't changed, Rose. You're not willing to make the slightest sacrifice, even to save yourself. It's all very clear now. . . . What a fool you must think I am! Did you really think I would write you a check for a hundred thousand dollars and send you happily on your way?"

"You needn't shout at me. I just don't see what good it would do to sell my jewels or my furs. I wouldn't get anything near what they're worth. Not now. Not while there is this stupid Depression."

Mary stopped pacing. Reluctantly she admitted a certain logic in what Rose said. It was a buyer's market; in such a market neither the jewels or the furs would bring even a fifth of their true value. "All right." She nodded. "I'll concede that point for the moment. Will you concede that you're living way beyond your means?"

"I'm thinking about renting the house," Rose replied quietly. She dried her eyes, looking up at Mary. "Amanda's cousin is interested in renting it, servants and all. I could get a good price."

"Oh?" Mary was suspicious, for Rose had made her suggestion too easily, as if it were part of a plan. "Where would you and Rosie live?" she asked.

"Well, I was thinking we would live here. It's such a large apartment. All these rooms going to waste."

"I see." Mary sat down, looking away from Rose. "I see," she said again, covering her mouth to hide her smile. "You are incredible, Rose! Let me be sure I understand this. In addition to paying your debts, I'm to put a roof over your head and food on your plate. Meanwhile you collect income from the trust and you collect rent. Is that about right?"

"Where else could I live? I couldn't afford another house. I certainly couldn't live with Georgy on his farm."

"Are you forgetting your dear friend Amanda? She has a splendid mansion on Fifth Avenue." Mary saw Rose blush. It was not like her; indeed, it was not like her to be embarrassed by anything. "Have you and Amanda had a falling out?"

"No . . . no, of course not. But I couldn't live there. Amanda's husband is too . . . fond of me."

"Really?" Mary looked closely at her sister. "I hope it isn't mutual."

"What a silly thing to say." Rose smiled, fluttering her golden lashes. "It's true I *like* Emory. He's terribly rich . . . but Amanda is my best friend in the whole world. I wouldn't do that to her."

"Wouldn't you?"

"Why must you always think the worst of me, Mary? Do you think I am a husband stealer?"

"I think money blinds you. . . . I advise you to be careful, Rose. Your reputation is all you have left. Don't ruin it. People are quick to gossip about pretty young widows. And you have a daughter to consider. Any indiscretion on your part will color her future too."

"I can't help it if Emory is . . . fond of me. It's not my fault. I've done nothing wrong. Why won't you ever believe me?"

"I want to believe you. But I know how your mind works. I know how you are when money enters into the picture. Well," Mary sighed, "never mind that now. We have more important things to discuss. Are you quite certain you want to live here?"

"It's the best solution."

"Yes, for *you.*"

"I promise I won't be in your way, Mary. You have your life and I have mine. Rosie won't be in your way either. She's so quiet you will hardly know she's here."

"I'm not worried about Rosie. I like the idea of having a child around the house again. *You're* the one who worries me."

"Why?"

"It would take me all night to tell you why." Mary looked at Rose for a long moment. Finally she smiled. "All right. You can move in here. We'll try it . . . but understand I'm going to be keeping a sharp eye on your finances. And understand you're not to charge *anything* to my accounts. Not even a spool of thread. Do I make myself clear?"

"You always make yourself clear, Mary."

"We'll go over your bills when I return from Boston. For now I want you to write me a list of your servants and the wages you owe them. You go about in diamonds and your servants go unpaid . . . doesn't that bother you? Even a little?"

It did not bother Rose in the least. She was going to say so, then prudently changed her mind. "I feel just terrible," she said instead.

Oliver was graduated from Harvard with honors. Mary savored every moment of the ceremony, giving in to tears only when Oliver received his diploma. Johnnie sat next to her and displayed no emotion of any kind. He glanced at Mary when the honors were read, but briefly and without even a flicker of a smile. He was polite, if cool, to Harley and to his half brother Spencer.

There were receptions after the ceremony. There were parties, on campus and off. Mary decided not to stay. She spent an hour with Oliver, then sent him off to have a good time. She chatted with Harley and took a picture with Spencer, but at six o'clock she was on a train back to New York. "This is ridiculous," Johnnie said as the train pulled out of the station. "We certainly could have gone to one or two of the receptions, Mother. It doesn't hurt to meet important people."

"You and your important people," Mary sighed. "If you felt that way you should have stayed. I told you to stay."

"The whole point of this trip was to give us an opportunity to talk."

"The point of this trip was Oliver's graduation. You remember Oliver, don't you? Your brother?"

Johnnie was not amused. "You promised we would talk," he said.

"We will. But later. I'm tired, Johnnie. Give me a chance to catch my breath."

"You're not tired. You're upset. Not that I blame you. Father was wrong to bring Spencer with him."

"Nonsense. Spencer is family. Why shouldn't he be at his brother's graduation?"

"Half brother."

"What difference does it make? Johnnie, I'd rather not talk about family matters in the middle of a crowded train. Spencer had every right to be at the graduation. He was happy to see Oliver and Oliver was happy to see him. Now let's say no more about it."

"I think you protest too much, Mother."

Mary turned her face to the window. She pretended to watch the passing scenery, though in fact she saw nothing. She was thinking about Spencer. He was ten years old, an appealing child, the image of Harley. Seeing them together had been a shock to her. Painful memories had been rekindled, memories of the day her marriage had come to an end.

"Did you hear what I said?" Johnnie asked.

"Yes, I heard. Are you trying to provoke me?"

"I am merely trying to get your attention, Mother. We have things to discuss. I've been patient, but you cannot keep putting me off . . . I must know where I stand. I must make plans."

"Plans?"

"Marriage plans. Elizabeth and I have been engaged for a year. It's time we married. That is not possible, however, until I am allowed to advance in the company. I've worked hard. I've earned advancement."

"Suppose you tell me what you have in mind."

"I want a vice-presidency. And a raise in salary of course."

"A vice-presidency at your age?"

"My age has nothing to do with it. I've worked hard. I've devoted myself to the company. No one knows its workings better than I. Certainly no one there has my abilities."

"Not to mention your modesty." Mary smiled.

"I see no reason for modesty."

"Well, at least you're honest." Mary stared thoughtfully at her son. "But what else are you? I wish I knew."

"That's an odd thing to say."

"You have always been a puzzle to me, Johnnie. So closed and secret. Sometimes I think I don't know you at all . . . perhaps that's the way you want it."

"Perhaps."

Mary rested her head against the back of the seat. "A vice-presidency is a big step," she said. "I'm not at all sure you're ready for it."

"I'm sure."

"I don't doubt your ambition. But there are other considerations. I'm not saying no. I'm only saying I need time to think. Give me a week or so."

"That won't do, Mother. I'm entitled to know where I stand. It's not too much to ask. You have had four years to judge my work. Time enough to draw accurate conclusions."

"Do you want to know what my conclusions are? Very well. Your work is excellent, Johnnie. You are, as you say, devoted. You have a quick mind, a business mind. That is all to your advantage. On the other hand, our employees dislike you. They seem to fear you. That's *not* to your advantage."

Johnnie smiled faintly. It was a cool smile, and derisive. His eyes, when he looked at Mary, were also cool. "Is it necessary for employees to like their employers?" he asked. "Did you always like your employers? Kilburne Bakeries isn't a social club, Mother. Our employees are not there out of friendship. They are there for the paychecks we give them. Generous paychecks, considering the times."

"I don't like tyrants."

"Are you calling me a tyrant?"

"You might easily become one, given enough power. There is something severe about you, Johnnie. I don't know where it comes from, but I have seen it. It troubles me."

Johnnie was silent. He did not dispute his mother's judgment of him, for he knew it to be correct. The sternness in his character pleased him. He deemed it an asset, in business and in life. It is a great asset, he thought now, but I cannot expect Mother to understand; she is only a woman. "Would you prefer me to be more frivolous?" He smiled.

"There is little chance of that, Johnnie. I would settle for more tolerance on your part. People are not machines. They make mistakes. *You* must learn to make allowances. You will get along much better with our employees if you do."

"Perhaps it's true I've been too . . . demanding of them. I will consider what you said. Your methods have worked well for you. You built the business, after all."

"I'm so glad you remember that . . . even if only occasionally."

Johnnie's eyes narrowed on his mother. "Do you think I'm after your place in the company?" he asked.

"Of course I do," Mary laughed. "But that time, if and when it comes, is a long way off. Be advised."

The old girl's no fool, thought Johnnie to himself. I must remember that in future. "You have spoken frankly, Mother," he said. "I will speak frankly also. It is not your place I'm after but a place of my own. I've earned it. I've worked hard, learning the business from the bottom up. You can't deny I've done everything you asked of me."

"No, I can't deny that."

"I believe it's time my efforts were rewarded. They would have been rewarded months go, were I not your son. Being your son has worked against me. You hold me to a higher standard."

"I can't deny that either."

"Well?"

"I still have a few doubts." Mary sighed. "But on the whole, I have to agree with you. I've already given the matter some thought." She opened her purse, removing a leather-bound notebook. "There are plans in here," she said. "I'm willing to make you vice-president in charge of acquisitions and planning . . . if you're interested."

"Certainly I'm interested! I made the original

proposal on diversification."

"It was a good proposal, Johnnie. Too ambitious for us right now. But the basic ideas were sound. We're using them as a guide to future planning. I'm willing to put you in charge."

Johnnie's expression did not change, though his pulse quickened and his breath caught in his chest. He took a moment to calm himself. When he spoke, his voice was carefully modulated. "I'm pleased," he said. "You've made the right decision, Mother. I promise I won't disappoint you."

"You will have the same authority as our other vice-presidents. No more than that. I will continue to make all final decisions on policy. Is that understood?"

"It is. Now I would like to discuss my salary."

"A modest raise is the best I can do. Naturally there will be bonuses for exceptional work. . . . It's not as if you need the money, Johnnie. You have the income from your trust fund."

"That's hardly the point. Do you pay all your employees according to need?"

"Executive salaries have been cut to the bone. I take very little in salary myself. You know how hard times are."

"I know you gave Oliver a trip to Europe. And Father gave him a new car."

"You have a convenient memory." Mary laughed, shaking her head. "Have you forgotten we gave you the same presents when you graduated from Harvard?"

"If you have money for trips—"

"Yes, I have money for trips. I don't claim to be poor. Far from it. But I run my business as a business. Your salary will be in line with those of other Kilburne vice-presidents. No higher, no lower. That's fair. If you object, you're free to refuse the job."

Johnnie recognized the tone in his mother's voice. It meant she was serious; no amount of arguing would change her mind. "I was only thinking about the future," he said evenly. "I will have many more expenses when I marry Elizabeth."

"What of it? Your father and I started out with nothing. He worked two jobs and was handyman of the building as well. I stayed up half the night baking cakes. We managed. We did pretty well for ourselves. Don't look so bored, Johnnie. It's the truth. We struggled for every penny. And because we did, you have a trust fund now. A handsome trust fund, may I add. You take things for granted. Your father and I worked day and night to give you all the things you take for granted. There are times I regret it."

"All that work, Mother. Wasn't some of it for yourself?"

"Yes," Mary replied quietly. "And there are times I regret that too."

But work had become a kind of comfort to Mary. It was the one thing, perhaps the only thing, she trusted. The long hours she spent at her office filled the empty spaces in her life. She had no time to think and that pleased her. She declined invitations to dinner, to the theater, to parties, preferring to return home to her own apartment. Rose was seldom there. Mary never knew where her sister was, nor did she ask. She spent her evenings with little Rosie. They ate together and listened to the radio together and were, in a way, companions.

There were no men in Mary's life. There were

memories—of Dan and Reeve and, most especially, Harley. She saw Harley at Johnnie's wedding in 1933. Again Spencer was with him and again she kept her distance. She saw him the following year when their first grandchild was born, a dark-haired, dark-eyed boy named Anthony Bradford Kilburne. It was a joyous occasion for them both though not really shared, for Harley left the hospital moments after Mary arrived. She wondered at his hasty departure. Later, over a celebration dinner with Anna, she asked about it. Anna hesitated before replying. She sipped her wine, fussed with her napkin. "Harley has things on his mind," she said finally.

"Don't we all!"

Anna was uncomfortable discussing Harley with Mary. She had been heartbroken when their marriage ended, for she loved them both; she had been determined not to take sides. She had succeeded, but only by refusing to discuss one with the other. "Tell me how you like being a grandmother." She smiled now. "You don't look the part."

"I feel it. I feel every one of my forty-three years."

"That's because you work too hard."

"I have no choice. The Depression very nearly put us under. . . . Of course things are better now. Our profits are climbing again. And the candy division Johnnie started is showing huge profits. With luck, and President Roosevelt, we'll be all right." Mary raised her wineglass to her lips, staring at Anna. She was in her late sixties, though she wore her age well. Her hair was gray and there were wrinkles about her eyes, but she was as active as she had ever been, her keen spirit undiminished. "You certainly don't look like a great-grandmother, Anna."

"I have a theory that children keep you young. I think it's true . . . you're the proof. You've been happier since Rosie's been here."

Mary's eyes lit up. She smiled. "Rosie's the most wonderful little girl. The problem is I'm beginning to think of her as *my* little girl. You know I always wanted a daughter."

"And now you have one."

"I have to keep reminding myself that she's *Rose's* daughter. But then Rose is so seldom home. She's quite the belle of New York."

"Yes, I read her name in the society columns all the time. She's in Cholly Knickerbocker's column almost every day."

"Well," Mary shrugged, "it's her life. I've urged her to spend more time with Rosie. I've nagged her. But you know Rose."

"I don't suppose she's changed."

"That's the strange thing . . . in some ways she *has* changed. She's paying back the money I advanced to cover her debts. And she hasn't cost me a penny during the two years she's been here. Not a penny!"

"Really?"

"Strange, isn't it?" Mary finished her wine. She dropped her napkin on the table and sat back. "If it weren't so late, I'd take you in to see Rosie. I swear she's grown another inch since last week. She gets prettier every day."

Mary rang and Greta came in to clear the dishes. "You will have your tea in here, Mrs. Kilburne?" she asked.

"Yes, thank you. Greta, are you sure there's been no word from my sister? She was going to meet me at the hospital today. She never arrived."

Greta frowned. "There . . . is a note," she said.

"Oh? Why didn't you give it to me before? Did you just find it?"

"I cannot give it to you yet."

"What in the world are you talking about? If there's a note I would like to see it. Now."

"Your sister . . . Mrs. Ellsworth made me promise not to give you the note until it is midnight."

"Midnight? But that's ridiculous."

"I promised Mrs. Ellsworth I—"

"Give me the note, Greta. *Now.*"

Greta took an envelope from the pocket of her apron. *"Ja,* here it is."

"Thank you, Greta. That will be all." Mary looked at the envelope for a moment. She looked at Anna. "I wonder what Rose is up to this time. I suddenly have the oddest feeling."

"Rose was always the dramatic one. It's probably nothing at all."

"We'll soon see." Mary tore open the envelope and read the note. "My God!" she gasped. "My God!"

"What's wrong? What is it?"

"It's Rose. . . . She's run off with Amanda's husband. She's run off with Emory VanDorn . . . they've gone to France."

There was a terrible scandal, a public scandal, for the tabloids rushed to splash the story across their front pages. *"Society Love Nest Revealed,"* screamed one headline; *"Society Lovers Flee U.S.A.,"* screamed another. It was a story of sex and betrayal and immense wealth. No one was spared. The Kilburnes and VanDorns were dragged through the mud, but so were the Wingates and Ellsworths. Simon Ellsworth's suicide was luridly detailed. One enterprising tabloid reporter even managed to weave Reeve Sinclair's death into his article.

The VanDorn family withdrew behind a veritable wall of servants, refusing all comment. Amanda Wingate VanDorn was more accommodating. She gave a score of tearful interviews, posing for pictures with her five children gathered around. Simon's mother came out of seclusion only long enough to threaten suit for custody of Rosie.

Those weeks were the most trying of Mary's life. She sent Rosie to stay at George's farm until the furor died down. She had repeated and extremely tense meetings with old Mrs. Ellsworth. She endured a barrage of nasty telephone calls. Three weeks later the tabloids moved on to their next scandal. Six months later, in a decision hardly noted by the press, custody of young Rosie Ellsworth was awarded to Mary.

Twenty-One

Rosie celebrated her sixteenth birthday in August of 1939. The following month Hitler invaded Poland and once again the dark specter of war fell across Europe. Rosie was too young to fully comprehend the horrors of war but she was troubled nevertheless, for she knew her mother was still living in Europe. She had mixed feelings about her mother. Certainly there was confusion, even resentment. Yet there was affection as well, affection remembered from childhood. "Do you think Mama's safe over there?" she asked Mary one afternoon in October. "It's beginning to sound dangerous."

"Of course she's safe." Mary smiled, sitting down on Rosie's bed. "Your mother is a survivor. Nothing so minor as war is going to get in her way. And she's in France, not Poland."

"The papers say war will spread."

"I wouldn't be surprised. Europe is always having wars." Mary sighed, no longer smiling now. "Each generation a new madman seems to rise up, determined to conquer the world. People follow along blindly, God knows why.... Though I can't imagine anyone following that dreadful Hitler. Just watching him in the newsreels makes my skin cràwl."

"The boys I know think war is exciting."

"There's nothing exciting about death. . . . But how did we get on such a depressing subject? At your age you should have only happy thoughts."

"Is that a rule?" Rosie laughed.

"It should be. You're only young once. I want you to be happy, Rosie. I want that more than anything."

Rosie bent, putting her arms around Mary. "You spoil me," she said. "You mustn't. I'm not a child anymore."

"Don't remind me." Mary smiled lovingly at her niece. She had Simon's wide gray eyes and Rose's fine golden hair though in truth she looked like neither of her parents. She had a look all her own, fresh and pretty and very American. Her golden hair was long, parted at the side and clasped with barrettes. Today she wore her favorite outfit: pink cashmere sweater, pleated skirt, bobby socks, and loafers. "Time goes by too quickly, Rosie. Just the other day you were a little girl in pigtails. Now you're a teenager . . . having dates and going to parties. I feel old."

"You'll never be old, Aunt Mary. Did you know that Kip Lansdale has a big crush on you?"

"Kip? The boy with all the freckles?"

"Watch him the next time he's here. As soon as you come into the room he'll start blushing and tripping over himself."

"You've made my day," Mary laughed. "And now that you have, I'll let you pack for your slumber party. Is Carol's father picking you up?"

"It's only ten blocks. I'll walk. . . . Don't frown. Carol's parents will be home the whole time. There won't be boys there anyway."

"I should hope not!"

"We couldn't talk about them if they were there.
That's what we do. We eat and listen to records and
talk about boys. Isn't that what you did in the olden
days?"

"We didn't have slumber parties . . . in the *olden*
days."

Rosie shrugged, smiling. She took a small suitcase
from her closet and began to pack. Mary watched her.
She remembered her as a child—quiet, almost solemn,
with few interests and fewer enthusiasms. Time had
changed that, and love. The scandal that had touched
them all in 1934 had been deeply distressing to Rosie,
but she had adjusted. Never, by word or deed, had she
shown any bitterness toward her mother. She replied
promptly and at length to Rose's monthly letters; she
took great care selecting Christmas presents for her. If
occasionally she lapsed into silence, Mary understood.

"Don't forget to pack your toothbrush," Mary said
now. "And you'd best take your warm robe."

"You worry too much."

"Worrying is my hobby."

Rosie snapped her suitcase shut. "Well, I'm all set,"
she smiled. "I'm off."

"Do you have enough money?"

"I have my allowance, in case we go to the movies
tomorrow."

Mary walked into the hall with Rosie, taking her
hand. "I want you to listen to Carol's parents while
you're there," she said. "Mind your manners."

"I will, Aunt Mary."

"Try not to stay up 'til all hours."

"But that's half the fun!"

"It is? Then I wish you a sleepless night." Mary held the front door open. "Have a good time, Rosie. Call me."

"I will. What are you going to do tonight?"

"I have a new mystery novel. *Murder Twice Removed.* That's my idea of fun. Don't start worrying about *me,* for heaven's sake. I'm a big girl. I've been alone before . . . just enjoy yourself."

"Okay." Rosie leaned over and kissed Mary's cheek. "I'll call you in the morning. Sleep well."

Mary waited until the elevator came and then closed the door. She stood there for a moment, feeling suddenly lonely. She knew she had to get used to Rosie being away. In no time at all Rosie would be off to college; after college, she would marry and start a family of her own. Mary sighed. Slowly, she walked through the hall to her bedroom. She was halfway there when the doorbell rang. "Don't bother, Greta," she called. "I'll get it. Rosie's probably forgotten something."

Mary was smiling as she opened the door. "Did you forget . . . ? *Oh!*" Mary took a step backward, astonished, for she was staring into the intensely blue eyes of Dan McShane.

"I really *was* in the neighborhood." Dan smiled. "In the building, as a matter of fact. You know that this building is to be torn down next year, don't you?"

"Yes," Mary nodded. "All the tenants were informed."

"Well, McShane Construction has nothing to do

with the demolition. But we have the contract for the new building. A sleek, modern building . . . thirty-two stories high. I've been here a few times to look over the site. I wanted to call on you, Mary. It took me a while to work up my courage."

"You never lacked for courage."

"Some things are harder than others . . . even after so many years."

"Yes."

Dan was seated on the couch in the living room, Mary on an antique silk chair across from him. Her initial shock had faded. She was calmer now, sipping a scotch and soda. "I'm glad you came by," she said. "I've thought about you often."

"Have you?"

"Of course." Mary gazed at Dan. He was still the handsomest man she had ever seen. He was in superb condition, his face bronzed from years of working outdoors in the sun and the wind. His extraordinary blue eyes sparkled. There was but a single streak of gray in the flame of his hair. "I have wonderful memories of you, Dan."

"And I of you. I lived on those memories for a long time. . . . During the days I had my work, but the nights were hard."

"You can be proud of your work. I see your signs at construction sites all over the city. You've made a great success."

"It's not Kilburne Bakeries." Dan smiled. "But I'm pleased. We're the third largest construction company in New York, and moving up. We do a lot of work in South America too. Believe it or not, this Irish lad from Yorkville has become a world traveler."

"That must be such fun, Dan."

"It is. At least I'm never bored. I wasn't cut out to go to the same office day after day. Tell me about your life, Mary. I want to know."

"I have two grown sons. I'm raising my niece Rosie. And I'm a grandmother three times over."

"Impossible!"

"You're looking at Granny Kilburne."

"No, I'm looking at a beautiful woman. You're every bit as beautiful as I remember. *More,* because you're a woman now, not a girl."

Mary laughed, though color flared in her cheeks and her eyes glowed. "All flattery gratefully accepted," she said. "You do have a way with words."

"Ah, but it's not flattery. It's the truth. I can prove it." Dan took his billfold from the pocket of his jacket. He opened it, removing a frayed and yellowed square of paper. "Look at this," he said. "See for yourself."

Mary unfolded the paper. "Oh, Dan . . . I remember the day this sketch was made. I even remember the funny Greenwich Village artist. You kept it . . . you kept it all these years."

"I took it around the world with me. Twice. Hold it next to your face and you'll see you haven't changed one whit. You're still my . . . You're still the same."

Mary continued to stare at the sketch, touched that Dan had kept it. She felt her throat tighten. "I don't know what to say, Dan. You've caught me by surprise."

"I hope I haven't upset you."

"I'm not upset. . . . Perhaps a bit off balance. You always had that effect on me. I suppose you have that effect on all women. You and your devastating charm."

"Would you be teasing me, Mary Kilburne?"

"Never. You were the one who did the teasing, as I remember."

Dan leaned back against the cushions. He took a long sip of his drink, staring at Mary over the rim of his glass. "I used to tease you about getting rich on Roly-Poly cakes. Little did I know I was being prophetic. You built a whole company on them."

"I had help. There was Elsie, and Mr. Basset . . . most of all, there was Harley. He made everything possible." Mary smiled slightly, shaking her head. "Without him, no company."

"But you were the driving force. You wanted more out of life than most people."

"I wanted money. In those days I thought money was protection. It is, in a way. But not in the way I thought."

"Are you happy, Mary?"

"Well, my company is prospering. We have four plants now. Modern plants with all the latest equipment. Our products are distributed coast to coast. That's not bad, considering where I started."

"And that's not answering my question." Dan's blue eyes were watchful, intent on Mary. "Are you happy?"

"I don't know. Sometimes. Sometimes not. I don't think about being happy anymore . . . I failed at two marriages. I failed with Rose. And my oldest son has very little use for me, though he pretends otherwise. There's nothing to be happy about in all that."

"If you had things to do over again—"

"There are no second chances for any of us, Dan. We do what we do, then make the best of it." Mary stood up. She took their glasses to the sideboard and refilled them. "But tell me about your family," she said, giving

Dan his drink. "How many children do you have now?"

"Four. Two boys, two girls . . . My wife died eight months ago."

"Oh, I'm sorry. I didn't know."

"It was quite sudden. A simple appendectomy, but there were complications. Kathy went into the hospital on a Wednesday and on Thursday she was gone."

"I'm so sorry. It must have been awful for you."

Dan glanced away. His face, in profile, was quiet. "I married late," he said. "I waited until I was sure the past was behind me. But we can never really be sure. . . . Kathy never said anything, but I suppose there were times when she sensed a distance between us. There *were* those times . . . What I'm trying to say is . . . I never forgot you, Mary. I look at you now, this minute, and I know I still want you."

Mary did not move for a full minute. She did not speak. Two spots of color darkened her cheeks, then slowly faded. Her mouth was dry, and her throat also. She felt weak. "You mustn't say such things, Dan."

"And why not? I'm free now. You're free. For the first time in our lives, there's nothing to stand in our way."

"There are years. Too many years."

"Do you think I care about years? The moment I saw you tonight I knew my feelings hadn't changed. I was a boy again, a boy in love with Mary Kilburne." Dan put his glass down. He rose, going to Mary. "There are second chances," he said softly. "This is ours. Ours to take."

"Dan, it's not that simple. It's . . ."

But Mary said no more, for Dan's strong arms were around her, his lips on hers. She was dizzy, her heart racing. Her thoughts were chaotic, slipping wildly between the present and the past. She remembered a long-ago spring day, a beach. She remembered the blaze of the sun and the crash of the waves and, as she did, she surrendered to Dan's kiss.

"I want you," Dan was murmuring. "Oh, my darling girl. My darling, darling girl. How I want you."

Mary's arms were locked about Dan but now, slowly, they began to fall away. Her mind seemed to clear and she felt as if she were awakening from the dark and swirling mists of a dream. There was amazement in her eyes when she looked at Dan. "No," she said, frowning suddenly. She broke free of his arms and walked across the room. With a sigh, she sank into a chair.

"Mary, what's wrong?"

"Everything."

"I don't understand."

"I'm just beginning to understand."

"You're not making sense, Mary. Tell me what's wrong."

"I don't know if I can explain it. I loved you so much, Dan. I loved you with all my heart. You must believe that." Mary paused, brushing tears from her eyes. She was pale, sickly pale. "Years passed and we went our separate ways . . . but still I told myself I loved you. Tonight, when you held me in your arms, it was like the answer to a prayer."

"It was for me too."

"I had imagined that moment a thousand times, ten thousand. I dreamed about it . . . but when it finally happened . . . Oh, Dan, I don't want to hurt you. Don't make me say any more."

Dan went again to Mary. He bent over her, staring into her eyes. "When it finally happened?" he asked quietly. "Are you saying you felt nothing?"

"I felt . . . the memory of love. That's what I've been feeling all these years. Not love, the *memory* of love. I suppose I'll always have the memory."

"That is all you felt?"

"We had so much, Dan. But what we had was over a long time ago."

"I still love you."

Mary took Dan's hand, pressing it to her cheek. "Maybe you love the idea of me. The idea of *us*, the way we were then. We were very special, Dan. A boy and a girl so desperately in love nothing else mattered. For a little while at least, the world was truly ours."

"We planned a life together. We can still have that life."

"It would have been a wonderful life. Then. Now . . ." Mary sighed. She gazed up at Dan, trying to smile. "Now we're two different people. I think we're probably lonely people. We can't build a life on loneliness. Or on memories. Don't you see, Dan? It's too late for us. . . . I should have turned my back on everything and married you. That was our chance, our only chance. I threw it away." Mary's tears were coming faster now. She took the handkerchief Dan offered and dried her eyes. "I couldn't bring myself to leave Rose," she said. "I didn't have the courage. It was my fault. All my fault. I'll regret it as long as I live."

Dan's blue eyes were clouded with pain. He bent closer to Mary, stroking her hair. "Don't cry, my darling girl. Please don't. I can't bear to see you cry."

"It's so sad. It's all so sad. . . . I didn't want to hurt

you, Dan. Forgive me."

"There's nothing to forgive. I understand how it was for you then. And I understand how it is now. You spoke only the truth, bitter though it was. I wouldn't have you lie. There were never any lies between us, Mary. I'm glad about that."

"Yes."

Dan walked a few steps away. He picked up his glass and drank. Mary could not watch. She lowered her eyes, staring at the pale, flowered carpet. Neither Dan nor Mary spoke for several minutes. They had their thoughts to cope with, their pain.

"Well," Dan said finally, turning to look at Mary, "I should be on my way. Will you walk with me to the door?"

"Of course."

Dan held out his hand. Mary took it, smiling. "You're a wonderful man," she said. "I must be crazy to let you go."

"Life is crazy. What can we do but laugh at it? Better to laugh than cry . . . I've done my share of both. So have you."

"More than my share."

Hand in hand, Dan and Mary walked to the door. She helped him on with his coat and tucked his muffler about his neck. "There," she said, "you're ready to face the cold, cruel world."

"A gloomy prospect if ever I heard one." Dan gazed deeply into Mary's eyes. He smiled. "Take care of yourself, my darling girl. Be happy."

"This seems so final, Dan. I don't want to lose touch with you. Can we . . . can we be friends?"

"Always." He tilted Mary's face to him, kissing her

lips. "Always and always."

Mary waved as Dan stepped into the elevator. She wiped her eyes and then hurried to her bedroom. A fire burned in the hearth. The bed had been turned down, the pillows plumped. Her mystery novel lay on the night table, next to a dish of peppermints. Mary hardly noticed those cozy touches. She went to the closet, taking a small metal box from the top shelf. The box was old, dented in spots, for it had traveled with her from apartment to apartment and even to Lucy's Court and back. Now she opened it, staring at the meager contents. There was a dried and faded bouquet of violets. There was a tiny silk butterfly. There was a sketch of Dan, companion to the sketch he had carried in his billfold all these years.

"Oh, Dan," Mary whispered. Slowly, deliberately, she dropped the faded violets into the fire. The tiny butterfly followed. Dan's sketch hovered above the fire for long moments, but finally Mary dropped it too into the flames. "Goodbye, Dan," she said.

Mary went to her bed. She fell upon it, weeping.

The fire was low, almost out, when Mary heard a knock at the door. She sat up, smoothing her tousled hair, her wrinkled and tear-stained blouse. "Yes?"

"It is Greta, Mrs. Kilburne."

"Come in."

Greta's eyes narrowed in concern as she looked at Mary. "You have been crying, *ja?*"

"It's nothing. I . . . I said goodbye to all my youthful dreams tonight. It hurt." Mary realized that she was confusing Greta. She shrugged. "Pay no attention to me. It's just one of those nights. And it's late. What are you doing up so late?"

"There was a cablegram delivered, Mrs. Kilburne." Greta took a tan envelope from the pocket of her bathrobe. "Here it is."

"Thank you." Mary opened the envelope. She read it, then read it again. "Dear God," she said, putting her hand to her throbbing head. "Dear God."

"It is bad news?"

"Yes, bad news. Cynthia Sinclair died in London yesterday. They say . . . it was a stroke. *Dear God.*" Mary flung the cable away. She jumped up, striding rapidly to the closet and pulling a dark fur coat from its hanger. "I'm going out, Greta."

"But it is late."

"I don't care. I have to get out of here. I have to. I feel as if the walls are closing in on me. I feel like screaming. And if I start screaming, I'll never stop."

"Please, Mrs. Kilburne—"

"Where is my purse? Have you seen my purse?"

"There, on the desk."

"Thank you. Go back to bed, Greta."

"Please—"

"Good night, Greta," Mary said, brushing past her into the hall.

Outside, the air was clear, sharply cold. Mary's breath streamed out in front of her as she walked through the deserted streets. She walked for a long time and, though she had had no particular destination in mind, found herself finally at the door of St. Brendan's rectory. "I must see Father Malone," she said when the sleepy-eyed housekeeper opened the door. "Tell him it's Mrs. Kilburne. Mary Kilburne."

The housekeeper frowned. She was accustomed to middle-of-the-night emergencies, but she was not accustomed to elegant women in fur coats standing on the rectory doorstep. "Mrs. Kilburne you say?"

"Mary Kilburne."

"Well, come in. You'll catch your death out there."

"Thank you," Mary said, walking into the semi-darkness of the hall. "I must see Father Malone."

The housekeeper's frown deepened as she regarded Mary's splotched, tear-stained face, her swollen eyes. "I'll call him." She nodded. "You can wait in the study. It's the third door."

"Thank you."

Mary stumbled through the hall to the study. She searched the wall for a light switch and then went inside, collapsing in a chair. The shabby room was full of memories, bad memories, for always she had come here during a crisis in her life. There had been her first parting from Dan. There had been Peter's death, and then her divorce from Harley. Father Malone was a frequent dinner guest at her apartment, but in a crisis she came here, to the rectory.

And now I'm here again, thought Mary to herself. I have nowhere else to go. It's as if I'm seeking shelter from a storm, but the storm is within me.

"Mary?" Father Malone rushed into the room. He was dressed in his black suit, his clerical collar in place, but his thick gray hair was uncombed and his glasses were tilted slightly to one side. "What's happened, child?"

"I apologize for coming here so late, Father. I didn't even know I was coming here. I was just out walking."

"Walking? At this hour?" Father Malone sat down behind his desk. Quietly, he studied Mary's stricken face. "Tell me what's happened."

"Cynthia Sinclair is dead. She died yesterday, in London."

"Ah, it's sorry I am to hear that. She was a good woman. A good friend to St. Brendan's too . . . we'll remember her in our prayers."

"Thank you, Father."

"But there's more than Cynthia troubling you. What is it?"

"I saw Dan tonight. Dan McShane."

"Did you?" Father Malone straightened his glasses. He sat back, folding his hands in his lap. "Tell me about it, child."

"For years and years I've been . . . fooling myself. I thought I still loved Dan. Then, tonight, I realized I didn't. It was a memory . . . a wonderful, romantic memory, but *only* a memory."

"So you've come to your senses at last."

Mary looked at Father Malone, blinking. "Don't you understand?" she cried. "I have *nothing* now. *Nothing.*"

"That's not true, Mary. It's never been true." He turned, smiling at the housekeeper as she entered the study. "It's kind you are to make tea for us, Mrs. Conner. Leave it on the desk here. . . . We'll manage."

"Good night, Father."

"Good night to you, Mrs. Conner." Father Malone poured the tea. He added brandy to it and gave a cup to Mary. "Drink up, child," he said.

Mary took the cup in her cold hands. She drank the tea without tasting it. After a while she returned the cup to the tray. She sighed. "Always, in the back of my mind, I thought Dan would come back to me one day and it would be the way it was. He came back to me tonight . . . and it didn't matter. I suppose it stopped mattering a long time ago. I don't know when exactly, or how, but it stopped. Now I have nothing, not even the dream . . . I'm alone." Through her tears, Mary looked at Father Malone. "Elsie is dead. And Cynthia Sinclair. My children are grown and gone. Rosie will be gone soon. I have no one."

"You're a smart woman, Mary, but not about yourself. The answer is so clear. If it were a snake it would leap up and bite you."

"*What* answer? You're always telling me about an answer. You don't tell me what the answer *is.*"

"Because you must find it for yourself. And you will. You need only search your heart."

"There's nothing in my heart anymore, Father. . . . I thought I loved Reeve. I didn't. I hardly knew him. I thought I loved Dan—"

"You won't find what you're looking for going from man to man. That's a bad road, Mary. Many a woman has lost her way on that road."

"Don't worry. I'm through looking. I'm through with men."

Father Malone was silent for a moment, though a faint smile lifted the corners of his mouth. "Through with men, are you?" he asked. "All men? Would that include Harley?"

"*Harley's* through with *me.* He refuses my invitations to dinner. He only calls when it has something to do with the children. I thought things might be different after he and Sally divorced. I was wrong. *Again.*"

"Harley has his reasons for staying away."

"Oh, I don't blame Harley. I'm the one at fault. I was

a fool. Worse than a fool. Now I'm paying for it . . . that's fair."

"I'm thinking you're still a fool. Anyone who throws happiness away is a fool. And you, Mary, you're throwing it away with both hands."

"What happiness?"

"That's the question you must answer for yourself. Sure and it's time." Father Malone leaned forward, staring hard at Mary. "You've come to the crossroads in your life. One path will lead you to a lonely old age. The other will lead you to happiness. You've a choice."

"I don't understand, Father."

"Search your heart. And your memory too. Go back to the beginning, to Dan. You say you stopped loving him. But you don't say why."

"I don't know why. Time—"

"No." Father Malone shook his head. "Time's the easy answer. The false answer." He stood abruptly, coming around the side of his desk. "I'll be leaving you alone now. I'll be leaving you to find the true answer in your heart."

"I'm afraid to look back, Father. I've always been afraid."

"You must do it. You must, to save yourself." Father Malone crossed the room and opened the door. "Trust me," he said, closing the door behind him.

Mary was very confused. She left her chair, pacing circles on the threadbare carpet. She heard Father Malone's words: *Go back to the beginning, to Dan.* It was painful and her mind resisted but finally her thoughts returned to earlier times. She saw herself as she had been then; she saw Dan, and Harley too. How young we were, she thought, how innocent.

A smile came to Mary's face when she recalled her Sunday walks with Harley. Her heart soared when she recalled her outings with Dan. But those were the last happy memories, for then the argument with Bob came into clear and terrible focus. There were gaps in her memory after that. She remembered her wedding day, the awkwardness of her wedding night. Dan had been much on her mind that night. Indeed he had been on her mind constantly in the first year of her marriage.

Mary's thoughts rushed ahead to the April day in 1917 when war had been declared. She had been hurrying home, her taxi stopped at a light, and she had seen Dan. She had made no move to leave the taxi, continuing on her way without speaking a single word to him. At the time she had considered her behavior strange. A few times she had questioned it, though never too closely.

Mary sat down again, huddling in her coat, for she was suddenly cold. She knew that day in 1917 was important. It was a key, the unturned key to her feelings. She thought: There was the war news and I was frightened . . . frightened that Harley might have to go off to war . . . *Harley,* not Dan. I gave no thought to Dan at all.

Other memories came to Mary then. She remembered buying new clothes, hoping to please Harley. She remembered fussing over him, brooding about his absences. She remembered her pain when she learned about Sally. Gradually, Mary began to see the pattern of her years with Harley. She began to understand. "Oh, God," she cried, tears misting her eyes once more. "It's Harley I love . . . I've been so blind. I've been such a *fool.*"

Mary slumped against the back of the chair, staring into space. Despair gripped her, for she knew her discovery had come too late. She had driven Harley away and, with him, her chance for happiness. A sigh shook Mary's body. She was so engrossed in her thoughts she did not hear the door open.

"Mary?"

"Harley!" Mary struggled to her feet, upsetting the tea tray, knocking her purse to the floor. "What are you doing here?"

"Father Malone called me. He said you were in bad shape. Obviously he was right. You look like you've been through the wringer."

"I have. It's not easy admitting the mistakes of a lifetime."

Harley shook his head, frowning. "I don't know what that means," he said. "I'm not going to ask. Come, I'll see you home. I have a cab waiting."

"Harley, I . . . I want to talk to you. There are a few things you should know."

"Talk to me on the way. It's late and I'm tired. You must be tired too. I understand you've had a busy night." He bent, picking up Mary's purse. "Take this and let's go."

Mary heard the anger in Harley's voice, the impatience. "I didn't ask Father Malone to call you," she said.

"I know that. That's not the point. I'm getting just a little weary of following in Dan's footsteps. You needn't look so surprised. Father Malone told me you saw Dan tonight. . . . Well, here I am. The second team."

"You don't understand."

"I don't *want* to understand. Your romantic melodrama is no doubt fascinating, but not to me."

"Harley—"

"Are you coming? The cab isn't going to wait all night."

"I'm coming," Mary sighed.

They left the study, walking through the hall to the front door. Father Malone was there, a questioning look in his eyes. "Did you do as I asked, Mary?"

"Yes. I can't say I feel any better for it."

"I'm thinking you need time. Certain things are inevitable, given time." Father Malone smiled, taking Mary's hand. "Don't be hard on yourself. There's been enough of that."

Harley opened the door. "Come along, Mary," he said impatiently. "Good night, Father. I won't thank you for calling me here."

"You may do just that, by and by. We'll see what we see."

"Irish riddles! How I love Irish riddles in the middle of the night."

"Go on with you, Harley." Father Malone laughed. "You've been up this late before, and for reasons not half so good. Put a smile on your face, boyo. I'm promising it won't hurt a bit."

"Good night, Father."

"Good night. Take care of our Mary."

Harley turned. He rushed Mary across the sidewalk and bundled her into the cab. He followed her in, giving the driver the address, then slamming the door. "I don't know how that man manages to be so damn cheerful all the time," he muttered. "And at all hours!"

"I'm sorry he called you, Harley."

"That makes two of us."

"I sent Dan away tonight."

Harley looked quickly at Mary. Just as quickly, he looked away. "What did you say?"

"I said I sent Dan away tonight. He won't be back."

Harley did not reply, though he was clearly surprised. He settled into the far corner of the cab, glancing out of the window. His face seemed to soften. The tight line of his mouth relaxed. Many questions occurred to him. They went unasked, for he did not trust himself to speak.

Mary saw Harley's surprise, but she could read nothing else in his expression. She wanted to explain, to finally put the subject of Dan McShane to rest. Will he understand, she wondered. How can I expect him to understand, after all these years?

They continued their ride in silence. When, a few minutes later, the cab pulled to a stop, Harley helped Mary out. He hesitated, then paid the driver. "I'll see you upstairs," he said.

"Thank you."

They did not speak during the ride upstairs. Once inside the apartment, they went into the living room and Mary poured drinks. "Still scotch and soda?" she asked.

"Scotch. No soda." Harley sat down on the couch. He lit a cigarette, inhaling deeply. There was some gray at his temples now and his forehead was lined, but otherwise he was unchanged. There was a look of maturity about him, though not the settled and tired maturity that had come upon most of his friends. Harley was fifty years old; he looked forty. "Thanks," he said, taking the drink Mary gave him. "I promised myself I wasn't going to ask . . . but I will go crazy if I don't. *Why* did you send Dan away?"

"There was no reason to have him stay."

"No reason. Since when?"

"Harley, Dan was a long time ago. A lifetime ago. It's true I loved him. He was my first love. And there's something special about first love. But that was *then*. I have fond memories of Dan, nothing more. Father Malone forced me to examine my feelings tonight. I'm glad he did. A great many things are clear to me now."

"Oh? What things?"

Mary sank into a chair. Slowly, she lifted her eyes to Harley. "I loved Dan once," she said quietly. "But I stopped loving him when I started loving you. . . . It's very sad, Harley, because I had the man I wanted. I had you. And I drove you away."

Harley was shaking his head back and forth, his eyes fast on Mary. "I don't understand any of this. It makes no sense."

"Tonight I took a hard look at the past. Do you want to know what I saw? I'll tell you. . . ."

Mary talked for ten minutes without interruption. She bared her heart and her soul, explaining all the things she could not have explained before. Harley listened. He did not move; he hardly breathed, so intent was he on Mary. He was conscious only of her, for the words she spoke were the words he had waited his lifetime to hear. His pulse had begun to pound. He felt a great lump in his throat.

"That's the truth, Harley," Mary finished, drawing a breath. "I was too blind, too busy with my shops, to see it. Then, as you drifted farther and farther away, I was afraid to see it."

Harley stood up. He walked over to the windows, staring outside. He knew what it was to be afraid. He was afraid now, afraid of more heartbreak, of trying again and failing again. Still, he could not deny the feeling of hope that surged within him now. He could not, would not, deny the stirrings of joy.

Mary went to Harley, resting her hand lightly on his. "You must believe me," she said. "I love you. Oh, I know that doesn't mean anything to you anymore but—"

Harley kissed her. He wrapped her in his arms and kissed her again. "Mary, it means everything to me. I never stopped loving you. Not for a day, an hour, a moment. I fell in love with you the first time I saw you. I love you now." Tears welled in Mary's eyes, slipping down her cheeks. Harley brushed them away. "I love you, Mary," he said softly. "But I warn you . . . if you let me back into your life, I'm there to stay. Forever and beyond forever."

"Is that a promise?"

"A most sacred promise."

"Thank God."

Mary snuggled against Harley. Her fingers caressed the back of his neck. Her eyes, gazing at him, were filled with the radiant light of love. She felt as if she had been given a wondrous gift, as if, in finding Harley again, she had found her life. All the doors to the past closed, never to be reopened, for in her arms she held the man who was her present and her future.

Harley held Mary close, stroking her hair, kissing her lips. He knew his dream had come true at last and his heart swelled with joy. "I want to make love to you, Mary," he whispered.

"Yes." She smiled. "Yes." She took Harley's hand and led him through the still and darkened hall to the bedroom. "Welcome home," she said.

Harley lit a fire in the hearth. He dimmed the lights and walked toward Mary. They undressed each other slowly, thrilling to each other's touch. They murmured softly but did not speak. They needed no words between them now, for their hearts, their bodies, told them all they needed to know and more. They made love long into the night. In the morning they made love again.

It was after ten in the morning when Mary brought a breakfast tray into the bedroom. "I wasn't quite sure how to explain things to Greta"—she giggled—"so I fixed this myself."

Harley sat up, clasping his hands behind his head. He smiled, a happy man warmed by love, intoxicated by it. Only yesterday, he thought to himself, I was alone and without hope; today I am king of the world. He gazed at Mary and his smile widened. She looked wonderful, her chestnut hair spilling over her shoulders, her eyes sparkling, her cheeks pink. "Did I tell you how beautiful you are?" he asked.

"A hundred times. But tell me again. I like hearing it."

"You're beautiful. 'Shall I compare thee to a summer's day? Thou art more lovely and more temperate.'"

"Poetry!" Mary smiled over her shoulder at Harley. "And before breakfast!" She put the tray on a small table and walked to the bed. "Would you like to sit down to breakfast? Or would you like me to serve you? Your wish is my command."

"Really?"

"Really."

Harley caught Mary's hand, lifting it to his lips. "My wish . . . my dearest wish," he said, staring into her eyes, "is to marry you. Will you marry me, Mary?"

"Yes. Oh, yes. I do love you, Harley."

"I love you." He loosened Mary's robe, slipping it from her shoulders. "I love you," he murmured, burying his head in the deep cleft of her breasts.

Twenty-Two

Mary and Harley were remarried just before Christmas in 1939. The candlelit ceremony was held in the chapel of St. James Episcopal Church, attended by three generations of Kilburnes. A champagne supper followed at the Hotel Pierre. At midnight, Mary and Harley sailed for Bermuda.

It was an idyllic three weeks, and if the Kilburnes were older than the other honeymooning couples they were no less romantic. Hand in hand, they strolled the pink and sparkling beach. They played in the bubbling surf. They drank magnums of champagne and danced beneath the vast, starry sky. In the small hours of morning, as balmy breezes stirred and birds sang, they made love.

Mary and Harley returned to New York in January. Their honeymoon trip was over, though not their honeymoon, for they seemed always to be touching and whispering and gazing into each other's eyes. Such displays offended Johnnie. He was, at thirty-two, a stern and unbending man, already graying. Harley began referring to him—sometimes affectionately, sometimes not—as "Gramps." But while Johnnie disapproved of his parents' behavior, the other

527

Kilburnes were delighted. Oliver and Spencer enjoyed teasing their elders. Rosie, an honorary Kilburne, often joined the game.

"I found the perfect house for us," Harley announced in the fall of 1940. And so he had. It was a handsome four-story townhouse on serene, tree-lined Sutton Square. It offered river views, fireplaces in all the bedrooms, and stained glass panels in the library. There was a wine cellar for Harley, a small garden for Mary. It was an old house, though no one knew precisely how old and no one cared. The moment they moved into the house, they knew they were home.

There was but one shadow on their lives as time passed, the long and ominous shadow of war. It had, in 1939, seemed inconceivable that America would again be drawn into Europe's problems. Now, in the waning months of 1941, it seemed ever more likely. Poland had already fallen to Hitler, as had Holland and Belgium. Britain was under siege, France controlled by the fascists in the collaborationist government at Vichy.

As the war news progressed, Mary made a determined effort to keep her family close. It was hard, for they had their own lives, their own interests, but she persisted; Sunday brunch at the house on Sutton Square quickly evolved into family tradition. Anna came with Jane and her husband. Johnnie and Oliver came with their wives and children. Spencer came alone and spent all his time with Rosie. Conversation was lively when they gathered around the table. Opinions on politics, business and the economy were traded back and forth. Always, it seemed, there was talk of war.

On Sunday, December 7, war became reality with

the Japanese attack on the American naval base at Pearl Harbor. Mary and her family sat glued to the radio, as did millions of other Americans. The first reports were horrifying. Later reports were worse. They told of bombs raining from the sky, of battleships going down in flames, their crews trapped aboard, of the death of more than four thousand men.

In the house on Sutton Square there was profound shock. There was grief and, at the last, anger. "The bastards!" Oliver cried, not once but several times. No one disagreed with him, least of all Spencer, who was ashen with rage. Johnnie alone seemed calm. And why not, thought Mary bitterly. He has allegiance only to himself. It is nothing to him that his country has been attacked, that his brothers will be going off to war.

Harley's thoughts were similar, for he knew Johnnie to be coldly unemotional about everything except business. He would wish his brothers well when they went to war, and mean it, but he would not be overly distressed if they failed to return. That was Johnnie. Sighing, Harley looked at Johnnie's wife Elizabeth, a very pretty, very quiet woman of gentle manner. Once he had hoped that her gentleness would soften Johnnie's heart. He had hoped in vain.

Hours passed and still the Kilburnes remained by the radio. Every bit of news, whether from Hawaii or Washington, was debated and analyzed, for there was an almost desperate desire to believe that things were not as grim as they appeared to be. But the truth, as news reports became less emotional and more hard-edged, was inescapable. Only the children—Johnnie's four sons, Oliver's daughter—were unaware of the significance of the day's events. They were tired, cranky. Seven-year-old Tony pulled three-year-old

Melissa's hair and she howled in indignation. Tony's brothers fought over a coloring book, tugging at it until it ripped.

"Enough!" Anna declared finally, rising from her chair. "It's time children and great-grandmothers were in bed." She was past seventy now and age had given her a certain authority. Her family deferred to her, even Johnnie, who deferred to no one. "You'll forgive us, Mary," she said, "but it's late."

"Yes, of course." Mary went to the radio and switched it off. She scooped little Melissa into her arms, kissing the child's pink cheek. "Let's get you into your snowsuit," she smiled.

"I'll take her, Ma," Oliver said. "She's kind of heavy."

"Heavy! I used to lift hundred-pound flour sacks in my shop. And I lifted you when you were twice Melissa's size. I'm hardly a delicate flower."

"Okay." Oliver laughed. "Okay. I'll buy you a set of barbells for Christmas. Will that make you happy? . . . What do you think, Pa? Should we build a gym for Madame Muscles?"

"Oh, by all means."

Mary shook her head. "Men!" she said, carrying her granddaughter from the living room.

There was quite a crowd in the narrow foyer of the Kilburne house as children were bundled into snowsuits, into leggings and mufflers and mittens, caps and boots. The adults struggled into their own coats, hushing the children while they searched for missing gloves, unpaired boots.

"Surely there's a more efficient way of doing this, Mother," Johnnie said impatiently. "It's the same chaos every Sunday."

"I'm surprised you haven't put your precious efficiency experts on the problem."

"Perhaps I will."

Mary glared at her son, silently, for Elizabeth was suddenly there, helping Johnnie into his coat. "The children are all dressed," she said in her whispery voice. She turned to Mary, smiling. "Thank you for a lovely brunch, Mother Kilburne. I apologize for Tony's behavior. He is too rough with Missa. I'll have a word with him."

"Come along, Elizabeth." Johnnie pulled at her arm. "Such foolishness over a boy's high spirits!"

Mary watched them go, feeling sorry for Elizabeth as she tried to cope with an impatient husband and four boisterous sons. Johnnie, she remembered, had been the quietest of boys; his children were just the opposite. And indeed the house seemed infinitely more peaceful with their departure.

"A penny for your thoughts." Harley smiled, taking Mary's hand. "Did you and Johnnie argue again?"

"Almost. It's a terrible thing to say about my own son, but he annoys me. Sometimes I think he does it on purpose."

"Well, you know he doesn't like being here. He'd rather be locked away in his study, working on his stamps and coins. Or on Kilburne Bakeries business. Those are his only interests in life."

"I wish I knew where I'd gone wrong with him."

"Gone wrong?" Oliver asked, winking at his mother. "Did I hear you say you'd gone wrong? You'll shatter all my illusions."

"Never mind that. I want to talk to you, Oliver. I hope you're not going to do anything . . . rash. I hope—"

"Pa's already talked to me. Just now, while you were helping the kids get dressed. I have some thinking to do . . . but I'll be in this war one way or another." Oliver stared at Mary, his blue eyes steady, calm. "I have obligations to Amy and Missa. I also have obligations to my country. . . . We'll see what we see, to use Father Malone's favorite expression."

"Think very carefully. *Promise* me, Oliver."

"I promise. . . . Now I must go. Missa was beginning to fuss. Amy's taken her to the car." Oliver hugged his father. He turned and kissed Mary. "Good night, Ma. Don't worry. Worrying does no good."

"He's right," Harley said when Oliver had gone. "It's out of our hands now."

"Yes."

They said good night to Anna and Jane and Tim. Tim was uncharacteristically subdued, the twinkle missing from his eyes. "I don't envy the young ones." He sighed, taking his leave.

That comment, more than any other, touched Mary. It was the young who would suffer, for it was always the young who suffered in wars. Young men would lose their lives, young women their husbands and sweethearts. Children would lose their fathers. Mary's throat tightened when she remembered the countless European children already orphaned by war; there would be others, many others. Nothing will happen to Hirohito or to Hitler, she thought, but in their wake a generation will be destroyed.

Harley sat in his book-lined study, gazing at Spencer. It was like gazing into a mirror, for the resemblance between father and son was astonishing.

Their coloring was identical, their features very nearly so. They were the same height, the same trim weight. Their voices were the same. But the resemblance extended beyond physical characteristics to such intangibles as disposition and temper. Spencer, like Harley, was slow to anger, quick to smile. He was patient. Few things seemed to bother him.

This was true despite the fact that Spencer had had a difficult childhood. The rift separating his parents had been apparent to him at an early age. At a slightly later age he had had to contend with the taunts of schoolmates who delighted in calling him bastard. He had never known his mother's family; his father's family, with the exception of Anna and Oliver, shunned him.

Harley had watched Spencer more closely than he had his other sons. He had watched for signs of bitterness, of rebellion against an unkind fate. To his great relief, those signs never appeared. Spencer had been a happy child. He was, at twenty-two, a happy young man. "We have to talk," Harley said now, sipping a brandy.

"It must be serious." Spencer smiled. "We have informal talks in the library. We have *serious* talks in here."

"It's been a serious day."

"I know, Dad. Perhaps it's wrong to joke. On the other hand, perhaps we should joke while we still can. Our lives are going to change. Probably not for the better."

"Probably not. We don't really know what's going to happen. We can assume, safely, that whatever happens won't be good." Harley took another sip of brandy, then put the glass down. "I take it you plan to enlist."

"First thing in the morning. I'm no hero, Dad. Nor do I believe there's any glory in war. But there's right and wrong. . . . I could wait to be drafted. I'd rather enlist."

"The army?"

"Navy."

"That means the Pacific."

"Sure. Where else? The Japanese started it. I imagine we'll finish it."

"Well, I understand how you feel." Harley sighed. "I tried to enlist during the last war. Part of the reason was that it was a bad time in my life and I wanted to escape . . . but the larger reason was that I wanted to serve. The army turned me down. And the navy. They discovered some sort of heart murmur. Oh, it was nothing important, but it kept me out of the war. I regretted that. I felt like a slacker. Little did I know I'd see my sons go to war one day. There weren't supposed to *be* any more wars."

"There will always be wars because there will always be madmen who start them."

"Then let the madmen do the fighting. Let them lay their lives on the line first. Not you, not Oliver."

"That's a nice idea, Dad. But too late. The damage has already been done. We have to deal with Japan. We have to deal with Germany. The sooner the better."

"Yes. I know." Harley leaned forward, looking into Spencer's soft brown eyes. "What thought have you given to Rosie?" he asked.

"I think about Rosie all the time. I love her."

"I hope you do, Spencer. If you love her, you'll be fair to her. She's very young, only eighteen. I expect you to remember that."

"I'm not likely to forget. What are you getting

at, Dad?"

"Just this . . . during the last war, a lot of young couples rushed into marriage. It was a romantic time. And there was a sense of urgency. The piers were full of starry-eyed brides waving goodbye to their starry-eyed grooms as they sailed off to war. It *was* romantic. It was touching. It was also foolish. After the war, many of those couples realized they didn't even know the people they'd married."

"I've known Rosie all my life."

"As a playmate, a pal. It's only in the past year that your relationship became something more."

"How long does it take to fall in love?"

"I'm not questioning your feelings. Or Rosie's. But she's very young, and you're hardly an old man yourself."

"When you were my age you were married and the father of three."

"That's right." Harley smiled. "I was. But things were different in those days . . . we went to work at an earlier age, much earlier. Responsibilities were thrust on us earlier. *And* worries. We were more grown up because we had to be." Harley sat back, laughing. "We were ten times more grown up than today's youth and a hundred times more innocent. We knew everything about survival, practically nothing about life."

"My generation is tougher than you think, Dad."

"Perhaps. God knows toughness will be needed in the months ahead. Don't misunderstand me, Spencer. I'm extremely proud of you. You made a great success at Harvard. Now you're making a great success at Kilburne Bakeries. I'm proud of your achievements. Above all, I'm proud of the person you are."

"If that's true, you must realize I wouldn't do

anything to hurt Rosie."

"Of course I do. But emotions run high during wartime. There's a tendency to live for the moment and let tomorrow take care of itself. I don't want you to make that mistake. It would be wrong to marry Rosie now. It would be unfair. She's too young. Only last year she was in bobby socks, swooning over Frank Sinatra."

Spencer laughed, for he remembered that phase in Rosie's life. He had taken her to the Sinatra show at the Paramount and had nearly been trampled amidst the rush of squealing, surging teenage girls. It had amused him, just as the movie star pictures on the walls of her room amused him, the stack of fan magazines a foot tall. He and Rosie had been friends, confidants, nothing more. Certainly they had not planned to fall in love. It had happened without warning. They had known each other all their lives yet, suddenly, they felt the magic in each other's touch, saw the magic in each other's eyes. Magic, thought Spencer to himself, is the right word. When we're together, it's magic. "Rosie's feelings for me won't change, Dad," he said. "Nor will my feelings for her."

"I believe that. Rosie is like her mother in one way only . . . she knows her own mind. You have always known your own mind. Once something is decided, it's decided forever. But marriage is far more complicated than either of you know. And to begin marriage with a separation of months, perhaps years, is a terrible mistake."

Spencer stood up. He walked slowly about the room, his hands in the pockets of his slacks, his head bent. "Marriage wasn't even in our immediate plans. Not until we heard about Pearl Harbor. That changed everything. Or I thought it did. Now I'm not sure. I don't know what to think." Spencer stopped. He turned, looking at his father. "I may not come back from the war, Dad."

"Of course you'll come back." Harley's voice was calm, though his hands stiffened and clenched into fists. "You must never doubt that. You'll come back and start a new life with Rosie."

"We could start our life now, before I go."

"And make your going all the more painful? Is that what you really want? Is that what you want for Rosie?"

"No."

"Then consider your actions very carefully. I'll support any decision you make. I hope it will be the right one."

Spencer returned to his chair. He sat down, reaching for his glass. "To decisions," he said.

"There's something else. . . . Your mother will want to see you before you take off for parts unknown. You'd better plan a trip to California as soon as you can."

"I'll think about it."

"Spencer, you haven't seen her in a year. I don't understand your reluctance."

"I saw Mother two weeks ago. I saw her in that Mickey Rooney movie. She played his aunt, quite well too. I called her and told her how much I'd enjoyed her performance."

"Seeing her in a movie is hardly—"

"I'll call Mother tonight. Perhaps we can work something out. We're both busy, after all. And California's a long way to travel." Spencer finished the rest of his drink. He poured another and then settled back in his chair. It was true, he thought, that he felt a certain reluctance about visiting his mother. They had been close once, when he was little, but as years passed, and she busied herself with her acting career, they had drifted apart. He had accepted that. What he could not accept was his mother's bitterness, a bitterness grown worse with time and age. The very mention of Harley, or any of the Kilburnes, sent her into furious tirades. Spencer granted that his mother had her reasons; still, he was uncomfortable. "Perhaps," he said now, smiling slightly, "we can arrange to meet halfway. Perhaps in Chicago."

"I know your mother is not fond of me, Spencer. But that shouldn't affect your relationship with her. She did ask you to move to California, if you remember. She wanted you to go with her. She wanted that more than anything. You musn't blame her if she seems angry sometimes."

"I don't. There are two sides to every story and she has hers. Unfortunately, her anger extends to Rosie, whom she's never even met. That makes it hard for me. . . . She's forever trying to fix me up with young actresses from her studio. Starlets, they call them."

"Really?" Harley laughed. "And you refuse her offers? What a sterling character you have. Some of those young actresses are delectable."

"I've noticed. My character isn't as sterling as you think. But even a casual flirtation could harm what I have with Rosie. I'm afraid that's what Mother wants."

"Well." Harley sighed. "I can't force you to go to California. I am, however, asking you to consider it. Will you?"

"I'll consider it." Spencer raised his glass to his father. "You've given me a great deal to consider.

Anything else on your mind?"

"I think we've covered everything."

"Hurray!"

"Come now, it hasn't been that bad."

"It hasn't been a day at the circus either." Spencer laughed suddenly, running his hand through his sandy hair. "Then again, maybe it has. We're all up there on the high wire now, aren't we? Working without a net."

"I'm sorry to say we are."

Harley and Spencer talked for another hour. Their conversation took the form of reminiscence and, on the eve of war, it seemed entirely appropriate. They remembered the good times, not knowing when, or if, good times would come again.

Spencer left shortly after midnight. Harley turned out all the lights and then climbed the stairs to his bedroom. Mary was at the door to greet him, anxiously searching his face. "Is Spencer all right?" she asked.

"He's fine. Bound and determined to sign up."

"He could wait to be called."

"There's not much point in that. And it's not his way. You look so tired, Mary," Harley said quietly, taking her into his arms. "You should have gone to bed."

"How can anyone sleep tonight? The whole world's gone mad!"

"I know. But there's nothing we can do about that. If I were a religious man, I'd pray. I suppose I'll pray anyway. I've heard it said there are no atheists in wartime. It's probably true."

"True, but small comfort." Mary left Harley, walking slowly across the room. It was a pretty room, decorated in shades of ivory and pale blue, with satin quilts upon the wide double bed and bowls of fresh flowers on the mantelpiece. A single portrait adorned the walls, an oil portrait of Mary and Harley seated side by side, holding hands. Silver-framed photographs of their children and grandchildren covered the tops of two bureaus. "I always thought of this room as our refuge from the world," Mary said now. "But tonight there's no refuge anywhere . . . I feel so guilty, Harley. If anything happens to Spencer I'll never forgive myself."

"Guilty? What are you talking about?"

"For years I treated Spencer like a pariah. He was just a child and yet I closed my heart to him." Mary sat down, warming her hands by the fire. She stared at the leaping flames and shook her head sadly. "I'll never forgive myself."

"Is *that* what's bothering you? But Spencer understands all that. You explained it . . . we both explained. He understands, Mary. He doesn't blame you for feeling the way you did then. God knows you've done everything in the world to make it up to him." Harley went to Mary. Gently, he stroked her hair. "You're silly to worry about past history." He smiled. "It's forgotten. And forgiven."

"Do you think so?"

"I'm amazed that you would think otherwise. Why *now,* of all times? What brought this on, Mary?"

"It's a night for reflection, I suppose. Certainly it's a night for regrets . . . Spencer and I were finally getting to know each other, making up those lost years. Now he's going away."

"He won't be away forever. He'll be back."

"Oh, I know he will," Mary said quickly. She grasped Harley's hands, looking up into his eyes. "They'll all be back. Spencer and Oliver and Johnnie too, if he goes."

"He won't. He's thirty-five and the father of four small children. That's a lot of protection. Should he need more, he has influential contacts in Washington. Our Johnnie won't hesitate to use them. Soldiering is the farthest thing from his mind."

"I wish they'd been born girls. We wouldn't have any worries now."

"Of course we would." Harley smiled. "We'd have different worries, but worries nevertheless."

"Yes." Mary nodded, glancing away. "Poor Rosie has been crying all night. I went to her room half a dozen times. She won't open the door. . . . I hope she and Spencer don't do anything foolish. She's so young."

"Those were my exact words to Spencer. Then he reminded me that, at a similar age, we already had a family."

"We were their age, but we were never *young*. There's no comparison."

"I agree. I think Spencer agrees too, deep down. Obviously, they want to marry right away. We can only trust in their common sense. Come," Harley said, taking Mary's hand, "you must rest. It's been a long, hard day."

"I'm not tired."

"Mary, you can't stay awake for the duration of the war. Off to bed and no arguments." Harley helped her out of her robe. He kissed her bare shoulder and then turned the covers back. "In you go. That's better. I think I'll make us a toddy. How does that sound?"

"You're determined to cheer me up, aren't you?"

"We can face what's coming with smiles or tears. Which would you prefer?"

"Is that my only choice?"

"Take it or leave it." Harley laughed.

"I'll try it your way, with smiles. But I'm making no promises."

"Fair enough."

Mary leaned back against the pillows, absently twisting a lock of her long chestnut hair. "You know, Harley," she said, "we're going to have problems at the company. We're going to lose a lot of our employees to the war."

"Not the old guys."

"I'm serious. We could lose the whole legal department, starting with Oliver. We could lose at least half of the advertising department. Half of sales. All of the executive trainees. I could be running a ghost company in no time at all."

"You're getting ahead of yourself. I doubt that every man in America is going to be on the next ship to the Pacific. Nor every man at Kilburne Bakeries. You'll have ample time to make adjustments, to reorganize."

"I've asked you this before . . . now I'm asking again. Will you consider helping me run the company? *Please?*"

Harley lifted Mary's hand to his lips. "I'll love you," he said. "I'll cherish you and honor you and adore you. But I won't work for you. That's final."

"Not *for* me. *With* me. You own fifteen percent of the company. Anna owns five percent. In a way, you would be protecting your interests."

"My interests are fine, thank you. And my *ownership* is merely a technicality. I never interfere in Kilburne Bakeries business."

"I'm asking you to interfere. I need you there."

"Flattery will get you nowhere. I had fun running Club Harley. It satisfied something in me. If I had something to prove, I proved it. But when Prohibition ended and Club Harley closed, I wasn't sorry. I have no desire to go back into business, Mary. I'm very happy with my investment office. Handling my own investments is a full-time job. Add to that the family investments, and you might say I have two jobs. That's quite enough."

"But the company—"

"You steered your company through the Depression. And came out of it showing substantial profits. You don't need my help. . . . Besides, you have Jane and you have Johnnie."

"That's what I'm afraid of. Johnnie never expected his brothers to come into the company. When they did, they acted as a kind of brake on him. He became more cautious in his maneuverings. When they leave, he'll have a clear field again."

"You'll handle Johnnie. You always have."

Mary shook her head. "It's more complicated now," she said. "He's more impatient now. He wants the company for himself and he doesn't want to wait."

"I know." Harley sat at the side of the bed. He smiled, running his hand lightly along Mary's arm. "But wanting and having are two different things. Who gets the company, and when, are matters for you alone to decide."

"Not Johnnie. Oliver or Spencer will get the company one day. Not Johnnie."

"That's no surprise to me. It will be an enormous surprise to Johnnie, however. You must warn me before you tell him." Harley laughed. "I want to be out of town. *Far* out of town."

"Oh, you're never serious."

"I've had enough seriousness today. I'm going to fix

us a toddy. We're going to drink it. We're going to put the war and Johnnie and the company and everything else out of our minds." Harley bent over. He slipped the strap of Mary's nightgown from her shoulder, kissing her warm, full breasts. "We're going to make love," he said.

Spencer was the first Kilburne to enlist. Oliver, after long and emotional discussions with his wife, enlisted the next week. They were assigned to Officer's Training School and, ninety days later, were on their way to war, Spencer as a Navy ensign, Oliver as an Army captain.

Mary, in her offices at Kilburne Bakeries, was busy every minute of every day. Once again, it was not choice but necessity, for the war meant shortages of labor and supplies and even fuel to keep the plants operating. The labor shortage was severe as employees were lost to the draft and to defense plants which seemed to spring up everywhere, almost overnight. The shortage of supplies was hardly less severe as the government imposed strict quotas on sugar and butter and eggs.

Mary visited all her plants, establishing a system of incentives for old and new employees alike. She saw to their morale too, financing company bowling teams, picnics, contests, and rallies at which war bonds were sold. Each plant had its own victory garden, its own collection center for packages going to servicemen overseas. Several of Mary's executives, Johnnie among them, openly scoffed at her efforts, though the scoffing ceased as production figures soared. "Well, Mother," Johnnie said in the winter of 1943, "you were right."

"Does that surprise you?"

"It astonishes me . . . bowling teams and victory gardens and bond rallies. It's all so awfully corny."

"Nothing that draws people together is corny. Even if it is, better honest corn than dishonest sugar. We have different theories of business, Johnnie. Mine is to draw people together. Yours is to go sneaking around Washington, trying to bribe your way into a larger sugar allotment . . . yes, I know about that. And if you ever try anything like that again I will fire you. Do I make myself clear?"

"I . . . I thought, with production rising—"

"Production will continue to rise. Thanks to our *corny* employees. But we'll make do with our assigned allotments. Somehow, we'll make do. There's a war on, Johnnie. It means nothing to you. It means a great deal to me. My country means a great deal to me."

Mary never wavered in her support of the war effort, nor in her determination to keep Kilburne Bakeries moving ahead. And move ahead it did. Sales were the strongest in its history, as housewives, coping with rationing and meatless meals, again discovered that a loaf of Country Bread went a long way. Packaged Roly-Poly cakes sold by the millions, turning up in pantries and lunch boxes all over America, in military post exchanges and in packages sent to husbands and sweethearts serving overseas. Mary sold all of her retail shops save one, the shop she still referred to as Mr. Basset's, and gave her full attention to the burgeoning Kilburne Bakeries.

But as hard as Mary worked, the war was never far from her mind. She and Harley pored over the newspapers, matching every dispatch to the large map they posted in the study. They arranged their schedules to accommodate the evening news broadcasts on the radio. Reluctantly, they learned to content themselves with these rituals, for the letters they received from Oliver and Spencer were heavily censored, offering few clues to the whereabouts of their sons.

Like millions of other Americans, they knew moments of great optimism and moments of great despair. 1942 saw major American victories at Midway and the Coral Sea, major defeats at Corregidor and Bataan. Casualty lists were long, some of the names familiar to the Kilburnes. One of Burr Sinclair's sons was killed at Bataan. Philip Claymore's only son was killed at Guadalcanal in 1943. Rosie's friend Kip Lansdale, barely twenty-one years old, was killed at Anzio in 1944.

Mary and Harley pretended to live life as usual, but the ringing of the telephone late at night, the arrival of a telegram at any hour, struck fear in their hearts. Their fears were confirmed in June of 1944 when Spencer was wounded during the battle of Saipan and Oliver during the invasion of Normandy. Oliver's wounds proved not to be serious; Spencer's wounds kept him in military hospitals for ten months. When, in 1945, he finally returned home, he had a severe limp and needed the assistance of a cane.

All of the Kilburnes were at the airfield to greet Spencer upon his return. They were a large and anxious group, unsure of what to expect, for he had forbidden them to visit during his ordeal. They knew the pain he had suffered, but they had no way of knowing what the pain had done to his mind, his spirit. Harley paced nervously. Mary stood at the railing, speaking only when one or another of her grandchildren asked a question. Johnnie and Oliver waited quietly with their wives. Rosie was absolutely still, part of the group, yet removed from it, her wide gray eyes scanning the sky.

At last a military transport plane appeared in the sky. Johnnie's young sons jumped up and down, cheering and pointing. Mary reached out, clasping Harley's hand. The plane descended and then touched down, engines roaring, wheels screeching. It seemed an eternity before the plane taxied to a halt, another eternity before the doors were opened. The crowd of people waiting for returning sons and husbands and fathers surged forward. Understanding attendants gently urged them back. Two sailors in wheelchairs were taken from the plane first, escorted to their tearful families by Army nurses. The Kilburnes watched as other servicemen began leaving the plane. They were sailors and soldiers and marines, officers and lowly privates, some of them young, some of them not so young. They were all smiling, for, after years of war, they were home.

"There's Spencer!" Oliver cried.

Oliver began to go toward the gate but Harley stopped him. "Let Rosie go," he said. "Let them have a few minutes alone."

And indeed Rosie was already through the gate, running across the field, her blond hair billowing out behind her, her arms flung wide. Spencer saw her and quickened his pace. His cane skidded on the damp tarmac, but only for a moment; in the next moment, he was in Rosie's arms.

Mary wiped away a tear. "Everything's all right," she said, gazing at Harley.

"He's so thin. All those damned operations . . ."

"Look at his *smile,* Harley. I know everything's all right just looking at his smile."

"Grandmother?" Seven-year-old Edwin tugged at Mary's sleeve. "Is that Uncle Spencer?"

"Yes, darling. He's home. Isn't that wonderful?"

"He has lots of medals."

"He certainly has." Mary swallowed hard, watching Spencer make his way across the field with Rosie. "He's a hero," she said.

Spencer was still smiling when he reached the gate. He was immediately surrounded by family: Oliver and Amy; gentle Elizabeth, her face wet with tears; Johnnie and his boys. The boys had never shown much interest in Spencer before, but now they were all over him, curious about his cane, awed by his bemedaled uniform. "Are you a hero?" Edwin asked.

"Of course he's a hero!" Rosie answered quickly, kissing Spencer's pale cheek. "We're all *very* proud of him."

"Did you kill any Krauts?" eleven-year-old Tony asked.

Spencer laughed, shaking his head. "I was in a different war. You'll have to ask Uncle Oliver about the Krauts." He looked past the children to see Harley and Mary breaking through the crowd of Kilburnes. He limped toward them, his eyes suddenly moist. "Hi, Dad," he smiled, embracing his father. "You can't imagine how glad I am to see you."

"How are you, Spencer? Are you all right? Really all right?"

"I'm great. There are advantages to this." Spencer laughed again, holding up his cane. "I bet I won't have any more trouble getting a seat on the subway." He turned to Mary then. He saw the concern in her eyes, the love, and he was touched. "Hi, Mom," he said.

Mom. Mary had waited six years to hear that word

from Spencer. It was to her a great gift, a miracle, for it was the final forgiveness. "Welcome home, son," she said through her tears.

The Kilburnes piled into their cars for the trip back to the city. They were halfway there when a bulletin on the car radio announced the unconditional surrender of Germany.

Three months later, after the bombing of Hiroshima and Nagasaki, Japan surrendered. The war was over at last.

Twenty-Three

The fifty-story Kilburne Building, all shining glass and steel, rose on Madison Avenue in the autumn of 1951. Its design was elegant, sleek of line, with recessed fountains bracketing the wide doors of the main entrance. The lobby was polished gray marble and had four banks of elevators attended by elevator men in crisp gray uniforms, the Kilburne Bakeries insignia on their lapels.

Mary's private offices were on the top floor of the building, accessible, though not accessible to everyone, guarded as they were by secretaries and assistants. She had decorated her offices herself, in soft tones of blue and green. The desk was antique, as was the carpet. The chairs were deep and comfortable. There were fresh flowers in vases and bowls and pretty clay pots. The many windows were uncovered, for they offered a breathtaking view of the city.

Mary stood at the windows now, her gaze fixed on the vast and cloudless sky. "I'll miss this view," she said thoughtfully.

"What are you talking about?" Jane looked up from her reports. She turned halfway around in her chair, frowning. "Are you going somewhere, Mary?"

"I'm going to retire one day. And don't smile. That day isn't as far off as you think . . . I'm sixty years old. I've worked all my life. There comes a time to retire. Harley will certainly be glad when I do."

"Will you be glad? You love your work."

"I did. I loved building the business. It was a challenge. It was a challenge keeping it going during the Depression, during the war. But now . . ."

"You have a multimillion dollar company."

"Exactly. My work's done. I've accomplished everything I set out to accomplish and more. *Much* more." Mary walked across the room. She sat down, facing Jane from behind her desk. "This company began in your mother's kitchen in Yorkville," she smiled. "Look at it now. We have plants throughout the country. We have thousands of employees. We even have our own building on glamorous Madison Avenue."

"That doesn't mean our problems are over. There are always new problems."

"Problems which interest me less and less as time goes on. I just don't care as much, Jane. . . . Perhaps it's this modern age. I walk through the plants and see machines doing the mixing and kneading and pouring. I see huge automatic ovens with control panels that look like the control panels in airplanes. I see automatic packaging machines, labeling machines. Assembly lines!" Mary sat back, folding her hands in her lap. She sighed. "I know it's necessary, but I don't like it. I don't like altering ingredients, adding preservatives to our products to give them longer shelf life . . . sometimes I wonder if I'm running a baking company or a chemical company. Have you tasted our Roly-Poly cakes recently?"

"I admit they're a little bland."

"A *little* bland?"

"It hasn't made any difference. Sales figures have been doubling every year. This year will be no exception."

"Our products are still the best packaged goods on the market." Mary shrugged. "But that's not saying much, is it?"

"You can't argue with profits."

"I used to believe that. I used to care. . . . I don't care anymore, Jane. I'm working as hard as I ever worked, but the pleasure's not there because the caring's not there. A clear signal, it seems to me, to start thinking about retirement."

"You're serious," Jane said, her clear green eyes studying Mary. "You're absolutely serious."

"Of course I am. It won't happen right away. There are decisions to be made. Difficult decisions, I'm afraid. I have three sons, but they can't all be president of Kilburne Bakeries. I'm going to have to make a choice."

"I don't envy you."

"It has to be done. Starting the first of next month, all the boys will have more responsibility. It will be good for them and good for me. In the long run, it will help me make the correct choice."

"If I know you, and I do, you've already made your choice. You're just bending over backward to be fair. Though I certainly can't blame you. It's a tricky situation. Johnnie *expects* to be president. There's no doubt in his mind."

"Johnnie never lacked confidence." Mary opened the top drawer of her desk, removing a single sheet of paper. She glanced at it and then gave it to Jane. "As you can see, I'm adding the candy division to Johnnie's responsibilities. He'll have two titles. Oliver will be promoted to vice-president in charge of legal services. That was anticipated. No one will be surprised. Spencer will become vice-president and general manager. That shouldn't come as a surprise either. He's been doing the general manager's job ever since Joe Royster left."

"Much to Johnnie's displeasure."

"Well, I can't help that. Johnnie is displeased by anything not directly related to his personal benefit. I know, in this case, he'll think Spencer has moved a rung above him in the overall scheme of things. That's untrue. But he'll think what he wants to think."

Jane looked at the list Mary had given her. "I see there are other promotions here," she said. "D'Amico to vice-president in charge of advertising. Ferris to regional sales manager. Davis to personnel director."

"We discussed those promotions, Jane. Two of them were your recommendation."

"I have an idea. Why don't we announce all the promotions at the same time? We could say they're part of a general reorganization. It's not far from the truth . . . more importantly, we'll avoid a lot of unnecessary conjecture. Johnnie's no fool, you know. If he senses you're even *thinking* about retirement, he'll be impossible to handle."

"Yes, that's a good point. We'll do it your way. A general reorganization it is. Better to keep Johnnie in the dark than to have him dogging my every step. He would, too."

"Johnnie was always quick to seize an opportunity," Jane smiled. "That's both his strength and his weakness . . . Oliver and Spencer are more measured. They may be just as ambitious, but it doesn't show."

"They're not as driven. They have pleasures in life other than business. Thank God." Mary stood up. She went to a small table at the side of the room and poured two sherries. "I think we ought to celebrate," she said, giving a sherry to Jane.

"What are we celebrating?"

"The future. All the futures. Tell the truth, Jane . . . aren't you tired of working? Aren't you tired of Kilburne Bakeries?"

Jane leaned back in her chair and sipped her drink. Her eyes were quiet, thoughtful. "The truth? It was more fun in the old days. It was more work, *harder* work. And it was more fun. We're big business now. Getting there was exciting. Staying there is another story."

"Did you ever think of quitting?"

"Sure. But I'm like an old fire dog. I hear the bell and off I go. . . . I suppose, at my age, I'm set in my ways."

"At your age?" Mary laughed, for Jane was a chic and elegant fifty-one. She was slender, always beautifully dressed, her blond hair in a sleek knot at the back of her head. "I know quite a few women who would kill to look like you, at *any* age."

"Kilburnes age well. You're proof of that, Mary. Harley's proof of it. Credit our genes."

"You're so like Anna." Mary laughed again. "Sensible and to the point."

"Ma used to worry that I was *too* sensible. I can understand why. When I was young, in my teens, I thought life was serious indeed. . . . It took Tim to show me that life is also funny and silly and . . . lovely." Jane's face softened, as it always did when she talked about Tim. There was a sudden bright light in her eyes, in her smile. "I'll never forget Ma's astonishment the day I told her I was going to marry Tim. She'd expected me to marry some humorless stick. Instead there was Tim. A dreamer. A romantic. A *poet,* for God's sake. Ma couldn't believe it. I could hardly believe it myself."

"And they all lived happily ever after."

"Yes, corny as it sounds." Jane finished her drink. She looked at Mary, shaking her head. "Though I'm not sure we would have been so happy if I hadn't had my job here. Here was the real world, the world of dollars and cents and hard decisions—that satisfied my serious side—at home was the dream world. The wildly romantic world. That satisfied my woman's heart. One world made the other world possible. You see, Mary, I owe Kilburne Bakeries a great deal."

"I think we all owe Kilburne Bakeries a great deal." Mary took their glasses and refilled them. "To Kilburne Bakeries," she said. "Come what may."

Ever increasing success came to Kilburne Bakeries as the 1950s progressed. It was truly an age of consumerism, for, after years of the Depression, after years of world war, Americans were ready to indulge themselves. Homes were purchased in record numbers, the dreams of young couples made possible by expanded credit and government loans. Car sales boomed. Television was a new and wonderful toy. Appliances of all kinds, from pop-up toasters to large and shiny refrigerators, were prized. Such extraordinary economic growth brought extraordinary rewards to business, Kilburne Bakeries included. Roly-Poly cakes became as much a part of the American scene as drive-in movies and backyard barbecues and "I Love Lucy."

Mary celebrated her sixty-fifth birthday in 1956.

Politely, she turned aside her family's plans for a gala party and spent the evening with Harley. It was a quiet evening, though a romantic one, for Harley bought out their favorite French restaurant, filling it with flowers and candlelight and stacks of presents. They had the small dance floor to themselves and, all through the night, they danced to their special songs. They had the strolling violinists to themselves, and the wine steward who brought bottle after bottle of champagne. They held hands. In the glow of hundreds of candles, they kissed. "I love you, Mrs. Kilburne," Harley said as they lingered over their brandy.

"I love you, Mr. Kilburne. You've made me the happiest woman in the world . . . you've given me joy. Such joy."

Harley gazed into Mary's dark blue eyes. He lifted his hand, tenderly tracing the curve of her mouth. "A poem has been running through my mind tonight," he said. "Grow old along with me. The best is yet to be."

"I'll love growing old with you, Harley." Mary smiled. "But as for the best . . . we already have the best. How could our life be any better than it is right now?"

"There's one way. We could spend more time together. We could spend all our time together. Does that sound tempting?"

"Very."

"I was hoping it would." Harley reached into the pocket of his dinner jacket. He withdrew a bulky white envelope and placed it on the table before Mary. "For you."

"What is it?" She looked at the envelope, poking it with her finger. "Not another present, Harley? I've never seen so many presents."

"Well, this is really for both of us. . . . Hurry and open it. I can't wait to see what you think."

Mary picked up the envelope. She broke the seal, spilling the contents on the table. "Harley," she gasped, her eyes widening. "I can't believe it! Tickets to Paris . . . London . . . Rome, Athens, Madrid. It's *wonderful.*" Tears came to Mary's eyes. She leaned closer to Harley, taking his face in her hands and kissing his lips. "It's the most wonderful surprise."

"Does that mean we can go?" He laughed. "Can we burn all our bridges and take off, just the two of us?"

"*Yes.* Oh, yes. I'm ready to go now, this minute."

"There's the small matter of hotel reservations. But as soon as they're made, we'll be on our way. . . . I was afraid to make reservations before. I was afraid I'd put a jinx on it."

"A jinx? Did you doubt I would want to go? Oh, Harley, we've talked about taking a trip for so long. It's a dream come true. This trip," Mary said, staring dizzily at the array of tickets, "is *all* my dreams come true. You must know that."

"Yes . . . but whenever we made plans in the past, something came along to ruin them. A sudden problem, an emergency. I wanted to be sure this time."

"You can be sure. I'd have to be crazy to refuse a trip around the world with such a handsome man. And I'm not crazy, not yet."

Harley smiled. "You're not retired yet either," he said.

"I would have been . . . I was all set to step aside. Then, the next thing I knew, we were in the middle of the Korean War. There were disruptions at the company. I felt I had to stay."

"That war's been over for a while, Mary. If we wait much longer, there will be another war, and another. There will always be something terrible happening somewhere."

"Come war, come hell or high water, we're taking our trip. That's a promise." Mary opened her purse. She removed a slim gold pen and gave it to Harley. "Choose the date of my retirement. . . . Go ahead. Choose a date, any date. Write it on the envelope. That will be the date I bid farewell to Kilburne Bakeries."

"Are you serious?"

"I've never been more serious . . . I've never been more in love, Harley. I want to sneak off to Paris with the man I love. What do you say to that?"

"I'm speechless. Though I'm *thinking* very naughty thoughts."

"Good." Mary nestled her head on Harley's shoulder. "The naughtier the better," she smiled.

"Do you really want me to choose a date?"

"Really."

"What an honor! But am I worthy of such an honor? I, a mere mortal from Sutton Square?"

"Don't be fresh." Mary laughed. "Just choose the date."

"All right." Harley considered for a moment, then put pen to paper. "There you are. It gives us enough time to make reservations, and to clear up any last business problems."

Mary glanced at the envelope. "Fine. I would have picked a closer date, but that's fine. And that settles the matter. . . . It's actually a relief."

"The hard part is still ahead, Mary. I understand why you kept delaying your retirement. It wasn't the company. It was the question of who would take over the company. However you resolve it, someone's bound to be upset. That's the hard part."

"Yes." Mary took a sip of brandy. She held her glass up, watching the play of candlelight on the dark liquid. "I made my decision some time ago," she said softly. "I believe it's the right decision. Right for the company anyway. I don't know how the boys will feel about it."

"Mary, they're no longer boys. We think of them as boys, and I suppose we always will. But they're grown men with families of their own. Johnnie will be a grandfather soon."

"Don't remind me. Time passes too fast."

"I mean that Johnnie and Oliver and Spencer are old enough to withstand disappointment. They know only one of them can have control of Kilburne Bakeries . . . of course Johnnie expects it will be him."

"It won't."

"I'm not surprised."

"I gave Johnnie every chance. I overlooked a great many things because I knew the company was all he had. His wife, his children mean nothing to him. Only the company . . . I wish I could turn it over to him, Harley. I can't. It's terrible to say about my own son, but he's greedy and unscrupulous. If a shady deal will bring a few cents more in profits, he'll take the shady deal." Mary sighed. She stared down at the table, fussing with the scalloped edge of the cloth. "He's not alone in that. There are other businessmen who operate the same way. . . . Am I wrong to want better for the company?"

"Johnnie has known your position from the beginning. He knows how you do business. He took a different path. He has only himself to blame. You built your company, Mary. And a reputation along with it.

You have the right to protect that. I would, in your place."

"Do you want to know my decision?"

"No. I'd rather hear about it when everyone else does." Harley stroked Mary's hand. It was freckled with age now, but smooth and warm to his touch. She wore a large sapphire on her right hand; on her left she wore the simple pearl ring he had given her more than fifty years before. "I might let the secret slip out. Loose lips sink ships," he smiled.

"Aren't you curious?"

"Quite."

"Then I'll tell you."

"Oh, no. What you really want is my reaction. I refuse to meddle in this, even indirectly."

"I want to know you approve."

"I approve of everything you do, Mrs. Kilburne. How could I not? I'm a man in love. And with my own wife! Isn't that remarkable?"

"Do you ever have any regrets, Harley?"

There was no hesitation in his reply. "I regret the years we were apart," he said. "They were bad years. Empty years . . . But in a funny kind of way they served a purpose. What we have now is all the more precious. From darkness came light."

"With a little help from Father Malone."

"Yes." Harley laughed. "Bless him."

They finished their brandy, smiling into each other's eyes. At midnight, the small orchestra played the first notes of "Always" and Harley rose, bowing ceremoniously to Mary. "May I have this dance?" he asked.

"You may. This and every other."

* * *

Mary's retirement party was a month in the planning. It was planned as a surprise, bringing friends and four generations of family together in the huge conference room of the Kilburne Building. The room, almost a block long and nearly as wide, had been stripped of its austere furnishings and dressed for a gala celebration. The many tables were covered with blue linen cloths, set with china and crystal and baskets of summer flowers. The walls were decorated with photo murals tracing Kilburne Bakeries from the very first pastry shop through the splendor of the Kilburne Building. White-gloved waiters stood ready with trays of champagne and hors d'oeuvres.

"Well, what do you think?" Jane asked, glancing anxiously at Oliver. "Does it look like a party?"

"It looks like the party of the year. You did a great job."

"Yes, considering that most of this had to be arranged in the dead of night. It's not easy keeping secrets from your mother."

"How well I know." Oliver nodded, laughing. "We could never have had the party at the house. Ma would certainly have caught on. I'm glad you thought to have it here."

"The obvious place."

"The perfect place. Those murals are a wonderful touch, Jane. You thought of everything." Oliver smiled at his aunt. She wore a long, slim gown of black silk. Diamonds glittered at her ears, at the curve of her throat. Her blond hair was drawn into an elegant French twist. "And you look sensational, by the way."

"I tried extra hard. There's a photographer here to record tonight's events for posterity. I want to make a good impression on future Kilburnes."

"You'll be the star of the family photo album."

"Mary's the star . . . speaking of Mary, she should be arriving any minute. She thinks she's coming to the monthly dinner meeting of the board and she's always on time for that. We'd best go inside and close the doors."

"Are all Ma's surprises here?"

"Safely tucked away in my office."

"It's going to be *quite* a night."

"That's the idea."

Oliver took Jane's arm and led her into the conference room. He gazed at the sea of expectant faces, smiling and waving. "Just one big happy family," he said.

"Big, anyway."

"We're a pretty happy family, as families go. Johnnie's the only grouch and even he's in a jolly mood tonight. I've never seen him in such a mood." Oliver laughed. "The cat that swallowed the canary. He's waited half his life for Ma to turn the company over to him and now the moment's finally here."

Jane looked sharply at Oliver. She was about to reply when a buzzer sounded in the room. "There's the signal. Mary's on her way up . . . Mary's on her way up," she called to the crowd.

There were excited murmurings in the room, then silence as all eyes went to the door. Moments later the door opened and Mary entered on Harley's arm. Everyone rose, applauding. Mary blinked. Her lips parted. She stood very still, too astonished to move, unable to speak. "Happy retirement, Ma." Oliver beamed.

"What?"

"This is your retirement party, Ma. We wanted to

surprise you and obviously we succeeded. Your eyes are as big as saucers."

"A party? For me?"

"Of course! No one deserves it more."

Harley put his arm around Mary's shoulder. "Oliver's quite right," he said. "We're here to honor a most special woman. You."

"Oh, Harley, I think I'm going to cry."

"Cry, laugh . . . just enjoy yourself. It's your night."

"Now I know why you insisted I wear my new gown. . . . How in the world did you manage to plan all this?"

"My sole job was to get you here. Jane did all the real work."

"Jane"—Mary turned to her, taking her hands—"it was so sweet of you. I'm . . . overwhelmed." Mary looked at all the smiling faces. Some of them she had seen only this morning, but some she had not seen for months, even years. "I don't know what to say. How can I thank you?"

"The expression on your face is thanks enough. But if you stay here another minute we'll both be crying. Go greet your guests."

Mary glanced at Harley. He kissed her, lovingly brushing a strand of chestnut hair from her brow. "It's your night, Mary. Your public is waiting."

Mary was smiling as the crowd engulfed her. She was radiant, a beautiful woman in a Dior gown of midnight blue chiffon, a matching cape drifting about her shoulders. Her hair was swept atop her head and dressed with jeweled combs. A single gardenia was pinned to her jeweled evening purse. She moved gracefully through the crowd, accepting kisses and hugs and congratulations, stopping now and then to exchange a few words. Again and again, tears came to her eyes.

My life is in this room, thought Mary, making her way to the flower bedecked head table. She saw Father Malone, her protector during the long voyage of the *Royal Star,* her protector still. She saw Anna, almost ninety years old, frail of body though not of mind. She saw Dan McShane and his wife Meg. She saw the Sinclairs, Burr and Emily. She saw her children and grandchildren. Lastly, she saw George, uncomfortable in his "city" clothes, his white hair clipped close to his scalp. George had never had a wife but he had a son, a gangly nineteen-year-old named Hexter. Now Hexter thrust a bouquet of flowers into Mary's hands. "Congratulations, Aunt Mary," he said, blushing deep red.

"Thank you," she smiled, wiping away another tear. "I'm so glad you're here, Hex. And you, Georgy. Did they have to dynamite you off your farm?"

"Eh, it's in a good cause. You're getting a vacation after all these years. I had to be here for that. I never thought I'd see the day." George's strong arms went around Mary. He, too, was remembering the past. His voice, when he spoke, was hoarse. "I'm happy for you, Mary. That's the truth. You came a long way in the world and you did it by yourself. Pa . . . Pa would be proud." He said no more, taking Mary's hand and leading her to her place at the table."

"Don't go, Georgy."

"I'm not going far, just to the other end of the table. We're staying for supper, Hexter and me. We'll all have a nice talk later."

Mary watched her brother walk away. She sat down, looking at Harley. "How did you get Georgy to come?"

she asked. "He hates the city."

"It was Jane's doing. Under all that silk is a will of iron."

Mary smiled. Her gaze roamed over the guests, now beginning to take their seats. "I still can't believe it," she said, shaking her head. "All these people . . . I've never been so surprised."

"Are you happy?"

"If I were any happier I'd burst."

Harley turned Mary's face to him, staring into her eyes. "You're a little sad too, aren't you?"

"Not sad exactly. I was thinking about the people who aren't here. Pa . . . Elsie and Mr. Basset and Mrs. Sinclair. And Rose."

"Jane tried to get Rose here. She tried very hard."

"Oh, I'm sure she did. I'm just being sentimental. I know Rose is quite the belle of Europe. I wouldn't expect her to leave her parties and her fun. I don't mind, Harley." Mary smiled. "How could I mind anything tonight? I feel blessed."

Mary looked up as a small legion of waiters entered the room. Dinner was served, a dinner of paté and veal and raspberries in cream. There was champagne by the magnum, and fine old brandy. After dinner, Father Malone rose to toast Mary. Oliver spoke next and then Harley. His was the last toast. He sat down and the lights were dimmed. A huge cake with sixty-five candles was brought into the room. "Oh!" Mary gasped, wiping her eyes once more.

Harley took Mary's hand in his. He leaned closer to her, smiling in the darkness. "Keep your eyes on the cake," he said.

"It's beautiful," she nodded.

Several moments passed. The lights were turned on

again and there, standing alongside the cake, was Rose. She was blonder than she had ever been, very slender, dressed in white from head to toe and ablaze with diamonds. "Hello, Mary," she said softly.

"My God!" Mary's hand flew to her mouth. "My God! It's you, Rose?"

"It's me."

Mary was out of her chair, around the side of the table in no time at all. She ran to Rose and the two sisters, apart for more than twenty years, embraced. "Oh, Rose," Mary said, choking back her tears, "I've prayed for the day I'd see you again."

"You're not angry with me, Mary?"

"I was. That's all in the past. All forgotten." Mary hugged Rose harder. "You don't know how happy you've made me."

"I'm glad."

"Rose, are you *crying?*"

"I have feelings too." She sniffled. "And it's been such a long time."

"We're all together now. . . . Have you seen Rosie? Have you seen her boys?"

"I saw them last night. Spencer picked me up at the airport. Mary, I'm a *grandmother*."

"So you are," George said, joining his sisters. "It's not a fatal disease, is it? Well, do you have a kiss for me, lass?" He opened his arms wide, hugging both Rose and Mary to his broad chest. "Eh, that's more like it," he smiled.

There was applause in the room as the Kilburnes were finally reunited. Father Malone watched for a moment and then turned to Harley. "Who said miracles don't happen?" he asked. "Falling into each other's arms after all these years. I'm thinking that's a miracle."

"At the very least." Harley laughed. "The *very* least."

"I suppose it's my turn to make a speech," Mary said, gazing out at her family and friends. "I'll try. . . . As some of you may know, I asked Harley to choose the date of my retirement. Although I didn't realize it at the time, he chose a most significant date indeed. Fifty-one years ago today, my brother and sister and I arrived in America. We might never have set foot in America but for the foresight of our pa . . . and the extraordinary kindness of Father Patrick Malone, who befriended us during our journey. . . . We arrived penniless orphans, strangers in a strange land. Anna Kilburne took us into her home and made us family. I will be forever grateful." Mary paused briefly and dabbed at her eyes. "I have, from the beginning, been blessed with good friends. Elsie Jadnick and Edwin Basset and Cynthia Sinclair, all gone now but still in my heart. With other friends, friends who shared the gift of laughter," Mary said, looking at Dan, "the gift of courage," she said, looking at Burr, "and of loyalty," she said, looking at Jane. "I have been blessed with a husband who brings joy to every moment of my life. I have been blessed with wonderful children and grandchildren . . . and, thanks to Tony and his lovely Kate, a great-grandchild. . . . I look at all of you in this room tonight and I see my life. A life I would not trade for any other. . . . Truly, I have been blessed."

There was a sudden commotion in the room as everyone rose from their chairs, applauding. Mary held up her hand. "Thank you . . . thank you"—she smiled—"but I have a few things more to say. . . . I'm retiring from the company tonight . . . I leave it in good hands. It's with deepest pride I make the following announcements . . . as of tonight, Oliver Kilburne is the new chairman of the board of Kilburne Bakeries. Johnnie Kilburne is the new president of Kilburne Candies. Spencer Kilburne is, in my place, the new president and managing director of Kilburne Bakeries. . . . Congratulations to you all." Mary heard several startled gasps. She understood them, for virtually everyone had expected Johnnie to become president of the parent company. She started another round of applause and then sat down quickly. "I don't dare look," she said to Harley. "How is Johnnie taking the news?"

"Well, he's not foaming at the mouth. But then that's not his style. . . . He *seems* calm."

Johnnie was outwardly calm; inwardly, he seethed. He had, in his dark and secret way, always disliked Spencer but now dislike turned to hatred. He looked at his half brother and his hands clenched into fists. He felt rage, a focusing of loathing and enmity long in the gathering. He thought: You have won. But only for the moment. I will destroy you, Spencer. If it takes the rest of my life, I will destroy you.

"Congratulations, Johnnie," Spencer was saying. He was as surprised as everyone else and, in truth, a little sorry, though not for himself, for Johnnie. He had no real affection for him but now he sensed his pain and he was sorry. "I know the three of us will work well together. Titles don't mean very much in a family company."

Johnnie smiled slightly, coolly. "Especially when some of the family is from the wrong side of the sheets."

"Johnnie!" Rosie cried. "How dare you!"

569

"That's all right, darling," Spencer said to his wife. "There's been a lot of excitement tonight. We're not ourselves, any of us."

Elizabeth was mortified by Johnnie's remark; she said nothing, staring past him into space. Amy was too angry to keep still. "Your manners certainly don't improve with age, Johnnie," she sighed.

"Nonsense! We all know . . . what we are."

Oliver decided he had heard enough. He stood up, shaking his head. "This is neither the time nor the place to argue," he said. "Besides, the photographer's calling us. Let's go have our pictures taken and let's be pleasant. *No one* is going to ruin Ma's night."

All the Kilburnes joined Mary at the far end of the room. Oliver and Spencer expressed sincere gratitude for their promotions. "Interesting choices, Mother," was all that Johnnie said. Photographs were snapped, dozens of them. There was more champagne, more talk, more laughter. The party went on and on, for nobody wanted to leave.

It was almost dawn when Mary and Harley left the Kilburne Building. The sky was a wonderful color, not quite blue or gray or violet but a little of each. The air was soft and warm. Mary took a deep breath, smiling at the fading shadow of the moon. "Isn't it beautiful!" she said.

"The sky?"

"*Everything*. Everything is beautiful this morning." Mary lifted her arms in a wide and sweeping arc. "Life is beautiful."

"I was so afraid you would have second thoughts

about leaving the company. Can it be you're actually glad?"

"I'm . . . in the clouds. See that pretty, puffy little cloud up there? That's where I am." Mary laughed, slipping her hand in Harley's. "Oh, I know there will be problems at the company. But they're not my problems, not anymore. And I'm delighted." She turned, staring up at the huge Kilburne Building, the tangible symbol of her achievement. She was proud of it. She would always be proud of it but, now, her happiness lay elsewhere. "I love you, Harley."

"I love you."

Mary kissed her husband. "Grow old along with me," she smiled. "The best is yet to be."

ZEBRA HAS IT ALL!

SENSATIONAL SAGAS!

WHITE NIGHTS, RED DAWN   (1277, $3.95)
by Frederick Nolan
Just as Tatiana was blossoming into womanhood, the Russian Revolution was overtaking the land. How could the stunning aristocrat sacrifice her life, her heart and her love for a cause she had not chosen? Somehow, she would prevail over the red dawn —and carve a destiny all her own!

IMPERIAL WINDS   (1324, $3.95)
by Priscilla Napier
From the icebound Moscow river to the misty towers of the Kremlin, from the Bolshevick uprising to the fall of the Romanovs, Daisy grew into a captivating woman who would courageously fight to escape the turmoil of the raging IMPERIAL WINDS.

KEEPING SECRETS   (1291, $3.75)
by Suzanne Morris
It was 1914, the winds of war were sweeping the globe, and Electra was in the eye of the hurricane—rushing headlong into a marriage with the wealthy Emory Cabot. Her days became a carousel of European dignitaries, rich investors, and worldly politicians. And her nights were filled with mystery and passion . . . .